The beginning of passion . . .

Dominic turned toward her and coaxed a fatuous smile from his stern lips. "Enough about me. Cold stone is a dull subject for a woman . . . especially a woman like you."

"A—a woman like me?"

"You don't need me to tell you that you are the loveliest creature alive, Lady Stavely. Such a cool name . . . I heard Mr. Gardner call you Clarice. It suits you."

"I don't feel you know me well enough to call me by my name, Mr. Knight."

"Perhaps not. Soon I hope to know you much, much better."

Magic
by
Daylight

LYNN BAILEY

JOVE BOOKS, NEW YORK

MAGICAL LOVE is a trademark of Penguin Putnam Inc.

MAGIC BY DAYLIGHT

A Jove Book / published by arrangement with
the author

PRINTING HISTORY
Jove edition / December 1999

All rights reserved.
Copyright © 1999 by Cynthia Pratt.
This book may not be reproduced in whole or in part,
by mimeograph or any other means, without permission.
For information address: The Berkley Publishing Group,
a division of Penguin Putnam Inc.,
375 Hudson Street, New York, New York 10014.

The Penguin Putnam Inc. World Wide Web site address is
http://www.penguinputnam.com

ISBN: 0-515-12701-9

A JOVE BOOK®
Jove Books are published by The Berkley Publishing Group,
a division of Penguin Putnam Inc.,
375 Hudson Street, New York, New York 10014.
JOVE and the "J" design
are trademarks belonging to Penguin Putnam Inc.

PRINTED IN THE UNITED STATES OF AMERICA

10 9 8 7 6 5 4 3 2 1

To my darling daughter,
BETTIE,
who brings me a magical world of joy every day.

One

⌢

The bride sparkled like a newly opened rose touched with dew. When she gazed upon her husband, the words of their vows still trembling in the air, all her adoration was written in her eyes. Clarice saw with approval that Mr. Henry returned her dear friend's love with full measure. Melissa perhaps deserved more than to share the future of a curate, but she would have at least the consolation of knowing he cherished her.

When the young couple emerged from the church, Clarice was the first to embrace the bride, veil, flowers, and all. "From the bottom of my heart, I wish you happy!" she said. She smiled down at her shorter friend. "Now didn't we vow we would not cry?"

"I can't help it. I'm so happy."

Mr. Henry shuffled his feet. Always a rather red-faced young man, he was blushing brightly beneath the indulgent gazes of the gentry and townsfolk of Hamford. Clarice turned to him with an outstretched hand and a warm smile. "Congratulations, Mr. Henry. I yield to you the dearest friend I have ever had. I know she will prove a great comfort and support to you all the days of your life."

"Thank you, my lady," he said, bowing as gracefully as a royal bishop. "I count the day I came to Hamford as the most fortunate of my life . . . until now."

Clarice laughed and let the bride and groom go to greet the rest of their well-wishers. As she turned to follow them, she very plainly heard a farmer's wife saying to her somewhat deaf mother, " 'Tis a pity she's no younger."

"Aye," the older woman said, nodding. "Young pullets do make the best layers. But she's a very pleasant-spoken lady for all that."

As Clarice watched Mr. and Mrs. Henry shake hands and smile, never leaving go of each other's arm, she could not help giving a sigh. Melissa Bainbridge was nearly a year younger than herself. If the townspeople of Hamford had long since given up expectation of seeing *her* wed, how much less hope had they of seeing the Lady of the Manor married? Their hopes could not be smaller than Clarice's own.

Fortunately, her position protected her somewhat from the pointed questions and sly comments that were too often the part of the unmarried at a wedding celebration. The fact that she was in somewise the founder of this feast didn't hurt either. But good wine and fine food was the least she could do to mark the wedding of the dearest friend she'd ever known.

"I'm afraid you'll be lonely now," her half sister said, approaching her after dinner. Felicia Gardner had the softest voice and the warmest eyes in the world. If anyone would understand Clarice's feelings it would be she, who had been almost a mother to her. For an instant, honest words rose to her lips. But then, over Felicia's shoulder, Clarice saw that Melissa was listening.

"Lonely?" Clarice said brightly. "Not at all! I shall positively relish the silence. You don't know, Felicia, how trying it is to live with people in love. If she was not sighing because he had not spoken to her in church, then she was singing because he had. If she was not over the moon with delight at receiving some little note, she was cast down into the depths because he had not written. I should appreciate some *level* ground after so many ups and downs."

"I have been a great trial to her ladyship indeed," Melissa said, smiling. "And she has borne all my foolishness most patiently."

"Only out of friendship for you, my dear," Clarice said, still merrily. "For I declare that my friendship for Mr. Henry has been severely tried."

"What's that?" Blaic Gardner came up, Mr. Henry just behind him. "You have sinned grievously, sir, if Lady Stavely finds fault with you."

"I beg pardon . . ." the curate began, not yet used to the jokes of the circle he'd joined by marriage.

"As you should," Clarice said, stern as a judge but for the twinkle in her eyes. "Why, you kept my dear friend waiting almost six months before you proposed, when anyone could see that you had fallen in love with her at first sight. That is a high crime, as you must agree."

"You are right. I felt an immediate inclination. However, I wished to give her time to know her heart," he said, drawing Melissa's arm through the bend of his elbow.

"I will not add to her blushes by saying that you waited three months too long for that!"

The bride hid her blooming cheeks in her husband's lapel. "You are too bad," she said in a muffled voice.

"That is nothing. Wait till you hear the speech I mean to give, being *in loco parentis* as it were to the bride. But now, there is to be dancing! Gentlemen, take your wives away unless you wish to incur more of my displeasure!"

She knew Mr. Henry did not disapprove of dancing, and indeed his rather large foot was already tapping to the sound of fiddles and drum. The early summer evening was warm, while moonrise and sunset met to give the sky a soft, opalescent gleam. Out on the lawn of

Hamdry Manor, twenty couples had already joined hands on the wooden platform Clarice had ordered built for the occasion.

Blaic too was whistling almost soundlessly along with the music. His eyes, green as new-budded leaves, looked at his wife with an eager light that not even ten years of marriage had dimmed. Felicia smiled back in a mysteriously tender way that seemed the special property of married women. Yet she took a moment to say, "Don't try so hard, Clarice. Everyone knows you are sorry to be losing your friend."

Before Clarice could answer, Blaic took his wife to the floor. Suddenly the joyousness of the music and the delight on her friends' faces was too overwhelming. Clarice turned away. The windows of her beloved home, welcoming with candlelight, beckoned to her but she did not go in. For the moment, she could not find comfort there. Too soon it would contain her alone, with no equal or even near-equal to share her days, her occupations, or her thoughts.

Slipping away unnoticed, and feeling absurdly neglected even though it was her own wish, Clarice wended her way through the garden. The gravel paths were laid out to wind and bend among an assortment of statuary, classical and modern. Though elegant and civilized in its contents, the famous Hamdry Gardens rested upon the very edge of a wilderness. The great moor rose beyond this hedge, seemingly wind-swept and empty, yet filled with secrets and danger enough to rival the deepest jungle.

Melissa, for one, had always thought Clarice's love for the moor bordered on the macabre. "How can you stand it, knowin' your ma . . . died there?" she'd asked once, not long after leaving Tallyford Orphanage to live with Clarice, orphaned herself.

"I don't mind that. I never feel unwelcome."

"You're Viscountess Stavely. Where do you ever feel out of place?" Melissa had been only a young girl then and, despite her illegitimacy and the hardness of her life, she'd still kept some illusions. Those few that Clarice knew had all been shattered the morning they'd found her mother's clothing beside one of the sucking green pools that looked so innocent in the sunshine yet concealed such deadly depths.

But she did not blame the moor for that.

The sounds of the party were dim as she walked out through the gap in the thick hedge at the back of the manor property. The wind pulled at the pale yellow silk of her gown, loosening the mass of curls piled upon her head. She had a sudden fancy to walk up to the top of the hill where the rising moon seemed to dance among the clouds like an Arabian princess among her veils.

Though the thin-soled slippers she wore were only good for dancing, she didn't notice any stones beneath her feet. Nor did she pay any particular attention when the moon hid herself away. She wasn't afraid of the dark. There was a greater chance of her losing her way in her own drawing room than here on the moor, even in the darkness.

As she walked, she thought about the men she knew and why she was not married to any of them.

They'd asked her. Ever since she'd come of age, there'd been a suitor or two to squire her to Assembly Balls, to routs, and to whatever other amusement this fold of the Devonshire landscape offered. But always when the moment had come to answer "Yes, I will," she had said, "You are very kind but . . . no."

Part of the problem was that she did not need to marry to better herself. "I have money," she said aloud to the night. "I have a title in my own right. I have everything a woman marries for, yet I also have the extra benefit of complete freedom of action. If only there was a man I could . . . respect."

She was thinking of the look on Melissa's face as she took the vows that made her a wife when she realized that she'd reached the top of the hill. For a moment, she stood with her eyes tightly closed as she caught her breath. Then she opened them, expecting to see the land she knew so well spread out before her like a giant's map.

But instead of familiar landmarks, she saw a tumbled, broken line of stones before her that looked black as obsidian in the moonlight. "But this is Barren Fort," she said. "I *can't* have walked five miles. That's impossible."

Yet even as she stood there, she became aware that the soles of her dancing slippers were worn right through. She felt the damp scrubbrushlike grass beneath the ball of her foot. A certain trembling in her lower limbs told her that she'd walked far, and at an unaccustomed speed.

She had knelt down to untie the silken laces of her ruined shoes when she felt the ground tremble. Once, while accompanying Blaic and Felicia on their wedding trip to Italy, she and Melissa had been on a Naples street when a tremor had shaken the city. This was the same vibration, yet who'd ever heard of an earthquake or volcano here?

Clarice looked around on instinct for someplace to take shelter. Except for the stones, the top of the hill was indeed barren. The trembling grew more furious, accompanied by a colossal groan as the earth twisted itself in resistance to its own violence.

Then she realized there was something oddly rhythmic about the way the ground shook. It was a beat she knew well, part of her blood ever since her father had put her on her first mare. Somewhere quite near, a horse galloped at a frenzied pace, coming closer by the instant.

But who would be made enough to gallop over treacherous ground beneath the insubstantial light of a coy moon? Clarice straightened up, shoe in hand, looking around for the animal and owner. She'd deliver a stern lecture to the foolhardy person! She cared little whether the rider broke his neck, but she cared deeply about the horse!

She saw nothing. A strong breeze blew up, blinding her with strands of her own hair. She pushed it back as the wind died away as abruptly as it had come.

Then he was there, taking the jagged stones of Barren Fort in a leap at least as daring as it was insane. The horse was black as the stones and from its back great wings soared out, flung wide in the tempest of its passing.

He passed so close that Clarice cowered, afraid of the slashing hooves over her head. They wrung red and gold sparks from the underlying stone as he landed.

Staring, Clarice saw the horse bore a rider. Yet the words she'd thought to say of his recklessness perished in her throat at the uncanny sight before her. Perhaps he wore only a hooded cloak. Yet the effect was that of a shadow riding a shadow. She could distinguish the outline of a figure astride the black animal, nothing more.

Rider and horse were as still as statues in the liquid light of the moon. Neither of them gave any sign of the strenuous exercise they'd just completed, by so much as a deep breath. The horse did not paw the ground, nor did the rider make any move to dismount. The dimly seen head moved as he seemed to scan the horizon for something.

"Shall we about it?" he asked.

The voice was so sudden and deep that Clarice jumped. The hooded face turned toward her despite her having made no sound beyond the thud of a shoeless foot in short grass. Clarice froze like a rabbit that feels the shadow of the hawk pass over. She even shut tight her eyes so that no gleam of white could draw his attention. Every tale of bogle or banshee that she'd ever heard in her life suddenly filled her head. She did not want to see whatever baneful face was hidden in the hood.

An eternal moment later, she heard again the ring of hooves striking rock beneath the thin covering of soil on the tor. She opened her eyes partway to see him ride down the hill, the sides of his long cloak flying open like wings upon a horse's back. She half thought he was looking back at her, so she shut her eyes tight again.

• • •

"Here she is!" a voice called on a note of triumph.

Clarice opened her eyes to find the handsome face of her brother-in-law bending low over her. The lines at the corners of his eyes deepened as he smiled reassuringly. "Sit up, Clarice. You're cold as ice from lying on the ground."

"On the ground?" she asked. She realized the strange prickling all over her body was from the blades of grass poking through the silk of her gown.

Blaic gave her his hand and pulled her up. She felt her head whirl. "Here now," he said, sliding his arm around her. "You're not going to faint?"

"I haven't fainted since I was sixteen. What happened? I was out on the moor a moment ago."

"Were you? Where?"

"Barren Tor. I don't know how I . . ."

"Barren Tor? But that's five miles away."

"I know. Yet I swear I was there. And a man on a horse came out of nowhere . . ." Suddenly, her knees seemed to lose all their stiffness. She started to sink.

"Hurry!" he called, even as he bent to pick her up. Though he was at least forty, his arms were strong and his shoulder broad enough to lean her head on. "You need a glass of brandy," he said more quietly.

"Oh, no. I loathe the stuff."

She could hear more voices, anxious, questioning voices, coming nearer. In the forefront was Melissa, closely followed by Felicia and several servants with torches alight. Their wavering light made the shadows move. Clarice gave a convulsive shudder, prey to the sensation known as "a goose walking over a grave," and tried to see past the shadows. Did someone in a black cloak stand there, concealed and watching?

"I'll carry you into the house," Blaic said. "You're not well."

Clarice shook her head with a smile. "Put me down, Blaic, do. I'm perfectly well."

"Is she hurt?" Felicia asked, her lovely face tight with anxiety.

"A little faint," her husband answered, ignoring Clarice's repeated request. "She's been overdoing it, I think."

"Don't spare my feelings," Clarice said, responding as always to any ugly emotion like this unreasoning fear that gripped her, fighting back with a smile and a joke. "Tell the world I'm naught but a dissipated rake. Can a woman be a rake?"

"Oh, it's my fault," Melissa said, wringing her hands. "She took too much on herself with this wedding."

"Carry her to the house, Blaic," Felicia said. "An early night and a glass of hot milk will do much to restore her. I'll make your excuses to the other guests, Clarice."

"Nonsense! Put me down. I'm very well able to walk. I merely wanted to be alone for a little. I had a bit of a headache, if you must know."

"Then why . . ." Blaic began, only to receive a nip of his sister-in-law's fingers all too close to his ear.

"Sssh," she hissed. "Don't worry them."

He only shook his head as he swung her down. Just as she stood on her own two feet, Melissa caught her breath on a gasp. "Clarice! What has become of your shoes?"

The grass of Hamdry Manor was cool and rich beneath her naked soles. Close-shearing made it as delightful to tred on as cut velvet. Very different from the dry, coarse grass on Barren Tor. Clarice looked down at her feet, white and long against the seemingly black turf. "I—I took them off. One of the laces broke."

"Would this be before or after you had the headache?" Felicia asked with the raised eyebrow and drawling tone of a skeptical older sister.

Clarice just laughed. She stepped over the grass to kiss Felicia's pale cheek. "Come along," she said. "I'm in no danger. I shall go to the house and find another pair of satin slippers. Then I shall dance with your gallant husband and he shall tell me all the doings of my brilliant nephew."

"Brilliant indeed," Blaic said, his fair brows twitching down in a way that promised and threatened all in one. "He takes after his father, who is not to be fooled."

When Clarice returned, last year's silver slippers safe upon her feet, her brother-in-law did not dance with her. They sat down together at a table with glasses of wine before them. Clarice imagined that to anyone else, they looked like a friendly pair of relations by marriage. Yet their talk was far from ordinary.

"So he appeared out of nowhere?" Blaic asked.

"It was dark. The moon had gone in among the clouds. I might not have seen a rider clad in black riding a black horse until he was upon me."

"Did he speak to you?"

"No. And I said nothing either. I—I was afraid." She paused an instant. "No, not afraid. Just . . . Anyway, what could I have said? I was not even certain of how I had come to be there."

"Clarice . . ." Blaic began. Then he shot a cautious glance over his shoulder. No one stood near enough to overhear. "Did you think at all that it might be one of the People?"

"One of the People?"

Clarice too, on instinct, glanced around before answering. Though many of the country-folk believed in the "piskies," most of their betters did not. Little did any of them know that Blaic Gardner, well-respected gentleman and author of the soon-to-be published *Notes on the Life-span and Social Structure of the British Bee,* had once been a prince of a mysterious race far older than mankind. Felicia's love for him had made him the man he was today, in more ways than one.

Clarice not only knew of Blaic's former station, she herself had had an enchantment laid upon her. Therefore, she considered Blaic's suggestion with due care. "No. Although . . . no. I didn't think of it; I don't think it."

"Barren Fort is a very ancient ruin. They are fond of such places. Some of them were built with our help, many thousands of years ago before King Boadach became so stern about enforcing the law against contact with mortals."

"You've never spoken to me much about this before, Blaic. Why not?"

The leaf green eyes of the singularly handsome older man turned in search of his beautiful wife. "I have not wished to remember. Even the near-paradise of the Living Lands pales beside my mortal life with Felicia and Morgain." He looked at Clarice. "Lately, however, I have been revisiting Mag Mell in my dreams. It troubles me. And now this . . . appearance . . ."

Clarice patted her brother-in-law's folded hands. "It's nothing, Blaic. I had an odd experience perhaps, but it isn't the first time strange things have happened to me on the moor. No doubt the explanation is perfectly reasonable. You and Felicia shall go to London tomorrow with a clear conscience.

"Besides," she added on a laugh, "I'd match my darling nephew against any magical creature from the depths of Mag Mell, or from the Book of Revelations for that matter. Morgain's a dragon, a gryphon, and a six-headed hydra all by himself. A pity he's not old enough for war. Wellington could use a weapon like Morgain. Napoleon would resign in an instant and be thankful for the opportunity."

Blaic could always be distracted by talk of his son. Just when Clarice believed she'd changed the subject successfully, Blaic came back to Mag Mell. "There is one way to tell whether someone is of the People or not." He paused impressively, an effect ruined by Clarice's impatient, "Well?"

"If you touch one, they are obliged to obey you in your next request, no matter what it may be."

Clarice nodded, giving Blaic the compliment of taking what he said in the same spirit in which he spoke. "I shall make it a point to touch every stranger I meet."

Soon, the fall of evening put an end to the festivities. The guests would have a full moon to light their various ways home. Melissa and her husband would spend their first night of married life in the little cottage allotted to him as curate. However, their bridal month would be spent in Bath, where Mr. Henry's invalid mother and two sisters lived.

Melissa gave her dear friend a warm hug and handed her the tightly gathered nosegay of pink roses that she'd carried that day. "I want you to have this," she said, her brown eyes sparkling with unshed tears. "You have been the truest, dearest. . . ." She swallowed with a noticeable gulp. "I never minded not having a family after I came here. Hamdry has been the nearest thing to a home that I. . . ."

"You'll make your own home now," Clarice said bracingly, though her throat was tight.

Melissa nodded. "I love him so much!"

"Then go to him. Be happy."

After the manor had settled down for the night, Clarice softly put the bedclothes aside. In her white nightdress, she knelt on the padded window seat in her room. She reached out to open the casement, letting the warm summer air perfume her chamber. Remembering how her former nurse would have died of horror at the risk of illness she was running, Clarice opened it a little wider.

She couldn't help thinking of Melissa, who was perhaps at this moment learning the deepest mysteries of married life. And from Mr. Henry! Though she'd never said anything of her feelings to Melissa, Clarice could not for the life of her understand what her friend saw in her new husband. He was, no doubt, very well in his way. But where were the depths that a woman could explore for life? Where was the spice of a clever mind, the challenge of taming a stronger will, the fascination of two completely dissimilar sexes finding a common ground on which to stand against the world?

Felicia and Blaic had these things. Clarice had seen their love grow from day to day, sometimes set back by adversity, sometimes by doubts. Always, however, they'd become stronger because of the struggle. Though

when they'd met she herself had been under a spell—
compelled to remain mentally a child despite the growth
of her body—she knew that Felicia and Blaic had both
desired and battled from the first only to reach a safe
haven at the end. But with Melissa and Mr. Henry, falling in love had been about as arduous as sleeping on a
new feather bed.

Clarice worried that without these necessary "growing
pangs" Melissa and Mr. Henry's first quarrel would
seem entirely out of proportion to the cause. She vowed
that she would never marry a man who did not argue
with her. Then she laughed at herself. Could she tolerate
having her decisions questioned when she'd been sole
mistress at Hamdry for so long?

The door behind her creaked in warning, a good reason for her always having refused to have it fixed. Just
for an instant, Clarice felt convinced that the man from
Barren Fort stood behind her, perhaps even reached out
to her. The feeling was so strong that it was like having
a wave break over her. She did not dare to turn her head,
though she despised herself for a coward.

A whispered "Clarice?" reassured her.

"Is something wrong, Felicia?" she asked.

"I was worried so I came to look in on you," Felicia
said. "You should be in bed."

"I couldn't sleep. Too much wedding cake, I think."

"You'll catch your death sitting there like that. At
least wrap up." Her sister pulled the neatly folded cashmere shawl off the end of the bed. "Tuck this around
you. What are you thinking about, sitting there like an
owl in an oak tree?"

"I was thinking about marrying, actually."

"Indeed? Anyone I know?"

"Marriage in general, I mean. How *do* you know
when someone is right for you?"

"You're thinking about Mr. Henry. Well, he wouldn't
have done for me and he certainly wouldn't have done
for *you,* but he's the precisely right man for Melissa
Bainbridge."

"Melissa's a dear girl."

"Very amiable. Now that she's not so bitter against life, she's a very amiable girl indeed. When I think how she snarled when I first met her at Tallyford Orphanage!" Felicia raised her eyes heavenward. "But no one could be more steadying and gently affectionate than Mr. Henry. That is what she needs and I, for one, am delighted that they found each other."

"But she seems to think of him as Apollo, Hercules, and Adonis all in one. He is not."

"Not to your eyes, perhaps. To each his own, my dear."

Felicia leaned closer to her half sister. In the moonlight, Clarice looked older than her twenty-six years, the lack of color emphasizing the slightly dark marks beneath her eyes and a tiny drawing in of a smooth cheek. These signs of weariness were not noticeable by day. All one saw then was the laughing beauty that was so startlingly perfect.

It was no wonder that all the young men—and quite a few of the older ones—came flocking to admire the exquisite young viscountess. The one Season she'd spent in London had caused pandemonium. At least one earl had been infatuated, as well as any number of lesser men. Yet in the end, Clarice had come home, unmarried, unengaged, and uninterested in trying the experiment a second time. She'd settled down with her friend and her old family retainers with every sign of contentment. But it was not contentment Felicia saw on that glorious countenance now.

"You *are* lonely, aren't you? Surely there must be someone you have considered marrying?"

Clarice switched her braided hair back and forth as she shook her head. Then she smiled impishly. "Melissa only left today. Give us a small respite before we have another wedding."

She looked into Felicia's eyes and seemed, for once, to be serious. "I am not afraid to be alone. In many ways, I have always been alone. If not for you coming to live here when I was a child, I should have died of loneliness. But I didn't. And I shan't die from it now either. Someday, if I wish it, I will search for a new companion."

"But not now?"

Somewhat absently, looking once more out the window, she answered, "No, not now. Let me. . . ." She caught her breath on a note of alarm.

"What is it?" Felicia asked, half-rising from the bed where she'd seated herself.

"Nothing. . . . I thought I saw a man."

"A man?" She came to the window seat to peer over Clarice's shoulder into the darkness beyond the open window. "Where? I don't see anyone."

"No . . . neither do I—now. It must have been a shadow . . ."

"I shall rouse the servants," Felicia said, heading toward the door.

"No! There's no need to wake them because their mistress hasn't enough sense to go to bed and instead sits dreaming of things that never were. You can hardly blame me if I see one lurking in the garden."

"Things that never were . . ." Felicia repeated.

"I'm only tired," Clarice said. "Don't worry about me. I've been in a strange mood ever since Melissa came to tell me she'd accepted Mr. Henry. I think I am just lazy and am blue-deviled because now I have all the difficulty of picking out another congenial companion. Don't you have some respectable widow among all your good works to fill this vacancy?"

"Yes, I do." Felicia's thoughts were busy with the lists of young bachelors that every woman has in her head. Kept, if not for herself, on the thrifty notion of "waste not, want not" for others. She decided that one of the objects of her trip to London would be adding significant numbers of young men to that list. Somewhere lived a man for Clarice—Felicia intended to find him if she had to track him through the Trossachs in the depths of a

January blizzard. Anything to banish the darkness at the back of the dear girl's eyes.

After Felicia returned to her sleeping husband, Clarice leaned her head on her hand and looked out the window. What dreams she'd entertained here as a young girl! Dreams of a dashing hero who'd dare anything for love! Her Season in London had taught her that there were no such men in these degenerate days. Plenty existed if she wished to be squired sedately around the park or escorted to choose a fashionable gown, but where were the bold knights and daring cavaliers of old?

Though it had never been said, Clarice knew that at nearly twenty-seven she was "on the shelf." Men preferred younger girls, fresh from the schoolroom, who could be molded and shaped into wives. Most women her age were already the proud mothers of hopeful families.

She leaned forward to close the window. "I think I shall buy a pug dog and raise roses," she said with a tiny, rueful laugh. "Better that than to settle for less than my dreams."

Some movement caught her eye. She paused, peering down like a princess in a tower. There *was* someone down there—moving slowly from shadow to shadow as though he did not wish to be seen. He was not moving toward the house, but away. It was hard to see through the distorting glass and the ethereal moonlight but Clarice felt certain she saw the trailing end of a cloak.

She sat up for a long time watching, even after she heard the sound of a horse's hooves traveling away.

Two

"Zee now, Jem. It's as I zaid it would be. High jinks, zame as any boy'd be."

"It's very good of you to look at it in that light, Mrs. Yeo," Clarice said. "I know my nephew didn't mean any harm."

"An' no harm was done. It was ever so good of you to come yerself, my laidy. Git up, Jem, do, an' zee her laidyship to the door. Ain't you niver laarned no manners?"

"Jem," who hadn't been permitted to speak two words by his good lady, rose to his feet from his seat by the cold fireplace. He towered over his round, pink-cheeked wife, yet it was plain who ran the roost. Mrs. Yeo stayed behind, waving a white dishcloth in farewell as her husband walked Clarice to the gate.

Clarice said, "I do hope the trees took no harm?"

"Nay. T'boy did not eat too many of the apples. Green 'uns . . ." He made a gesture in the direction of his third waistcoat button. His wife had obviously hurried him into his Sunday clothes as soon as the viscountess had appeared.

"I'm afraid he did. If it's any consolation, he's lying

down upon his bed at this moment feeling as though he
had three cats fighting inside him."

"Poor lad. Laarn him a lesson, though."

"That it has." Mr. Yeo assisted her in mounting her
cream-colored mare, Bess. "Good day, Mr. Yeo."

"Yer laidyship."

She rode away with a ladylike salute. If Morgain's
escapade of the morning had not left him with a stom-
achache, she would have brought him along to make his
own apologies to the Yeos. As it was, she would have
to explain that one did not take advantage of one's tenants. From a legal standpoint, the apples in Mr. Yeo's
orchard belonged to her, as the owner of the property,
and, if she so chose, her rights could be extended to her
nephew. But the labor, and the love, were Mr. Yeo's
own.

The summer afternoon was almost too warm for exercise. Clarice adjusted the brim of her hat to allow more
of a breeze to caress her face. If not for the movement
of Bess, there would be no air stirring at all. Between
the hedgerows, all was still as a painting, though the
birds were merry among the branches. Above her, the
sky was cloudless, looking like the merest wash of blue
on some maiden lady's watercolor.

She was growing steadily warmer. Loosening the
frogs across the throat of her riding dress did little to
relieve her. She wished she'd called out the carriage this
morning, for then she would have worn a lighter dress,
but she had been afraid that too much pomp would alarm
the Yeos unnecessarily. Besides, both she and Bess
needed the exercise. Perhaps a gallop, once they
emerged from this narrow track bounded by the hedges?

As if in answer to her thought, she heard the pounding
of hooves coming up fast behind her.

Though it had been more than a week since Melissa's
wedding, the odd events of that day and evening had not
faded in Clarice's memory. Every night found her still
at her window, though she saw nothing.

The moment she heard the hooves she *knew* that the

rider from Barren Fort had found her. Half-panicked already, she glanced desperately about for someplace to hide. But there was only the narrow road and the impenetrable hedges.

When the rider appeared, coming at a full gallop, Clarice felt true fear for the first time in her life. She'd always prided herself on her courage yet now knew she'd never been tried. Frozen, she could only stare back over her shoulder, waiting for the black horse to overtake her. Her chest felt heavy and tight, as if her lungs had shrunk, leaving her nothing to breathe with.

Then Bess whinnied, not the friendly call of one horse to another but at a higher pitch. Without waiting for the clap of a heel to her side, she leapt forward.

Clarice, taken by surprise, nearly tumbled off. Then she tightened her hands and leaned close to Bess's neck. The lashing of the coarse mane helped to jolt her from her paralysis. She'd ridden almost before she could walk and had been in the stables the day Bess had entered the world, daughter of her own beloved Meg and Tom O' Bedlam. When they rode together it felt as if they were one, a mythical being of horseflesh and human, and never more so than now with terror riding close behind.

She glanced back through the dust they'd raised and saw the black rider like a hunting shadow among the white clouds. He was close, and coming closer yet. She found herself panting, the tightness in her chest increasing, as though she were being laced much too tightly in her stays.

"Come up!" she gasped to Bess. "Come up, my own, my dear, my love."

The long legs flashed out in a yet more furious rhythm. Exhilaration drove out fear in Clarice's heart. They'd never touched this speed before. There'd never been the need.

Then Bess swerved, heading toward Daly's three-bar gate. Clarice shut her eyes and prayed. She felt the mare's muscles beneath her gather for the spring.

Bess took the gate as though she'd sprouted invisible

wings. There came a long, floating moment in which time seemed to stop, held forever between one breath and the next.

Then the mare landed, neat as a cat, with an impact that Clarice felt from the base of her spine to the top of her head. All would have been well had Clarice been riding astride as she sometimes did while alone. Even a hunting sidesaddle would have been safer than the plain one the mare had been fitted with that morning. But the grooms had not guessed that their mistress might take a fence in the course of a simple morning's ride.

Her foot came free of the single stirrup. There was nothing to keep her from falling to her death but her other leg around the pommel and the grip of her hands on the reins. Neither one felt adequate, especially since Bess's pace had not slackened. But the mare was tiring. Her sides heaved, while her neck had a froth of sweat upon it.

Clarice looked back and saw nothing and no one. She sighed in relief and noticed that the terrible constriction around her chest had eased. She felt rather disgusted with herself for having lost her head so completely. At the same time, however, she found herself amazingly relieved to see no bay horse behind her.

When she finally returned to Hamdry, the head groom himself was standing in the courtyard of the stables, polishing the sides of his pipe with a bit of cloth. Mr. Drake's idly curious eyes sharpened when he saw the state of his mistress and her horse.

"Did she run away with you?" he asked, hurrying up. He whistled for his sons to come as he reached up to Clarice. She was all too grateful to fall into his arms and be swung down to the ground. She had to clutch the spry man's arm to keep from falling.

"Clem! Fetch her ladyship a chair."

She forced a laugh. "No, I'm well. I don't need it. Whew!" She tried to blow a lock of hair out of her eyes but it was damp with sweat and would not move. "Extra treats for her tonight, Mr. Drake. She deserves it."

"For running off with you? I've zaid it afore, ma'am, and I'll zay it again . . ."

She said the words with him, "You must always take a boy with thee . . ."

"There's no use in scoffing at me, my lady. Yer own father would have no different opinion."

"Undoubtedly true, Mr. Drake, but the Gypsies haven't stolen me yet though he swore they would one day."

Bess looked glad to hear her foot strike once again on her native cobbles. She twitched an ear toward the younger grooms exclaiming over the sweat that had frothed and dried on her coat. Yet she still had attention to spare when Clarice smoothed her velvet nose and whispered, "You saved my life or perhaps it was only my soul. Thank you."

As she walked from the stableyard, she said briskly, "Give her extra treats tonight, Mr. Drake. She deserves spoiling."

"But what's she done?" the put-upon groom called after her. "An' where's yer hat?"

Camber, her youthful butler, appeared no less astonished by her appearance than had Drake. But since Camber's great ambition was to be the complete butler at all times, he said a good deal less than the free-spoken groom. Remembering when Camber had been no more than gawky William the Footman, Clarice took pity on his unspoken curiosity. "I had a little trouble with Bess today. I'm unhurt, even if I must look a fright."

Catching sight of herself in the gilded mirror in the center of the hall, she caught her breath. Her hair, charmingly casual when she'd left that morning, could be rented out at a noble figure to any homeless bird. As for her habit, no two points of it hung straight. The carefully tied cravat hung like a bandage around her neck while a shoulder seam gaped where the strain had been too much. Add to this a thick coating of road dust to dull her hair and redden her eyes.

"Where's Pringle?" she asked in a conspiratorial whisper.

"Doing the mending," Camber answered, "in your room."

"Oh, lor'. Well, might as well face her now. She'll see the habit later anyway."

Camber cleared his throat when she would have hastened away. "What it is?"

"A gentleman to see you, my lady. He has been waiting some little time for your return."

"He's fortunate that he didn't miss me altogether. He might very well have . . ." For an instant the feeling of terror engendered by the shadowy rider enveloped her again, suffocating her attempt to appear as she usually did. Clarice swallowed hard and tried to speak naturally.

"What's the gentleman's name?"

"A Mr. Knight, my lady. He brings a message from Mr. and Mrs. Gardner."

"Oh, then, it's for Morgain. Is he moving about yet?"

"Not yet, my lady. Mrs. Pringle has given him some oil of walnuts in the hope of easing him."

"Poor boy. As if green apples weren't bad enough." She began to move toward the stairs. "Pray tell Mr. . . . Mr. . . . "

"Knight, my lady."

"Yes, tell Mr. Knight that I shall be with him as soon as I repair myself."

She did not find it easy to escape from her former nurse's cluckings and questions. "I had a little trouble with Bess. No, I'm not hurt. No, she didn't come down with me. Yes, very dusty. No, Mr. Yeo's not angry with him. I'll wear the blue one and wash my hair tonight. Yes, it may rain but I will still wash it. I have to hurry, Pringle, there's a man waiting for me."

"A man? Who?"

"I haven't any idea. A Mr. Knight."

"Oh! I saw him arrive. Such a fine-looking . . . horse."

"You noticed his horse? What's he like?"

All of a sudden, Pringle became flustered. "You must wear your black lace scarf. It looks so pretty with that deep blue gown. Let me . . ." She draped the Spanish lace from her mistress's elbows, smoothing the fringe so that it made a neat swag from side to side.

"You always have such a cunning way with scarves and such, Pringle. I never manage it half so well when you're busy elsewhere."

Pringle colored to the eyes. "It's just a knack."

Realizing how much she'd pleased her former nurse, Clarice promised herself that she'd take the other woman much less for granted in the future. She'd made such promises before. It was fatally easy to forget how sensitive Pringle really was. She didn't *look* much like someone with an excess of sensibility—appearing much more solid than that—yet she would cry at the first hard word and weep sentimentally over every kind one.

Sometimes Clarice thought how pleasant it must be to have a stern nurse who would scold and slap rather than sigh and cry over her charge's misadventures. But Pringle had never been stern or no-nonsense. Quite the contrary.

She was plump and dark-haired, with slender hands and feet. She could not have been called attractive by her dearest friend, except when she smiled. Thanks to a rather melancholy disposition, she rarely smiled wholeheartedly. Every day, it seemed, reminded her of the essential sorrow of life. No more than forty, she should have been married off long since were it not for her tireless desire to do good for others. Once she had confided to Clarice that she'd been on the point of being engaged once but her snoring drove her suitor off.

"How did he know you snored?" Clarice had asked, agog.

Pringle had blushed sallowly. "He stayed the night at our house once when my brother was visiting. I—I woke him up with my snoring and he never proposed after all."

She no longer snored, having gone in one night from

making more noise than a piston-driven loom to making no more noise than any other sleeper. It had been like a miracle, engineered by Blaic while still enchanted, but no other suitor had presented himself.

Clarice came downstairs, her mind still given to the problem of Pringle. Somewhere there had to be a man. . . .

Then she looked around and there was a man, standing in the middle of the entry hall, staring up at her. But he'd never do for Pringle. He seemed too stern, too ramrod straight, his feet firmly planted on the black and white tiles of the hall. His dark brows angled downward and Clarice felt strongly that he disapproved of her at first sight.

"I'm terribly sorry to have kept you waiting, sir, but I had an accident with my horse."

"Are you unhurt, my lady?"

"Yes, thankfully," she said, trotting lightly down the last few stairs as if to prove it. "I am, as you have guessed, Lady Stavely."

"It was presumptuous of me," he said, his brows lowering further, if such a thing were possible.

"Not at all, Mr. Knight. Won't you join me in the library? I'm sure Camber will bring the tea tray at any moment."

He followed her silently, his steps hardly making a sound over the tiles, though he probably rode fourteen stone. Once they trod on carpet, Clarice had to glance back to be sure he was there. He caught her eye and she smiled, forcing it a trifle. "These busts are of my ancestors," she said for the sake of saying something.

"Most impressive. And this?"

He stopped before a painting of a small gazebo or temple on a mist-shrouded hill. Tiny figures in Renaissance dress danced and cavorted on the lawn, while a ribbon-decked pleasure-barge waited to take them across to the temple.

"My sister painted that before her marriage."

"To Blaic Gardner."

"Yes. Do you know him?"

"He is why I have come."

She waited for him to say more but he simply stood there, gazing into the painting as though he were memorizing it.

No woman would say he was handsome, yet no woman would have denied he was attractive. That is, Clarice fumed silently, if one could be attracted to an irritatingly taciturn block.

His dark hair was brushed straight back, short at the nape and clipped close by the ears. The men she knew clung to the styles of their youths, with queues of their own hair or tie-wigs. His short hair accented the smooth planes of his face, emphasizing his strong cheekbones and those flaring eyebrows. She realized she was staring at him, and dropped her eyes one split-second before he glanced at her.

"Shall we go on?" she said, leading the way.

She doubted there was a spare ounce of fat on his frame. His riding breeches fit his muscular legs closely while his dark blue coat lay smoothly over the width of his arms and the breadth of his back. Everything about him, from his boots to his stickpin, spoke of quiet good taste.

Yet it was not his sartorial gifts that kept Clarice aware of just how closely he walked beside her. For one thing, he stood some four or five inches taller than she, no mean consideration to a girl who could look just about any man in the eye. Furthermore, there was no softening or blurring of any line of his face or body— no roll at his waist, no loose flesh on jaw or throat.

Clarice decided she'd been spending entirely too much time with old men and boys if the sight of one man at the peak of health and maturity could set her cataloging his body like a connoisseur. A blush still heated her cheeks as she ushered him into the library. Sure enough, Camber was already there, placing the heavy silver tray just so on the low table. She seated herself on one side, indicating gracefully that Mr. Knight

should sit across from her on the green damask upholstered settee.

She could tell by the way that he didn't cast so much
as an eye in Mr. Knight's direction that Camber had
already judged the man to be worthy of breaking bread
with Lady Stavely.

She drank her piping hot tea with a due sense of
thankfulness. Had it really been less than an hour since
she was riding like a madwoman in fear of . . . she knew
not what? After all, what had there been to frighten her
in the sight of a rider, however eccentrically dressed?
True it had been hot enough to make her wish for lighter
clothing but not everyone must feel that way just because she did so.

She smiled more warmly at Mr. Knight. "How may I
be of service to you, sir?"

For an answer, he handed her the letter he kept in an
inner pocket of his coat. It was from Blaic, introducing
Mr. Knight to her notice. With all the signs of being
written in haste—blotches, crossed out words, and in-
sertions—it was still as though Blaic himself were
speaking to her, recommending his acquaintance. He
also said that if he had been at home, he would not have
hesitated to offer Mr. Knight a room for the duration of
his visit to the west country, though he realized that a
scandal would result from the same offer being made by
his spinster sister-in-law.

"So you are also an author, Mr. Knight?"

"I have had two books accepted by Mssrs. Tompkins
and Hurlock, the first of which is presently enjoying
ready sales. *Viking Relics of York* has been praised by
Mr. Charles James Fox himself."

"Indeed," she said, knowing from Blaic's experiences
that the praise of a notable figure could do much to
elevate even the dullest book to public notice. "Have
you known my brother-in-law very long?"

"No, ours was a chance meeting in our publishers'
office the last time he was in London. When I saw him
again on Tuesday and told him that I hope to write my

next book on the relics to be found in this country, he
insisted that I visit Hamdry. As I was to be passing this
way, he gave me that letter of introduction."

She never would have guessed him to be one to make
a living with a pen. Not with those shoulders . . . though
Blaic was no puny fellow either. She promised herself
not to be so prejudiced by appearances in future. Authors
must come in all shapes and sizes like any other men.

"Do you mean to make a long stay in Devon, Mr.
Knight?"

"Some weeks, I fancy."

"So long?"

"I intend to be very thorough in my research, Lady
Stavely."

"You must let me help you. I know the moors very
well."

"So I have heard."

"Blaic told you?"

He glanced at her with laughter in eyes that were suddenly quite clearly an unusual shade of brown. "He said
you are the best guide anyone could hope for and that
if you agreed to come with me, I should count myself
fortunate."

"I should be happy to help you. Although several of
my servants are as familiar with the moor as I am."

"In that case, I shall plead for the company for such
a one. I'm interested in finding out any old legends or
tales connected with the relics. A native—especially
someone who cannot read—will have a better tale to tell
than you might, Lady Stavely."

Clarice realized what was troubling her about Mr.
Knight. He was not admiring her. This was very remarkable.

Though she was not vain, she did possess an unspot-
ted looking glass. Impossible to look into a mirror and
not be confronted with a visage that had been lavishly
praised since her birth. Much bad poetry had been written to pay tribute to her even white teeth between a pair
of sweetly curving pink lips, a straight nose rising flaw-

lessly between rose-flushed cheeks, eyes as blue as Mr.
Wedgewood's pottery, and hair variously described as
"wheat," "honey," or "gold."

As for her figure, once she'd outgrown a rapacious
appetite for sweets, it had remained in all respects the
same as when she was eighteen. If her dresses from that
period had not been grievously out of the present mode,
she could have still worn them without lacing her waist
even one inch.

Clarice asked herself if she'd suddenly developed
vanity. Perhaps it was just that Mr. Knight didn't find
blondes appealing. Yet it piqued her interest when she
saw that he didn't try to flirt. She could hardly recall the
last man she met who didn't at least make an attempt to
compliment her at their first meeting. Certainly none that
so obviously would prefer the company of a servant to
her own self.

"I shall ask Collie Camber if he is free to accompany
you. He is my butler's brother and a most reliable man."

"Your butler's brother?"

"We at Hamdry hire from among our own when we
can."

She glanced at the nearly transparent porcelain cup in
front of him, resting untouched on its saucer. "You don't
care for China tea, Mr. Knight? A glass of sherry, perhaps, instead?"

He hesitated before reaching for his cup, looking at it
as if he'd never seen one before and needed a moment
to study it discreetly before approaching. Clarice lifted
her own cup and took a quick sip. The tea was hot and
wonderfully refreshing, the warm smoky scent calming
her overwrought nerves.

Watching her carefully, Mr. Knight also drank. His
mobile mouth twisted wryly at the taste. "This tea is new
to me," he confessed.

"Lapsang Souchong," she said musically. "I acquired
a taste for it during my Season."

"Ah, yes, your Season. You must have enjoyed that."

Clarice began to answer lightly but paused. Was there

something faintly patronizing in Mr. Knight's tone?

"London is most interesting," she said. "Yet there is nowhere in the world I would rather be than here at Hamdry."

"The world is very large. Don't you think you should see more of it before deciding?"

She could be in no doubt of it now. He smiled at her with the arrogant loftiness of the man-of-the-world listening to some insipid virgin lisping out her trivial dreams.

"I have seen more of it, I fancy, than most women. I was fortunate enough to accompany my sister and Mr. Gardner on their wedding trip. We traveled to Italy and Greece, and even penetrated into Egypt. My friend, the present Mrs. Melissa Henry, and I had many fascinating experiences."

"No doubt you have recorded all your impressions. A sketchbook, perhaps. Or a diary? When are we to see *your* work in print?"

"I have no such talents," she said. "Nor have I the arrogance to think any such work of mine would have enough merit to trouble the public. I leave that to the real artists . . . and authors."

Changing the subject, she asked, "Where are you stopping, Mr. Knight? The Ram's Head? You'll find Brewster sets a good table."

"The Ram's Head is apparently full, Lady Stavely."

"Full? Why on earth . . . ?"

"The landlord said that several of his relations were expected and he doubted he'd have houseroom for anyone else."

"Odd," Clarice said. "He never mentioned it to me."

"Perhaps he thought it not worth troubling you, being a purely personal and minor matter."

"If so, it's the first time someone *hasn't* troubled me for something minor." She laughed a little, self-deprecating laugh, still determined that he should realize with whom he was dealing. "I am not only Lady Stavely, you see, I am also Lady of the Manor. I settle most of the disputes, hear all the gossip, and am usually their first recourse in times of trouble. The Ram's Head too full to lodge a guest? I should have heard something about that by now."

"Don't you find all that responsibility a great burden? After all, you are very young."

She did not, as a rule, encourage personal comments from strangers. There'd been too much of that in her life, and London had given her a lasting dislike of staring, whispering, and pointing. Between her looks and the rumors of her mother's unpleasant decease—presumed drowned in a sinkhole on the moor—she'd soon found it necessary to purchase a series of hats with veils in order to maintain some illusion of privacy.

"Oh, I'm older than I look," she said with her hands folded primly in her lap.

"So am I," Mr. Knight muttered. If Clarice had not exceptionally quick ears she would have missed it.

She couldn't help glancing at his face. He still looked to be about thirty years of age, though the fine lines at the outer corners of his eyes might more than just be a consequence of the same sun that had left his face slightly brown. After all, a writer who studied ruins and relics must be forced to spend considerable time out of doors. His hands too showed brown against a border of white emerging from the sleeves of his coat.

Clarice studied his hands secretly under cover of pouring another cup of tea. His fingers were blunt with well-trimmed but not buffed nails. Well-defined veins ran over the backs of his hands, giving them a look of strength, while she recognized the pattern of his calluses as being the same as those she herself had begun to develop before Pringle had become so strict on the subject of wearing gloves for riding.

With a look at his boots, Clarice confirmed her suspicion that he also had been riding today. She was about to ask him a question about his horse when another, darker suspicion occurred to her. Something she'd observed but not considered drew her attention again.

She glanced once more at his hands, at their warm brown tone, their clean nails. Too clean. Even Blaic, who was meticulous, couldn't keep the ink stains off his hands. Pens spluttered, ink not yet dry smeared under the swipe of a careless hand, while ink poured from bottle to bottle spattered cuffs. Even if Mr. Knight had not written for some time there should still be stains. Whatever Mr. Knight was, he was not an author.

Could this Mr. Knight, sitting so quietly in her library, be the mysterious rider who'd appeared seemingly out of the very stones at Barren Fort? Could Blaic be right in assuming that such a rider would come from the world of the Fay? Had he pursued her today? The cloak had concealed much, but surely his shoulders were just as broad. And there was something terrifyingly familiar in the cock of his head.

Suddenly, Clarice was filled with an inner certainty that had nothing whatever to do with observable facts. Every instinct cried out against him. Outwardly calm, inwardly screaming, Clarice rose slowly and walked over to the cold fireplace to give several emphatic tugs on the embroidered bell-pull.

"I have a sudden fancy for macaroons. My cook has a miraculous touch with such things," she said, trying to recapture her easy smile. Please God that Camber would respond to the sudden vicious jangling of the bell with both footmen and the house pistol! She doubted either would be of any use against one of the immortal Fay, but all she longed for now was the sight of another human being.

Three

~~

When the door burst open, she began to say gratefully, "Oh, Camber . . ."

Her words clashed in midair with a higher voice saying, "Aunt Clarice, I have come—"

Morgain Gardner stopped in midsentence, his heavy brows coming down over his nose. "Who's this?" he asked with a nod toward Mr. Knight.

"A friend of your father's," Clarice said, hurrying over to stand between the boy and the man. Whatever dark purpose Mr. Knight had, Clarice must protect Morgain.

She said, "Didn't I tell you to remain in your room until such time as you felt you could apologize to me?"

"Indeed, yes." He straightened his shoulders and began an obviously preset speech. "Aunt Clarice, I have come before you to apologize unreservedly for my foolhardy and inconsiderate behavior. Knowing full well that a good laborer is worthy of his hire, it was most wrong of me to pillage Mr. Yeo's apple trees without consideration. As Seneca rightly says—"

"Yes, yes, Morgain. Apology accepted. Now, if you please . . ."

As usual, he paid no attention. Clarice looked at her

nephew with love, mingled with worry and exasperation. Morgain was short for his nine years, with a pale, freckled complexion and a snub-nose that showed no signs of growing into his father's more aquiline profile. He wore the reddish hair he inherited from his mother somewhat long, to hide projecting ears. His brows were thick, which tended to distract attention from the remarkably quick deep green eyes that had been his father's legacy. From babyhood, he had never known any qualms about demonstrating his large vocabulary in a clear, beautifully inflected voice. His first term at school had been sheer hell.

But eventually he'd won the respect of his cruel peers by a talent for uncomplimentary verse directed at masters, and by a fist that proved capable of striking both very straight and very hard. Within a year, he'd gone from being a pariah to being one of the notables of the school, an outcome which, though fortunate in itself, had done nothing to limit a self-opinion that had started out tolerably high.

Morgain, perhaps feeling that he deserved more of an introduction than he had received, neatly avoided her by going around the other end of the settee. "How do you do, sir?" he said again. "I'm Morgain Gardner. You know my father?"

"I'm Dominic Knight. Yes. We have the same publisher."

The two shook hands. Clarice froze as Blaic's caution came back into her mind.

"There is one way to tell whether someone is of the People or not. If you touch one, they are obliged to obey you in your next request, no matter what it may be."

If Mr. Knight were not a human being, he would have responded to Morgain's handshake with an offer to do his bidding. Even without her fear of Mr. Knight, this seemed a terrible prospect. Her mind reeled at the thought of the damage Morgain could do with even one wish, let alone the traditional three!

However, rather than appear ready for wish-granting,

Mr. Knight had become distracted by some crumbs clinging to his breeches. He brushed them off, while Clarice wondered if this law of which Blaic had spoken only worked for human beings. Morgain, after all, was half-Fay.

She recalled her promise, so lightly given. *"I shall make it a point to touch every stranger I meet."*

She considered touching Mr. Knight herself. A brush of the fingers might tell her everything she needed to know. She took her seat again behind the tea tray, plotting.

Morgain was seated crosswise on the opposite settee, asking Mr. Knight questions about his books while eating preserved meat sandwiches at a great rate, despite his already maltreated stomach.

"Legends?" he said, arching an eyebrow. "I've heard a few. The maid at Tallyford Orphanage is a great hand at stories. She used to work for my mother before I was born."

Mr. Knight nodded solemnly. "I would very much like to meet her."

"She might talk to you. Mary doesn't care for strangers as a rule but she's always said 'a man may do as he likes with me . . . within reason.' " Unlike most boys, Morgain didn't speak too high or flutter his lashes when he imitated a woman. Yet for an instant his imp's face took on the character of a maid who'd achieved middle age without losing any of her charm or vivacity.

"Morgain, you'll give Mr. Knight the wrong impression," Clarice chided him gently. "Mary is a treasure," she said, turning toward the man. "Though the sister of our local physician is nominally in charge at the orphanage, I believe Mary truly runs the school. Morgain's mother began as directress there before her marriage and Mary went with her. Felicia left; Mary stayed on. I don't know how we should get along without her."

"This orphanage is a charity of yours, Lady Stavely?"

"Of my father's, rather. I continue his good work." She glanced up at the small clock upon the mantel as it awoke to sprinkle small silver notes over them. "Where *is* Camber?" she asked. "I rang for him quite ten minutes ago."

A moment later, he came in. "I beg pardon, my lady. Some Gypsies came to the back door and I found it necessary to deal with them myself."

"Gypsies? How odd. Well, never mind. Some macaroons, if you please, Camber. Oh, and pray bring another cup for Master Morgain."

"Yes, please, Camber," Morgain said, twisting around to look at the young butler, always one of his favored people. "Would you bring me a pot of stout Indian tea? I can't abide this smoky stuff. I don't think he likes it much either," he added, jerking his thumb toward his aunt's guest.

"On the contrary," Mr. Knight said, for which politeness Clarice honored him, even if he wasn't human. He took another sip, only his second. "I'm beginning to acquire a taste for it."

Clarice smiled at him and saw him blink with surprise at her sudden increase of warmth. "You shall have Indian, if you prefer. See to it, Camber."

"Yes, my lady."

She left it to Morgain to carry the conversation, something well within his powers. He too loved the vastness of the moor, the sense of centuries bearing down upon one, and also knew a surprising amount about the sheep that wandered the hills and dales. Whether Mr. Knight had any such interest, Clarice could not tell. Certainly he was polite when Morgain veered off into a monologue regarding the various merits of one kind of fleece over another.

She noticed, however, that Mr. Knight's smile had lost that patronizing quality that she had objected to. Obviously Mr. Knight only thought little of women. Anything *male* was worthy of his respect.

When Camber carried in the second round of refreshments, she broke in. "I think you'll quite like these. I can't tell you how many times my neighbors have tried to wrest the recipe from my cook. Isn't that right, Camber?"

"Yes, my lady. She stands proof against them all. Even bribery has failed."

Clarice put several of the browned puffs on a plate and offered it to Mr. Knight. When he reached out for it, she quite blatantly allowed her fingers to brush his as he took the plate.

His skin was warm against her own. It was the most fleeting of touches, yet the impression lingered so that she wrapped her left hand over her right to banish the sensation.

He stared down at the macaroons, his brows twitched together. Just as he had when she'd given him his first cup of tea, he seemed to take a moment to judge, to measure, and to ask deep questions of himself.

Then his dark-lashed lids lifted and he subjected her to the same look. He studied her carefully and at length, his eyes both dark and clear like smoky quartz. Clarice felt the hot color mount to her cheeks but she could not look away. She felt that he knew what she'd attempted by her touch and why.

But that was madness. If he were only what he seemed, then he could not know. Certainly he'd not leapt to offer his services in accordance with any faery Law.

At last, he turned again to listen to Morgain. Clarice let out her breath in a silent sigh, satisfied that he was no more than a man. She couldn't help, however, looking at him again, reappraising his person.

"But how foolish!" Morgain said, like a man of fifty reproving a youngster. Before she could chide him, he turned to her. "Now, Aunt, isn't it the height of folly to travel ten miles or more every day when a simple arrangement can be made to stay here?"

"I'm sorry, Morgain, I don't follow you."

"Mr. Knight intends to put up at the Magpie in Tallyford, seeing as the Ram's Head is full. Why shouldn't he stay here?"

"Here?"

"My father would have him to stay, I know he would."

"Undoubtedly, but . . ." She didn't quite know how to explain propriety to Morgain. After all, Mr. Knight was a stranger. To have an unknown man stay in her house, where she had only a boy and servants to chaperon, was not to be considered for an instant. On the other hand, he was an acquaintance of Blaic's and surely her credit was high enough to withstand any rumors that might fly about her. Best to make the offer and leave it to him refuse as no doubt he was eager to do.

"Mr. Knight is welcome to stay, of course. I should have thought of it myself."

Now was his opportunity to decline with thanks. Instead, he said, "Is Tallyford truly ten miles off?"

"Yes, it is. Vile bad roads too," Morgain said.

"I don't mind that. I came on horseback."

Clarice stiffened. "A dark bay?"

"Yes."

She wanted to ask if it was he who had chased her and why, but not in front of Morgain. Mr. Knight watched her curiously. Clarice did not meet his eyes again, though she was very much aware of their regard.

Morgain said, "There's half a dozen remnants of early civilization not half a mile from the gate here at Hamdry. I know every one of 'em and can take you to 'em."

"Your good aunt has already offered me the help of one of her tenants." Clarice thought this designation made her sound sixty years old if a day.

"Oh, she means Collie," Morgain said. "He's good. But not even *he* knows as much as me."

" 'As I,' " Clarice corrected.

"That's right," Morgain said. "She knows even more than I do. I've only been allowed to go alone on the moor in the last few years. *She's* been up there hundreds of times."

"I manage to totter up there once in a great while now I'm in my dotage," Clarice said, laughing at the boy.

At last, Mr. Knight said what politeness demanded. "I

cannot impose on your aunt, kind though she is to offer."

"It's hardly an imposition," she answered, having had a moment to consider. "I have more than enough room, and Morgain is right. Lodging in Tallyford will leave you to spend half the day coming and going. You should stay here. I am persuaded my brother-in-law expected me to offer you hospitality else he would not have introduced you to me at all."

"I assure you . . ."

"Cease to wriggle, Mr. Knight. I'll have Camber show you to your room."

Once again, she tugged the bell-pull. Mr. Knight rose to his feet and took her hand. "You're very kind, Lady Stavely. I feel quite at home already."

He raised her hand and bowed over it, a strangely courtly gesture from so ungallant a man. Yet that was not quite fair. He had an impassive countenance which made it nearly impossible to read what he was thinking. For one moment, though, she'd felt so strongly that he'd wanted to kiss her hand that it was almost as if he had done it. Certainly she was as flustered as though he had. She hardly had enough sense to direct Camber appropriately.

The moment the door closed behind the butler and her guest, she turned on Morgain. "You wretch!" she said, half-laughing.

"I, Aunt?"

"Don't look so innocent! What are you about, inviting a complete stranger to make himself at home in *my* house?"

"Don't you want Mr. Knight to stay? Why didn't you say so?"

"In front of him? That would have been prodigiously polite!"

"Oh, were you just doing the pretty with him?"

"Doing the what?"

"You know . . . saying what you don't mean to—er—jolly him along?"

"Where do you learn these terrible phrases? Never

mind; don't tell me. Does your mother know you speak like this?"

"No. Besides, I've heard you say worse things when you're at the stables."

"That's because . . . never mind!" She knew how fatally easy it was to let Morgain take command of a conversation and steer it all over creation. "You had no right to make so free an invitation to a man about whom I know nothing."

"*I* like him. He's an honest man. Besides, my father wrote you a letter about him. He doesn't make mistakes about people."

"No, he doesn't." She turned her head, looking around. "Where is that letter? I thought I put it down on my desk, but it's not there now."

Crossing the room, she looked under the mahogany desk that had been her father's. She even pushed back the sage green velvet drapes that hung in the double-height windows to see if it had flown off to lodge behind one. The letter had gone as utterly as if it had been dropped onto the fire.

"How odd."

"It'll turn up," Morgain said, completely uninterested. A moment later, he burped discreetly. He tucked his hand between two buttons of his waistcoat and put the other to his forehead. "Oh, Aunt Clarice . . ."

"I knew those sandwiches boded ill! Come along to your room. I'll find Pringle."

"Not more oil of walnuts, please . . ."

The long summer twilight hung like a shimmering veil across the sky. With an hour before him until supper, Mr. Knight walked in Hamdry's justifiably well-reputed garden. His hostess had intended to show it to him herself, but the renewed illness of her nephew had detained her. Dominic was just as well pleased to be alone.

He knew the names of none of the flowers that bloomed in merry profusion in the neat beds, and had no aesthete's eye for the sculptures that stood among the tall green hedges. Botany and art had never come much in his way. Yet something about the combination of cool stone and joyous color did seem to summon some appreciation from the depths of a soul uncultivated. If he had not had vital business in the grotto, he would have passed a happy hour there.

But his duty summoned him to the grotto at the bottom of the garden, not far from where a laughing streamlet flowed. He glanced around him to be certain he was unobserved. All his carefully trained senses were on the alert. He went into the grotto, satisfied that no one watched him.

The grotto was built of manmade stone, cunningly crafted to look quite real. Inside, it was snug enough, but only about eight feet deep, though twice as wide, with a high ceiling and a sanded floor. The opening allowed plenty of light to enter. The air inside felt pleasantly cool on his cheek. He was quite alone.

"I am here."

A queer echo brought his voice back to him almost as soon as he'd spoken. For a moment, nothing happened.

Dominic said again, "I am here."

This time, there came no echo. His words were snatched from his lips by a sudden wind that sprang up within the grotto. It sent his cravat flying into his face, flapped the tails of his coat about his sides, and brought with it a fragrance that shamed the scents of the Hamdry garden.

The back wall of the grotto vanished and a light as opulent and brilliant as the reflection from pure gold shone in. A shadow moved against this light, coming nearer. Dominic went down on one knee, his head bowed. A pair of velvet boots, the same soft brown that covered stag antlers in the spring, stood beside him.

"My king," he said humbly. "All is well. The mortal woman has taken me into her house. She does not suspect me."

"Excellent. You have done well."

Dominic could not accept praise that was not his due. "I have done nothing. She would not hear of my residing elsewhere."

"She is kind?"

"Most kind. Yet I think the false letter I showed her did more for me than even her kindness."

King Forgall sighed. "Yes, it was a ruse unworthy of us, useful though it may have proved."

"The boy too spoke for me. He is half-Fay, is he not?"

"I am certain I told you so."

"Never a word, my king."

Forgall's foot moved restlessly. "No? Well, 'tis true enough. His father was a prince among us and surrendered everything sooner than lose a woman. This woman you guard is at least halfway in love with him herself."

"I have seen no sign of this."

"But you have learned so much of war that the lessons of love have passed you by." The Fay-King's laugh was a whisper. "She is fair as well as kind, this Clarice Stavely?"

"Fair enough for a mortal woman, yet to one whose eyes have feasted on the beauty of the People, there can be little to desire elsewhere."

"Well answered, Dominic."

"How goes it on the Other Side, my king?"

The toe of one boot tapped the sand impatiently. "Our enemies are massing in the fastness of La'al. Many misguided brethren have flocked to the Pale Banner but without the key they seek, their treason will not succeed."

"They will not capture her while I live," Dominic swore.

"All I ask is that you keep the mortal woman safe-hidden until I have need of her." The soldier felt the press of his king's hand on his head like a benediction. "I have chosen well, o best of my soldiers."

"I hope that you have, my king."

The hand was withdrawn. "What? Do you doubt me? Or is it yourself you doubt?"

"Neither. Yet I wonder if I might not do more good by remaining with my cadre. I have lived only to be trained for war. Shall my arm, my strength all be wasted watching over one mortal woman, however vital?"

"This is strange talk from you. I chose you because you were the most loyal of all my knights—and the boldest. Now you question me?"

"What good is my boldness here?" Dominic clenched his fists and spoke in little more than a growl. "I have told some few lies to gain entrance to her house. Having done so, what now? Must I sit at my ease while my dearest comrades go to face battle? Eat and drink luxuriously while they suffer hardships?"

"I believe that it is they who pity you, my son. They remain in Mag Mell while you sojourn in the Lands of Sorrowing."

"You are pleased to jest, my king. Yet . . . yet . . ." Dominic spoke the thought that tortured him the most. "Shall not some fall that I might have saved had I been there?"

King Forgall's voice deepened. "Do you ask me to foretell the future? Not even I, most cunning of all the People, can do that. Yet this I will say . . . there may yet be a battle in which you will serve."

Dominic lifted his head, the light of hope in his eyes. "If it were true . . ."

"For now, you serve me best by obeying my behest. Stay here. Guard the woman. With good fortune, this war will be resolved in one or two weeks, as the mortals reckon the days. You will lose no honor by remaining here instead of waiting out the days encamped among your comrades."

"As your will commands, my king. Yet—"

Forgall's laughter was a trifle louder. "Still you contend with me?"

"Let me have word at times of how it progresses."

"You shall have that. Aught else?"

"A sword, so that if the day should come I shall not be slack through lack of training."

"You need not ask the King of the People for cold iron, Dominic. Look within that house, for it has withstood war before now."

Dominic raised his head still further to look upon his king. Forgall was broad across the shoulders and somewhat heavy through the middle, which his long tunic did in some measure disguise. His brown beard showed not a sign of gray, despite his years beyond counting. Only his eyes, deep as the unplumbed depths of the ocean, showed that he was other than a man of about forty.

He was now the eldest among the People, having succeeded to the kingship when the Oldest of All, Boadach, had resigned to become one of the Sleepers, wrapped forever in slumber with his long-since sleeping wife. It was said the Sleepers traveled in the world of dreams, visiting both mortals and immortals to weave their wonders.

Dominic did not think he would like to receive a dream of Boadach's weaving. The former king had hated humans with a vengeful passion in his life, all the more violently when he'd lost his own dearest child to a mortal man's love. Not even Dominic's long service as a warrior to the People would excuse his humanity in Boadach's eyes.

But Forgall never gave any sign of hating humans. He had invented the spell that made it possible to bring mortals into the Deathless Realm of Mag Mell. Some few had passed therein in days long past, brought by their faery lovers, and made immortal Fay themselves. But Forgall had found a way to bring mortals in, keeping their human qualities over lives stretched far beyond the normal span of days. The reason was simple. No one of the People could wield iron without suffering torments. Humans could.

So Forgall created a small standing army of *werreour,* stealing mortal boys from their own times, training them, and using them for tasks which the People could not perform—tasks requiring cold iron. When a dragon had gone mad, the *werreour* had subdued it. When the Dark

Forest had tried to encroach upon the peaceful orchards of the Westering Lands, they had come with ax and sword to drive it back. Despite their strength and their valor, they had never yet stood against the kind of army that was massing against the rightful king.

"It enrages me," Dominic said. "All was well until *she* came among us."

"Not so. The signs of decay had already begun. Matilda has merely hastened it. Perhaps—once we are successful—the process will reverse itself and all will be as once it was. If not, then at least we shall have peace for our last days."

"Is peace enough?"

"Ask those who have it not." Forgall's head turned and his bird-bright eye sharpened. "One comes. The woman. Be wary. These mortals have charms that we of Mag Mell know not."

The golden light faded and with it passed the king. The grotto wall was as solid as the day it was first built. Dominic rose slowly, the burden of what he knew heavy in his breast. He put on a show of examining the walls of the grotto.

Lady Stavely—with that name she should have been some middle-aged woman, ripe with dignity and poise—poked her fair head in. "Here you are, Mr. Knight. Admiring the family folly?"

"For what purpose was this place constructed?"

"My grandfather had a foolish fancy to install an ornamental hermit at Hamdry. This was the poor man's residence, at least during the summer months. What a miserable time he must have had!" She looked about her, and shook her head.

"What is an ornamental hermit?" Dominic asked, watching her carefully.

"The idea was, it seems, that if one is going to build a ruin that favors the picturesque, one should have the proper personages about to set the tone. I believe one duchess had live sheep and shepherds to provide a living fabric for her rustic folly, while another had girls in an-

tique costumes to stand about her *faux* Greek temple.
My grandfather preferred a hermit."

"None of these people objected to be used in such a
way? It seems most careless of these duchesses and,
though I don't wish to speak slightingly of your family,
your grandfather."

Clarice bowed as if in agreement. "I imagine they
were glad enough of regular meals, and one can't say
the duties were onerous. Rather boring, perhaps."

Casting another glance around, she added, "Almost as
boring as this empty place."

After a moment, she smiled at him. He could not recall anyone ever smiling at him in just that way before—
as if she wanted to be friends. Among the *werreour*,
there was an unspoken comradeship based on shared
training and those travails they'd undergone. Dominic
owed his allegiance to his cadre and to his king. Yet
there were no friendships, no seeking out of one particular person over another. His memories of a life before
he was stolen away were so dim as to be all but mean-
ingless.

Nonetheless, something in Clarice's beautiful smile
warmed him. He wanted to return it, but he was unused
to the exercise. He unbent his lips a trifle, all that he
could manage for the moment.

"I find this grotto to be most interesting," he said.

"My garden is much more beautiful, and not nearly
so stuffy! Besides, I believe I saw a spider move in the
corner and I abominate spiders."

"Why? They are useful creatures."

"Undoubtedly. Yet I am—to be frank—terrified of
them. Shall we?"

Dominic found dining to be something of a trial. Not
only did he eat no meat, but there were so many tiny
rules of etiquette—the breaking of which would instantly expose him as a fraud. Fortunately, the boy was
still indisposed and the table was sufficiently long so
that, between the flickering candles and the dim shad-

ows, he felt Clarice could not distinguish the errors he made.

He'd never seen so much metal at one time as was spread out on the tabletop before him. Gold was used a little among the People; silver rarely; iron never. Steel was unknown except in the finest *werreour* weaponry and that was all stolen from mortal treasuries. Yet here were steel-bladed knives, sterling silver vases, cups, flatware, a candelabra, and even a salver or two. The sight of all that highly polished splendor overwhelmed him and made him feel ever so slightly nervous.

Dominic tested a knife on the ball of his thumb. "Blood-steel," he said to himself.

"I beg your pardon, Mr. Knight?" Without waiting for his answer, Clarice said, "I really must scold Camber for this ridiculous arrangement. He must have added two leaves to this table. We might as well be seated in different rooms!"

"He is concerned for your reputation?"

"Yes, but they go too far. All of them. That is one of the difficulties with old family retainers, Mr. Knight. They forget that I am mistress here." She softened. "I cannot blame them, I suppose. They have known me since my childhood and cannot forget it. In somewise, I will always be little Miss Clarice to them, in need of protection."

He felt her gaze upon him and knew that he had missed again some vital cue. Constantly trying to determine what he had left unsaid or undone was a great strain. An ordinary mortal would have found his path much easier than he, who had to stop and think what would be appropriate.

"You have no need to fear me," he said and saw her grow haughty once more. When her merry eyes turned cool and her head went up, Clarice resembled very strongly the witch-woman Matilda who threatened the peace and security of the Wilder World. It was a sharp reminder of what he was doing here.

"I need fear no one," she said. "I have protectors enough."

Some bustle and noise at the front door caused her to turn her attention away from him. "I wonder what . . ."

"It's the doctor," Dominic said, his sharp hearing distinguishing this phrase amid the hum of several people talking at once.

"Doctor Danby? I haven't sent for him." She rose from her chair just as the door opened. Camber bowed from the waist and announced the doctor.

Clarice advanced, her right hand held out. Dominic also stood up, holding his knife half-concealed in his large hand, yet at the ready. The enemies of King Forgall might take on any form, even of a wizened old man with no hair. This doctor looked entirely too much like a warlock for Dominic's peace of mind.

"I'm very glad to see you, Doctor," Clarice said as the old man bent to kiss her hand. "This morning, Morgain ate entirely too many green apples. . . ."

"I know about the young fool's behavior at the Yeo orchard. Discovered a bellyache among the branches, eh?"

Dominic found himself being appraised by a piercing pair of eyes under a disconcerting pair of white eyebrows. The doctor was entirely bald on top, with a mottled head. His eyebrows, however, were elegant plumes of white not unlike egret feathers. His voice was harsh and surprisingly deep. Snuff powder marred his old-fashioned waistcoat and black velvet suit. Dominic, who had been carefully tutored in the appearance of a gentleman, wondered at the adept's untidiness. He bowed when the doctor's eye fell on him.

Dr. Danby said nothing to him, however. "Yes, I'll go up and check him over. Young idiot ate what? Why on earth didn't you stop him? What am I saying? Who ever stopped Morgain from doing as he pleased."

"Certainly not I," Clarice said. "He tolerates me, only just, because his parents tell him to."

Doctor Danby's rasping sniff might have been meant

for laughing agreement. He said, "I'll report on him before you've finished your pudding."

Clarice seated herself again and indicated with a gesture that Dominic should copy her. "Speaking of protectors . . ." she said wryly.

"Yes, we were."

"He's one. Doctor Danby. I'd wager he came here
with the express purpose of seeing you."

"I?" No one had warned him that these strange cravats
could suddenly grow too tight. "I am in no need of a
doctor."

Her cheeks looked quite pink. "I'm sure he's come to
make sure you are a suitable person to shelter beneath
the Hamdry roof. I am such a poor innocent, you see,
that any smooth-tongued gentleman may worm himself
into my good graces with no more than a compliment."
Suddenly her voice carried without in any way growing
too loud. "Isn't that correct, Camber?"

The butler came in, carrying a gaily decorated china
epergne stacked with fruit. "I felt it incumbent upon me
to inform the good doctor of your guest. Please forgive
me, my lady."

"Oh, Camber, you're impossible when you're humble.
Go on with you."

She pulled a freakishly charming face at Dominic,
who was at first taken aback to see her pleasing countenance so distorted. Yet in a moment, he found himself
smiling at the memory.

"I told you I was not without protectors," she said.

"I see it to be true indeed," Dominic said, wondering
how he was supposed to guard her from the king's enemies when she had so very many friends.

Four

~

Doctor Danby stumped into Clarice's sitting room. "Agreeable fellow, that."

"Morgain? Agreeable is hardly what you called him last time."

"Not that scamp! Nothing ails him that a little fore-thought would have avoided. So I told him. Yet he'd hardly be a boy if he didn't fall into these scrapes. I was speaking of your unexpected guest, Knight."

"He seems a little . . . I don't know . . . patronizing?"

"Not a bit of it! Feels just as he ought about staying here. Told me he'd leave in a heartbeat if I thought it wrong."

"And do you?" Clarice asked, smiling up at him. She sat in an easy chair, a lamp close by on a little table. Her book was held in her lap, with a finger between the pages, and her reading spectacles had slid halfway down her nose.

"I confess I was thinking it at first, but, lord, Mr. Knight's no hothead to fall in love with your face and make himself a nuisance to you. A sober, intelligent fellow, and a friend to your own brother-in-law."

"Exactly what I thought when I'd given the matter a

moment's consideration. It is not as though I were alone here, either."

"Servants. Hmph." The doctor folded his lips together as he thought. "I could wish Mrs. Henry were still residing here. A genteel companion is just the thing to keep tongues from wagging."

"My dear doctor, tongues have wagged over me so often that I have very nearly accustomed myself to the hum. You know to the hour how old I am. If a spinster lady of nearly twenty-seven years cannot entertain a man in her home without being thought *fast,* when can she?"

"Aye, I know to the hour your age, m'dear, and I tell you frankly there's not many would take you to be more than nineteen."

She took her glasses off and folded the stiff wire temples together with a sigh. "Some days I feel forty-five."

"Eh?" He came near and took her wrist in his cool fingers, counting her pulse. "Slow and even. Can't be illness."

"I'm well enough."

"Bored, eh?"

"Terribly so. I did not know how much I would miss Melissa until she'd gone. Now I have no one to talk to."

"With Morgain in the house? He talks enough for two."

"Yes, he can carry on both sides of the conversation without my adding a word! He's a dear whom I love for his own sake, quite as much as for his mother's. Yet, he is just a boy and I want someone . . . someone . . ."

"You should marry, m'dear."

"Find me a husband, darling Doctor Danby, and I shall stand in your debt." She rose gracefully to her feet, leaving her book on the cushion. Walking to the window, she pushed aside the blue velvet curtain and looked down into the garden, though she could see little beyond some streaks of pink and gold in the sky. "I envy Felicia so. Her husband came to her like a miracle. I can't even find one when I search."

"You should return to London. You had offers. . . ."

"*Such* offers! A fortune hunter looking for a snug harbor, a dissolute nobleman whose praise of my person bordered on the vulgar, and a couple of youngsters who fell in love with my face. The rest were too frightened of my family's reputation for eccentricity to come nigh me, though pleased enough to stand up for a quadrille. There was no one to know me and no one to care. I will never go on the Marriage Mart again, Doctor."

"You'll never find a husband while you stay holed up in Hamdry."

This was so true she could not bear to hear it. She forced a laugh. "Never mind me. I'm in the sullens and feeling quite sorry for myself. I'll come right tomorrow. Now! About Mr. Knight. Though I find him rather arrogant, you think he is entirely harmless?"

"Oh, as harmless as a man could be, I fancy, especially if you've taken a dislike to him. And yet it's a pity we can't put it about that he's your cousin or some such."

"We could . . ." Clarice said temptingly. She could see Doctor Danby consider the notion.

"Won't fadge," he said after a moment. "Everybody knows your father's sister's children all died young. If we went any further afield than that, it'd be just the same as it is now. You wouldn't perhaps marry your *first* cousin, though I've known it done, but there's nothing to prevent you marrying a second or third cousin."

"I wish I had one to marry," Clarice said, only half in fun.

"There, now. Sooner or later, Providence will provide."

"I live in hope. In the meantime, I will give houseroom to Mr. Knight, as it is what my brother-in-law should like. I only wish I could find that letter so I could show you it."

"Probably the maid tidied it away. They're forever doing it to me. Can never find a thing after they've been through."

Clarice knew better than to let the good doctor start

one of his favorite hobbyhorses. She stood up to take him to the door. "Morgain will be well by morning, do you think?"

"Keep him on a low diet tomorrow and don't let that nurse of yours quack him. He'll be all right and tight by dinnertime tomorrow."

"You relieve my mind. He should hate to be kept cooped up for long. He wishes to accompany Mr. Knight on some of his expeditions up the moor."

"I see no harm in that, if Collie Camber goes along to haul him out of whatever trouble he's bound to find. Mind you, this Knight fellow seems capable enough. Indeed, does it not seem to you that he is a thought muscular for a man who lives by his pen?"

Clarice hid a smile behind her hand, turning her face away as though to glance at one of the pictures hung along the upper hall. Doctor Danby sometimes did her the honor of forgetting that she was female, and unmarried as well. Others might ask her opinion of a horse; only the doctor would dare ask her about a man's physique.

"No," she said, lying, "I hadn't noticed particularly. Perhaps he has some hobby that would account for it."

"Hmm, 'tis possible. I understand that pugilism is increasingly popular among the young bloods though this fellow hasn't the look of one of those wastrels."

"I don't know about boxing," Clarice admitted.

"No, of course not. How should you? I dare say that Mr. Knight rides and walks a great deal which would naturally improve his health."

"No doubt. After all, he must trek over hill and dale to find the subjects he writes of. Viking relics and such don't come calling on a man."

The doctor nodded yet still he frowned. Clarice said, "You are quite sure that I have not done wrong in permitting Mr. Knight to remain at Hamdry?"

"I—no, not wrong. Imprudent, perhaps. But you may rely on me, m'dear. Once I tell my good wife that I find

Mr. Knight unexceptionable, I'm sure the county will follow my lead."

This was true. Mrs. Danby never gossiped about her husband's patients' ailments. The rest of their histories proved not only fair but irresistible game. If she could be persuaded to take a lenient view of Mr. Knight, her attitude would color all her tales and thus influence her hearers. "Do bring her to luncheon tomorrow. I don't believe that we have met since Melissa's wedding."

"She would like it above all things. Only not tomorrow, my dear. She's making an expedition in to Exeter to buy a wedding present for her niece." They passed a few moments talking about the prospects for happiness of the doctor's wife's niece until Camber appeared with the doctor's greatcoat and stick. "Your gig is at the door, sir."

"Thank you, Camber. Good night, m'dear." Pausing on the threshold, the doctor took two or three deep breaths of the warm summer air. "Wonder if any of us will keep our engagements for tomorrow. I smell fog in the air."

"Does fog have a scent?" Clarice asked, diverted.

"Aye. So does rain and snow if you stop a minute to think. I've lived on the edge of the great moor longer even than your ladyship. I may have learned a thing or two in that time. There will be fog tomorrow, sure as a gun."

"Do you come anyway, if it should prove not too thick," Clarice urged.

The doctor only waved his stick noncommittally as he heaved himself into the gig. Clarice stood in the lamplight, waving, as he drove away down the drive. When she breathed in, there was a definite scent, misty and ill-defined but undeniable. "Can you smell fog, Camber?"

"No, my lady. But my grandfather could."

She cast a look around, half-considering a short stroll before retiring. A trifle of exercise often kept her from a restless night. Then Clarice remembered the shadowy figure of a cloaked man watching the house. She wondered if he were out there now.

The evening air suddenly seemed much cooler. Clarice shivered and retreated into the house, letting the butler close the door. "I mustn't neglect my guest," she said. "Where is Mr. Knight?"

"I believe you will find him in the Red Chamber, my lady. He desired me to inform him whether there were any antique weapons in the house."

"Oh, yes. Of course."

"My lady?" Camber spoke just as she was turning toward the stairs. "Will the gentleman be staying?"

"Yes, Camber. Doctor Danby sees nothing amiss in his staying on, nor do I. You exceeded your duties when you sent for Doctor Danby, you know."

"I thought it wise, my lady. We know nothing of this Mr. Knight."

"Never mind, Camber. I'm not angry."

She knocked on the door before she went in. The Red Chamber was undoubtedly the most formal room at the Manor. It had been her father's room and his father's before him. It was hung with dark red silk wallpaper with openwork paneling in a vaguely Chinese style. The black oak bed that occupied the center of the room was large enough for four people to lie down side by side. The other furniture was not nearly so massive, having been in the best of taste of sixty years previously.

The thing that had most interested her father was what held Mr. Knight in fascination now. He stood before the outer wall, looking with awe at an interlocking pattern of swords, daggers, and knives that filled in the space between the windows.

"My grandfather collected them," she said, coming to stand beside him. He'd given no sign that he'd heard her tap at the door, yet neither did he start in surprise when she spoke. "He was a great traveler. I don't know what they all are. My father told me once. I only wish he'd written it all down."

"This one is Arabian," Mr. Knight said, lifting his

lamp higher and reaching out to trace the shape of one curved blade. "You see the writing?"

The letters seemed as sharp and warlike as the sword itself. "I thought that was just decorative."

"No, it's Arabic. It says, " 'The lamp of heaven is fueled by the blood of my enemies.' "

"My goodness! You read Arabic?"

Ignoring the questions, he turned to point out another blade, shining with a pattern of gold inset in the silver. "This one is from Spain. See the crowns? Andrea Ferria, greatest of the European swordsmiths. And that one, with the black and gold cords traversing the hilt? The Japanese have their own methods and their blades are all but unbreakable."

"You are an enthusiast, Mr. Knight."

"I have studied. Do they come down from the wall?"

"I suppose they must. May I beg a favor?" She felt vaguely piqued that he did not turn to her when she spoke. "As I say, I have no catalog of these weapons. Perhaps during your visit, if you'd be so good, you could list those that you know. If we number each sword and write down the corresponding number in a book, then I would have at least a partial listing. It's a great shame when knowledge is lost irretrievably, don't you think?"

He turned toward her then, the lamplight shining on his face. There was a smile on his lips and a warmth in his eyes that quite transformed him from the arrogant man she'd seen earlier into someone entirely delightful. His enthusiasm was as warming as a fire. "I should be delighted, Lady Stavely. And honored. It's an excellent collection. Your grandfather had a discerning eye."

"Not too discerning," she said, responding to his warmth. "He also chose all the furnishings for this room."

Mr. Knight held up his lamp to survey the bed. "He must have had a great many friends come to stay."

"I doubt they all shared that bed, Mr. Knight."

"They could have done. Easily. And stabled a few horses as well."

She couldn't help being amused by the picture conjured in her mind of a bed crowded with her grandfather's haughty and noble acquaintances and their
livestock. She fought down a giggle and the urge to continue in this humorous vein by adding a few elephants.

Instead she said prosaically, "The maids hate this
room. All this dark wood makes it so gloomy and the
deep carving on the bed is very difficult to dust. I daresay they're right and yet I don't believe I ever shall
change it. It has been in that spot since the house was
built and came out of the manor that was here before
that."

"It's a good room and the bed is the key," Mr. Knight
said, responding to her sober judgment. "I imagine it
would be easy to look upon it and feel as though one
were part of something greater than oneself. I am sorry
I made a foolish jest about it."

Clarice glanced at him. She'd hardly seen enough of
him to know whether he was a man of deep feeling or
no feeling at all. Yet there'd been understanding and
more, a kind of empathy that she'd never met with before, in his voice.

"That is precisely how I feel. When I come in here, I
think of all the other Stavelys who have slept there or,
for that matter, who have dusted it. I am part of them,
just as they are part of me. Is there anything in your
home that gives you just that feeling?"

"Nothing."

"I'm sure there must be, 'else how could you know?"

He shook his head gravely, his dark hair catching the
light and sending it back with a faint red glow. "My
home is far away by any reckoning. I have not been
there in many years."

"Are your parents still living?"

"No. They are long-since gone."

"I am sorry. I lost both parents myself when I was
but sixteen."

"I was younger even than that. Shall we go out? I feel
certain your doctor would not think it proper for us to

be discussing beds, however old and venerable." This was delivered with no hint of humor, rather as a mere commonplace.

"Safe" in the hall, Clarice said, "Usually at this time I spend an hour or so with the account books. I am, however, more than willing—nay, eager!—to put them off if you would care for a game of chess."

"Are your accounts so trying?"

"I confess I do not love mathematics. I can do it, but I do not enjoy it."

"I enjoy chess. However, I don't wish to keep you from your duties and the day has been long. Perhaps we can play a match tomorrow?"

"Yes, tomorrow."

It was the first time since Melissa's wedding that Clarice looked forward to the day ahead. After paying a brief visit to Morgain and Pringle to be certain all was well, she retired to her own room. There, she sat before the mirror, brushing out her hair, while her maid, Rose, bustled about, putting away gown, fichu, and stays.

"Who is tending to Mr. Knight?" Clarice asked.

"Mr. Camber himself, ma'am."

"I had no idea Camber knew anything about valeting!"

"Oh, yes, my lady. When the fine gentlemen would come to visit yer father, he'd always be takin' time to speak with them haughty fellows as what come to tend 'em. Learned more'n a little 'bout them things."

"He never confessed a yearning to be a gentleman's gentleman to me. I always thought the height of his ambition was to fill Mr. Varley's shoes, which I must say he does better than Varley ever did."

Rose gave a delightful giggle, quite at odds with her matronly appearance. "I was niver zo glad in all my borned laife as when he took hisself off. Gloomy as church in the rain, he was. We all below stairs like Mr. Camber ever zo much more, even if he was just a footman afore."

Clarice laid her brush down and removed her combing

mantle. With a stretch, she said, "I shall sleep well to-night!"

"I'm zhure you is worn to the nubbin. You'm must be ever zo feart when your horse run away with you, my lady."

"Who told you that?" Rose gave her only a blank look and a shrug. Clarice knew it was impossible to keep anything from her servants. What they weren't told they discovered by other means or invented. Unlike some other tales which she'd only laughed at, this one rankled. She hadn't been run away with since she mounted her first saddle.

"Good night, Rose," Clarice said, knowing any explanation would only make matters worse. Her reputation for horsemanship would just have to suffer this one backcast.

"Sleep well, my lady." The maid dipped a curtsy and left, carrying away my lady's shoes to be cleaned. One beeswax candle burned away behind a screen, the sweet honey scent delicately perfuming the air. The night was still, without even the sighing of a breeze sweeping down from the moor. Clarice realized she had not looked out of her window to see if the doctor's prophecy of fog had come true. If she were not lying in the most deliciously comfortable position, she would have instantly thrown off the bedclothes to find out. Before she was well-launched into a rebuke of herself for being so lazy, she was asleep.

Not until she had awakened the next morning did she realize that she had not, after all, sat by her window looking out for the mysterious watcher.

She rose earlier than was her usual practice. Dawn had just begun to lighten the gray of the night. On the rare occasions that she did awaken early, she usually lay about in bed, trying to recapture sleep, for there was little point in getting up before any of the house servants accomplished their morning rituals. It would discommode them in their daily duties to have her underfoot.

This morning, however, she felt as if someone had

called her name. The moment her eyes opened, she tossed aside the confining counterpane and all but leapt from the low white bed. She dressed herself in the same light blue silk gown she'd worn yesterday, lacing her short overjacket rather more loosely than Rose or Pringle would have thought seemly. All the while she dressed, she felt an inner urgency.

While she pulled back the curtains, she realized that she'd not thought about the watcher in the garden after she'd met Mr. Knight in her father's room. Suddenly she felt no doubts of the wisdom of having offered him hospitality. If there were housebreakers or dangerous persons about, it would be protection to have a gentleman in the house. Dominic Knight could quell a housebreaker with a cold glance and a few disdainful words.

She tied a lace-trimmed cloth over her free-flowing hair and opened the door. It was the work of a moment to slip her feet into her newly cleaned shoes and trot down the hall. As she reached the top step, she heard the gentle bong of the tall-case clock in the entryway. It sounded only once.

"Half-past what?" Clarice wondered. When she reached the ground, she wished very much for her spectacles. She went close to the clock to be certain. "Half-past five? Heavens, the last time I was up so early, I'd been out all night."

She hardly had time to marvel before some inner compulsion drove her out of doors. The big front door had several locks. Camber held the master keys, while Clarice had a set of her own that jangled on the end of her chatelaine. She rarely wore the heavy silver chain and always became confused among the many tiny implements a proper lady carried. She'd pull out her toothpicks when a tweezer was wanted and find her corkscrew when she needed thread. The belt and the keys were in her room. Clarice felt too restless to hurry back for them.

Instead she opened one of the tall windows and slipped out onto the grass. Her shoes were instantly wet with dew. Her hems were not in much better condition. It had either rained heavily in the night or Doctor Danby was a better weather prophet than she'd ever guessed. As she came around the corner of the house, she knew Doctor Danby's reputation was secured.

Veils and shreds of fog lingered in corners where the newborn sun did not yet reach. Festoons of vapor still ensnared the trees and lay in wait in treacherous low spots. For the most part, however, the fog had cleared. She would not have gone on if it had remained thick on the ground, for that was a sure way to wind up confused, lost on the moor.

Her sense of summoning remained as she hurried into the garden, turning down the center path. The sun rose a little higher, gilding the mist. Like faery gold, it vanished as soon as Clarice came near, turning cold and gray when it seemed she had it within her grasp.

She'd come to a blind corner among the green yew hedges when she understood that the deep rhythmic sounds she'd been half-consciously hearing for some time were the breaths of someone laboring hard. She looked around the corner just as the sun lifted above the low-lying clouds and sent shimmering beams into the dark places. She caught her breath at the sight before her.

Dominic Knight stood there, naked to the waist, his broad chest gleaming with sweat. In his left hand, he held a sabre, a two-and-a-half-foot long swath of brutal steel. Each wrist was bound with white bandages, crisscrossing their way around his wrists.

Yet it wasn't the sword or the bandages that enthralled her and kept her so still that she could not have spoken for her life. It was the sight of his magnificent body. She'd been raised to appreciate the arts of the sculpture above all others, though she'd always felt that no one could live up to the fabulous likeness in stone. Now she saw a man who surpassed the images.

He did not bulge in any vulgar way. He resembled in no way the overdeveloped brute of the tawdry traveling fairs. Dominic's body was all sleek circles and defined planes. Every muscle seemed to flow into the next in a manner exceptionally pleasing to her eyes. She wanted to stare endlessly, noticing the ridges of his stomach and the light furring of dark hair on his chest.

Clarice closed her eyes and told herself she was a fool. *She* who always hated being stared at and judged on her face alone now did the same thing to this poor man. This severity did her little good when she could see Dominic nearly as well with her eyes closed as with them open. The sight of him would not soon be forgotten.

She looked again, quite against her better judgment, and gasped.

He had picked up another sword from the ground, which had been lying there unnoticed by Clarice. It was a scimitar, equal in size to the sabre, though with a more pronounced curve to its shining blade. Now without a moment's hesitation he began to swing the two swords around his body.

His bare feet were set wide apart, as though anchoring him to the earth. He began quite slowly, moving the two blades in a simple pattern. With each repetition he moved more and more quickly and added complications to the basics. Soon, his arms and hands moved so fast that the sword-blades soon seemed little more than flashing silver wings. He slashed them about his sides and appeared to spin them from hand to hand far too quickly for her to be certain that a switch had been made.

Clarice's heart felt squeezed by an equal mixture of admiration and terror. She knew perfectly well that her father had ordered the swords maintained in what he'd called "fighting trim" despite the hundred other calls on him. Therefore, the point and half of each blade was ground to an unnecessarily sharp edge. One mistake and Dominic could find his arm or his head on the ground beside him. A warning strangled in her throat. If only she could be sure that her interruption would not cause the very fatality she wanted to avoid.

Dominic paused for an instant and Clarice hoped he was finished. But the pause seemed only to serve to increase the speed and vigor of his cuts through the air. His lips were drawn back in a tense approximation of a grin while he did not seem to look at the swords at all. He stared straight ahead, his eyes fixed on nothing while the sweat poured off him, darkening his waistband.

Clarice wondered how long he could keep it up. The weight and length of the swords must require tremendous strength to whip them around as Dominic was doing. He was grunting now with the effort, stomping his naked feet in repetitive patterns as the weight of the swords pulled him this way and that.

She found herself, all unconsciously, rocking back and forth in concert with his movements, as though she were lending him her morsel of strength. She'd never seen anything so terrifying and yet so beautiful as this exotic practice. It had something of the mystical about it, for Dominic Knight seemed transfigured—changed by the magic of steel from a gentleman to a warrior out of legend.

With a suddenness that left her breathless, Dominic pulled the swords close to his body, catching them up tight under his arms. She winced, thinking that the slightest error would have brought the cutting edges against his flesh, but apparently he'd maintained such concentration that he must have known it was the blunt side.

He shook the sweat out of his eyes. It was only then that he saw her, though she'd been in plain sight all the while. Clarice saw him blink, saw him start, as though he'd come back suddenly from a great distance. He dropped his hands, the swords carrying his arms downward.

She hurried toward him, pulling the cloth from her hair. "Mr. Knight, I . . . I've never seen anything like that."

She extended the cloth to him so he might wipe his brow. His broad chest still rose and fell to the deep breaths of exertion yet he was recovering more quickly than she would have believed possible. With reverence he laid the swords down on a blanket that he'd spread out nearby. "Do you mind that I borrowed these?"

"No. How could I? I've always thought of my grandfather's collection as merely overgrown knives but now . . . now I understand."

He looked at her with his dark, yet brilliant eyes. "Do you?"

"Yes. They're almost alive, aren't they? When you use them, they come to life."

"So I have been told." He wiped his face and draped the cloth about the back of his neck. Though the sight of lace on his firm body was a notable contrast, Clarice felt no desire to laugh.

"Told? But you must see it for yourself? When you are in the midst of all that . . ."

"No, it's not like that for me. I can't explain. There are my hands and the blades. I can see them, I know where each one is at any moment but I am not thinking of them. I am not thinking of anything during the discipline. It's like that in war too . . . so I am told."

"Who tells you? Who taught you?"

"My father was my first teacher. He died when I was very young, but he had fought once upon a time."

"It must have been exciting when duels were common. I cannot argue with the idea that such violence should be outlawed and yet what daring we have lost!"

He chuckled, a trifle grimly perhaps. "Are you one of those who would be elated to find two men dueling to the death for a rose from your breast?"

"To the death? Oh, no. I shouldn't like anyone to fight over me at all, merely to have the opportunity to do so if they wished!"

Dominic laughed, as though delight took him by surprise. Clarice colored. "You must think I sound bloodthirsty."

"Charmingly so."

Clarice shied away from the return of his patronizing

tone. Or perhaps that was Mr. Knight's idea of flirtation. Either way, she did not like it. "You shouldn't stand about like that. You'll catch a chill and with all this fog it will go directly to your lungs."

"I am in remarkable health for a man of my age," Dominic answered.

He knelt on the grass and began to roll up the blanket. Each sword, and she saw that there were several more in addition to the sabre and the scimitar, was wrapped around before the next was added to the bundle. He made no particular work over this, and Clarice wondered how many times he'd collected weapons in this fashion. In the end, he stood up with a neat package just as long as the longest sword and thin enough to tuck comfortably under his arm.

"Have you ever fought anyone?" Clarice asked, realizing she sounded a disingenuous seventeen.

"Yes, but not over a woman."

"I did not ask you that."

He turned his head to smile at her. She had not noticed yesterday how straight and white his teeth appeared. Nor that he bore a scar, long-faded, at the outside corner of his right eye. Only the level beams of the morning sun revealed it to her now. It drew down the outside edge of his lid a trifle, giving him a slightly wary expression, as though he looked out of the corner of his eye at everything. She wondered if it was that, however faint an impression it left, that made her think yesterday that he was guileful.

He stood up with an easy, confident grace that made no apologies for its beauty. Nor did he make any excuse for his half-dressed state. Clarice understood that it must be nearly impossible to achieve the kind of speed with which he'd drilled while wearing any restrictive clothing. Even the best tailor would be in a puzzlement over how to stitch a shirt to permit such arm movements.

"You must be hungry," Clarice said, starting toward the house. "If anyone's awake, I'll order breakfast to be served at once."

"I need little," he answered. "I do not wish to burden your household."

"Don't be absurd. You are my guest. Ask for what you will."

"Very well, provided I may say the same to you, if ever you visit my home."

"Where is your home, Mr. Knight?"

"I was born in a small village called Priory St. Windle. It is in the north."

" 'Priory St. Windle'? Forgive me; I'm unfamiliar with it."

"Few people are."

"You have some family still residing there?"

"My family? No. We were cast to the four winds long ago."

"When your parents died." She shaded her eyes, apparently against the sunshine, now pouring like honey over the grass and dazzling against the windows. "I know what it is to be alone."

He did not speak again until he stood back to let her enter the house first through the window. Then he said, "There are worse things than being alone."

Five

~

Clarice had little loneliness to complain of that day. In the morning, she had Morgain, fully restored to his usual rude good health, to bear her company. They had their favorite pastime to occupy them—the invention of a fabulous geography. Ever since the winter that Morgain was six, a hard winter when Clarice had been unexpectedly snowbound at the Gardners' small but pleasant home, nephew and aunt had enjoyed creating these "maps." Morgain had inherited something of his mother's talent for art, though he preferred pen-and-ink to watercolors and oils.

"I think we need to add another Pit of Peril," Morgain said. "Over here by the Sugar Swamp."

Clarice knew well that her part was to approve Morgain's suggestions and to rein in his natural boy's tendency to create zones of havoc rather than peaceful realms. His imagination had been fired by the adventures of King Arthur's knights and other tales of high daring.

"That's a good place for a pit, dear. But don't forget that you've put a nest of basilisks there. Don't have them fall into the pit."

"Oh, basilisks never fall in! If it were gryphons, that would be a different tale. Gryphons! I forgot them. I'll put them down here, by the mountains. They'll like it there."

She felt deeply sympathetic toward the invented residents of any land that Morgain drew. Between the bubbling volcanoes where the dragons dwelt and the forests of innocent appearance but deadly misdirection, they had but little chance of living to an imagined old age.

After an hour or so, Morgain began slaughtering his population with too liberal a hand. Clarice intervened, suggesting that they go riding after luncheon. The boy looked up from his map, saying, "Are you certain, ma'am? After yesterday . . ."

"I do wish everyone would forget this ridiculous notion of my having been run away with!"

"Then what did happen?"

"Nothing of importance. At any rate, I should like to go riding and would appreciate your companionship, if you wish to give it."

"You know that I should like it above all things, only . . . I did in somewise offer my services to Mr. Knight, though he seemed to have little wish to go up to the moor today."

Thinking of now exhausted anyone would be after taking the sort of exercise he had, Clarice could not be too surprised. They had spoken little after entering the house, separating to go to their respective rooms. He had taken the swords with him. Clarice had barely shut her door behind her before Rose had come up with a cup of tea and a can of hot water. She'd exclaimed at finding her mistress up and gowned, though she'd been appalled to find that Clarice had already been out and had spoiled her dress. How much more she would have exclaimed and scolded if she'd known Dominic Knight had been out as well. It would have looked ill, as though they'd had a clandestine meeting.

At the luncheon table, she greeted him with an unexpectedly shy smile. Though he was once again properly dressed in neat, dark clothing, she saw before her eyes the expanse of his chest, the shifting highlights on his working muscles and the beautiful lines of his back and hips. It was with something of a blush that she took her seat.

As usual, Morgain came scrambling into the room just as Camber began serving the soup. Taking his seat, he said, "Are you going up to the moor today, Mr. Knight?"

"Not today, if that is acceptable to your aunt. I want to talk to this Collie Camber before I go wandering."

The butler gave no sign that he'd heard this reference to his brother but went on serving rolls and butter as imperturbably as though he were deaf.

"Good!" Morgain said. "You can come riding with us. When I was down in the stables this morning, Jem and Jasper were singing the praises of your horse. He's a bright bay," Morgain added for his aunt's information.

"Is he?" Clarice's suspicions had been insensibly allayed by Dominic's performance this morning. Now, though, she wondered what other secrets he might be concealing.

"Yes. Two white stockings and a clever nose. He found the sugar I had in my pocket quick as winking!"

"Two white stockings," Clarice echoed, thinking back. She felt certain that the horse that had chased her in the lane had been without markings of any kind.

Dominic chuckled, a deep, warmly masculine sound. "Yes, Captain is notoriously greedy. Take care he doesn't knock you down in his zeal."

"Do you hunt, Mr. Knight?" Clarice asked, tearing her roll.

"No. It's too expensive to keep hunters and there's little sport to be had on a hired horse."

"Then you *have* hunted?"

She glanced at him when his answer did not come at once. He looked confused and slightly embarrassed. Clarice urged, "Mr. Knight?"

"Forgive me, Lady Stavely, for speaking more authoritatively than I have a right to. I had read that somewhere once and it seemed very sensible. I have no knowledge of hunting at all, not even the cost of keeping such horses."

"Pray don't think of it." Clarice glanced at him, confused. The arrogant man she'd met yesterday would not have known how to make such a handsome apology for such a minor matter. Had she misjudged him? Perhaps the patronizing tone he'd used had been born of nervousness and was not an example of his true nature at all.

The rest of the meal passed quietly. A chance question gave Morgain the opportunity to talk extensively about his fanciful maps, even half-rising from his chair to fetch his most recent creation. Clarice would have let him go; Dominic stated unequivocally that he never could give his attention to anything else during a meal except the food. Morgain sat down, promising a sight of the map as a special after-luncheon treat.

It was not to be. Before they'd entirely finished a dish of meringues, Camber announced a visitation by Mr. and Mrs. Lasham. They were Felicia and Blaic's dearest friends, Mr. Lasham being a gentleman farmer like Blaic. Per force, Clarice introduced Dominic to them. Mr. and Mrs. Lasham asked no impertinent questions yet did their best to draw the stranger out. They found themselves stymied by his cool politeness.

"I don't believe so," he'd answered when asked if he was any relation to a Mrs. Burlington-Knight she'd met during her London Season.

"I am from London, ma'am," he'd said when asked to commiserate with the thought of Blaic and Felicia so far from home in this delicious weather.

"Then you've no hay to look after as I have," Mr. Lasham said heavily. "Come along, Louisa. A pleasure to have met you, sir. Lady Stavely, a delight as always. Be good, youngling! I'll send Harry over tomorrow. You'll be the better for a bit of company your own age."

Morgain could only accept with thanks, though he whispered to Clarice as soon as the drawing room door had closed, "Harry Lasham's an empty-headed lout who thinks of nothing but girls."

"He's only thirteen!" she said with a rueful glance at Dominic. "Morgain, don't exaggerate."

"I never exaggerate. The last time he came by, I spent the whole afternoon watching for Marthy Seppings's brothers while he tried to kiss her. She never would so we were all three of us wasting our time."

"Oh, dear," Clarice said. "I had no idea . . . I shall tell Felicia when she comes home and have her drop a word in Mrs. Lasham's ear."

The Lashams' chaise had no sooner rolled away than Mrs. Wisby and her four charming daughters arrived. They were only halfway through their courtesy call when Mr. Hales, the vicar, and the bashful young man who was substituting for Mr. Henry during his wedding trip paid a call. The Wisby girls were delighted to see Mr. Tapping, for single gentlemen of breeding and education were hard to come by in the limited society of Devon. Now two could devote themselves to Dominic, while the other two could listen agog to Mr. Tapping.

At first, Clarice was at a loss to explain why she'd become so popular. The morning had seen more callers than a week usually brought to her door. Her conversation with Mrs. Wisby gave her a hint.

"Have you heard from dear Mrs. Henry?"

"Nothing as yet. I expect to receive a letter at any time."

"Such a perfect wedding! Enough to make even a sober matron such as myself believe in fairy tales." Mrs. Wisby gave the mauve silk twisted about her head in an approximation of a turban a demure pat. Ever since her oldest daughter had emerged from the schoolroom, Mrs. Wisby had begun dressing like a dowager despite Mr. Wisby's continuing in robust health.

"I think we all have a taste for anything that savors of romance."

"Ah, yes. Of course, one must allow that dear Mrs. Henry had nobody to please but herself. She has no family to disoblige." She lowered her voice and launched a significant glance at Mr. Tapping. "I vow I hope for better things for my girls than a curate, although there's no denying that there is *something* most attractive about a clergyman. . . ."

"Melissa had to please Mr. Henry. It seems she did so as he married her."

"A most suitable match. She receives all his respectability while he gains a delightful bride. A great pity about her parentage, but in these lax days . . ."

"I'm sure Mr. Henry did not regard Melissa's parentage when he asked her to be his wife."

"Oh, but I thought her family was quite unknown to her. Was there some message on the occasion of her marriage?"

Not for worlds would Clarice divulge that Melissa Bainbridge's father was a duke who had contributed a yearly sum to her keep through a solicitor but who also had sent a beautiful set of silver spoons to the natural daughter he'd never so much as seen.

Mrs. Wisby took Clarice's silence for an answer. "Well, no doubt they did not mind whom *she* married so long as she was settled respectably. But then! Mrs. Henry has always impressed me as a most level-headed, sensible girl. Not the sort to fling her heart over the windmill, as the saying is."

Clarice wondered who in their circle was about to contract a less-than-sensible marriage. She was not overly fond of Mrs. Wisby who, she felt, took the natural ambition of a mother with four daughters to absurd heights. Gossip was the stuff of life to her, for through it she could keep current on who was married and who was not. Though only her eldest was "out," Mrs. Wisby kept a sharp watch for lords who had not yet reached their maturity, those gentlemen in line for a fortune, and widowers both titled and wealthy.

She turned an indulgent eye on her two youngest daughters, chatting happily around Dominic. "Such an amiable young man, Lady Stavely. A friend of dear Mr. Gardner, I apprehend."

"That's correct. As he is visiting the area to gain information for a book . . ."

"What could be more natural than that he should stay here? Have you known him long?"

"No, we only met yesterday."

The laughing look she received in reply told her that Mrs. Wisby didn't believe a word of it. "One can always tell a man of good breeding by his ease of manner. Look how little Patty is warming to him and you know she is the shyest thing!"

Clarice looked and had to stifle a laugh. At first she'd been afraid Dominic would give the two girls an example of how cold he could be. Considering, however, that both Dilly and Patty had let their tongues run like fiddlesticks, leaving him nothing to do but nod and begin sentences that were doomed to fade into nothing, Clarice could find it in her heart to feel sorry for him. It wasn't so bad when just one of the girls spoke but when they both chimed in, Dominic looked a trifle desperate.

At that moment, their eyes met. Mrs. Wisby's busy voice faded in her ears. Clarice had seen him dressed and seen him half-naked yet until that instant she had not seen him at all. She felt that he alone, of all the people whom she'd known for so long, understood her. Sympathy shone in the back of his smoky brown eyes and a current of encouragement and strength seemed to flow between them. They smiled at one another in the same instant, as the feeling was recognized and accepted.

Then he looked down into the face of the youngest Miss Wisby and their contact was broken.

Mrs. Wisby's voice became quite clear again. Plainly at the end of a long monologue added, "Of course *no one* could think ill of you, Lady Stavely."

Mr. Hales, after the ladies had gone, said much the same thing. He had been vicar for at least a dozen years, had read the services over her father's body and at the memorial for her mother, as well as standing her friend and advisor any time she'd needed one. She'd seen his hair grow gray and his stomach larger. He was unmarried, the young lady he'd set his heart on dying before their wedding day. He and Doctor Danby were forever quarreling in a friendly fashion over where their duties to the parish overlapped.

Now he took her hands and looked searchingly at her. She laughed a little under this scrutiny. "Don't tell me you too have heard this silly rumor?"

"Rumor, my lady?"

"About my horse running away with me."

He released her hands and sat down beside her. "No, I had not heard that one."

"You appall me! I should have sworn you would have heard many a tale by now. Can the ladies of the village really be growing so lax in their duties?"

"It's not the ladies; it's the doctor."

"Doctor Danby gossiping? I thought it against his principles."

"On this occasion, he made an exception. He wanted me to come out and take a look at the young man who is visiting you." He held up his hand. "Not Morgain."

"I thought not."

"There are always persons willing to be censorious on very little evidence, dear Lady Stavely. Rest assured that we who are your true friends can see nothing in this but your wonted generosity of spirit."

Clarice gave him a light answer. "Do tell me, now that you have seen Mr. Knight, what is your opinion?"

"A gentleman and a scholar," said the vicar, a graduate of Oxford. "I doubt you'll be troubled by any more inquisitive visitors."

"I'm sure I won't, as soon as you tell Doctor Danby what you've told me."

By the time the last guest had left, they'd relinquished the idea of riding in favor of the tour of the gardens Clarice had promised Dominic last night. Morgain had taken himself off to visit the Lashams despite his complaints, Mrs. Lasham having let fall the fact that her cook was making cheesecakes—above all things Morgain's favorite.

Clarice had been pointing out the various statues with commentary on their histories and probable age when a disturbed chorus of magpies put Dominic forcibly in mind of the Wisby girls. "I have never met that kind of girl before. Are they very common?"

"Yes. Very." Instantly she said it she was reminded of all the kindnesses Mrs. Wisby had shown her after the disappearance of her mother. "I should not say that. They are generally held to be charming young ladies. Quite handsome too."

"Were they? There certainly seem to be a great many of them."

"Only four."

"Is it customary for so many people to call on you at once? Or do you hold Open House frequently? I cannot imagine that Mrs. Lasham's thirst for knowledge can be satisfied with a less regular diet."

"I am sorry," Clarice said. "It's only that they want to meet you."

"Meet me?"

Whatever flash of sympathy had passed between herself and Dominic had gone. He only looked at her blankly. She found herself floundering in the midst of an explanation. "It is so kind of them to worry about me. How I wish they would not."

"I would think that friends are your greatest treasure, Lady Stavely."

"They are. They are indeed. However, having known me virtually since the cradle—and in Doctor Danby's case for some time before that!—there is not a one who doesn't treat me as a foolish girl who must be protected and defended. They none of them remember that I am considerably more than seven . . . !"

"Does someone think you need to be protected and defended against me?" He stopped in front of a lion recumbent on a pedestal of pink marble. "Do you think so, Lady Stavely?"

"Perhaps I was hasty in accepting you purely on the word of my brother-in-law. I asked myself what harm can there be in my offering you hospitality. Now I am afraid I have learned the answer to that question."

"What is the answer?"

"Great harm," she said, looking into his eyes. Some hope lived in her that she would again feel that sense of having found someone who could comprehend her without having every joke or passing comment explained. He said nothing and she realized that she must not hope. It had been the same way yesterday, when for a moment in the Red Chamber they'd seemed on the point of a good understanding, only to lose the feeling a moment later.

She said, "Mrs. Wisby as good as told me she suspected that I had known you before. Mr. Hales thinks no ill of you or me but then he is next-door to a saint."

"A saint lives—" He broke off and smiled at her a touch more broadly than seemed usual for him. "Surely what the vicar thinks today, the village will think tomorrow."

"Perhaps. After all, I have something of a reputation as a woman who does not truckle under to the dictates of society. Oh, but how I hate all this whispering! If I had one wish in this world it would be to pass by unnoticed, unregarded, and unmentioned!"

"It would be easier," he said thoughtfully, "if a few less persons interested themselves in your affairs."

"Precisely. But I might as well wish for the moon. There's so little to do in the country except pry into your neighbor's doings."

She thought she heard someone shouting in the distance. The sound was so faint that she would have dismissed it, if Dominic hadn't turned toward the house, saying, "Here's your butler. He looks distressed."

Camber remained too far away for Clarice to understand what he was shouting and certainly too far away behind screening hedges to be recognized. She shot a confused glance toward Dominic and began walking toward the house. "You must have remarkably sharp hearing, sir."

"I do. It's mostly a matter of training, however."

The usually calm butler was in a rare taking. "Come at once, my lady," he panted. " 'Tis Master Morgain."

She didn't wait to hear another word. Throwing the bulk of her skirt over her arm, she sprinted toward the house. Coming behind her, she heard poor Camber trying to gasp out some tale to Dominic but she caught only one word in three.

Morgain lay on the black and white tiles in the entry, his feet halfway out the door. No one had thought to carry him in further. His freckles stood out like fallen leaves on snow, his complexion having lost all color. His eyes were closed; his jaw hung open a little. He looked tiny, for without his vibrant personality to distract one, his true size was revealed. For an instant, Clarice's heart died within her breast.

She threw herself down on her knees beside him. Pringle, weeping weekly chafed one of his hands. "Oh, my dearest . . . I'm afraid . . . I'm afraid he's . . ."

"Nonsense!" Clarice said firmly as though by her resolution she could drive off death. She paid no attention to her own tears, splashing on the lace that framed her bodice, and had little patience with Pringle's. Smoothing the tumbled hair from the boy's brow, she saw an ugly bruise on his temple, the flesh puffing around a perfectly straight cut, two or three inches long. Though the sight was gruesome, she yet rejoiced, for blood trickled slowly from the wound.

"Have none of you any better sense than to let him lie here? Don't be fool, Pringle! He's alive. . . ."

Taking him by the shoulders, she struggled to raise him. Hardly had she begun to do so, however, than Dominic appeared and lifted the boy high against his chest. "I'll take him to his room."

"Yes, at once. Camber—send Jem Drake for the doctor at once. Have him take my horse; she's the fastest. Then bring up some brandy. Pringle—some water to bathe Morgain's head and the hartshorn." She threw her nurse a fulminating look. "If you cannot make yourself useful, have Rose do it, or the cook if necessary! But don't stand there weeping in that singularly useless way."

"I'm certain he's dead!" Pringle wailed.

"He shan't be if I have aught to say of it!" More gently she said, "I know you are overset. So am I. Go and lie down until you feel more the thing."

She hastened up the stairs, taking them two at a time as she had during her days as a hoydenish child. She hardly realized she was doing it.

Dominic stood by the boy's bedside, looking at his head wound with a dispassionate, appraising air that struck Clarice as a welcome example of coolness in a situation in which everyone else seemed to have gone utterly to pieces. "It's not so bad," he said. "The skin is broken, but I do not believe he has suffered any lasting damage to the skull itself."

"Are you a doctor too?"

"No."

"You have seen such things before, though?"

"Not that either. But I am not without experience of wounds and battles. Your nephew was struck down, my lady, with considerable violence."

"Struck down? By whom? No one would . . ."

This information, however dispassionately delivered, shook her as the sight of her unconscious nephew could not. About this, she could do nothing. There were no orders to give, no strength she could exert. She tottered to a chair, laden with books, and pushed them off with a clatter so that she might sit down.

Dominic stepped over to her and took her hand. "I should not have said it so plainly. Forgive me."

"No . . . don't regard it. As soon as I saw . . . it was too straight to have come there by accident. Who could have done such a terrible thing? He's only a ch-child."

When the brandy came up, Dominic made her have the first taste of it. Though she coughed and choked as the aromatic liqueur burst in her throat, it did steady her. She could apply without an outward qualm a sponge, dipped in the hartshorn and water, cleansing the horribly neat wound.

The doctor came, bustling and rough, only to turn grave and silent after a moment standing beside the bed, examining the boy in the yellowing sunlight that came through the open curtains. Danby's lack of bluster frightened Clarice more than even the sight of Morgain's bruise.

Dominic put his hand on her shoulder. "He's an excellent doctor. All will be well."

The weight of his hand seemed to anchor her in a world whose very foundations were shifting beneath her. The warmth of it thawed the chill of her blood. She reached up, wanting to cover it briefly with her own, only to start forward when the doctor's familiar "Hmph" reached her ears.

"I've seen worse," he said, turning from the small figure of the boy. "When Ames hit out at Tully with a plowshare, for instance. I daresay Morgain'll have a scar he'll bear to the end of his days but he won't mind that! Claim he was abducted by pirates or some such nonsense."

"What about this unconsciousness, Doctor?"

" 'Course he's unconscious. Just as well. I'll have to take a stitch or two to close the cut. It's best he be senseless for that." He glanced around. "We'll need more light. A lamp would be best, or several branches of candles. Someone will need to hold the boy's hands and someone else needs to keep his head steady. Can't have him thrashing about, you know."

Dominic said, "If you require help, I shall be happy to assist you."

The sharp blue eyes, undimmed by years, slanted at him. "Any experience?"

"I have sewed up a wound or two."

"Did your patient live?"

"I have been my own patient and I live, as you see."

Doctor Danby pursed his lips but let Dominic stand by him while he pulled together the wound's lips with the black silk thread he'd had Clarice find in her sewing cabinet. "There," he said, making a neat knot. "That'll hold through anything. Easy with such young skin."

Clarice had also remained, holding Morgain's hands down when he'd become restless as soon as the second stitch was set. Her fortitude, however, had escaped her when the doctor began stitching. She dared not look at what was happening, finding it necessary to keep her head down. She prayed.

More quickly than she'd dared hope, Doctor Danby pronounced himself finished. "It'll be sore for a bit, and he'll probably wake with the devil's own headache, yet I have every confidence he'll recover. Boys bounce back, m'dear, never forget it!"

"I'll show you to the door, dearest Doctor Danby."

"I know my way by now. You sit down and wait for the boy to come around. Have a glass of wine. Some of that Burgundy your father was always boasting about. That'll bring the stars into your pretty eyes again! I'll tell Camber about it as I go."

Clarice poured the Burgundy when it came, saying, "Won't you have a glass, Mr. Knight? I'm sure you must stand in need of one."

"I do not drink wine."

"Neither do I as a general rule, but when one's physician insists . . . !" She sipped it while looking toward the boy. "I thank God he is not seriously injured. I thought for an instant that he—that I should have to tell his parents what had happened. I do not think I could have faced them. He is their only child."

She did not know what he would have said in answer for he had said nothing but, "Lady Stavely . . ." when a moan from the bed brought her instantly to Morgain's side.

"Head . . ." he sighed.

"Yes, my love. You've hurt yourself."

"Hurts."

These one-word answers, so unlike his usual style, brought the tears springing into her eyes once more. With a great effort, she forced her voice to remain calm and even. Not for anything would she frighten her nephew by showing any trace of her own fears.

"I know, my darling. Lie still."

Dominic approached and stood above her. "Can you tell us what happened?" he said gently.

Clarice flashed him a raging look. "Don't worry, Morgain. Don't even think about it. Doctor Danby has already been to see you. You'll be perfectly well before you know it."

Morgain seemed not to have heard her advice or her prophecy. He tried to raise a hand to the bandages swathing his brow. She caught it and pressed it gently back atop the cover of his light wool blanket. "Mustn't do that, dear."

"Tired . . . hurts . . ." he said in a voice, burdened with the soft thin wail of one who knows the world is unfair but has never imagined such inequality being applied to himself.

"Who did it?" Dominic asked again.

Clarice pointed an imperious fingertip toward the bedroom door. A moment ago, Dominic had been an unexpected support, lending her something of his strength. Now he was a nuisance. How dare he presume to overrule her?

Dominic shook his head at Clarice's demand. It was only when she stood up with the avowed intention of *pushing* him out—despite the difference in their sizes—that he made as if to go. Clarice went with him as far as the door. In a ruthlessly suppressed voice, she said, "I will not have you . . ."

Most rudely, he stared past her. "What did you say, Morgain?"

Very faint, Clarice heard the boy say, gaspingly, "Devil . . . the devil on horseback. Couldn't breathe. He hit me."

Six

Dominic caught Clarice as she swayed. He picked her up as easily as he had the boy. "I'll take you to your room."

"You may put me on my feet again, sir. I am well."

"You were about to fall down."

"But not in a faint. It is simply that my knees do not seem to be working properly."

"Then let me assist you."

"Quite unnecessary."

Ignoring her, he carried her out of Morgain's room. Finding Camber on the point of entering, Dominic said bluntly, "Stay with the boy 'til the nurse comes."

"Yes, sir."

Clarice called out as they passed him, "I shall return directly, Camber!"

"Very good, my lady."

It was beneath her dignity to kick and scream in protest as Dominic carried her irresistibly to her room. She sent him as vicious a glance, however, as she could muster. Being so near, with her eyes only two inches or so away from his impressive jaw, she could see the advent of his smile though he fought hard to repress it.

"Do you find something amusing, sir?"

"No. I hope I am respectful."

His arms were strong under her knees and around her rib cage. She could feel the spread of his warm fingers just under the weight of her breast. He bore an elusive fragrance, clean and windswept like the air at the top of the hills. Finding his shoulder so near, she dropped her head onto the smooth woolen cloth, though her appearance would have been more impressive if she'd kept rigidly upright. "I wish I knew . . ." she said aloud.

"Knew what?"

"Whether I like you or not."

"I hope you do," he said levelly. "Here is one who does not."

"Goodness gracious me!" Pringle said, emerging from her room like an overwound jack-in-the-box. "Never say she's taken ill, too?"

"There's no 'too' about it, Pringle," Clarice said, raising her head from its comfortable position. "Morgain is not ill; he has had an accident. I am not ill; my knees have failed. Mr. Knight is merely being kind."

"Kind?" Pringle spread her arms wide across the door. "He'll not enter here! It isn't decent!"

"She is right," Clarice admitted. "Put me down."

Dominic's eyebrows drew together. For a moment he stood looking between lady and nurse. "Very well."

Clarice smiled. "Thank you; I'm certain that . . ."

The smile fell from her lips the instant her feet touched the ground. Her knees buckled and Pringle cried out in shrill alarm. Once again, Dominic swept her up into his arms.

"How perfectly absurd," Clarice exclaimed. "Such a thing has never happened to me before."

Dominic said, "There is no impropriety when someone is ill. Stand aside; I'll put Lady Stavely on her bed."

Pringle let him enter, then chased around the man and his burden like a yapping pug dog. Her voice had a particularly sharp pitch when excited or nervous and she was both now. With flustered hands, she sought among Clarice's bureau drawers for her smelling-salt bottle and her *eau de cologne*. "Dear me, dear me . . ."

"Never mind, Pringle," Clarice said.

Dominic carried her to the bed and placed her gently down atop the counterpane, sliding his hands away. He found a shawl over the arm of a chair and tucked it in from throat to waist. For a moment, he leaned over her, blocking Pringle's view. She looked up into his face, so near, and saw—or fancied she saw—a tender light in his eyes. "You must think me a perfect fool," she said huskily.

"No. It often happens that a person's knees give way after a time of strain. I, too . . ."

"When?"

"I'll save that tale for another day. Are you comfortable now?"

"Entirely. Thank you, Mr. Knight." Though his words had been accompanied by a warm smile, she recognized a set-down when she heard it.

Pringle stood by, cut-crystal bottles at the ready. "She needs rest," Dominic said.

"I'll be the judge of that," Pringle said stoutly. "I've cared for her since her childhood. I know her character through and through and I'll never desert her. Why, even during those three years when she was out of—"

"Pringle!" Clarice snapped. "If you please, Pringle. Mr. Camber is alone with Morgain. Please go and help him."

"And leave a man in your room with you? Never fear, my lady, I stand on my duty!"

Dominic's quiet yet dominating voice broke in. "You'll do as your mistress commands. Send up her maid if you are afraid I shall ravish her the moment your back is turned."

Pringle gasped, flushing red. It seemed as though he would find himself carrying another fainting woman. Instead, he took her by the shoulder and turned her toward the door. "My lady?" she squeaked.

"Go on, Pringle. Morgain needs you more than I do."

Dominic ushered the nurse into the hall, closing the

door in her face, while her mouth opened and closed as soundlessly as a fish's. "Do you need any of the things she took with her?"

Clarice sat up, supporting herself on her elbows, letting the shawl slide down. "I should say no in any case, lest you bully them out of her."

"Bully? I?"

"Perhaps that is too strong a word."

"She would have stood there 'til the end of time if I hadn't encouraged her to leave. Why do you keep such a foolish woman about you?"

"She has been, as you heard, my nurse since my childhood. I cannot very well turn her off merely because she is what she has always been. When I was a child, before Felicia came to live here, Pringle was the best friend I had and truly the only one who gave me the sort of unconditional love a child needs. If she is sometimes overwrought and silly, well, so be it."

"You're the one who suffers because of it."

"Suffer? How? By being kind to her in my turn?"

Rather to her alarm, Dominic did not seem in any hurry to leave her room. He strolled about, looking at her collection of her half sister's watercolors, running an absent finger along the spines of the books on her shelves, and glancing out the windows. He should have looked ridiculously out of place in her feminine boudoir; instead his masculine aura had the effect of making all her refined decor look flossy and overdone.

"By sometimes feeling more than a little bored and irritated? I have no doubt she is a very good sort of woman, but not the kind you should have about you."

"What kind should that be?" She did not think she spoke coyly. She could not imagine him trying to flirt with her.

"I'm not certain." He came over to her and without asking a by-your-leave, he sat down on the edge of her bed. The mattress creaked under him. "You should have clever, honest people around you. Not fools who flatter, and fault-finding neighbors who can't see past their ends of their prejudices."

Now was the moment to depress his pretensions. Clarice knew that, yet she said, "You don't flatter me."

"No. I never will."

"How ungallant."

"Not at all. I simply do you the credit of believing you are too intelligent to be swayed by flattery."

"No woman is *that* intelligent."

"What of men? Can we be swayed by flattery?"

"I suppose you can. For instance, I might say to you 'You are very attractive, Mr. Knight, and you have un-rivaled prowess with the sword.' I was most impressed this morning."

"It seems I am not as intelligent as I thought. Thank you, Lady Stavely." He bowed his head in a most regal fashion. Then she caught sight of his glinting eyes. "I might say, however, that I am too intelligent to believe that your knees failed to support you because of an excess of nerves."

"But you yourself said . . . ?"

"That was to rid us of the nurse. Now tell me why you were so overcome by Morgain's words."

Clarice wished she were not lying on the bed. There was nowhere to escape to. His eyes had the brown mistiness of peat smoke as they gazed down on her. "I—"

" 'The devil on horseback.' What did Morgain mean? I feel certain you know."

"I do not." Clarice lay back, straight as an effigy on a medieval tomb. "I wish you would see how Morgain is."

"He's asleep again."

"Well, I have the headache."

He went on sitting there, impervious to hints. "You were very interested in my horse until Morgain told you it had two white stockings. That first day, you came home in a hurry from a riding and Camber tells me your horse threw you, a thing that had never happened before."

"I was *not* thrown!" she said, struggling up again. "If you must know, I took a gate badly on my way back from an errand to a tenant."

"This tenant lives off the main road?"

"Yes. What is your point?"

"The only gates I saw between Hamdry Manor and the main road were to let farmers through fields. Why did you jump a gate into a field?"

"Because I was in the mood to do so! What is wrong with that?"

He shook his head slowly. "You are not so impulsive or heedless."

"You presume to know me very well on such short acquaintance! Pray be good enough to touch the bell and summon my maid."

"In a moment. I am still puzzling out your character."

"A gentleman would do as I asked."

He grinned, a peculiarly youthful and engaging smile which sat oddly but attractively on his chiseled features. "But I'm no gentleman, my lady. I'm an author."

"Whatever you may be, kindly touch the bell! If Morgain was attacked, we must summon the constable." She swung her legs to the side of the bed, nearly kicking him. As soon as she attempted to stand, his arm came around her waist to steady her on her feet. She was both grateful and exasperated. "There. I am perfectly well and able to take up my duties. It has been a pleasure to listen to you, Mr. Knight. You may be mad but you are an entertaining guest."

"Where did you see the Rider, Lady Stavely?"

How unfair of him to ask that question while his arm was still steadying her! He must have been able to feel the agitated rhythm of her heart. Nonetheless, she attempted a blank stare even as she schooled her body to icy rigidity. "What rider, sir?"

"The cloaked Rider. Need I describe him? Very well. No one has ever seen his face—or if someone has, they had no chance to describe what they saw. His horse is about the size of a cart horse but swifter than you can

believe possible. It's either black or a deep bay the color
of dried blood. When you are before it, you feel as
though you cannot breathe for the very air seems to be
swallowed by the speed of his coming."

Though his description filled her with remembered
dread, Clarice laughed coolly. "Do you take me for a
gullible child, frightened by a ghost story? There are
many such tales told in this region, Mr. Knight. Perhaps
while you are here you would enjoy making a study of
them."

"You have a facile tongue, Lady Stavely, yet your
heartbeat betrays you."

As though she were peeling a wet cloth from her skin,
she lifted his hand from her waist. "You take liberties,
sir."

"Tell me—"

"Don't think you can bully *me*, Mr. Knight! I find it
very suspicious that you should know so much about
this person who struck down my innocent nephew!
Nothing like this has ever happened at Hamdry until you
came among us!"

He stood up and Clarice was aware anew of his
height, his breadth, and the strength that powered the
muscles she'd seen that morning. He could break her
with one hand, smash her to the earth and never known
he'd done it. Yet she faced him, head high, and if she
was afraid, only she knew it.

"Do you truthfully believe I am in league with the
Rider?" he asked, his voice hard as stone.

His voice was hard, yes, but Clarice saw some other
emotion in his eyes. The exact meaning eluded her, as
fugitive as the exact composition of the aroma that clung
to his clothing. She felt as though he were willing her
to say that she believed him. It was as if he were pushing
at her with his thoughts, urging her toward some agreement that he could then use against her. Stubborn as she
was, she could feel all too strongly the urge to give in.

Clarice looked away from his compelling gaze. "I do

not know you well enough to answer. I *hope* that you are not."

His mouth and brows turned down as though he were disappointed in her. "I am so little his ally that if I see him, I will dispatch him for you."

That made her look at him again with doubting eyes. "I am afraid, Mr. Knight. You make this 'Rider' sound like something no mortal force can stop. Where does he come from? Surely he is only a man like any other?"

"The world is wide, Lady Stavely. Not all your 'ghost stories' are lies."

"Then what can you do against such a one?"

"I can do more than your constable can. You *did* see him?"

She nodded. "Yes. I saw him. He chased me. I leapt the gate to escape. But if he is as powerful as you say, why would that be enough?"

"What was the gate made of?"

She had seen Daly's three-bar gate a hundred times in her life, yet she had to think before she could answer. "Wood, of course. Painted red, though it's mostly faded now."

"Just wood? No nails?"

"Naturally it has nails."

"Creatures like the Rider can't abide any form of iron. It burns them. I have heard they can learn to bear to be in its vicinity, given enough time and a strong enough reason, but they do not love it and are never comfortable near it."

"Creatures?" Clarice gazed at him in suspicion and wonder. "How do you know so much about such things?"

Now it was he who could not sustain her gaze. "I have studied much. The tales of the simple people have much to tell us if we only study them."

He walked across the room to look out of her window. As though the words were forced from him, Dominic said, "If the Rider is hunting you, then you are not safe here."

"Not safe at Hamdry?" The thought was utterly alien to her. She wanted to scoff at the very idea of a mysterious Rider with mystical powers, but her frantic ride and the loss of breath she felt while being chased were too recent to be easily dismissed. After all, her own dear brother-in-law had come from another Realm; darker things might dwell in that world as well. If he could come here, so, perhaps, could they.

"Go nowhere alone, not even into your own garden. Carry iron on your person at all times." There are some small Elizabethan ladies' knives in your grandfather's collection with handsomely wrought sheaths. You may not be able to stab the Rider but you can burn him with the cold steel."

"And if I touch him," Clarice said wonderingly, "will he do my bidding?"

His grin flashed out again and Clarice found herself responding to it with a smile of her own. "So that is why you touched me at our first meeting," he said in a tone of enlightenment. "I wondered at it, for such a bold gesture seemed most unlike the prim and polite young lady I saw before me. You need not worry, my lady. *I* am human enough."

Clarice couldn't help the flush that heated her face. "I thought that you were the one who chased me. You see, I had seen something else most strange a few days before . . . something so uncanny that I . . . I . . ."

"What was it?"

"Nothing . . ."

"You must tell me everything," Dominic said. He came to her side and took her hand. His clasp was warm and strong, making her feel that her own far-from-petite hand was small and helpless. She could almost wish that she were not Lady Stavely, a viscountess in her own right, but a meek and fragile creature who required a man's strength in order to face a brutal world.

She slipped her hand out of his grasp. "You are the oddest creature," she said lightly. "I know nothing of you, yet I am to trust you with all my secrets?"

"If I am to protect you, I must know everything."

"I have not asked for your protection, sir."

"Not for yourself, no. But what of Morgain?"

Thinking of her defenseless nephew, Clarice sighed and nodded. "You are right. Very well."

She collected her thoughts. "The evening my dear friend was married, I found myself upon the hill we call Barren Tor. There is an old stone fort there—or at least the tumbled stones that may have once been a fort."

"I have seen such things." He did not look as though the memory of them was happy.

"While I was there, a rider appeared, cloaked even as the one I saw yesterday. He said, 'Let us be about it' and rode away. The curious thing—or rather one of the curious things—is that I did not see him arrive, only his departure. It was as if he came from the stones themselves."

"Most curious. Is that all?" Dominic turned once more to look down into the garden border below. Yet in the instant before he turned away, Clarice could have sworn she saw a tinge of burning color rise in his smooth cheeks.

"Nearly all. I believe that I saw the same figure in the garden every night for a week after. But perhaps that was my imagination at work?"

"Perhaps." He raised his hand when she would have spoken again. "Someone is coming."

A scratch at the door an instant later verified his warning. "My lady?" Rose said, peeking in. "Master Morgain do be callin' for thee."

"Tell him I'm coming, Rose."

The maid glanced between mistress and man with a glint of pleasure in her dark eyes. "He'll niver take no manner o' haarm if you be a bit behind-like. He'm be lyin' with a cool cloth on his brow that Pringle done put there, and Cook be squeezing lemons for all she's worth iffen he takes a fancy for some coolin' drink. A prime favorite with her now that he's poorly."

"Thank you, Rose."

Dominic said, "Just a moment," when Rose spread her white apron in a curtsy prior to dismissal. He came quite close to Clarice and said in a low tone, calculating to reach her ears only, "Your stable boys are likely looking lads. They'd make excellent guards against unwanted visitors."

"Rose," Clarice said immediately, "pass the word that I would like to see Mr. Drake as soon as may be convenient to him."

"Yes, my lady," the maid replied, dipping another country curtsy. Out in the hall, her giggles came clearly even to Clarice's ordinary hearing.

Dominic said in a much lighter tone than he'd used throughout this interview, "Does she believe she has interrupted some tender scene?"

"No. She hopes that she had."

"Why so?"

"These people were born on Hamdry land. They and their families are my tenants as their ancestors were tenants and servants to my ancestors. They would like to believe that I am irresistible to men. After all, if I die unwed and without children, what is to become of them?"

"Whoever inherits your property would care for them, no doubt?"

"It would not be the same. At present, my heir is a distant cousin in Lancaster. The people here do not know him well and he would always be a 'foreigner.' "

"Would the man you marry be in any better position?"

"Of course. They'd accept my choice, though I'm sure prayers are offered nightly that I chose well." She bent rather cautiously to pick up the shawl that had slid to the floor when she'd stood up. To her relief, her head did not spin and her knees stayed true. She wrapped it about her shoulders, for her earlier weakness had left her feeling a trifle cold. "I must go to my nephew."

He went ahead of her to open the door. "May I be present when you speak to your groom?" he asked.

"Certainly. Though do not expect my men to know

anything about sword-play." She smiled automatic
thanks to him as he stood aside to let her pass.

Dominic watched her go down the hall to the room
where Morgain lay. He did not for a moment believe
that she had told him everything she'd seen that night
on Barren Tor. One thing he was certain of, however.
She had not recognized him as the rider she'd seen in
the midst of the moor's desolation. It was there that he'd
traveled by a secret way between Mag Mell, the Vale of
the People, and the mortal realm. How the Black Rider
of Vedresh had crossed was a question only Forgall
could answer. Dominic made his way to the grotto.

When the King of the People at last appeared, the sun
had all but sunk below the western horizon. This time,
when Dominic went down on one knee he spoke first.
"You did not tell me everything, my king," he said.

"Is this how you speak to me? What have I not told
you?"

"You did not inform me that someone else has crossed
into this world from the Deathless Realm." Dominic
raised his head. He wanted to see the king's face when
he spoke, little good though it might do him. Not for
nothing was he known as Forgall the Wily.

"Someone else? Who has dared?"

When Dominic told him, the king paled behind his
brown beard. "Vedresh . . . Vedresh has crossed into this
realm? Impossible."

"The boy lies in an upper chamber, his forehead
scarred by the wyvern tail whip. The woman too has
been chased. He only missed her by a fortunate chance."

"How can this be?" From nothing, the king conjured
a stool, beautifully carved with runes of wisdom. He sat
down heavily, his hands on his thighs. To look at him,
despite the silk of his tunic, one would almost take him
for a farmer, tired after a day's toil, taking his ease at
his own hearthside. That is, if one overlooked the lines
of tension about his eyes and brow and the fact that he
sat on the very edge of the stool.

"I know little of spells and enchantments, my king, but may it not be possible that when *I* crossed over, some loophole was left open?"

Forgall smiled, a little patronizingly. "No, that is not possible. When I beguile time and space, nothing happens that I do not will to happen."

"Yet Vedresh is here."

"This can only mean that *she* has learned how to send her soldiers into this realm. Vedresh must be the first, the experiment. Once Matilda knows she has succeeded, she will send others."

"Let them come!" Dominic said, the prospect of battle heating his blood. "I will do your bidding in the face of a thousand such!"

"Go mildly, good knight, go mildly. I will think what is best to be done. Guard the woman and the boy. Come again tomorrow and I will tell you what I have decided."

"I could flee with Clarice," Dominic said. "Vedresh would surely follow. . . ."

"Clarice?" the king asked, his eyebrows raising high. "You have grown wondrous great with her if she makes you a gift of her name."

Dominic said, "It is difficult to think of her as 'Lady Stavely.' She is young to bear such a title."

"I saw her once, you know." The king crossed his legs and sat back a trifle. A wooden goblet, carved of oak, appeared in his hand. Though plain stuff, it was cunningly turned so that it caught and seemed to absorb the golden light that poured through the grotto. "A mere child, she was. She came riding down one of the hills not far from here and had the fortune, good or ill, to disrupt one of our revels. Even as a child only on the cusp of womanhood, she was lovely."

"Interrupted a revel? I thought . . . why did you not kill her?"

"Kill her? I am not Boadach. He would have done it quick enough—left her lying a blasted, twisted thing on the heath. Or mayhap he would have taken her sight, or maimed her mind so that she became a thing of horror.

I have known him to do all these things and more to
your poor mortal brethren."

"Then what fate did you set her?"

The king drank while Dominic awaited an answer. He
felt that Forgall was debating within himself. "We erased
all memory of herself, taking her mind back to that of
a child. I believe her family thought her mad, but she
did not suffer. Every day was joyful for her. She was
too beautiful, almost like one of our own, to destroy."

Dominic could believe that Clarice had touched the
heart of the king. "She seems well enough now."

"So she is. Thanks to Blaic. He defied us all to bring
her back to herself. It is to that misplaced kindness that
we owe all our misfortune now. Were it not for that, and
the outcome, Matilda would never have crossed into our
realm and become one of us."

"I have not asked before, my king. Now I must know.
How is the woman, Clarice, linked with our enemy, Matilda?"

"I may as well tell you. It may keep you from falling
into a trap that she is not even aware she has set." Forgall raised his hand to prevent Dominic's protest. "You
may have dwelt for many years in the Realms of Gold
but you are still a human. You may fall in love despite
yourself. Do not make that mistake for no joy can come
of it. Clarice Stavely is Matilda's daughter."

"Her daughter? The hag's daughter?"

Forgall chuckled and Dominic threw him a glance of
dislike. "You have not seen her, good knight. I have.
She is not as beautiful as her daughter, but she is no
creature of nightmare. Her heart is dark; her face is fair."

"You should have told me this before, my king."

"Do you presume to dictate to me? I told you what
you needed to know, no more, no less. You may take
what I tell you now as a warning. Your blood is human
and it can all too easily warm to a woman of your own
kind. I would tell you the same if Clarice Stavely were
a hag herself, for it is not in beauty alone that love is
found."

"I am in no danger," Dominic said, bowing.

Dominic thought of Clarice as he'd seen her last, her golden hair slightly disheveled as though by the hand of a lover, her blue eyes enhanced by the twilight colors of the soft shawl she'd put about her shoulders. He knew she had pride, yet he'd seen her charm as well. How could she be the child of a woman whose greed and violence had brought Mag Mell, haven of Peace and Beauty, to the brink of war?

made, her plump hands resting atop her r...
her plump hands resting atop her stalwa...
made, her plump hands resting atop her ...
It felt and smelled late. His ...
It rarely had been up past ten. His ...
A rarely ...
after everyone else had ...
legs out of bed and ...
head did not a...
enough to g...
thing...

A ca...

He ...

Morgain lay in his bed, feeling as though he were floating on the ocean. The pain in his head that had made
him cry like a baby earlier had all but vanished, thanks
to some potion Cam... had tipped down his throat. Most
likely laudanum, Morgain mused, remembering a tooth-
ache from some years previously. The stuff they'd used
then to quiet him had given him the same strange sense
of distance from his own emotions and body.

The bed seemed to rock up and down, not unpleasantly, but in the manner of a boat under sail. He could
hear a repetitive sighing, like the sound of the wind and
the waves. A gentle, soothing sound, it should have
made him sleepy, as should the sedative. Strangely
enough, he felt quite wide awake.

Opening his eyes, he sat up stealthily. No voice cried
out upon him. Pringle had charged him to stay in bed,
but there wasn't any point in just lying there sleeplessly
hour after hour.

He peeked out from among the damask curtains hung
around his bed. Pringle slept, her cap pushed askew by
the supporting wing of her armchair beside his bed. Her
soft burring breaths were the sound of the sea-breeze.
Morgain smiled, not unkindly, at the absurd picture she

...und stomach.
... sleeper, Morgain
...chool did not encour-
...ys been glad to seek his
...thrill to be out of bed so long
... gone to sleep. He swung his bare
... stood up, delighted to find that his
...ne. His stomach, however, was empty
...rgle. Maybe he could find a little some-

...ndle burned on the small table next to Pringle.
...picked it up and walked over to the square mirror
...at hung above his bureau. Holding the candle high, he
saw his bloodless reflection. It was as if the ghost of
some murdered twin had come up suddenly before him.

"Coo-er. . . ." he said, peering closely. The line of the
wound in his forehead looked black by candlelight, the
track of the doctor's black silk thread adding a particularly horrid touch. His face was so deathly pale it seemed
almost to glow, while his eyes appeared to have sunk to
the sockets. One bore the beginning of a fine black eye.

"Wait 'til Harry Lasham sees this!" he said aloud,
then threw an anxious glance at Pringle. She sniffed and
muttered but went on sleeping. Morgain turned again to
his reflection and the thing smiled back at him with a
death's head grin. "He'll be green," he said more softly.
"*Pea* green."

He raised his hand to touch the bruise on his forehead,
just where his hair sprang back off his forehead. "Mother
won't like it," he said. "With luck, it'll be gone before
she comes home."

A bit of incautious pressure sent a throb of pain
through him that not even the drug could stop entirely.
He felt a little sick, so he promptly touched the same
spot again.

He set the candle down on the bureau, suddenly weak
as a kitten. The bed seemed to be much further away
than when he'd so blithely left it. He staggered back to
it, his bare feet cold. Lifting the covers to swing them

under took almost the last of his strength. He felt nauseated, worse than he had after devouring green apples and potted meat sandwiches. He thought about calling Pringle, but it wasn't the nurse he wanted.

"Mother . . ." he whispered, feeling the tears gather at the outside corners of his eyes. He blinked and they trickled coldly down, wetting the hair at his temples. Morgain closed his eyes, hoping that would stop the unmanly tears.

He'd been hit before, by the bullies at his school during the first six months of his sojourn there and at least once or twice by a master—for impertinence. But his father had never struck him nor had any stranger. He could not imagine why anyone who did not know him would want to harm him.

For a moment, he seemed to hear the thunder of the hooves and feel the tightness in his chest as he fought for breath. Then the shadow of the horse fell over him and he saw the rider raise his arm. What a strange shape his whip had been! Thick, scaly, with an arrow for a tip . . . it had lashed down out of the sky and he'd not even had enough air in his lungs to scream.

Who was the rider, Morgain wondered. A madman? A monster? The hand that held the whip had looked human enough, though the nails had been perhaps a trifle long. He didn't want to think about the "thing" that sometimes populated his imaginary landscapes to the detriment of his citizens, yet now that he'd begun to think about it he couldn't seem to stop.

Even Pringle's chatter would be a welcome diversion to the direction of his thoughts. He drew breath to call her, but stopped with a squeak before he'd forced the first syllable out, suddenly too frightened to speak.

A window rattled. A floorboard creaked in the hall. Some fragment fell, landing with a sound no louder than a whisper, in the chimney. Pringle's little noises seemed to grow noisier, as though something bigger than the nurse were breathing in time with her. The light of the candle on the bureau seemed too dim and far away to reveal whatever it was that he suddenly felt was right inside the room. Did that shadow move?

A deep instinct held Morgain frozen to the mattress. He bit the edge of one of his pillows to keep from crying out. A tiny moan escaped him, but Pringle—usually so attentive—still did not wake.

He squeezed his eyes shut and waited, with the helpless trembling of a rabbit in a trap, for the horror that stalked him to strike again. It was all the worse, in that he knew what to expect this time.

Long, shivering moments passed. When Morgain couldn't stand another second of suspense, he peeped through his lashes. No dark figure stooped over his bed to strangle him. His relief was such that at first he hardly noted the change in his bedchamber.

He sighed, a long, long release of unbearable fear. Stretching out arms and legs, he reached into the cool recesses of the bed linen, feeling drowsily comfortable. His next deep breath brought with it the wild scent of pine needles and an entire lack of the smells of camphor and hartshorn.

Morgain's eyes popped open. He sat up in bed, realizing that over him—where once a painted ceiling had provided shelter—there was only sky. Not a sky of night, either. It arched over him, a pure, clean, dizzyingly deep blue. Hugely tall trees swayed and whispered above him to a breeze only they could feel.

His bed of polished oak, complete with the initials he'd carved into the bottom right bedpost to try his first pocketknife, stood in the middle of a forest. There were spongy pine needles underfoot, the detritus of the great ████████ aller than a mast-oak. Here and there, where sunlight fell to the forest floor, other trees had taken root in the shadow of the giants.

As he looked around, a small woodland creature of a sort he'd never seen before, stopped to observe this oddity, waving its long-fingered paws about as if to say "My goodness me!"

Morgain laughed, for the creature looked like nothing

so much as Mrs. Wisby exclaiming over a bit of gossip, only Mrs. Wisby wouldn't be wearing a little black loo-mask like this fellow. His laughter frightened the creature and it ran off with a peculiarly humorous waddle.

When Morgain had finished laughing, he realized that his headache had gone, quite as if it had never been. He still felt very hungry, however. As if to call his attention to this problem, his stomach let out a gurgle that flushed a chattering flock of birds from their roost behind him.

Morgain started in disgust as a pattering sound fell to the counterpane all around him, but it was not what he'd feared. The birds had dropped nuts on his bed, though not one had fallen on him. Morgain shrugged. Nuts were better than nothing.

He cracked one, using two others. To his awed surprise, he did not find a nut-meat, but a tiny jam tart no bigger than the end of his finger. Realizing that in a dream nothing could harm him, he ate it.

In a few minutes, there was nothing left but empty shells. Morgain licked a bit of strawberry off the corner of his mouth and looked about him for something to drink. No more birds flew and the small creature he'd seen before did not seem inclined to return with a pitcher of milk or a cup of tea.

Morgain swung his feet out of bed and stepped out onto the carpet of pine needles. They were surprisingly soft beneath his bare feet. Glancing down, he saw that, though most of the needles lay tossed about in a chaotic muddle, some of them formed chevrons and that these interlaced needles formed a path. It began small at his feet, but within a few yards the braided-together needles formed a path about two feet wide.

He began to walk forward until he reached the trees. Morgain glanced back over his shoulder, feeling a little hesitant about leaving his bed behind. It was, after all, the only familiar thing in an unknown landscape. However, he could not think of a way to bring it with him.

One clearing lead to another. Morgain thought he could hear the sea, but it was only the tossing of the wind in the trees. When he stepped out into the second clearing, he saw that the grass had been cut very short. It tickled the soles of his feet and he laughed.

As if his laughter had been a signal, the doors appeared. One instant there was only the short grass ringed by trees; the next, the doors. They were immensely tall, made of some dark gray stone that had been so highly polished that Morgain could see his reflection in their smooth places as he approached.

There were not a great many smooth places. Nearly every inch of the doors seemed to writhe with incredibly intricate carving. He could not trace even one line to its conclusion for everything was lost in a tangle of birds, flowers, small beasts, and vines.

Morgain could not imagine how long it would have taken for someone to carve such things. The second thing he'd done with his new pocketknife had been an attempt to carve a dog for his mother. It had taken him *days* and that had merely been a block of wood.

The round, smooth texture of the stone door nearest him seemed to invite his touch. His mother had often entreated him to "look with his eyes, not his fingers" and as always she was wise. He'd no sooner run his finger over the slightly oily stone, than the door swung open, nearly striking him! If he'd not jumped back, he would have received the door on his nose.

All was silent, even the breeze having died. Morgain peered into the opening. His forehead wrinkled with confusion and he noted dimly that his wound had stopped hurting altogether.

Surely—*surely*—what he saw was the back garden at Hamdry? There was the big larch, the statue of that Frenchman, and the tennis ball he'd lost last summer.

He poked his head in a bit further, noting that the sun shone brightly on the stone, yet when he'd left it had been nighttime. He wondered if he walked in through the opening, would he find himself at play? That would be amazing and an end to loneliness.

"No!" someone said from very close at hand.

Morgain jerked back, casting a guilty, yet relieved, glance around. At this moment, he'd be happy to see the least unsympathetic housemaster or the gruffest tutor. "Who's there?"

No voice answered. While he was thus looking about him, the doorway had closed. Nothing he did—not even a kick that bruised his toes—made it open again.

Slowly, he made his way back to his bed. Suddenly, he felt quite sleepy. He lay down under the clothes and must have shut his eyes for only one instant before deciding that he'd given up too soon. Perhaps he should try once more to open the doorway. But his foot had no sooner touched down on the pine needles that he found it instead on his own bedside rug. Pringle peered at him from under heavy eyelids. "You must lie down, Morgain. Doctor Danby made that very clear."

"Oh, but Pringle, I'm so thirsty."

When Clarice came to spell Pringle in Morgain's room, she found her yawning and blinking red eyes. Clarice would have felt more guilty about the nurse's long, sleepless vigil were it not that Pringle herself had insisted on taking the night watches.

"How is he?" she asked in a low voice.

"Very well, so far as I can see. He's hungry and thirsty, though I brought him a cup of tea last night."

"Tea? Was that wise, Pringle? Tea is rather stimulating."

"He took no harm," she said. "I put plenty of milk in it. *He* slept well enough, barring a nightmare or two. . . ." She yawned again, hugely. Rather belatedly she patted her lips and murmured an apology. She added another "I'm sorry" about the untidy state of Morgain's room.

"You're asleep on your feet, poor dear," Clarice said. "Don't give Morgain or anything else a second thought! A nightmare or two is perfectly natural under the circumstances."

"He'll tell you all about them, given half a chance. I

told him it's best to forget about things like that; dreams go by contraries and we are not intended to know what they mean."

"I thought you believed in dreams," Clarice said lightly, wanting to move on to Morgain's bedside. "At any rate, I hope your sleep is untroubled. Do eat first. I've given orders that you are not to be disturbed once you've closed your door, and you may very well miss luncheon."

Pringle could hardly stop yawning long enough to thank her. Feeling that in another instant she too would be cracking her jaws, Clarice closed the door behind Pringle with a feeling of profound relief.

Thinking of how dreadful Morgain had looked the day before, Clarice approached the bedside, steeling herself against any display of excessive sensibility. When she put back the curtain, what she saw so amazed her that she simply stood like a stock, staring down at her nephew.

He sat up, propped behind by mounds of pillows, a sketchbook on his knee. His hand fairly flew over the page, with never a pause for consideration. Except for his still being in his nightclothes at this hour of the morning, instead of up and doing the instant his eyes opened, everything about him looked the same as on any other day.

"Morgain?"

The boy glanced up just long enough to recognize her. "Aunt, are there one 't' or two in 'detritus'?"

"Two," Clarice said, spelling it. Then she added, "How do you feel today?"

"Excellently well, thank you." He wrote the word. "Thank you for spelling that! Pringle can't and she wouldn't fetch me a dictionary. Said reading would make me feverish."

Clarice had only the single instant when he glanced up to see the boy's forehead. She could not accept what she saw. Now she pulled the bed curtains all the way back to allow extra light in. "How can you see what you are doing, scribbling away in the dark?"

"That's just to keep Pringle out with her fussing. She talks all the time, but she's so good-natured I hate to give her a set-down."

He put his head to the side and shut one eye to better judge his work. Clarice reached out and caught his face between her hands. "Morgain, what happened?"

"I'm surprised you don't remember!" he exclaimed, wounded.

"Of course I remember! I shan't ever forget it."

"Looked horrible, didn't I?" His tone was pleased. "Did you think I was going to die?"

"I thought you *were* dead, my dear."

"Did you?" He grinned at her, as conscienceless as a monkey. "What a bore I wasn't awake. Did Pringle scream?"

"I think she did, now that you mention it, and you're a dreadful boy to look so happy about it!"

Morgain shrugged, all loose-limbed. "Doctor Danby put these stitches in, I collect. Or did you do it?"

"No, I'm not that brave. I couldn't even watch while the doctor did it." She sat down beside him, watching his face change. "No, I'm not poor-spirited," she said, answering his thought. "And you wouldn't have enjoyed being awake for *that* one little bit!"

"It's not your fault," he said magnificently. "You can't help being a girl."

"No. If you want all the horrid details, you'll have to ask Mr. Knight. *He* showed great presence of mind and even passed Doctor Danby the scissors!"

She gently brushed the hair back from his forehead and confirmed what she'd thought she'd seen. Of the huge black-and-blue bruise that had begun to blossom on his face last evening, there was not a sign. Of the promised black eye, only a little greenish mark, as of a bruise several weeks old, showed. The wound itself had faded to a soft red, covered with a scab, old-looking and dried. Only the black silk stitches still seemed like new.

"Pringle said you had a nightmare," she said.

"How would she know? She was asleep and snoring in that chair before the hour had struck twelve."

"She doesn't snore anymore," Clarice said.

"No, now she whistles through her nose!"

"You're monstrously unkind to poor Pringle and she loves you very much."

"She fusses. . . ."

"And you adore her for it. Who else spoils you so? Not I, *Monsieur Monstre*."

At this childhood pet-name, Morgain grinned again. "No, why should you spoil me? You listen to me."

"Thank you. High praise indeed. Are you hungry?"

"Starving! I didn't have anything last night except for some—" He stopped short.

"Pringle said she gave you some tea." She gazed at him with quiet alarm. Maybe this sudden healing only meant there was something wrong with him on the inside. All her fears of how to tell his parents returned. She'd spent half the night wondering how she could bear to break it to Blaic and Felicia if their only son had been killed. The other half she'd spent starting at every creak of a floorboard or rattle of a window. If the Rider could stoop to harming an innocent boy, heaven only knew what other outrage he'd commit.

When not tossing between these two points, Clarice found herself wondering about Dominic Knight. Had he come as a savior in the nick of time, or as the traitor who would open her gates to the enemy? Half a dozen times she made up her mind to send him away, only to change it in favor of his strength and the inner knowledge he seemed to have. How had he come by it?

Morgain made a face. "Milky tea," he said scornfully. "Pap for babies!"

"Then you are hungry now?"

"I could eat a roasted ox!"

"I'm afraid the cook didn't expect that request. Some coddled eggs and toast?"

"I'd rather have gammon and eggs. . . ." Morgain

caught his aunt's eye and sighed in the tone of one who suffers much from the well-meaning. "Very well. Coddled eggs and toast."

As she stood up, Clarice knocked the sketchbook to the floor. She picked it up and it fell open to the page he'd been working on. Clarice turned to Morgain and asked, "May I look?"

"If you want to. It's just another imaginary scene."

The circle of trees had been lightly sketched as though they stood beyond the footboard of his bed. Little arrows pointed here and there with one- or two-word descriptions written in beside them. In the corner of the paper, sketched larger than life-size and out of proportion to the rest of the scene, was a nut, more or less like a walnut and yet smoother-skinned and more rounded.

"Excellent perspective." Clarice handed it back to him. But nothing too fanciful about it, except the doors."

"Doors? I didn't want to put—"

"No? Then what are those?"

She pointed to the page. Off between the trees, two large rectangles appeared half-hidden by the forest all around and also well-concealed by the design of leaves and branches that covered the surfaces. It was impossible to tell if they were of stone or of wood.

Morgain stared at them as though he'd never seen them before. Her worry returning, Clarice took the sketchbook from him and closed it firmly. "No more until you've eaten and had Doctor Danby come again."

She took his pencils and sought among the sheets for his eraser-gum. "How you can lose things without ever leaving. . . . What's this?"

Opening her hand, she showed him the nut she'd found under his pillow. "I found it," Morgain said, reaching for it.

"I'm not surprised you drew a picture of it; it's too unusual not to keep a record. Isn't it enormous? I've never seen a walnut that size before." She admired it for a moment more, then said, "Don't keep it under your pillow anymore, though. That will give you the head-ache all by itself."

Clarice rang for Morgain's breakfast and sat beside him while he ate every bite of it. When he wiped his mouth and said, "Now may I have some bacon?" She laughed and agreed.

"I'll nip down myself and bring it back. Everything is at sixes and sevens this morning, no thanks to you!"

"Me?" he said innocently.

"Yes. Maggie had hysterics—not that she saw your bloody corpse but she had them anyway—it's all very well for you to giggle, Morgain Gardner, but you were more trouble to us than you were to yourself at that point. Where was I?"

" 'Maggie had hysterics,' " Morgain said helpfully.

"Yes. While she was screaming the place down, Cook gave notice. . . ."

"She took it back again though, just as always?"

"Just as always but not until Camber reached the point of all-but breach of promise! Then Collie came in, limp-ing, because he'd worn his boot-sole through looking for the man that—" In her eagerness to see Morgain laugh, she'd gone too far.

"The man that hit me," he said, finishing for her.

"Yes. Did you see him, dear? Can you tell me what he looked like? The constable must know if he is to have any chance of finding him."

"I didn't see anything, Aunt Clarice. He came from nowhere, riding that horse. I can describe the horse, if that's of any help. It was as big as a carthorse, with huge feet. When it reared up over me, I thought I was dead for certain."

"We told Constable Newkirk about the horse. No one seems to have seen it since last night, or its rider."

"I only saw his whip, Aunt."

"His . . ." She'd always thought the sensation-mad writers of Gothic horror tales were exaggerating when they spoke of "blood running cold." Now she knew she had maligned them. A chill seeped out of her heart and crept into every fiber of her body.

A rap at the door made them both look around. Dominic looked in. "How are you, Morgain?"

"Well, sir, thank you."

"I wonder if I might speak with your aunt a moment? Just if you can spare her."

"Certainly, sir."

"Thank you very kindly the pair of you," Clarice said more briskly than she felt. Collecting her nephew's tray and sketchbook, she bore them both away. "You need to rest, Morgain. If you sleep, you may come downstairs later for tea. No milk, however."

Morgain grinned, very nearly in his old way. Yet she realized that some measure of its impish brightness had dimmed, lost to his new knowledge of the easy brutality of the world. Balancing the tray on her hip, she pulled the bedclothes up around his thin shoulders and dipped to kiss his cheek. She did not cry, for he hated that, but she couldn't restrain an unladylike sniff of emotion as she walked away.

Dominic waited there in the doorway, reaching out for the tray as soon as she came near. "Allow me."

"Leave it there on the table. Rose will tidy it away."

"And his book . . . may I? Or would he object to my seeing these sketches?"

"Morgain? He's more likely to hound you with explanations of each little flourish."

"I don't understand art," he admitted. "I like portraits."

"We have a few at Hamdry, ancestors and such, but most of our art is sculptural. What did you want to see me about?"

"The doctor cannot come today."

"I beg . . . why not?"

"Look out the window."

She saw that Dominic stood and looked at Morgain's pictures by candlelight. A branch of candles stood on the table where he'd placed the tray, and another stood waiting a light in front of her own bedroom door. Leaving Dominic to flip through the pages, she walked to the window and held the curtain back with one hand.

Before her was another curtain, of pearly mist and swirling opal. This one no mortal hand could hold back. It concealed more than the lighted interior of a house from prying eyes. The fogs of the Devon moor were more dangerous than tor, or stream, or the will-o'-the-wisp. In the deep fog, every landmark blurred, every sound died, even the sun vanished. The most moor-wary individual could lose her way and fall in a long, rolling tumble to the bottom of a tor, or wander so far off the beaten path that she'd never find her way home.

Clarice let the curtain fall. "No, he'll not come today. Nor I think will anyone else."

"No, it's thick. Where does it come from?"

"I don't know. The Old Ones will tell you—"

"The Old Ones?"

She glanced at him, for there'd been something startled in his voice. "Old wives and old men. They'll tell you either that the fogs have grown steadily worse or that what we have today is hardly worthy of the name." Her voice dropped into a croak. "Niver zeen it zo bad in all me borned laife an' I been zeen the Duke o' Monmouth ride by with his gay cockade a-stuk in his hat." Resuming her natural tone, she said, "Or they'll say, 'Fog? Call this 'un a fog? B'ain't no more'n a bitty mist this is. Iff'n you'm be more'n a finger, you'd a-zeen zome fogs! We used t'*eat* t'fog when it come down from moor . . . crawl right into yer bowl. Iss fai'!"

" 'Iss fai'?"

"It means a statement for which there is no argument and I don't suggest you try to find one."

She noticed that he had one finger holding his place in Morgain's book. "Did you find a sketch you especially like? He's not above giving his work away, you know."

Dominic hesitated so infinitesimally that she was left more with the impression that he'd wished to avoid her looking at the page than with any actual perception. "This one is . . . different from his other drawings."

He showed her the very one Morgain had been working on that morning. It was still unfinished, the sky only a blank, the trees not polished with the high attention to detail Morgain could command. She felt as if she were looking at a direct sketch, rather than one done from Morgain's formidable imagination.

"It is different," she agreed. "He doesn't usually sketch so roughly. He prefers to do things 'properly,' which simply put means that which gibes with *his* measure of propriety."

"I'm fascinated by these doors, here behind the trees."

"They are interesting. Morgain only said that he wanted some doors there. I don't pretend to understand art . . . or at least not Morgain's."

Dominic raised his gaze from the page to her face. Clarice shifted on her delicate shoes and gave him a warmer-than-usual smile. She said, quickly, "Why not that game of chess, Mr. Knight? There's little else we can do until this fog lifts."

"I take it these fogs do not abide for long? The one last night, for instance. Not a wisp left by the time luncheon was served yesterday."

"There was still more than a little about when you were—practicing." She cleared her throat of whatever made her voice so low. "Yet that was only a light touch. A heavy fog like this might last two or three days."

"So long as that? And me eager to find my way back to the monuments up there." He waved his arm in entirely the wrong direction, pointing somewhere off the Isle of Wight by her dead-reckoning.

"The monuments will still be here when the fog lifts."

He gave her a warm smile, so warm that even her feet, grown a little cold in a draft whispering over the floor, promptly thawed. She felt a slight sense of light-headedness, not unlike when she nearly fainted last night. The cause was so opposite, however, that she didn't dare let him sweep her off her feet again. Surely she was not so spinsterish that one utterly charming smile from a personable man was enough to turn her head. Not even from the most personable man she'd met in years.

"Then let us play chess." He held out his arm as though he were about to lead her into the *Grande Ronde* at some society hostess's perfectly planned ball.

She swept him a right regal curtsy, as one might do for a royal gentleman conveying a signal honor upon one beneath him. "You are too kind, sir. The library?"

With some inner trepidation, she laid her fingers atop his hand and together they walked away, quite in the grand style. Halfway down the stairs, however, Dominic said something almost unforgivable.

"I like the way you laugh, Lady Stavely. You should do it more often."

Eight

Clarice had never thought of herself as a poor loser. She never minded paying out her pence at the resolution of a game of copper loo, and was more likely to laugh with delight than frown with pique should Morgain defeat her at croquet. Blaic was an especially fine player, with a fiendishly straight eye. No, she did not mind losing.

She hated being annihilated. Dominic played chess as though he'd been tutored by Attila the Hun. His was not a game of hours, but of horrible minutes in which pawns were slaughtered, knights unhorsed, castles destroyed, and royal families ruthlessly overthrown. She could only fall back, step by step, fighting to save this square or that piece, feeling all the while that she and they were doomed.

"Checkmate."

"Where?"

"That bishop and that knight hold you in checkmate."

"Oh, I saw the knight but . . . oh. Oh. I see."

"Again?"

"Certainly."

It was frustrating to set up some cunning set of moves and countermoves only to see him come whirling through like a sickle among standing corn. He hardly seemed to think at all. She might sit there for long minutes, planning out each stage, usually with disaster awaiting on every side. Then, she'd no sooner move than his brown hand would flash out, arrange one piece, and take another. He almost always found something to take away from her ranks while his remained at full strength.

Desperate, she had begun to play recklessly, knowing that he was using her long pauses to plan his own attacks. She spent less time considering the moves and did what seemed good at the time. The only benefit she reaped was that the torture ended more swiftly.

"Again?" he asked, his brown eyes alight.

"No. Thank you. You're very good."

"I'm afraid I become carried away a trifle. 'Take no prisoners' and all that."

"Are you always so competitive?" She glanced at him as she gathered up the remnants of a once-proud army. Unlike the game, this question made him think.

He shook his head. "If I play, I play to win. That's the way it should be. After all, chess is just war in miniature, don't you think?"

"I disagree. I play for enjoyment or to pass an idle hour. And, at least partly, to honor my father's memory. 'Twas he who taught me the game."

"Did he give you these pieces? They're fine." He held up one dashing cavalier from the red set. The tiny horse reared up, every hair in his mane clearly carved in the ivory. A rider clung to his back, very martial in Greek helmet and shield.

"They were his. Please . . . Mr. Knight. Put that down."

He looked at her with a frown. She supposed her voice must have sounded rather odd. Hurriedly, he set it in the space outlined for it in the velvet-fitted drawer under the game table. "Pardon me," he said, his head bowed. "I should have realized how much it looked like the Rider."

"No, how could you? I think you must pardon me.

I'm not usually so fanciful. There's really no resemblance at all."

She put the rest of the white pieces away. In the hearth, a fire popped and sizzled a few feet away. When she was done, she sank down before it, leaning her arm on a hassock, her blue silk shirt billowing in waves around her. "How wise of Camber," she said. "It might be the height of folly to have a fire on a beautiful June evening but when the fog is pressing against the windows, what could be more cheering?"

Dominic sat down and sipped the red wine in his glass. The flavor still did not appeal to him, yet the liquid was capable of lending a certain warmth to the limbs. Though he'd expected the weather to turn after his talk with Forgall, even fog created by the king's own will had a depressing effect on the spirit.

Clarice sighed, her eyes dreamy in the firelight. He wondered what she saw in the heart of the flames. The red light played over her profile, highlighting first her warm pink lips, then the curve of her cheek. Her eyes sparkled, only to be cast into the shadows again as her hair glistened with gold and red strands. One instant, the hollows of her face predominated, making her look like an old crone; the next instant, her face glowed like that of a girl in the first blush of beauty.

He gazed at her, thinking that this was Clarice herself, ever-changing, ever-intriguing. She was like a diamond, held up to the light. Depending on how it was turned, different colors would flash from its heart, everything from green to rose to sapphire blue. Like a diamond, too, she could not be cut except by her own like.

He thought of her future, how one day she would marry. He toyed with a portrait of the right husband for her. Someone worthy, of course, with a resolute spirit. He'd need that for she had been too long Lady of the Manor to take lightly to interference, unless it came from someone she loved with her whole heart. Someone young enough for her too, to bring the laughter into her eyes and awaken her passions.

His gaze traced the long curve of her back, admiring the edges of her shoulder blades under the smooth silk and the proud carriage of her head, her soft golden hair piled high. If only she weren't the daughter of his sworn enemy . . .

Dominic sighed, resolutely turning his thoughts from the envious direction they'd taken. Taking another sip of his wine, he said, "Tell me a little about your parents."

She started, as though his voice had broken some dream she'd fallen into. "My father . . . had a wonderful sense of humor. Dry wit. He'd say something to set the room aroar and then look about him with a bland expression as if unsure what had set everyone off. He always had a word of greeting for everyone, high or low. The local people all loved him. They could tell, you know, that it wasn't something he put on for the occasion. He knew everyone's concerns intimately."

"He loved Hamdry?"

"Oh, yes. We all do. We Stavelys have lived here for many, many centuries, even before we received the title." She rose up and went to the bookshelves. Choosing a large folio volume, she brought it down and laid it open on the smooth leather desktop. The book was closed, a faded red ribbon tying the covers together. She said, "This is the patent."

He rose to look over her shoulder while she tried to untie the ribbon. The silk ties had worked themselves into a tight knot. "How vexing," she said in smiling exasperation. "I never leave it like this. If Morgain has been in here, we'll probably find hippogriffs and phoenixes scrawled over it and I will have to contain my anger because he's unwell."

"Allow me," Dominic said. His big hand moved and suddenly the knot on which she'd been nearly breaking her fingernails came loose. She smiled her thanks and opened the book.

It contained only the one uneven sheet of vellum, once a new white lambskin now turned mellow and tan with great age. The thin black lines of handwriting traced away down the page, crooked and straight, some initial letters as big as his thumb. A date leapt out at him in red ink. "Fourteen fifty-two?"

"Yes. You'll see it's signed by Henry VI. His mind broke just a few months later, in 1453. There are those who will tell you that his signing this patent for my ancestor was the first sign of his approaching insanity. You see, the title can descend to the eldest child of either sex. Unheard of, at the time."

"Not so common now, I think," he said in the same tone.

"No. Just as well. I should hate to have been 'Miss Stavely' all my life."

"I thought your sister was the elder," he said idly.

The laughter died in her eyes. She closed the book, tying the ribbon neatly at the side. Smoothing the limp leather cover with the flat of her hand, she said, "She should have been Lady Stavely. My father loved her mother first, before he married my mother. If he'd married Maria Starret instead . . ."

She picked up the book and carried it back to its place on the shelf. "I didn't know about Felicia until the year I was ten. Her mother died and she came to live here, at Stavely."

"That must have been a shock."

"To my mother, yes. A very considerable shock. Felicia was not at all . . . that is, she had not been raised with advantages. To me, however, her coming was sheer delight. I hated being the only child rattling around in this house. When Felicia came, it was as though all my dreams of having an elder sister were realized. I loved her at once."

Dominic guessed that she was leaving much unsaid. From what he knew of Matilda, the presence of an unwanted, illegitimate child of her husband's getting must have been a perpetual thorn in her side. He doubted that Clarice's realized dream of having an older sister had been untroubled by dark looks and disdainful words.

How easy it would have been for Clarice, no more than ten, to have followed her mother's example and make Felicia feel her inferiority. None of the information he'd been given had indicated that she had done so; quite the opposite, in fact.

"I take it that Mrs. Gardner doesn't look upon you as an usurper of her rightful title?"

Clarice shook her head, laughing at the very idea. "Felicia would hate it. Not the responsibility for she is both dependable and honorable but the other duties that attend a title. The very idea of being in the House when the Session opens, sitting among all the notable lords petrifies her. She says she can never speak naturally to strangers. She only accompanied Blaic to London this time because it is the book's debut."

Dominic realized later that it might have been wise to make some complimentary comment about Mrs. Gardner, who, after all, he'd given the impression of having met. Instead he said, "So everything falls out as it should. You are Viscountess Stavely and she is married to Blaic Gardner."

"Yes. Yes, everything is as it should be."

"Do you ever wonder, I wonder, what it would like if *you* had married him?"

"Of course not," she said incredulously.

"Surely, he appeals to you. It's only natural that you should look on him with admiration."

"I do admire him. As though he were my older brother. Any other notion is absurd. Whatever would make you say such a thing? Wait . . . let me guess. One of those silly Wisby girls, no doubt expressing *her* wish disguised as mine."

"You've guessed it," he said, lying through his teeth.

"No great effort was needed to guess. I admire Blaic greatly, as I would anyone who wooed and won my lovely Felicia. But that those girls should try to . . . don't they know I was not yet seventeen when Felicia and Blaic were wed and he was . . . well, he must have been all of thirty!"

"I would guess Mr. Gardner to be older than he looks."

Her brilliant gaze flicked toward his face as though suspecting him of some inner meaning. He schooled his features to show nothing beyond a mild interest. Her eyes narrowed as she tucked in her rose lips. It was a look he'd come to know over the chess table this very afternoon. Clarice was about to try an audacious gambit.

"I am most curious, Mr. Knight, about your work. Tell me all about it." She seated herself on the comfortable settee, gathering her whispering silks to make room for him next to her. When he didn't at once join her, she patted the cushions invitingly.

As warily as though he were walking into a seemingly empty dragon's lair, Dominic approached her. He sat down, thinking there was sufficient distance between them, but somehow winding up much closer to Clarice. Suddenly, he was highly aware of the soft, powdery fragrance of her skin and the swanlike beauty of her throat. The whiteness there was rivaled only by the purity of her rounded breasts, the tops screened by the muslin fichu about her shoulders in a way that seemed both to conceal and reveal.

She did nothing vulgar—neither licking her lips nor taking deeper breaths than usual to emphasize her figure. Yet Dominic found himself aware of her as a desirable woman as he had not been until that moment. He remembered Forgall's warning. It steadied him, despite the instincts that were screaming at him that this was some particularly subtle trap.

His voice remained deep and steady. "I intend to discover whether the builders of these ancient forts used any particular pattern or style of building. For instance, if each one is the same circumference, it would tell us that these 'forts' were built by the same groups of people or, at any rate, people who had a great deal of contact amongst themselves."

"How fascinating. You'll measure each fort that you find, then? What if they are not complete?"

"There . . ." Strange how he had suddenly to clear his throat. "There will be other evidence, dips in the ground where a former stone compressed the earth and such. Even if a stone has fallen over, I will be able to determine which way it fell. Naturally—ahem—naturally, I will have to chart each fort with the greatest care."

"What fascinating work. I don't believe anything like it has been done here before, though I saw some similar archaeological work being done at Herculaneum."

Clarice did not reach out and touch his hand as she'd done at their first meeting to test him. Yet something in her smile made him feel as though she might at any time. He tried to remember everything he'd been told about the wiles of mortal woman. As soon as the king had chosen him as Clarice's guard, he'd been sent to study all he could of human history and behavior. Though he was human, he knew little beyond the art of war. What else he had learned flew out of his head the moment Clarice had patted the cushion.

He would have to recapture his cunning while at the same time give her enough of a fright to stand off from him. Safer by far if she wanted never to be alone with him again—safer for them both.

Dominic turned toward her and coaxed a fatuous smile from his stern lips. "Enough about me. Cold stone is a dull subject for a woman . . . especially a woman like you."

"A—a woman like me?"

"You don't need me to tell you that you are the loveliest creature alive, Lady Stavely. Such a cool name . . . I heard Mr. Gardner call you Clarice. It suits you."

"I don't feel you know me well enough to call me by my name, Mr. Knight."

"Perhaps not. Soon I hope to know you much, much better."

Clarice would have vehemently denied that she'd been flirting with Dominic Knight. She'd been raised to believe that only light-skirts flirted with a man; nothing could be more vulgar. Yet she'd also been told that nothing was more appealing to a man than a woman who took a genuine interest in his pursuits.

Not pugilism or gambling, perhaps, but if a man were a collector of snuffboxes or a lover of fine music, it behooved a clever woman to cultivate those tastes as well. Not with the intention of surpassing a man—never that!—but so that one could ask intelligent questions, for men also loved to instruct ladies in their own particular field.

"Pray believe me. I am truly interested in your work, sir. How old, do you think . . ."

"At the moment, I am interested only in you. How can you bear living so retired when London waits to throw itself at your feet? Such beauty and charm shouldn't be wasted in this backwater."

"I go to London now only when my duty demands it. I've no ambition to make a great noise in the world."

"I cannot be sorry to hear that. Such a prize as you are surely would have been won by some titled gentleman and we should not be here now, together."

Clarice tried to move farther down the settee, but found herself already wedged into the corner. Her motives had been less to learn about his book than to draw him out. She knew little about him, only what he'd let slip. She thought if he started talking freely on the subject of his work, it would be easy to persuade him into discussing whatever subject she fancied. Instead, it was she who was telling him more than she'd wanted to.

She said lightly, "I suppose the titled gentlemen were all married already. Not so much as a single duke proposed during my Season. Pray tell me, Mr. Knight, what is it you do when not pursuing your researches?"

"I live very quietly, but not so quietly as you. No dukes pursued you, you say? Then all the nobles of England must be blind as well as foolish. Not one made a push to secure the loveliest prize of all?"

"I do not think myself so very lovely. Once, perhaps, I was." She held up her hand to keep him from uttering any more empty compliments. "If I had a wish, it would be to find someone to love me for those qualities which linger. Beauty fades."

"You have nothing to fear in *that* direction for some time to come." His gaze wandered over her, and suddenly she wished she'd put on her heaviest woolen gown despite the calendar.

Clarice described her behavior to herself as having become a trifle more unabashedly feminine than was her habit. She only understood that she'd raised her feminity too much when he had turned to her with that fatuous expression. She'd wanted to set him talking freely about himself, only to find that he did not want to stop at talking.

Dominic slid a trifle closer to her on the settee. There was literally not an inch of space between his thigh and hers. His rich, low voice carried warmly to her ear. "Clarice . . . don't be bashful."

She knew she should rise to her feet, rebuke him sharply, and sweep away out of the library. Instead, she sat immobile, not even turning her head away. She felt his hand steal about her waist while his other hand covered hers on her knee. She'd never been touched so intimately by a man before.

Clarice remembered the strength of his arms when he'd carried her to her room, and felt a curious flutter deep inside as though her heart had trembled. She hesitated, fatally.

Dominic had thought that she would have run away by now. He could see the tension in every line of her beautiful figure. When his arm encircled her, he felt her quiver as though with disgust. Yet she didn't move. Frowning now, he said in a well-feigned loverlike tone, "The moment you agreed to let me stay here at Hamdry, I knew what you wanted."

Surely *now* she would run away?

He added, "I wanted it too. We are entirely alone. Shouldn't we seize the moment that has been granted us?"

She turned her head and looked him full in the eyes.

Her expression was not something his study had prepared him for. Half-eager, half-frightened, wholly determined, she studied him. Her face was so close to his that he could all but taste the violet pastilles she'd taken while playing chess.

Then, in a clumsy lunge, she reached out to grasp his lapel. With a surprising strength, she pulled him nearer, leaned in, and kissed him. Her lips landed on his chin. They were soft as rose-petals.

Drawing back, she appeared to be appalled by her own brashness. Her cheeks glowed feverishly from sheer embarrassment and she ducked her head. "I'm sorry . . . I don't know. . . ."

Dominic's arm encircled her waist. Still acting on pure instinct, he tightened it, bringing her abruptly against his chest. Her head flew up while her hands fended him off as best she could. He had never kissed a woman before in his life, yet he aimed with both speed and accuracy. His kiss did not go awry.

Her lips were even softer than he'd thought. Warmer, too, with a sweetness that struck right into his soul. When the same odd little quiver ran through her body, it awoke a response in him. Her hands tightened on his coat as she kissed him back. New instincts came roaring into life. For the first time, he felt the desire to possess, to claim this woman for his own.

For a moment, he broke contact with her lips. Was this wrong? The pause lasted less than a heartbeat before he knew he did not care. He wanted to go on kissing her, exploring this new experience. Aware of nothing except Clarice, he tasted her lips again, trying a different pressure, a different angle, and finding it also good.

He wondered why his eyes closed naturally the moment their lips met when it would be so much more wonderful to see her lovely face. He opened them, but saw over Clarice's shoulder the black expression of his king.

Forgall stood in front of the fireplace, his arms crossed over his chest, his head held down so that his beard bristled over his arms. His voice sounded in Dominic's head. *"Stop that immediately!"*

Clarice must have noticed his sudden loss of interest. Her hands released his coat and she turned away, straightening her arms until he no longer leaned over her. Her breath still came a trifle fast.

"I do not know what came over me. Pray forgive my forwardness, Mr. Knight."

Dominic wished futilely that even a single drop of Fay blood had mixed with his own somewhere in his ancestry. Without it, his thoughts were open to the king. If it were not for that, he would be thinking what a darling Clarice was. As matters stood, however, he had to act the part of a self-satisfied lout for her, while playing the calculating soldier in his thoughts for the king.

"There's nothing to forgive," he said. "You couldn't help yourself."

"Couldn't I?"

"No, little silly! Many women have found me hard to resist. You might say I've made something of an art of seduction." To Forgall he sent the thought, *"That should give her a suitable disgust of me."*

"Ah, was that your intention? Strange methods, sirrah."

"Have you, indeed?"

"Oh, yes. You'll be in good company, dear heart."

She rose regally to her feet. "Be good enough to excuse me, sir. I find I have neglected some minor duties that must be seen to."

"Ah, no," he said, rising too and catching at her hand. "Never mind such foolishness! What's housewifely duties compared with the rapture we find within each other's arms?"

"Overdoing it?" the king asked.

"Trust me, o King."

"So I do, as much as I trust any man."

That made Dominic wince. Clarice, however, was beyond noticing his expression. She pulled her hand free with the expression she would have worn had she found a slug crawling across her fingers. "You mistake me, sir. I gave in to a moment of weakness—my curiosity has ever been my downfall. I found no rapture, no pleasure in your arms. I have not the slightest wish to repeat the experiment."

"But . . . but . . . Clarice . . ." he stammered, locking his true feelings in his heart. He cocked an eye toward the king, to see what his reaction was. The royal eyes were narrowed.

Clarice stood very tall. "I am the Viscountess of Hamdry, sir. You will call me Lady Stavely or you will leave this house at once." The king gave a nod of approval at the imperial ring of her voice.

"You mean, I can remain here?"

"I do not forget, sir, that the weather is such that I would not turn a dog out-of-doors. Furthermore, despite your behavior, you are still an acquaintance of my brother-in-law. For his sake, you may remain. But never again dare to lay a hand on me!"

She turned to sweep from the room, her back as straight as a queen's. Reluctant though he was to spoil a fine exit, he said, "Lady Stavely, have you taken a knife from your father's collection yet? You know we discussed that you should keep one for protection."

He was grateful that she was not one of the People, for he surely would have been turned to ashes by the flash of her brilliant eyes. "I shall certainly carry one from this hour forward! Indeed, I wish I'd had one but five minutes ago!"

She strode away, leaving him bowing after her.

When he could look about him again, Forgall had gone. Dominic could not even be certain that he'd seen him in truth. He might have been no more than the figment of a guilt-ridden conscience.

He sat in the very spot where Clarice had embraced him. It would never happen again; she'd vowed it, but the memory was inexpressibly good. She'd taken him by surprise, a defeat for the soldier but a definite victory for the man. He grinned at the thought, even as he realized what a strange one it was for him to have.

He'd never thought of himself as a man, mortal though he was. Trained from childhood for one purpose, his humanity had never entered into it, except for two facts: his lack of power and his ability to handle steel.

He could not stay here, wallowing in sensual memories. He would go and practice with the swords from the Red Chamber. Standing, he stretched out his arms, feeling remarkably healthy for a man of his years.

Then the door opened. He turned, hoping against hope to see Clarice. But it was Camber. The thin, youthful butler looked over his shoulder stealthily, then came in. "Are you alone?"

"Yes. Come in. What have you to report?"

"All is well. This mortal lady suspects nothing."

"There will be difficulties ahead, especially for the maid. How will she perform her duties without touching Lady Stavely?"

"She will wear gloves, explaining the action with a facile tale of blisters on her hands from handling some noxious plant or other. These humans are prey to many such weaknesses."

"Don't forget to whom you are speaking, if you please."

The butler's lips twitched. Then his face changed and over the crisp white collar of the servant, Dominic saw the luminous countenance of a Fay. Everything was different; the long-lashed eyes, the vaguely pointed ears, the upswept brows. Only the laughter remained. "It is easy to forget that you are one of them, Dominic."

"For me also, Chadwin. Their ways are strange to me."

"How long has it been since you dwelt in a human home?"

Dominic had to think about it. "Some four hundred mortal years, I believe. And this manor is nothing at all like the smoky hut where I was born. That had naught but a fire in the center of the floor and a hole in the roof to let the smoke out. My mother had but one bed, a table, a stool, and a pewter spoon. Yet she was of good family." He shook his head. "It has been long indeed since I thought of her. How she would stare to see the books in this room!"

"Yes, I suppose they have managed some progress over the centuries, though it seems but slight to me. I know this much. Of all the uncomfortable clothing . . ." He tugged at the butler's cravat. When it was loosened, his features had once again taken on the semblance of Camber.

"It won't be for very long, Chadwin. Soon the hag will sue for terms."

"I hope you are right. Ah, well. To work, to work." Pointing a finger at the fire, he restored the half-burned log to its unburned state. After a nod, the hearth was clear of ashes and another nod straightened the cushions on the settee, placed the box of chessmen on the shelf, and the tea tray vanished, leaving not a crumb behind.

Nine

~

Clarice debated having dinner on a tray in her room. If it were not for Morgain and the trouble it would give the servants, she would have done it. How could she face Dominic Knight, coolly and collectedly, when her face still burned with embarrassment an hour or more after leaving him in the library?

What had come over her? Never in all her life—well, not since her mother had died—had she acted so impulsively. She had learned to control her wilder notions while under the severe gaze of society. Flinging herself into his arms . . .

Clarice could not sit still. She paced in the clear space between bed and bureau, her skirts swishing in agitation. Again and again, she replayed the scene in the library. Though she would have liked to blame Dominic for the entire dreadful business, she could not. True, he'd acted badly. She never would have guessed that he could sound so vain, driveling on about how irresistible he was.

Even more than disgust, she felt disappointed. He'd been so helpful when Morgain had been hurt; exactly the kind of friend she'd needed most. There'd been a warmth in his eyes when they'd rested on her as he brought her to her room that had created an answering warmth in her heart. She'd cherished a hope that his former patronizing tone had been born of shyness or diffidence at meeting a stranger. Now to find that he was vain enough to believe himself the perfect lover for *any* woman. . . . Perhaps he was a man who could only look at a woman in two ways—as a creature of a lower order than man, good only so far as she was docile, or as a convenience for a lustful male. She had met that kind before.

Though she blushed, she conceded that he might have a reason. She still could not say why she'd done it, except that all the while he'd been talking she'd seemed to hear another voice, a small voice whispering in her ear. It had urged her to accept his challenge, to make him prove what he said about desiring her. Slowly, she'd felt creeping over her a sense that her will was draining away. When the little voice had told her to kiss him, she'd had no self-direction left.

She'd sat motionless while the spell was woven about her until she was compelled to grasp his lapels and pull him close. What he must think of her had been proved when he'd kissed her in response, only to push her away a moment or two later. Her sense of self had returned in a flood, bringing with it hideous humiliation and the knowledge that she'd sunk herself beyond hope of redemption.

Clarice flung herself into a chair, and sat in the very attitude of despair. Placing her hands over her eyes, she groaned aloud. She could not face him. It would have to be supper on a tray after all. Breakfast, luncheon, and tea would also be taken here. She might never emerge from her room again in her lifetime. "How fortunate that I like the view," she muttered.

"Aunt Clarice . . . ?"

Morgain stood in the doorway, his red robe caught around his middle with what looked like a twisted cord taken from a drapery. With the faint remains of the bruise on his face, he looked like a very small, rather dissolute monk none too sure of his reception by the abbot.

Putting aside her disquiet, Clarice hurried to slip her arm about his shoulders and lead him into the room. "Are you feeling well enough to be out of bed, Morgain?"

"I don't feel at all bad. I was tired—I don't think I slept well last night so I'm the better for having rested."

"You look far better than I expected." Clarice cupped his face in her hands and turned it toward the candles burning on the table beside her chair. "I don't understand how this wound can look so well the very day after you received it. Your face is hardly swollen and there are only faded bruises. I have never known you to heal so swiftly before."

Morgain tossed his head to be free of even the lightest touch. He stuffed his hands into his pockets, further distorting his robe. Digging one toe into the carved carpet, he said, "I don't. Nobody does, except perhaps those who do not die. The immortal ones must have amazing powers of recovery from such minor wounds or how do they live so long?"

"These are questions for your father, Morgain, not I."

The thin shoulders lifted and fell fatalistically. "He doesn't tell me anything about those days, except how *not* to . . . you know."

"Yes, I know. But I cannot help you. I know only the very little your father has told me. Your mother may know more yet."

"She won't tell me. She's afraid, I think, that if I know too much I'll want to join *them*. But that's silly. I never should, you know. Father's told me enough for me to know that the ways of the People will never be mine. What kind of a wasted life I should have if all I need do is wave my hand and whatever I desired appeared to me."

He made a fine gesture to show what he meant. A moment later, Clarice and Morgain froze as they heard from behind them a sniffling whine and a slither. A long red tail slid over the carpet toward them from behind, a sharp triangle on the tip. At the same moment, they were aware of a smell as of brimstone and burning.

"Morgain . . ." Clarice said in a low voice. She didn't dare look around to see whatever it was he'd brought forth from his mind. She only hoped it didn't commit an indecency upon her new Aubusson carpet.

"It wasn't *me*!" he said in an agitated whisper. "You know I don't do that anymore."

"I don't care who did it! Get rid of it!"

He closed his eyes so tight that lines appeared in the corners. Taking in a deep breath, he released it very slowly. Then twice more. "There!"

"It's gone?" She looked over her shoulder. Except for a light haze around the candles, which might have been fog, whatever creature had stood for an instant behind them was there no longer. Then she looked down and saw traces of its presence—great four-clawed impressions that had flattened the intricate cut-pile of her carpet. Each claw-mark was larger by far than her hand. She sighed heavily.

"Morgain, what happened?"

The boy raked his teeth over his lower lip in thought. "I haven't the remotest notion. Ever since my father taught me how to control my 'gifts,' such a thing has never happened to me. Something odd is occurring in this household; I intend to discover what it may be."

Clarice sat down in her chair. "I think I shall write your parents and tell them to return. . . ."

"Ah, no. . . ."

"They must be told that you've been injured, Morgain. I should be neglectful in my duty to them and to you if I did not write to them. Already, I may have waited too long."

"But I am well. You can see I am. There's no need to alarm them unnecessarily."

"I'm not certain it is unnecessary. You had a nasty blow to the head, dearest. Who is to say it was not that which has reawakened your dormant gifts?"

"It hasn't! I would know . . ."

"You thought you knew you could control them. Yet what was that thing that stood behind us? Of what were you thinking just then?"

"Of . . . of a wyvern, Aunt."

"Of a . . ." She closed her eyes, thinking of slashing beaks and tearing claws. "That's a type of dragon, is it not?"

"Yes, Aunt. Whenever I imagine one, mine are always red."

"And harmless, of course. Yours are always entirely harmless?"

"Actually, I have always thought a fire-breather would be most handy on those occasions when the firewood is wet. . . ."

Clarice's hands tightened on the upholstered arms of her chair so much that she was afraid she'd slit the fabric with her nails. "You conjured a fire-breather into my boudoir?"

"I'm sorry, Aunt. I was not intending to."

"No, of course not. You shall have to exercise the greatest caution until your father returns." Putting on her spectacles, she flipped open the lid of her writing case and took out a square of paper and a pen. "I feel I must write them. Of course, until the fog lifts, I shan't be able to send the letter."

"Is it foggy?"

"Yes, silly. Why else would we have the candles lit so early on a summer's evening *and* have the windows closed?"

"Oh. You see, I have such a realistic dream. . . ."

"What about, dear?"

"The picture I drew . . . but I left many things out. The little animal, for instance. It was rather like a cat, but it wasn't really. . . ."

"You should look it up in the library. We've a book on different animals—when you were very little you loved to pour over its pages."

"Oh, yes. I remember. I'll do that at once."

Clarice was only half-attending, her focus on the letter. It was surprisingly difficult to form into sentences the happenings of the last day or so. She wanted the prompt return of the Gardners, but did not want to alarm them unnecessarily. She found her first effort to be so full of reassurances that she knew it was more likely to throw them into a panic than any bald statement of the facts. She crumpled it and laid it aside.

When the door closed, she glanced around. Morgain had gone. "I do hope he puts on some clothes first."

Morgain had not stopped for that. He didn't even think of it. His leather slippers slapped along the stairs and the tiled hall but he went silently enough over the wooden floor. Therefore, as he passed the dining salon, the two men within did not look up. Morgain had gone by before he'd realized what he'd seen had seemed most unusual.

Carefully, he kicked off his slippers and crept back, keeping low. He poked just enough of his head around the corner to see without being seen.

"Have I put the goblets in all the right places?" Mr. Knight was asking.

Camber held a book open in one hand, while he traced his finger over a page. "I believe you have the wine and the water reversed on the left side of the table."

"Over here?"

"That's better. Now, the silver and we must hurry, Dominic. There's not much time before the woman comes down."

"If she comes down at all. I won't be surprised if she takes supper in her room."

"What *did* you do to her? No, the blade of the knife faces the plate."

"I kissed her."

"Did you? How odd of you. Those small forks lie next to the larger ones, on the outside."

"I had a reason," Mr. Knight said.

"Of course. Why would anyone do such a strange thing without a good reason?"

"When I know, I will explain it all to you. Are you certain we put all these things on the table at once? Where will the food set?"

Morgain could not imagine why Camber would have a guest put out the table settings. It made no sense. Camber—while off-duty was not above helping a boy build a model boat or hunt bird's nests—was jealous of his professional abilities. He permitted no one to polish the family silver but himself and never allowed another soul to touch a bottle of wine.

"There will be room enough," Camber said, closing the book with a snap. "Serve from the left, remove from the right," he muttered. "Serve from the left, remove from the right."

Mr. Knight was rolling up the rest of the silver flatware in their special flannel bags. "Don't worry so much. If you make a mistake, I'll be there to distract her attention from it. She doesn't like compliments; I'll make a few, the grander, the better."

"If she'll speak to you at all."

"She doesn't have to speak to me, just not look at you."

"There is another alternative," Camber said, and raised an eyebrow. Morgain caught his breath and scuttled back out of sight. Their voices went on, but he paid no attention, unable to hear anything over the blood drumming in his ears.

Five minutes later, when the coast was clear, he returned to his aunt's room. He all but fell at her feet.

"Morgain?"

"Aunt Clarice . . . something . . . something strange . . ."

"Not the Rider?" she said, starting up in alarm.

He shook his head. "No, not that. It's Camber—I mean, it's *not* Camber."

Clarice raised the boy to his feet and guided him to a chair. "You're shaking. I feared you were overdoing.

Is that cordial still in your room? I'll ring for Rose. . . ."

She found the boy clutching her arm as she began to move away. In a low, hoarse voice, he said, "Don't ring for anyone. I'll sit right here while you go."

"I don't want to leave you. Rose will be happy to—"

"No! You can't trust her. We can't trust anyone." He seemed to realize that his fingers were digging into her arm and released her. He gripped the stuff of his robe in white-knuckled hands as though the tighter he hung on to something the easier it would be to keep calm. "I'll sit right here."

Clarice didn't like his color, for he'd gone from naturally pale to white as wax. His green eyes were like a hunted creature's, never still, darting about as though seeing motion where none could be. She should be firm, ring for Rose, and squash his foolish notion. That blow to the head must have disordered his senses even more than she feared. However, rather than agitate Morgain further, she said, "Very well. I shall return in a moment."

She walked past Pringle's door and into the room Morgain used during his visits. The dark bottle of cordial stood on a lacquer tray with two glasses, one with a trace of the deep red liquid dried to a sticky blob in the bottom. Leaving that one behind, Clarice carried the tray out.

Pringle stood in her doorway. "Why, my lady, let me carry that."

"No, thank you, Pringle. Are you feeling more rested now?"

"As well as ever," she said, smiling warmly. "Is Morgain still sleeping? I almost couldn't fall asleep myself for worrying about him so."

"No, Morgain's awake," Clarice said. "He's waiting for me in my room."

"Is that wise, my lady, after such a terrible thing! He should stay in bed until Doctor Danby can visit him. Goodness know what fancies he'll take into his head. I never told you about my cousin Maggie, did I, my lady?

Well, *she* was hit on the head when a rock fell out of a tree and she started *seeing* things—things that just could never be! Why, she even saw Uncle Arthur pinch the governess and you know he was a married man."

Interested despite herself, Clarice asked, "Why was a rock in a tree?"

"That's exactly what we asked ourselves. My cousin thought that a squirrel must have carried it there mistaking it for a large nut."

Clarice knew she should have never asked. "I must go back to Morgain now, Pringle. He needs this cordial."

"I'll come too. He mustn't be given too much!"

"I can pour out the proper dose. He asked to be alone with me."

"How you coddle him, my lady!"

"When he is unwell. . . ." She walked away, leaving the sentence unfinished. She had gone only a few steps when the strangest feeling swept over her. Suddenly, she felt as though she'd been walking forever down this hall, carrying this tray, as if she would never come any nearer to her own room. She'd had this feeling in dreams, laboring all through the hours of the night and waking no more rested than when she'd laid down, but she'd never known it while awake before.

A mirror hung on the wall beside her. She turned her head, so slowly, to look into it. Between one blink and the next she saw, not her own blond head and fair face, but a woman wearing a dark veil thrown over her hair. Dark eyes gleamed in a face she knew as well as her own. "Mother?" she asked, her voice barely a croak.

"My lady?" Pringle called from behind her. "Are you well?"

"Quite well," Clarice said, after a cough. The face had evaporated at the sound of Pringle's voice. "Put on your dinner gown. You will dine with us tonight."

"Won't that throw Camber's plans out?"

"He won't mind. He loves a challenge."

Quite firmly, she shut her bedroom door behind her. She put the tray down on a table near the door. With a hand that shook only slightly, she poured out a glassful of the cordial and tossed it back in one gulp. It tasted, not unpleasantly, of anise and cherries as it glided over her tongue, but there was a strong aftertaste of charcoal.

Morgain watched her intently. "What is it? What happened?"

"Nothing at all. Drink this." She poured him a dose in the same glass and handed it to him. "Go on. It will put heart into you."

"My heart's a little squalmish, for certain." He made a face as the licorice flavor went down.

"It's not that bad," Clarice said with a smile.

"You pulled a worse face when you drank it!"

"Well, perhaps a little. Now tell me. What's all this about, Camber?" When he told his tale, she listened quietly. At the end, though, she said, "And is that all?"

"All? Isn't it enough?"

"No. Camber raised an eyebrow and you come here claiming that he is *not* Camber. Dear Morgain, you are usually the first to point out a flaw in someone's logic. Permit me to tell you that you sound a trifle unbalanced."

"You don't understand. You don't know Camber so well as I."

"I have known him considerably longer."

"But as his mistress, not as a friend. Aunt Clarice, Camber cannot raise only one eyebrow. Both always go up. He told me once that he wished he could, even tried to train himself to do it. He spent weeks in front of a mirror trying to develop the knack."

"Why on earth . . . ?" Clarice asked with a choked laugh.

"Because of somebody who stayed here once when Grandfather Stavely was alive. A—a—oh, what's the word for a fellow who runs around after another fellow straightening things? A—a valet, that's it! Some valet who stayed here used to make Camber feel very small and provincial whenever he raised one eyebrow at him. Camber told me all about it. The fellow's master could do it too, only he did it through a quizzing glass and used to ruin reputations with it or some such nonsense. Sounded silly to me but Camber thought that if he could do it too, it would help him rise in the world. But he *couldn't* do it—no matter how hard he tried!"

"Perhaps he has learned." She thought about it. "I have never seen him do such a thing, though perhaps he would not raise an eyebrow at me. Still it is hardly enough to say that the butler downstairs is not Camber."

"Why is he having Mr. Knight set the table? Why was he reading from a book the proper placement of the flatware? Camber knows protocol as well as he knows his pantry. He wouldn't have to refresh his memory with a peek in some book—not for a quiet family dinner!"

"I cannot answer that, but Camber can and he shall." She turned away to reach for the bell-pull.

"No! It's not Camber and heaven only knows what he will say—or do." More quietly, he added, "Give me until tomorrow. I will find out what is happening. Maybe I am out of my head and this is all some fabulous dream or if strange things are happening, who better to discover this than me?"

"No." Clarice hated to say it. "I have a responsibility to you, Morgain. If you are 'out of your head' then I shall send at once for Doctor Danby, fog or no."

"And if I am not? Do you remember when all the world said you were out of your mind? Were you?"

"That was different, as you know perfectly well."

"Granted. But what if I say is true? What do we do then?"

Clarice's hand fell away from the bell-pull, leaving it unrung. "Very well. We will pretend, for now, that we suspect nothing. Do you feel that you can face going down to dinner, or shall I have something sent up to you?"

His childish chin stuck out. "I can face it—if you are with me."

She came to him and kissed his cheek. "Go to dress, then."

For herself, she debated awhile before ringing for the maid. Rose came in with nothing less than her usual firm step. Clarice glanced at the candid eyes and rosy cheeks of the middle-aged maid and knew a moment's doubt. Could any impostor, even with the aid of powers beyond mortal ken, appear so much like the genuine person? "I must dress, Rose."

"In what, my lady?"

"The newest one, from London."

"Oh, my lady! 'Tis ever zo nice." In a few minutes, she'd brought the dress out from the dressing room and laid it out on the bed. "I niver zee 'un laike that 'un afore. 'Tain't no top to it!"

"It's entirely respectable," Clarice said, more sharply than she would have if her own doubts in that direction weren't so great. Then her eyes narrowed. "Rose, you're wearing gloves?"

"I thought it best, my lady. Oh, my hands be mortal-bad with the blisters!"

"Blisters?"

"Iss, fai! I was pickin' the burdocks out of the horses' tails. . . ."

"You were? Why were you? Cannot Drake and those sons of his do it?"

Rose looked shyly down at her large feet. "I wanted a good reason to talk t'oldest 'un," she said. "As he were doin' it, I did too. But, oh! The blisters! Niver could touch a burdock, not even when I was a little one. An' now I don't want to be a-spoilin' thy new gown, my lady, zo I be-thought me of these gloves of Mr. Camber's."

"They are Camber's gloves?"

"Iss, my lady. They'm be clean."

"Very well." She turned her back to Rose, letting her unfasten the lacing up the back of her afternoon dress. With the taking off of that dress, she crossed the line from the eighteenth to the nineteenth century. She hoped it would prove a propitious omen.

The modes were changing with bewildering rapidity

that year. Her modiste had talked her into buying one of the new Grecian dresses of sheer white muslin but even wearing it in the privacy of her bedroom left her feeling far too naked. She'd sent it back with regrets all the greater because to some extent the dress was flattering. The new raised waist had given her a pleasing line and the straighter skirts had made the most of her figure. The purity of the white cloth had accentuated her own classical features.

After some discussion, the dressmaker and the viscountess had come to an agreement. With the addition of an overdress of black drugget, showing the white muslin only in front and with long sleeves instead of absurd puffs at the shoulder, she felt both fashionable *and* clothed.

Tonight, after she dismissed Rose, she added two accessories that would have left her dressmaker aghast. One was a cut-steel chain looped twice about her neck, which Morgain had given her for her last birthday. The other was a knife sheath hidden under the overdress.

As she left her room, Clarice reflected that this would be the first time she'd ever gone armed to dinner. Was that an omen too?

She rapped on Morgain's door and, at his call, went in. "You look most dashing," she said, appraising him. He wore his school uniform, black coat over knee breeches with blue stockings tied with blue-green garters. It was an old-fashioned style, set down by the original Board of Governors when such clothes had been the height of fashion. Morgain was secretly very proud of this attire, as Clarice knew.

"Are you ready?" he asked.

"Are you frightened?"

He thought about it. "No. It's rather exciting."

"I suppose so," Clarice said with a secret smile. Trust Morgain to find some bizarre good in a difficult moment.

In the hall, with a nod of reassurance to Morgain, Clarice knocked on Pringle's door. There was no answer. "She must have gone down already."

Morgain looked relieved. "She may be one, too."

"So might I," Clarice said. "How do you know I am not?"

"Because of this." Morgain reached out to touch the chain of alternating black and bright steel that flowed down to Clarice's waist. "You wouldn't be able to bear it against your skin if you were one of *them*. Nor when you touched me did you instantly agree to grant me a wish."

Clarice patted his cheek. "Grant me one wish, Morgain. Don't make any attempt to expose Camber. If he is not our butler, he will betray himself in a thousand little ways. I will be watching."

"I'll try. What about Mr. Knight? Do you trust him?"

"I touched him once. He stayed the same as before."

"Good. Shall we go?"

It would not have helped him to know that his aunt was growing so light-minded that she'd kiss a near-stranger on no more than an insane impulse.

When they reached the bottom of the stairs, Camber was waiting for them. He bowed and said, "My lady, before you proceed, a word?"

At her side, Morgain stiffened. Clarice put an arm about his shoulders and drew him closer. She could feel his heart beating as swiftly as a rabbit's, but his face remained serene. She realized he'd learned much more at school than reading and the Rule of Three.

"Certainly, Camber. What is it?"

"A small tragedy in the kitchen, or so the cook would have it."

"What? Is someone hurt?"

"No, my lady. Forgive me. I did not mean to alarm you. It is merely that somehow all the meat in the cellar has been stolen."

This was so much less than Clarice had feared that for an instant she goggled at the man. "I beg your pardon?"

"We cannot determine how such a thing happened. No one admits to having left the door unlocked or open.

Yet when Cook went downstairs to fetch the joint for this evening, every steak, ham, and chop was gone. For myself, I have no doubt it was those Gypsies who came to the back door t'other day."

"Then what, pray tell, are we eating tonight?"

Camber became even more confidential, leaning forward and speaking in a greatly lowered tone. "Cook informed me that as a young woman she was kitchen maid in the house of a gentleman of rank. Being quite remarkably wealthy, he could afford to indulge in some eccentricities. One of which—the *mildest* in my view, my lady—was an abhorrence of anything remotely savoring of meat. Cook spent several months in this unnatural kitchen until she received an offer to go elsewhere. Though she never liked to add the experience to her references—such a thing being thought so odd— she did learn how to create a great many dishes made solely of vegetables and fruit. The gentleman of rank had no objection to nuts, either, being especially fond of that strange American nut, the—ahem—goober."

"But we cannot eat nuts and vegetables alone. What a preposterous notion!"

"Until the fog lifts, my lady, we cannot send for the butcher."

"True. Very well. Having no choice, I suppose we must do the best we can. Kindly convey my thanks to Cook."

Camber bowed. Clarice and Morgain walked ahead of him toward the dining salon. She glanced down at her nephew to give him a reassuring smile, only to see him doing the same for her. She squeezed him about the shoulders, and let him go.

"Good evening, Pringle. Good evening, Mr. Knight. So sorry to have kept you waiting. Shall we begin?"

Ten

The three days that followed were the most trying Clarice had ever known. The heavy fog clung to the earth like a wet pillow, muffling everything, even breath. Clarice could scarcely tell night from day. The hours seemed endless between waking and sleeping again. The house felt stuffy and grew steadily colder.

At first, she'd ordered fires be lit in all the bedrooms. But the low clouds kept any wind from blowing away the chimneys' smoke and the stink of the fires further exasperated her strained nerves. She couldn't even open a window, for the fog came wending silently in, hardly noticed until she looked up to see a room full of shrouded ghosts. It was most odd, how long it took for the fog to dissipate, once it was inside.

"I've never known a fog to last like this," she ranted, taking her fortieth turn at the end of the long hall. Morgain, curled up in an armchair like an elf encircled by warm lamplight, hardly looked up from his book. He'd embarked upon a course of extensive reading for the duration, strange tomes, some bigger than himself.

"I'm tempted to try for a walk in the garden," she added, nearly brushing over a Chinese porcelain vase as she made a wider turn than usual at the farther end of the hall. "You know, it sometimes happens that a fog will settle over one spot, while not a hundred yards away it will be clear."

She stopped before him and pushed down on his book with one extended finger. "Morgain . . ." she said dangerously.

He blinked up at her, like an owl awake in the daytime. "You won't be permitted to go that far," he said. "But make the attempt if you find it entertaining."

Clarice was not convinced, as Morgain was, that anything was wrong at Hamdry Manor that would not be speedily solved by a shift in the wind. She had observed Camber and the other servants closely, and had seen nothing very much amiss. After that first dinner of herbs and vegetables, Clarice had waited until after she'd seen Morgain asleep to ask the butler what he'd meant by permitting a guest to set the table. His answer had been very smooth.

"Mr. Knight asked me to allow it, my lady, and so I did. He had, it seemed, some concerns about the proper use and order of utensils—not an uncommon worry among persons who do not go into good society very often, I believe. Naturally, I assisted him in so far as it lay within my poor powers. I have not done wrong, I trust, my lady?"

"Not at all, Camber. You are very good. Please tell Cook I shall come down in a few moments to discuss what is to be done about the food supply."

"Very good, my lady," Camber had said with just the right inflection as he wiped up a drop of milk that had fallen from the spout of the china milk jug. The tea-tray, brought into the drawing room after dinner, was all that it should have been. It bore the Camber-like touches of a rose in a vase, and a basket of little cakes arranged just so.

As a proper hostess, she served her guest tea, saw that Pringle had begun dealing a hand of patience, while Mr. Knight spread his coattails before the fire, and excused herself. She'd found reason to excuse herself early every evening thereafter. She had grown used to nut-cutlets and vegetable terrine for her evening meals; she had *not* grown used to seeing Dominic Knight's face across from her over the centerpiece.

Leaving Morgain to his book, she stopped in her room only long enough to pick up a red shawl. She draped it over her head and tossed one end over her shoulder. Downstairs, not a soul was to be seen. Dominic was allegedly studying maps of the surrounding area in the library, while Pringle took a nap. The servants were all busy with tasks in various corners of the house.

Clarice slipped along to the small, cold gallery at the back of the house where a door let out into the garden. The fog looked thick and opaque, like dirty ice. She was surprised by the ease with which the door opened; the fog seemed solid enough to push on the glass, yet when the door swung wide, there was none of the half-expected resistance.

She could see little ahead of her, but if she looked down, she could just make out the herringbone pattern of the bricks that made up the walkway. She followed it slowly, one hand questing out in front of her. If she looked up, she instantly lost the gift of sight. The world was hidden behind white swathings, like bandages over her eyes.

She kept her eyes on the last visible brick on the path, watching as another appeared beyond it. Though she knew perfectly well the path extended from the house to the garden's border, she couldn't help thinking that it looked as though the path were building itself, one brick at a time, just beyond the edge of her sight. No sooner did she think this than the thought took possession of her mind. She could almost see the brick form just before her foot came down upon it.

At first, the idea amused her. She walked faster, watching the bricks appear, but such a pastime was dangerous in the fog. When she slowed, the illusion was perfect. There was nothing but the mist over the black earth, then a brick appeared fulfilling the pattern in the walkway. "Nonsense."

Her shawl had become beaded over with mist the instant she'd set foot outside. The mist had quickly coalesced into drops of water that were soon absorbed. The wool grew heavier, proving no protection, and soaking her clothes. She began to pull it off, only to have it become entangled with a hairpin. Sighing, Clarice began trying to disengage the strand of wool. It would not free itself.

This petty annoyance combined with the concealing, confusing fog and became a hell-brew of frustration. Clarice began ripping out the hairpins one at a time, trying to pull free the one that had caught. "Oh, blast!" she said, this hindrance setting the match to an already exasperated temper.

Her hair was coming down, and growing wet, clinging to her face. Then she felt a gentle hand on her shoulder and another sorting through the damp golden mass.

The shawl fell away and her hair tumbled down her back in an undisciplined cascade. What dismayed her even more than being caught at such a disadvantage was that she knew that touch. She would have instinctively known it under any circumstances, though she'd only experienced it once.

Clarice turned around to face Dominic. His coat too was damp and droplets clung to his hair and the ends of his lashes. He did not smirk at her, or condescend to her. He said gently, "I came out for some exercise. It's so stuffy inside."

"I wanted to see if it was clearing at all."

"It isn't." He raised his hand and traced the curve of her cheek with the joint of his bent forefinger. "You're cold."

"No . . ." Clarice heard no little voice urging her to throw herself into his arms. She reminded herself that she did not even like Dominic. He could be pompous, patronizing, unwontedly amorous, and he had hardly spoken a dozen words to her in three days. Yet she could not take her eyes from his, nor stop her heart from catching when he touched her.

Dominic retrieved her shawl and swung it about her shoulders. She reached up and grasped it close to her throat. He said, "This fog can be dangerous. We should go in."

"Oh, no," she said. "I can't bear it inside. I love Hamdry but not when I can't get out! The house is becoming like . . . like a cage."

"A cage?"

"Yes. I feel like a prisoner in a cage and I can't escape. Not even to walk in my own garden."

"At least all the moisture is good for the flowers," he said and she smiled at him for trying to cheer her.

"Plants need sunshine too, Mr. Knight, and there's been little enough of that lately."

"I know it won't be too much longer, or so I hope. One breath of air and it will all be swept away. Then the sun will shine again."

"Sunshine—I hardly remember it. It came from up there, somewhere, did it not?" She cast her head back to look up in the general direction of the sky, though all directions were the same in this fog-boltered world. She couldn't even be sure of the earth under her feet.

"I believe so," he answered in the same joking way. "But for all I know, it's presently the middle of the night."

"I do not mind the nights so much as the days. When I'm asleep, I can at the least dream that the sun is out. It is a great shame, Mr. Knight, that this should happen during your visit. Usually our summer weather is far more clement."

"I too must regret it."

"Because of your work. All this time wasted!"

"No," he said. He reached out to drop his hand lightly over hers for an instant, where she clutched her shawl to her breast. "You have not let me come close enough to you over the last few days to permit to apologize. My actions were not those of a gentleman and I deeply regret . . ." He stopped, frowning as if listening to the echo of his own words.

This apology both gratified and pained her. "You are very good to take the responsibility but the fault was partly mine. I led you to believe that I would not be repelled by an advance. I want to correct that false impression."

"You would be repelled by an advance?" Dominic said. She would have thought he was making a game of her were it not for the earnestness of his expression.

"Not 'repelled,' " Clarice hastened to say, realizing she was now insulting him. "It is merely that I am not a woman to be treated in such a fashion."

"No, you are not. For that idea, I apologize unreservedly. But not for kissing you, Clarice. I cannot regret that. I have never known such a moment before."

She backed away from him, straightening to her full height. "Kindly recall that you have boasted to me of your conquests, Mr. Knight. . . ."

"Conquests? Yes, a few. What of them? They have nothing to do with you."

"Men say that as though it were enough. But what woman wants the love of a man who has known nothing beyond easy pleasure? Not I, Mr. Knight."

She spun about on her heel and walked away. In less than two strides, she could not see him when she glanced back. But then he emerged from the fog, hurrying to catch her. "Be so good as to leave me, sir," she said.

"Not in this weather. Come back to the house."

"I have come out to find the sun. I shall not go back until I find it. These fogs are unpredictable."

"They are," he said grimly, seizing her arm. Only his strength kept her upright as she caught her toe on a raised brick. "What next? Will you break your neck?"

"I might have tripped in broad daylight just as easily." She couldn't free her arm without a vulgar struggle so she simply looked at him with disdainful eyes.

"What did you mean by 'easy pleasure'?" he asked.

"I'm sure you know the meaning far better than I. Look. We have come to the end of the path. This is the gravel walk that leads to the statues. Shall we go?"

"You can't see any of them in this. Come back to the house. Be sensible."

"I'm very tired of it. I am used to a fair amount of exercise, Mr. Knight, and refuse to spend another moment pacing in the hall. As it is, I shall have to order a new carpet as I've quite worn a track in it. Now, if you don't mind—"

"Hush!"

"Well, of all the . . . !"

He pulled her back against his body and clapped a hand over her mouth. "Hush! Do you hear it?"

His tone was so intent that she lost her anger. She listened, her ears straining against the all-enveloping silence of the fog. Clarice heard Dominic's short breaths, the crunch of their feet on the gravel as they made involuntary movements, the beating of her heart—or was it his?

She shook her head and he took his hand away. Moving slowly around her in a circle, his body taut and hunched, he said, "Something's out there."

"You can't see anything. You can't see your hand at the reach of your arm." To prove it, she held her arm out straight to the side. Her hand was lost to view, concealed by the white mists.

Something grabbed it!

"Dominic!"

She threw out her other hand to free the first. Her fingers hunted over the strange, tight band that held her fast. A pebbled texture, cold to the touch . . . then the thing about her wrist began to pull her invincibly forward.

She struggled, digging in her heels, but her feet found no purchase on the gravel. Dragged forward, she could not draw her arm in. She still could not see her hand before her. She felt the strain on her overextended elbow and wrist pass into pain.

Except for the single shriek of Dominic's name, Clarice could not scream again. Her breath strangled in her throat, permitting nothing to escape but a hoarse gurgle. She fought for breath, knowing that the horrible Rider of the Vedresh had found her.

Dominic ran past her. She could only turn a pleading look on him, but she was sure he did not see it. He wore a teeth-baring grimace as he flung himself into the fog.

For an agonizing moment, the pull on her arm continued. She felt as though her joints would give way, tearing her arm from her body. Then, abruptly, the pressure eased. Though no longer dragged forward, she still was unable to draw her arm close to her body to soothe it.

At the same instant the pressure eased, she found she could again draw in painless breaths. Once again, she sought with her left hand to determine the nature of the band that had captured her right. She explored the pebbly, yielding surface, finding neither beginning nor end, her eyes searching the fog for Dominic. All was still.

Then he came flying out, hurled by some great force. His coat was slashed across the breast in three parallel lines as though by sharp claws. Blood trickled from his right brow and the corner of his mouth. His hands were clenched in fists, the knuckles already battered.

Landing with a slide across the gravel, he rolled to his feet in a graceful movement almost too fast to see. "Hold on, Clarice!"

"To what?" she demanded, as once again the fearful dragging began again. This time, the choking was worse from the first instant. She could almost feel a band tightening around her throat as well as her wrist. Her fingers were numb.

She threw Dominic a pleading glance and saw him gather himself for another spring into the fog. Fighting the instinct that told her to continue struggling to free her hand, she used her left to fumble in her bosom. There, like a busk to thrust apart her breasts, was the small dagger she'd taken from her father's room. Pulling

it out, sheath and all, she flung it across at him, only to
misjudge the distance through the black mist rising before her eyes. Tumbling over and over, it flew past him.

By some legerdemain Dominic reached out and
snapped the knife out of midair. He drew it, tossing aside
the sheath, and leapt once more into the concealing fog.

Exhausted, Clarice dropped to her knees when the
pulling stopped again. She began to pray, snatches of
Psalms and Ecclesiastes, hoping for deliverance. The fog
made her dizzy, as it swirled in seemingly meaningful
patterns. Were it not for the force keeping her arm up
and out, she would have fallen facedown on the gravel
walk and been content to stay there until the grass grew
over her.

But where was Dominic?

She heard a shout, or was it a grunt? The sound-
baffling qualities of the fog made it impossible to know
how loud the cry had been. Or whether it had come from
nearby or faraway.

"Dominic?" she said, then shouted it. There was no
reply. She began to hunt over the band around her wrist
once more. If only there were some way to free herself!
Then she sucked in her breath sharply as some little edge
caught her finger. She brought it close to her eyes and
saw the bright blood welling from her fingertip.

The slice awakened her wits and her determination.
Searching the fog was profitless. She rose up, wearily,
rising first on one knee, then standing, like an old
woman. Carefully, anticipating another painful dragging,
she began moving forward. Though she twitched at
every random billow, she moved into the thickest part
of the fog, calling for Dominic.

She found after a moment or two that she could bend
her elbow. The relief was enormous. Bringing her hand
in toward her face, she saw at last the black band that
held her captive. It was attached to a long coil that disappeared into the fog.

The surface looked as though it had been oiled, yet it
was not smooth. Bringing it nearer into focus, she re-

alized it looked very much like snakeskin. Turning her wrist over, she saw the bulging triangle that overlapped the rest like the clasp on a bracelet. It was sharply pointed and thicker than the rest of the skin. Trying to pick at this clasp cost her another cut on her finger.

"Dominic?" she called, believing she heard a noise near at hand.

A darker shadow fell across the billows of fog. An instant later, the shadow resolved itself into two men, fighting in vicious silence. They rolled on the ground, contending for the knife clutched in Dominic's hand.

Clarice jumped aside, or they would have rolled over her. She'd never seen such violence and she winced every time a fist landed. Dominic struggled to shake off the Rider's grip on his right wrist. The blood from the cut over his eye had smeared his face, making him appear fiercely savage, or was it the glare in his eyes?

She could see nothing of the Rider—his cloak concealed all, entangling Dominic in its toils. It made him look bigger than Dominic. Clarice did not see how the man could contend against whatever the Rider was—not alone.

She began tearing at the band, not caring if she sliced every finger to the bone! "Hold him!" she called. "I'm coming!"

But the band would not release her. She sobbed in frustration, watching as the Rider pinned Dominic to the gravel, using his greater weight. With an effort that made the cords strain in his throat, Dominic hurled him aside.

"Well done!" Clarice called.

The Rider landed, sprawling like a spider on its back. He seemed stunned. Dominic rose to his feet, still holding the knife. His footsteps wavered as he approached the Rider.

Clarice caught her breath. Would he stab the cloaked man?

"Yield," Dominic said. "Yield to me or die in all worlds and for all time."

"Yes . . ." The voice was as thin and bodiless as a spirit's.

The band around Clarice's wrist opened. The long black coil snaked away into the concealing mists. At once, she cradled her hand against her breast, rubbing the impression left behind on her flesh. Though she marked herself with blood, it felt heavenly to be released.

She walked over to where Dominic stood, still panting, over the motionless form of his enemy. "What will you do with him? Turn him over to the constable?"

Dominic looked at her in disbelief, putting up a hand to wipe his cut brow. "What would your law officers do with him? There is nothing that can be done."

"Nothing? But . . . I don't understand."

He bent down and picked up the cloak as he'd picked up her shawl before. It came up as easily for there was nothing in it. The Rider was gone as thoroughly as breath-mist breathed for a moment upon a mirror.

"I don't understand," Clarice said again. "I saw him fight you. There was something wearing that cloak."

"He has returned to the time and the place from whence he came."

"Where is that?"

"I do not know, Clarice. He was one of your mother's soldiers, not one of ours."

Eleven

~

"My mother is dead," Clarice said.

"You know that is not true." Dominic saw that she was still dazed from the nightmare scene she'd just lived through. He dared to hope that he might now hear the truth from her. Perhaps he was still a little confused himself. It had suddenly become very important to him that Clarice trust him.

"No, it isn't true. That is a tale we told to satisfy the curious. She was lost to me ten years ago when she went up to the moor and . . . vanished. We put it about that she fell into a sinkhole. For all I know, that is what happened."

"You let people believe she committed suicide."

"Yes. We—Felicia, Blaic, Doctor Danby, and I—let the world believe she was despondent over the death of my father, but it wasn't that. Her lover had been killed after stealing our money. He deserved it; she agreed to that. I never knew what prompted her to go."

"I can tell you. It was. . . ."

"How do you know so much?" Clarice demanded. "For once and for all, Mr. Knight, who are you?"

He longed for her to trust him; he did not dare tell her all in return. "I came to protect you."

"From that?" she asked, nodding toward the cape he held.

"Partly from this. Also from other dangers that surround you, things you are not even aware of."

"I can believe that there are many things that I am unaware of, but I find it difficult to believe that you have come here to protect me. Your behavior has not been that of a protector, for all that you saved me today." She looked down at her wrist.

Dominic took her hand gently in his own. Though his fingers were stiff and torn from hitting the Rider, he did not mind his pain as much as he minded hers. All around her wrist the skin was red and sore. There'd be a bruise encircling there before long. "It looks worse than it is."

She asked, "What was that thing?"

"A whip made from a wyvern's tail. It is the same thing that struck down Morgain."

"A whip? Impossible. How could it hold me?"

"If its master wills, it can hold forever to what it has caught or until that will is broken. When the Rider returned to his own place and time, the wyvern whip no longer had anyone to obey."

"What about the horse?" Clarice asked, and he smiled down at her for it was a question no one else would have asked.

"It has returned to the stable from which it came."

"Wherever that may be."

"Wherever that may be."

"How *do* you know so much, Mr. Knight?"

"I have studied," he said. Bowing slightly, he raised her hand to his lips. He very gently kissed the mark of the whip. "If I could have done, I would have spared you this."

"It—it isn't your fault," she said, slipping her hand from his. "I should have taken your advice and returned to the house when you said we should. I apologize for not listening."

"I should have asked more politely, perhaps."

Her eyes held a glint of returning humor. "If it is all

the same to you, we can argue over that issue later. Now, I feel strongly that we should go in."

"That is wise."

She reached up to his face with the corner of her shawl and patted his brow, wiping away a little of the drying blood. "How do I explain that my guest comes in so much the worse for wear?"

"Don't say anything. I'm sure your servants are too well-trained to ask any questions."

"Rest assured, Mr. Knight, that I am not so well-trained. However, those questions will have to wait until we are somewhere warm and considerably drier."

"You called me Dominic before."

"Did I?" she asked, and blushed faintly. "I've no recollection of it. Which way to the house?"

Ordinarily, Dominic could rely on his sense of direction, even among the shifting fog. But the frenzy of battle and the heavy blows he'd taken had shaken him more than he liked to admit. The tracks of Clarice's heels as she'd been dragged by the whip gave him his start.

He drew her cold hand under his arm, feeling that she could use the reassurance of a human touch. This time, she did not try to withdraw it. It warmed him to be able to give her even that much comfort.

"I think you'll need another glass of Burgundy," he said as a joke.

"I'll drink it to your good health." After a moment, she said, "I haven't thanked you."

"There's no need. I did what I was trained to do."

"Trained? By whom?"

"Trainers."

"You might as well just say that you aren't going to tell me anything."

"Very well. I'm not going to tell you. . . ." He laughed as she pinched his arm.

But there was no answering laughter in her voice when she said, "Surely we should have reached the brick path by now? I know I was not dragged so far as this."

"It's difficult to judge distances in the fog, Clarice."

"I know that. But I also know Hamdry. We've walked a long time and the gravel path is only a few yards wide. Perhaps we have gone the wrong way and are now walking *around* the garden."

"Very well. You stay here and I will—"

"No. If we go, we go together."

They tried making one sharp turn and then walking forward a ways. But neither brick path, nor wall, nor house, nor even grass underfoot met them. They made another cast, with no better result. The gravel path seemed to have grown wider, despite all Clarice's protest that it was at most nine feet across. They wandered on until even Dominic, with all his strength, began to feel weary. She must have been nearly exhausted. No complaint escaped her lips; indeed, she was ready to joke.

"What a pity we haven't a better day for a stroll," Clarice said. Her lips were pale, with a blue shadow underneath. At some point, he'd stopped walking with her hand on his arm, taking her hand in his instead. All the same, her fingers had grown steadily colder. His clothes were as wet as though he'd been swimming and she was in no better case, her hair streaming with collected moisture.

A little while later, she said, "Perhaps I should, after all, wait here while you find the house. Or we could try shouting. If we are close, Camber or someone might hear us."

Dominic stopped in his tracks. "I should have thought of it before."

"What?"

"This isn't the path around your garden, Clarice."

"Yes, it is. Please don't start talking like a crazed lunatic. I—I don't think I could stand it."

He cupped his hands around his mouth and shouted, "Halloa! *Oyez*, the king!"

Faintly came an echo in reply. Clarice raised her face from her hands. She breathed in deeply. "What is that fragrance?"

For the fog no longer smelled of damp and mire, but

of flowers. It no longer hung in impenetrable folds, but thinned, changing from heavy curtains to tattered veils. Where it parted, flashes of brilliant colors could be glimpsed, but her mind did not move swiftly enough to put names to them before they were gone.

Clarice stepped close to Dominic, taking his arm again. Though she did not trust him completely, he was the one familiar thing in a universe suddenly altered. He smiled down at her, and for once she did not mind the hint of patronage in his eyes.

The breeze that stirred the fog also dried her clothes or so she thought until she looked down. Her bedraggled dress of black silk had changed without her even being aware of it. She wore a white satin gown of an antique cut. The neck was square and low, the waist just under her breasts. Full flowing sleeves were pulled in tight above the elbows by ribbons of gold whose ends fluttered in the sweet-smelling breeze. Fitted sleeves of cloth-of-gold peeked out beneath the others. These were embroidered over in scarlet thread, strange, complex patterns that seemed to both reveal and conceal vast mysteries.

"Don't be alarmed," Dominic said. "No one means you any harm. Whatever else you believe, believe that."

He had not changed. He was not even dry. The blood had stopped flowing from the cut over his eyebrow and the collected water of the fog had washed away the worst of the stains on his face. Though he wore the tattered remains of a gentleman's attire, he looked utterly disreputable, as barbarous as a Visigoth striding through the streets of Rome.

The sun came out, catching the drops in his hair and making them glitter. She stared at him as though she'd never seen him before. When she looked around her, she realized that she had not, indeed, seen the true Dominic Knight. For he was a product of world other than her own.

She looked across a field of green so intense that the sun seemed to strike sparks from it, as though the grass

were made of individual emeralds. Banners rippled like
pure silk above half a dozen oblong-shaped buildings.
She could not tell whether they were of stone or of cloth,
for she was distracted by their roofs. Each one was var-
iegated, a blur of pure hues that blended into a whole
so harmonious that she felt the changing of one tint for
any other would have thrown off the entire beauty of
the scene.

Clarice found herself walking down a gentle slope,
Dominic at her shoulder. She glanced back at him, find-
ing that she had to push aside her flowing hair. He said,
"Go on. You are expected."

"What makes the roofs glimmer so?"

"Haven't you ever wondered why, with all the untold
millions of birds in the world, the earth is not waist-deep
in lost feathers?"

"No, I cannot say that I have. Are you telling me that
those roofs are made of feathers?"

"Thousands of them, from a condor's flight-feather to
a hummingbird's pinfeather."

"Incredible."

As she drew nearer, she heard music, no more than
pipe and drum, yet she found her feet dancing as her
heart lightened step by step. The tune was simple, merry,
and somehow familiar. She wondered if she'd heard it
at some rout-party or other, but the feeling she took from
it did not seem related to the overheated elegance of a
ballroom. Perhaps it was at Vauxhall, for she seemed to
associate the tune with outdoor amusements, with the
grass under her feet and a free breeze blowing through
her hair. Some words went with it. She sought in her
memory.

Her lips found the words before her mind could catch
them. *"In Mag Mell, the king does dwell; on his cedar
throne, he sighs alone; heigh-ho the day-oh!"*

"You know the words? I used to sing it when I was
a boy but since I came here, I haven't been able to remember them. Sing it once more, if you please."

Dominic joined her as she sang it through, though he

did not dance with her. He laughed and she thought that she liked the sound even more than the music. Her feet, however, obeyed only the sound of the pipe and the drum. He asked, "Are you certain it's 'cedar throne'? I seem to recall it being 'silver.'"

"I have it on good authority that it is made of wood."

"Well, yes. I've seen it myself many times, but I thought that in the song. . . ."

"Blaic taught me the proper words when I was still under an enchantment. I believe I am enchanted again now."

"Oh, no," he said. "Don't be confused. This land and all who serve it are enchanted, but you are not. You are a human being still. Hold on to that. Prince Blaic would say the same were he here now instead of me."

She wanted to turn to look at him, to ask him what he meant, but the pull of the music grew as she came closer. She could not make herself circle about until the dance that flowed through her body permitted such a move. By then, it was too late. He'd resumed his stolid expression.

Clarice danced all across the field. She did not feel the least bit tired anymore. Nor was she growing short of breath or dizzy, no matter how many pirouettes, leaps, or curtsies she performed. When she became aware that quite a few persons stood about watching her progression, she wanted very much to stop. Being stared at was no more pleasant here than at home. However, she could not will her muscles to cease their motions until she'd danced up to the very entrance of the largest and most dazzling building.

This one was neither decorated with bird feathers nor richly carved. It was a mere marquee—if the word "mere" could be used to describe a tent of the finest silk. It was a pure and stainless white that glistened as the fabric billowed in the sunlight.

Once she stepped foot onto the magnificently woven carpet that led to the entrance, her dancing feet slowed step by step until they carried her with no more cadence than that lent by a very graceful walk. She drew a deep breath and turned to smile at Dominic.

Through it all, he had stayed at her side, to the right and slightly behind. Now, he stepped forward. Bowing low, he swept back the silken hanging before the entrance.

"Go in," he said. "Don't be frightened."

"And what," a voice demanded, "has she to be frightened of?"

Clarice wondered about that herself. So far, everything had been delightful. Yet undoubtedly, she felt some fear. Every tale she'd ever heard of the "piskies" had warned of their extreme trickiness coupled with a notorious level of irascibility. It would behoove her to go most warily.

"Come in," the voice beckoned. "Come forward and let me see you. We are related, you know."

Being inside the tent was like walking into a great pearl. The sunlight was softened through the silk, lending it a luminescence not unlike moonglow but far more alive. At the far end of the enclosure stood a man, just that instant risen from the chair behind him. As in the child's rhyme, the chair was indeed of white cedar. Somehow, Clarice knew this throne was of great age and yet still a faint fragrance of the wood reached out to her.

The man came forward, stepping firmly on the grass. He wore no crown, no splendid robes of ermine and velvet, and no courtiers stood about him, laughing with delight at a joke or weeping with fear at a frown. Yet, on instinct, Clarice swept him the same deep reverence she would have given to George, King of England.

"But no, my dear!" The king tut-tutted like a fond uncle. "Did I not say we are related? I do not ask such things from my family, do I, Dominic?"

"No, my king."

Clarice glanced back, only to see that he had dropped on to one knee and now knelt with his head bowed low. She did not like to see him so humble. Though she was loath to admit it, she would have preferred a resurgence of his arrogance.

Clarice had to clear her throat before she could speak to the fatherly gentleman who stood smiling down on her with such genial delight. "You say we are related, sire? How is that?"

"She calls me 'sire'!" the king said to no one in particular. "One can always tell the true nobility."

He made no grand gestures, no veins stood out on his forehead, yet a moment later Clarice found him ushering her to a chair that had just that instant appeared beside the throne. The king said, "Oh, long ago—even by my standards!—one of your ancestors married one of my house! A complicated business that no one remembers now except those of us with the longest memories. And yet, there is a nearer tie as well."

"A tie by marriage, perhaps. Through Blaic?"

"It seems but yesterday that our former king, Boadach, enchanted him. Then your lovely sister enchanted him once again and, it would seem, even more fatally." Forgall turned the full attention of his sherry brown eyes on her and Clarice was conscious of a shock.

The king appeared in all respects to be a human being. He had the right number of limbs, his features were bland but pleasantly arranged in the usual order. Not many men of her acquaintance wore a beard, yet there was nothing strange about choosing one. If she'd passed him in some quiet lane, she would have taken him for a farm-laborer.

Yet when she looked into his eyes, she knew without a doubt that he was not of her kind. Mists of memories floated there, shadowing deep wells of experience, created from a mixture of warm appreciation and cold, cold knowledge. Here was not some innocent creature of wood and dell as the fairy tales would have it, nor was he the devil's tool as the ignorant would call him. He was his own master, and master of the world as well.

She could not begin to guess the limits of his power, or even if there were any limits. For the first time, she felt a whisper of a threat, like a chilled blade brushing against the back of her neck.

Forgall said, "I want to apologize to you, my dear child, unreservedly."

"But why, sire?"

"For the regrettable incident just now with the Rider of Vedresh. Believe me, if I had not believed his escape to be wholly unconnected with you, I should have put a stop to him at once. As it is, I can see to it that you and Morgain Half-Fay shall have no ill-effects from my poor judgment."

Clarice felt a tingling sensation about her wrist. When she pulled back the sleeve to look, it appeared quite as usual. The redness and swelling had gone away. Glancing at Dominic, she saw the cut on his head was still unhealed.

"Is he not worthy of such an apology?" she said, lifting her chin in Dominic's direction. To her surprise, she saw a slow crimson rise into his cheeks.

The king did not glance at him. "He is my servant and was complaining not long ago of a lack of excitement in his assignment. The wounds he suffered in your defense may remind him not to question the wisdom of his king."

"But how should they?" Clarice replied. "When it was your wisdom that placed him where he might defend me from your lack."

She did not look at him, being busy smoothing her sleeve, yet beneath her seeming calm she was quivering, tense as a stretched bowstring. She wondered if it hurt very much being blasted by the wrath of the Fay-King. The last time, there'd been only a gentle languor that had passed into slumber. When she'd awakened, she'd had the mind of a toddling child despite her thirteen years. She doubted the king would be so kind this time.

Then he laughed, clapping his hand softly against his knee. "Well-answered, my lady. Come! We shall dine together."

"With the greatest pleasure in the world, sire."

She rose to follow him. As he passed Dominic, still on one knee, the royal hand brushed his shoulder. "Don't be such a fool next time," the king said.

Clarice saw the wound on Dominic's forehead heal cleanly, as well as his bruised knuckles. The instant the king went by, Dominic raised his head and watched her come forward. His expression was grim. Clarice half-expected him to berate her in a harsh whisper for embarrassing him. Instead he caught her hand as she passed by and swiftly pressed his lips to it.

Stunned, she hardly caught his whisper, "Eat what you like; drink only water."

As they traversed the glade between the two tents, Clarice said, "This is not, I believe, the first time you and I have met, sire."

"Ah, no. I remember you very well. I was sorry for you and rather hated to put you under a spell, but you interrupted one of our revels, and the Law is very strict. Had you touched me or any of my People, I should not have harmed you, but you did not. I cannot apologize."

"You permitted me to live. I took no very great harm, for which I thank you. At any rate, I was eventually freed from your spell, thanks to Blaic."

The king's mouth might have twisted for an instant under his beard. Certainly he made no further answer. When he entered the vast tent where the banquet was served, a roar of welcome arose from every throat. He stood with his arms raised to the sky, accepting the cheers of his citizens, while Clarice gaped in amazed wonder. What had looked like a moderately sized marquee must have held a thousand persons. Though her mind reeled at the notion, she could not deny what she saw. This pavilion was bigger on the inside than on the outside.

No meat was served at the feast, but the fruit, the vegetables and the bread had a savor like no other food she'd tasted before. She realized that she'd been eating like a Fay for several days, ever since the fog had shut the roads and the meat in her cellar had so unexpectedly vanished. The cook had created marvelous meals out of far less than Clarice would have believed possible. But here in the heart of the kingdom, everything had a rich, rare flavor far surpassing the things of the world she knew.

The king's table was in no way singled out by finer clothes or tableware. Even its position was ordinary, down amongst the others, and he was served in his turn like the rest with the same foods. She sat at his right hand. Dominic, so far as she could tell, wasn't even at the same table.

Glancing up and down the table, she noticed with a flutter of humor that she was, without a doubt, the least attractive person there. On each face, she saw ageless, poreless skin with every brow and lash achieving perfection without cosmetics or, so far as she could tell, assistance of any kind. Teeth were white and even, eyes bright, large, and clear regardless of shade, whether lapis, coffee, or emerald. There was a vast variety among them—skin and hair of every color from an alabaster white to a lustrous ebony. Their voices were musical and whenever one of them laughed as they often did, Clarice could imagine that angels must pause in their flights to listen.

The king saw her shake her head ruefully and demanded to know what amused her.

"Oh, sire," she said, "if ever I suffered from vanity, this last hour has cured me."

"Why so?"

"I know at this moment how ugly I am."

"Ugly? Not a bit of it. You are very well to pass, for a mortal."

"That is what I mean, sire. Even now, I am aging, whatever beauty I possess fading from instant to instant."

"That must distress you."

"On the contrary, it is a great relief."

The lovely creature seated across from them leaned forward to say, "How can that be true? Do you not live in terror of the moment when you are quite old?"

Clarice smiled at her for she'd never seen a female more enchantingly lovely. Her face was sweetly heart-shaped, her brown hair rising from a widow's peak on her brow to tumble in long closely curled ringlets to her waist. The dark green of her gown emphasized the deep tan shade of her smoothly rounded bosom and elegant throat. She looked no more than nineteen but Clarice had to assume that she might have been thousands of years old.

"I confess that I used to stare into my mirror wondering when I would show age, but now I think I shall welcome my first wrinkle and gray hair. There is no point in struggling against my fate for, try as I might, I shall never equal the least of you."

The breathtaking maiden in the green gown laughed, rendering herself even more exquisite. "A toast against that hour! Come, pour wine for the Lady Mortal."

One of the servitors, less elegantly gowned but no less beautiful than the ones who sat and ate, appeared at Clarice's shoulder, a magnificently turned vessel of wood in her hand. She poured an opaque red liquid into the goblet before her.

The king raised his wine-cup, as did the Fay on either side of him and across the table. Remembering Dominic's warning, Clarice did not lift hers. "Among my people, we dare not drink a toast to ourselves. It brings ill-fortune."

"No ill can befall you here, but I respect your custom," the king said. He rose to his feet. "A cup of honor to the Lady Mortal!" he called.

Though his voice was not loud, it seemed to carry to every ear. All the Fay rose to their feet. The sound of their voices was like a storm falling upon the sea. They raised their cups and drank to her. When they resumed their seats, a silence came over the banquet. Clarice felt them all watching her and knew again a moment's fear as though she felt a trap closing about her. She had no choice but to return the compliment.

The king nodded encouragement when she caught his eye. With a smile she was very far from feeling, Clarice stood up in her fine white gown. She hardly knew what to say. It was customary to wish good fortune or long life to one's hearers but these people already had all of that.

"I feel I move in a dream far too wonderful to long for waking," she said, wondering if the magic that had amplified the king's voice worked as well for her. "You are very kind and I thank you."

She reached out for the goblet, hoping she could pretend to drink and not be detected. The wine-cup gleamed as though it were hammered out of highly polished gold, yet the grain under the polish told her that it was made of wood as well. She lifted it and the heady fragrance of the wine—raspberry, honey, and oak—made her dizzy as soon as she breathed it in.

At that instant, she heard a mighty voice shout "Stop!"

The very air seemed to ring with the sound. Clarice was so startled that she dropped the cup before the wine touched her lips. It fell to the grass and split in two, cleanly from top to bottom, splattering her white gown with the red wine. At once, the stains vanished, leaving not even a damp spot behind.

Clarice looked around, hoping insanely that it had been Dominic who had stopped her, defying his king and his service, but it was not. She stared in amazement at the man who stood behind the king, her heart leaping at the prospect of rescue from a danger all the more real because it was hidden behind smiles.

"Blaic?"

Twelve

"His father," the newcomer said with a bow.

Clarice stared, rudely but helplessly. The resemblance was extraordinary. The same dark hair curling to the shoulders, the same eyes of forest green, and the same aura of hidden strength made the father his son's image.

Yet there were differences as Clarice now saw. Her brother-in-law was a man of about forty; his father appeared to be approximately thirty, Blaic's age when Clarice first knew him. His height was perhaps a trifle less, his shoulders not quite so broad and his hands, she noted, were much better kept than those of her dear sister's husband.

The king's smiling geniality left him. "You here?"

"I am come to assist you, my overlord, in your struggle."

"You are welcome in Mag Mell, Morgain of the West. You have brought troops, I take it?"

"I have, many and a many. They await a word of welcome from their High King." Blaic's father smiled at Clarice with a warmth so genuine that she found herself smiling involuntarily in answer. "I will myself take charge of your charming guest, Forgall. I believe we have much of interest to say to one another."

Forgall did not seem very content to leave Clarice in Blaic's father's hands. His beard bristled as he sank his chin against his chest. "You are come opportunely," he said in a deeper voice than he'd used hitherto. "There is much to be said, and much not to say."

He turned a hand over on the table and it, all the others, the guests, and the food disappeared. Clarice found herself alone with Blaic's father in the midst of an empty meadow.

Morgain of the West sighed. "Forgall is known as the Wily for good reason, my dear. Do not imagine for a moment that he is not listening."

"I do not know why he should take such an interest in me."

"Unfortunately, I cannot tell you that or this interview would be cut short, probably unpleasantly. But come, sit and speak with me. We have never met, yet I feel I know you tolerably well, my dear."

He made a courtly gesture, as though encouraging her to be seated. She glanced automatically behind her, only to see the earth heave up silently, forming a kind of winged armchair covered with short grass, soft as velvet, for upholstery. It was exceedingly comfortable and she did not fear that it would mark her gown. Such annoying things were not possible in the fay world.

She asked, "I'm sorry to be so rude, sir, but who are you?"

"I am Blaic's father, King of the Westering Lands and vassal to Forgall, who is lord of Mag Mell and High King of the People and of the Living Lands."

Clarice put her hand to her temple. "I don't understand anything."

"You shall ere long know all, I'm certain."

Without disturbing her in the slightest, the earth-chair lengthened and became a settee. The King of the Westering Lands seated himself beside her, regarding her with a pleased smile. "I am certain of more than that, my dear Clarice. I know you are dear to Morgain Half-

Fay's heart. For that reason, if no other, you may count me as your friend."

"Of course," Clarice said as a spark of illumination lit her thoughts. "You are Morgain's grandfather!"

He inclined his head. "Yes, strange though it is to say it, I am. They named him for me."

"Do you ever visit him?"

"I have seen him from time to time, but I have not intruded upon him since he was an infant in arms. Once he began to notice and remember, I ceased to play with him."

"That is too bad. I cannot help but feel that he would benefit from knowing you, sir. He is growing up with a far too serious a view of existence."

King Morgain chuckled. "You judge me rapidly, my dear."

"Do I do it wrongly?"

"On the contrary. You are right; I have something of a frolicsome nature. It has often landed me in difficulties with those of your race prior to the law forbidding contact between our peoples. Now it lands me in difficulties with my own people. I should like, indeed, to grow to know my grandson better. However, it is his parents' wish that Morgain grow up as a mortal and it is not for me to meddle in that."

"Perhaps Morgain is more like his father than anyone else. I would not say that Blaic was ever of a sportive nature."

"Once upon a time, my dear . . . but he loved a princess of the People who could not return his feelings and then . . ." The slim shoulders lifted and fell fatalistically. "One must admit that being turned to stone for several centuries *does* take quite a lot out of one."

"I suppose it would do so to anyone of any nature."

"Now I, on the other hand, loved a maiden who gave her heart to me at first sight! So I was far more lucky than my own dear son. Ah, Amphysis! They call her the Incomparable and for good reason. She had something of your coloring, my dear, and seeing you brings her back to me in some part."

"She is no longer with you? Surely she did not die?"

"No, nor yet did she join our former king and queen among the Sleepers." The smile which seemed to hover perpetually about his mouth faded almost to nothing. He stared straight into her eyes and Clarice realized he was trying to convey something of importance. She remembered how he said their conversation might not be as private as it seemed.

She asked, "Who, or what, are the Sleepers?"

King Morgain relaxed. He gave a tiny nod of his head as if in approval. "Oh, when one of the People grows weary or can no longer bear some heavy sorrow—yes, we have our burdens too!—they lie among the Sleepers, drifting eternally in dreams. Have you never been asleep and experienced a life not your own? Seen ravishing images, wandered in strange paths, worn a face utterly unlike that which you bear in waking hours?"

"Of course. Who has not?"

"Then in all likelihood you have been touched by a Sleeper in your dreams."

"Fascinating. But you say your wife is not among them?"

"No, she would find it far too dull!" Once again, he took to looking at her steadily as though urging her in some direction. Clarice remembered what Forgall had said about being unable to read her thoughts, thanks to some long-ago fay ancestor. Thought-reading would have been most useful at this moment.

King Morgain said, "My wife enjoys visiting the far-flung courts of the Deathless Realm. At the moment, I believe she is visiting her distant cousin, the Snow-Queen. Amphysis does so revel in the winter sports. She won a medal for skiing the Northern Lights the last time she was there. She could have never done *that* lying at the bottom of a lake, you know."

"The bottom of a lake?" Clarice echoed, her brain reeling.

"Where the Sleepers lie, my dear. You can see them lying there, so they say, when the sun goes behind the clouds. I have not gone to Homashyl, the Depthless Mere, since our former king went to join his queen there. It is a beautiful place, very silent, the water entirely still; sad, you know, but peaceful."

"I think all of this world is peaceful," Clarice said dreamily, and was surprised to find him looking at her with renewed approval.

"It has been called so, yet all things change, even this aerie of we immortals."

"I think I can guess what has changed, sir. Mr. Knight, the soldier who was sent to guard me from the Rider, he said that my mother lives still."

"Forgall sent you some protector, then? Are you certain he was sent for that purpose?"

"What other purpose could he have? At any rate, he did protect me. He defeated the Rider when he would have carried me off. Dominic was injured. . . ."

"I have heard much of this mortal's prowess. They do whisper that he is the best of the *werreour* and that Forgall would make him immortal soon."

"Isn't he?"

"No, Forgall has learned a hard lesson about making humans into People. Dominic Knight is a human being like yourself. His lifespan has been lengthened by Forgall's will. Forgall is long-sighted and he saw that the day might come that we would need soldiers who can handle cold iron in our defense."

Though Clarice's curiosity was aroused by this description of Dominic's place in this Realm, she found herself wondering, "About my mother, sir . . . Dominic said that the Rider was one of her soldiers, even as he himself is one of King Forgall's. Can you tell me, sir, why does my mother have soldiers? She is not a general or a queen."

"Now we come to the crux. . . ." King Morgain, looking very much like his grandson when contemplating the results of some piece of mischief, did not complete his sentence at once. He glanced about him as though expecting an interruption.

Clarice, without thinking, reached out to lay her hand on his, wanting only to urge him to speak. Before she could touch him, King Morgain faded away like mist before the morning sun. She saw him grow fainter. It was only then she recalled that to touch a Fay was to make him her servant.

When he reappeared, he stood a few yards off, his back to her. She called, "I apologize, sir; I did not . . ."

Then she saw that instead of dark hair curling to his shoulders, her new visitor had hair clipped close to his nape and his shoulders were wider than King Morgain's by far. "Dominic!"

She was up and halfway to him before she knew she'd meant to go. He spun about abruptly at her shout. "Clarice! I did not know what had become of you."

"Nor did I know what happened to you. Where were you?"

"Where were you? Here all the time?"

He caught her hands in a welcoming clasp, bringing them to his chest. Clarice hadn't realized how much she missed the warm fellowship of her own kind until that instant. The People of Mag Mell were beautiful beyond compare, but she had nothing in common with them. However unusual Dominic's life had been, no matter how old he was, he and she shared something fundamental. They were both human.

Yet no sooner had she thought it than she knew their shared humanity was only part of the reason she was so happy to see Dominic. If it were only because he was a fellow human being, why did she doubt that seeing a prize fighter, her aunt Amabel, or a Chinese mandarin would have made her equally happy? They were all humans too, yet it was not any other face she wished to see nor any other touch she wanted.

"Dominic," she asked, "what is all the mystery?"

"Mystery?" He seemed to notice that he still held her hands and let her go. "You walk in a world of mysteries and demand answers of me. I do not know that I can satisfy you, Clarice."

"You can. Tell me. What is my mother doing?"

He too glanced about him in the same fashion as King Morgain. "I don't know if I am permitted tell you."

"If you are worried about Forgall, it doesn't appear that he intends to tell me anything himself. He should know I am not the sort of woman who takes silence for an answer!"

His smile came slowly. "If he does not know it, rest assured that I do. Come, sit down, and I'll explain, though the king's wrath may strike me a moment after."

He did not sit beside her. He rested his foot on the seat and crossed his arms, frowning at the grass. Clarice waited impatiently for him to collect his thoughts. But when he spoke, he did not bring up her mother.

"What do you think of King Morgain?"

"He seems a most droll gentleman. I can see my nephew in him."

"Is that all?"

"Why, what else?"

His smoky eyes studied her as though attempting to plumb the depths of her spirit. "You marked his resemblance to Blaic?"

"He is very much like him. At first, I thought it might *be* Blaic, transferred here by some magic or miracle."

"You thought he'd come to your rescue."

"I'd hoped. So much is strange here that the sight of a familiar face is very reassuring. I should love to see Blaic come striding over that hill." She studied him, noticing how his lips had tightened into an expression of pain. "Did the king heal all your wounds, Dominic?"

"Yes."

"I hope you know how grateful I am that you rescued me from the Rider. I was terrified—I don't believe I've ever known such terror before. I hope I never shall again." She shuddered at the memory. "I dare not wonder what would have become of me if you had not followed me out of the house."

He pushed away from the grass-covered settee and turned his back on her. In a bitter tone, he said, "Better you do not know."

"That's what I thought."

"You say you are grateful to me; I wonder how long that will last."

"I am not, in general, thought to be an ingrate." She stood up, unable to understand him. "Everything is so strange," she said again, reaching out to put her hand on his shoulder. The muscles there bunched and jumped under her touch as though to throw her off. "I don't even feel strange calling you by your name and I was taught from girlhood that a woman doesn't even address her *husband* so familiarly. My mother was always very strict about such things."

He did not turn to face her, so she walked around him. "Tell me what you know, Dominic. I am not afraid of the truth."

"Very well. I have promised to tell you what I know and I will. But first . . ."

Dominic stepped closer to her, his eyes so intent she thought she saw the fire that made them smoke-colored. Moving slowly, as though to keep from frightening some wild creature, he slid his hand over her cheek and into the depths of her hair. She reached up, wrapping her fingers around his wrist but not with the intention of pulling his hand away.

"Forgive me," he said, "I may never have the chance again."

Clarice hesitated at that, but he did not. His mouth covered hers, moving with exquisite hunger that invoked her own desire. His arm closed around her waist, pulling her against his hard body. She gasped at the impact, her lips opening.

At the same instant, Dominic made an effort to taste more of her yet. The touch of his tongue in her mouth should have filled her with disgust, but it did not. Clarice was flooded with the knowledge that the power of the

Wilder World was nothing compared with the passion of two people linked so closely.

Bent slightly backward, yet supported completely by his strength, Clarice slipped her hands up his arms to caress the back of his neck. She imitated the thrust of his tongue, wanting to know if Dominic felt something of the heat that threatened to burn away all the control she'd spent years building up.

Dominic broke the kiss but not the embrace, holding her against his shoulder, his cheek on her hair. "You'll never forgive me, Clarice. But I beg you to try. I couldn't resist the temptation to kiss you as myself, just this once."

"I knew you were playing a part before. You couldn't have been as cruel and boastful as you seemed, not after you'd been so very kind."

"I have never been kind to you."

His voice was harsh. Clarice shook back her hair to look up at him, confusion making her voice soft. "What is it, Dominic? Please, tell me."

He held her for one more moment, savoring until the last the warmth of her nearness, the orange-blossom fragrance of her hair, the sweetness of her breath. The memory of this moment would have to last him, he feared, for an horribly long time.

Dominic would have rather felt the lash of the wyvern's whip a thousand times than to force Clarice away from him. The whip would have pained him less. Gently, he grasped her shoulders—how well they fit into his hands!—and pushed her back.

She stared at him in hurt wonder. It would have been so easy to kiss her again, to delay the inevitable moment when she learned the truth, to sink into the sweet sensuality of love and let duty go by. He was tempted beyond anything he'd ever known to do just that.

Yet he knew he could not live with himself if he shirked this burden. Better she should learn the truth from the man who loved her, than from one of the Fay.

"Clarice, I am your enemy."

"My . . . ?"

"I was not sent by Forgall to protect you; I was sent to keep you as a hostage."

Now he felt the lash sting his soul. It was there in her eyes as she took a step away from him. "My enemy? A hostage? I don't understand. This has something to do with my mother, I take it. Everyone hints about her but no one says anything. What dreadful thing can she have done?"

"She has destroyed the peace of the Living Lands. Even now, she sits in her fortress plotting the overthrow of King Forgall and all that we have built here. This has been a place of peace and a refuge of the People for centuries. She has destroyed that in less than ten of your years."

Clarice passed her hand over her brow. "Perhaps you should start at the beginning, Dominic. My mother came into the Living Lands ten years ago, though we put it about that she had died. What happened then?"

"She wanted to be turned into one of the People. Everyone said Forgall was besotted for he granted that wish. Such a thing hadn't happened in centuries, and then only when a human wished to joy a Fay lover. Usually a human will demand riches or power, not the chance to give up their souls."

"I am not certain that my mother's soul was ever her chief concern."

He reached out to take her hand for comfort, but realized that she would surely recoil from his touch. He clenched his fist instead, hoping the bite of his nails would cover the agony in his heart. "You told me about your father, but you hardly mentioned your mother."

"That's not important now. Go on. Did she say why she wanted to change?"

"At first Matilda spun a tale of wanting to be free of earthly cares and pains, but it was not long before everyone saw the truth. She wanted 'faery gold' and gems. She bedecked herself in them and spent all her time creating them."

" 'Creating them'? That must have made her happy. My mother was ever fond of jewelry. She could never have too many rings. Her fingers were always covered with them."

"Greed like hers can never be satisfied. Soon we found she had developed some remarkably strong powers, strong as one of the oldest among the People. Almost as strong as Forgall. No one knows how she did that, but there have been whispers that she has allied herself with some dark power out of the Long Ago Before."

"The days of legend . . ." she said, half to herself.

"Yes. How did you know?"

She blinked. "I'm sorry. Please go on. What did my mother do next?"

Her tone was hard, almost flippant, but Dominic was not fooled. There was hurt at the back of her words, and he felt it as though it were his own. He could do nothing, though he longed to take her in his arms once more.

"Matilda took over an abandoned fortress called La'al. Long ago, a mighty sorcerer lived there on the cusp between the Wilder World and your own. Slowly, she has drawn to her the discontented among the People. . . ."

"I would not have thought that there could be discontentment here."

"You like what you have seen of Mag Mell?"

Clarice said softly, "It's beautiful, even more beautiful than Hamdry Manor, but it could never be my home. If I had been born here, however, I could think of nothing better than to dwell here for eternity."

"That is, I daresay, how most of the People feel about Mag Mell. But there are always those who are disgruntled. In this instance, there are those among the People who want Boadach to return from Homashyl and take up his duties again. No one has ever returned from being a Sleeper. Your mother claims she has found a way to force his return. Though Forgall succeeded to the kingship in accordance with the Ancient Laws, not everyone was pleased. Boadach was our first king. He was harder than Forgall and he hated your kind."

"*Our* kind. Sometimes you speak as though you were one of *them*."

"Mag Mell is the only home I remember, Clarice. Long ago, they found me, a boy of no more than six, wandering on a dunghill, lost, hungry, and filthy. My parents died in some plague or other and there was no one in all the world to care for me. If it were not for the Fay needing warriors, I should have died long ago."

"King Morgain said . . . he said they have kept you alive all this time to fight for them."

Dominic inclined his head proudly. "It would be a waste of time indeed to train a warrior as I have been trained, only to see him die of old age before he can be useful. So they have given me the gift of long life and of honorable service. At least, I believed it to have been honorable. . . ."

"How old are you?"

"I cannot say for certain. I believe that I am about four hundred years old as time is measured in the human way. Time is different here."

"Four hundred years old?" She closed her eyes and swayed.

Dominic guided her to the seat. She did not avoid his touch, though she stiffened and shrank away when he tried to put his arm about her. "Please don't. . , ."

"As you wish."

He sat beside her, watching her with careful solicitude. Her eyes were closed yet he could see their dark centers move beneath the translucent lids. A pulse beat in her white throat, a tiny rhythm of time unaffected by the magic of the Lands of Fragrance.

She leaned her head upon her hand, her eyes still shut. "You said something of my being a hostage. I assume that you were sent to Hamdry for that reason."

"Forgall thought that if your mother knew we held you, she would sue for peace."

"Has she done so?"

"No. Her answer was to send the Rider to find you. If you had been captured by him, you would at this moment be speaking with your mother."

"I see. Now I understand. Thank you for explaining everything." She stood up, her gown displaying her magnificent figure to perfection. But it was not her beauty that made Dominic love her.

His love had been born as she had struggled so hard against the wyvern's whip about her wrist. She had fought it every step, though it was a weapon completely alien to her world and her ways. No one could have blamed her for panicking, or screaming, or indeed for any reaction born of her fear.

But Clarice had dug in her heels, resisting valiantly as she'd been dragged, inch by inch, into the unknown. She had not surrendered.

Dominic knew little of women, yet he had no doubt that not one in a hundred would have fought so hard for her freedom. He had been trained all his life to follow the orders of the Fay king, yet every human instinct he possessed had cheered for her. He'd never felt more human, or more ashamed when he defeated the Rider, knowing that he was keeping her from what she must wish for most, a reunion with her mother.

Now, he realized that such a meeting might be bittersweet for Clarice. Nonetheless, he still felt that she should see Matilda if she wished. It was wrong for the king to keep her as a hostage for her mother's good behavior.

Clarice turned to him. "What becomes of me now, Dominic? My mother will undoubtedly try again to capture me. I have become, it seems, a valuable pawn in a game I did not even know was being played. What comes to me now?"

"Believe me, if it were my decision, you would go free."

"Then I wish that it were your decision. As it is not . . ."

"No, it is not. We are both pawns, Clarice. I cannot move except as my king commands."

"What does he command you do with me now? Or am I not to know."

"He wants me to take you home to Hamdry Manor."

Clarice walked a few steps with him. Then she said bitterly, "Only it isn't the Manor, is it? It's a clever copy, and my servants aren't really Camber, Rose, and the rest but Fays made up to look like them. What has become of my servants?"

"I will show you." He cupped his hands about his mouth and shouted to the sky, "My king?"

As though a curtain parted, the sky split in two. Forgall walked through the gap, seeming to bundle the sky and the meadow up in his arms. Where the sky had stretched to infinity in an intense swath of blue and where the meadow had seemed to flow away toward the horizon, there was now only fabric being pleated smaller and smaller. Just before he'd folded up the last corner, he gave the sky a shake and out rolled a silvery globe. Then the meadow and sky disappeared, perhaps up Forgall's sleeve, perhaps into thin air.

Clarice and Dominic stood again outside the dreamlike buildings of Mag Mell, their roofs merry with bird feathers. Forgall passed them, headed for the white tent. As he went by, he tossed something to Dominic, saying, "Take care, my son. I am not so hard as Boadach, but I have my limits."

Dominic bowed from the waist. A trifle late and very haughty, Clarice swished her skirts in the smallest of curtsies. Forgall only laughed at her insolence and went inside his tent.

"Come and look, Clarice," Dominic said.

He held in his hands a clouded crystal ball. At first glance, it looked like a small model of the moon. Though still broad day, Clarice could tell by looking at his hands that the globe was giving off light, as pale and celestial as moonlight.

Dominic said, "This is a scrying stone. It is unheard

of for anyone but the king to look into it. You are honored."

He held it out for her closer inspection. It must have been surprisingly heavy for its size, for Dominic's arms shook with the strain of holding it and she knew that he was exceptionally strong. Clarice looked into the stone and saw swirling vapors that glittered with a silver light.

"You wanted to see your servants. . . ."

"Yes . . ."

She did see them. Camber sat with his elbows on the table, his cravat hanging. Lela sat like a coquette on the table beside him, flirting as hard as she could. Cook, her face disapproving enough to have curdled milk, beat something vigorously in a big copper bowl. They did not look worried or troubled in the least.

"Have you put someone in my place?" she asked. The silvery mists swirled again and she saw Rose, busily brushing her mistress's favorite riding habit. Because the stone gave very sharp, if tiny, images, Clarice could see quite clearly that the habit did not require cleaning.

"They don't know you are gone. They do the same tasks as always, serve dinner, take it away, lay out your night rail, bring up your water—everything. They do not notice that you are not there. They do the same for Morgain Half-Fay."

"But surely someone must call on me . . . ?"

"Your servants deny you to everyone. They say you are indisposed. Doctor Danby is away, as he told you. No one else doubts your servants. Would you?" The scrying stone's inner clouds returned, covering over the tiny picture of Rose. "What else do you want to see?" Dominic asked.

"Nothing more."

"Not even . . . Blaic?"

"He cannot help me. No one can."

"You are right. No one can help you."

"You can't keep me forever!" she said, her frustration mounting.

"We don't have to. Your mother has failed to capture

you. I doubt she'll try again. Now she must certainly sue
for peace." He tried to think of something to say that
would comfort her. "Don't be frightened. The king will
not harm Matilda. That is not his way."

Clarice took a last look about her. Mag Mell was as
beautiful as an opium-eater's dream of paradise. Everything bore a luminous shine, rainbows seeming to flicker
along every edge. The air was filled with the fragrances
of a thousand flowers and everyone was beautiful and
blithe.

Turning to Dominic, she begged, "Take me back to
Hamdry, or at least that Hamdry you have made for me.
Please."

Thirteen

◦⌇◦

Clarice found herself outside her own front door. Though the fog had not lifted, it had moved farther off, so that Hamdry Manor stood in a circle of clear air. She could see all of the round drive before the house and a good piece of the lawn beyond it. She was entirely alone, wearing her own clothes, which had miraculously dried. Even her shawl was back about her shoulders.

Taking a few steps away from the house, she leaned backward to look up at the roof. There were fantastic creatures sitting on the chimney pots, just as always. Unicorns, basilisks, chimeras, and more, decorated the edge according to the fancy of an ancestor. Once, one had led her to a treasure that had restored her family wealth when her mother's lover had stolen everything. That had been the beginning of this odyssey into realms of legend.

She'd always loved the creatures on the roof and it warmed her now to see them still, though they were no more than copies. Or were they? Suddenly, she became convinced that those beasts were not carved of stone anymore, but were entirely real. Real, and watching her.

Opening the door, Clarice went inside quickly. Now

that she knew the truth, she marveled at the perfection of detail. The Fay overlooked nothing.

Catching sight of herself in a mirror, she noticed that she was frowning. Perhaps this *was* her real home. Perhaps they'd sent her back to her own place, hoping that she'd believe them and not try to leave to find help. That would be like them, cunning to the end.

She crossed the entry hall, looking for some flaw to tell her the truth. Hurrying down the corridor, she entered the library. The warm smell of the leather bindings took her back to the days when her father was still alive. How often had they pored over some intriguing volume with the aid of his magnifying glass, for his eyes had been nearly as poor as hers when it came to reading.

Clarice pulled open the center drawer of his desk, which stuck just as always, and sought for the brass-handled glass. The drawer was nearly empty. A few loose and dusty pastilles, a crumpled page or two was all that met her questing fingers. The drawer stuck so tightly that she did not use it, though this was now her desk.

Just as she was trying to force the drawer closed, a glint as of glass caught her eye. Reaching in again, she found the lens, but not the handle. Yet she was prepared to swear that the lens had not been there in any condition one moment before.

Still fighting against the truth, Clarice told herself that she might have overlooked it. As for the metal handle and rim having gone missing, any one of the servants might have dropped the magnifier and rather than own up to the deed, had taken away the battered brass.

Even as she came up with this notion, she dismissed it. Her servants knew they'd not be turned off for such a trivial mishap. No, if the brass handle and rim were missing it had to be because the Fay could not summon up metal.

To test her theory, she rapped one of the bronze jars that stood on the mantelpiece. It gave out a dull thud. Using the lens, Clarice saw that the "bronze" was carefully painted wood. She heaved a great sigh. Morgain had been right. She would tell him so at once.

As she turned to go, a book fell off the shelf on the far side of the room. Clarice considered ignoring it. If she had to remain here at this imitation manor, she could only retain her sanity by disregarding anything that could not have happened in her own realm. That was when the book began to thump itself repeatedly and insistently on the floor.

Clarice left the library but she could still hear the thumping. Perhaps it would continue interminably. Tightening her lips, she returned and went over to where the book lay. It stopped making noise as she came in, opening of itself and riffling through its own pages.

"What next, I wonder? Will quills tickle me until I write letters, will my needle prick me until I ply it, will the pianoforte frolic about me like a foolish dog until I play? I have been dictated to by more than my share of people lately; must I now truckle to inanimate objects as well?"

The book lay open, supinely offering itself for reading. "I suppose you are not so inanimate as all that," Clarice said, still aloud as she picked up the book. "Very well; let us see what you have to say."

Using the lens, Clarice saw that this was the first volume of a history of England. The book felt comfortable in her hand, as though it settled down with a sense of pleasurable anticipation of use. "I don't know what you want me to read," Clarice said.

One page rippled. "Oh, thank you."

She rattled off the words aloud, " 'In the dark years following the arrival of the Black Death in England, the customs and orders of a society predicated upon the manorial system were irretrievably damaged. Entire households were lost, from babe in arms to venerable grandfather. The histories of a household's proper service vanished with the souls who accepted them as the standard for civilization. Even more damaging was the desertion and eventual destruction of many villages, where the death-toll was so complete that there were none left alive to bury the dead. A famous example is that of Priory St. Windle. . . .' "

Clarice's voice faded. Her eyes moving more quickly, she read how the village had been abandoned to its dead, leaving such desolation that even the sheep reverted to a wild state. When the monks who owned the village at last crept out from the security of their stone walls, they found dead bodies lying in the snow all the way from their gate to the village.

Painstakingly, the monks, guilt-ridden at having failed their community, buried each of the dead in individual graves, unlike the hurried mass graves of so many other places. Each name was recorded, all were accounted for with the exception of a small boy who, it was assumed, had been carried away by feral dogs. The monks of St. Windle said prayers every day for the souls of the plague-dead until Henry VIII dissolved the monasteries in 1536.

Clarice returned to the top of the page and read it again, carefully searching for the name of the boy. The historian who had summarized this sad tale did not mention it. Closing the book, she restored it to its place on the shelf. She did not really require confirmation; she knew the boy's name already.

She could not imagine what it must have been like for Dominic, seeing each of the people he knew sicken and die in such a hideous way. Children lost their parents even today; she herself supported a local orphanage. Yet how much worse to have *everyone* around him die, his parents, his neighbors, his friends, young and old. Her heart ached for him, though his suffering had been long, long ago.

He had said that the Fay had taken him when he was six years old. From a distant memory of a never-well-liked governess's teaching, Clarice recalled that the plague had struck England in the year 1350.

All at once, Clarice needed to sit down. She put her head down on her knees. Though King Morgain had told her Dominic's age, and he'd mentioned it himself, it was not until she herself did the math that it came home to her. Dominic Knight, looking no more than thirty, he who had guarded her, kissed her, and made her furious, was four hundred and fifty-five years old.

When the dizziness passed, she wondered who it was that had wanted her to see that particular book. Glancing surreptitiously about her, Clarice asked herself if she was, even now, alone in the library. Was someone standing over her, watching her as she struggled to accept what she had learned? Why had someone wanted her to know so much about Dominic? Even more than this, Clarice wondered why Dominic had kissed her there in the make-believe meadow.

This time, when she left the library, no book pursued her. She was curious to know whether Morgain was having the same trouble with his books. Did books grow jealous when one was preferred over another? Would they jostle frenetically for position, each seeking to be read first? Clarice felt sure Morgain was capable of keeping them in order.

He was not in his room, nor in any of the corners that he'd taken to reading in of late. After she'd searched fruitlessly for some little time, she was disturbed by a gentle, attention-awakening cough in the dust-sheeted nursery.

Camber—or whoever—stood beside her. "May I be of assistance, your ladyship?"

"There's no need to keep up this pretense," she said coolly. "I know you are not my butler."

"But I am." He smiled when she would have protested. "For the time being, I am most certainly your butler. I find it quite amusing. How may I help you?"

It would be childish to continue to argue. Clarice said, "I am looking for my nephew."

"Ah." The Fay who wore Camber's countenance looked about him. He bent his head slightly to look under a table and even strode to the double-doored wardrobe to examine the inside. One eyebrow rose. "He does not seem to be here."

"I realized that myself. And I should mention that Morgain knows all about you as well as I."

"Does he indeed?"

"You don't believe me? Then you should know that Camber cannot raise only one eyebrow. No matter how hard he tries, both always go up together."

He pursed his lips and nodded. "That would explain several things. I thought Morgain Half-Fay was strange in his distrust of me. I am grateful to your ladyship for pointing it out. How true that it is the little mannerisms that betray us." Without another word, he closed his eyes and let his head loll on his neck.

"What are you doing?"

"Hush. I am casting forth my consciousness."

A silence as heavy and tactile as a velvet cloak closed around her. That, more than any single thing, taught her that this was not her home, no matter how like all the contrivances of the Fay could make it. Hamdry Manor, the *real* Hamdry Manor, had never seemed to her to be less than welcoming, more accepting than her mother had ever been. Yet in this silence, she felt no comforting aura gathering about her. She could not forget that she was the daughter of Forgall's enemy and that these Fay playing the part of her servants were Forgall's most trusted people.

When heavy footsteps approached, she could feel them shake the floor. "That's not Morgain," she said, fear rising in her throat. If the Rider could come so close to taking her, what else might try?

When Dominic opened the door, she was so glad to see him that she became angry at him for worrying her unnecessarily. "The least you could do is knock!"

He glanced between her and the butler. The definition in his jaw grew more noticeable. "I'm interrupting you?"

"We were looking for Morgain."

"He's in his room."

"No, I looked."

"Then he's in the library."

"No. Don't you think I looked there as well?"

Clarice knew she wasn't angry with Dominic either for his obtuseness or for scaring her. If she hadn't been so abashed at seeing him again, she wouldn't have spoken so. Seeing him, she felt she could almost read his thoughts. He must be thinking of those stolen moments when he'd kissed her and she had so wantonly kissed him back. At the remembrance of how she'd clung to him, answering his passion with her own, she didn't know whether to run away, slap his face, or throw herself into his arms.

She did neither. Hating herself for being such a shrew, she challenged, "Instead of suggesting places I've already searched, why don't you and your confrere here do something useful? Going away comes to mind."

The butler opened both eyes. "Are all mortals so uncontrollable, Dominic? You are not thus. It must be the females of your species that behave so. Troubling. No wonder you never have peace."

Clarice advanced upon him. "Considering how I have been put upon, sir, I suggest you take your patronizing tone elsewhere."

"Or what, my dear child?" His austere smile did not long survive her next words and the threatening gesture that went with them.

"Or I'll touch you!"

The Fay-Camber stepped back a pace. "Come, Dominic. Let us search for Morgain Half-Fay as she wishes. I do not want to be trapped by the Ancient Law into accepting the command of such a wild-hearted creature as this."

Dominic said, "Careful, Chadwin. I am sworn to protect her, even against you."

"But who, pray tell, will defend me against her?" The butler strode to the doorway. "I'll find Morgain Half-Fay for you, my lady. Then we may all be comfortable again. This masquerade need not last much longer. Thy mother, Lady of the Pale Banner, will sue for peace soon enough."

When he'd gone, Clarice demanded, "What is 'soon' to an immortal? Two hundred years?"

Dominic closed the door behind Chadwin. He stood with his back against it, gazing at her with a smile lurking in the depths of his dark topaz eyes. He seemed entirely at his ease. He'd left off his cravat and had unbuttoned the top two buttons of his waistcoat. This relaxing of the gentlemanly code gave him a rakish air that she should have found vulgar, but that appealed to her natural taste more than an overparticularity of dress.

His gazing on her so steadily unnerved her. She thought that he knew that it had that effect on her and believed that was why he did it. She snatched her hand away from where she'd quite unwittingly been coquettishly smoothing her hair. "Why do you stare at me so? It's exceedingly rude."

"You may stare back if you like."

"I don't. I don't see anything of interest in your face."

"No? Well, it's the only face I have so I'm sorry if it doesn't please you." His shoulders came off the door and he began to advance on her slowly, giving her plenty of time to run from him. Clarice wanted to stand her ground, but she had a strange, hot, jumpy feeling in her stomach and it demanded that she back away if only to see how far he'd follow.

"It's not the only face you have. You've shown me half a dozen since you first came to Hamdry."

"Perhaps I have. But this is the true one you see now."

"How can I tell? Tomorrow you may wear another."

"I give you my word." Dominic took her hand. She pried it loose from his lax grasp. Yet before she had an instant to feel gratified, he reached out for the other. He brought it to his lips and brushed the back of it. She had a little more difficulty getting free, but not a great deal.

"Clarice," he said with teasing reproach.

He took her left hand again. This time, his warm mouth moved against the tender underside of her wrist.

A thrill of desire seemed to shoot up her arm, overwhelming her senses. She realized slowly that her increasing difficulty in freeing herself was not because Dominic held her too tightly. Rather, her will to resist weakened every time he touched her.

Clarice felt trapped in a dance of ritualized movements, the steps of which she had never been taught. Dominic, for all his years in the Living Lands, seemed to have mastered not only the desirable moves but also the countermoves.

She searched his eyes. They'd lost their smiling look. Like a magnifying glass, their intensity narrowed to focus on her mouth. She could feel her lips growing warmer under the concentration of his gaze and knew that however much he might want to kiss her, she wanted it just as sharply.

When he bowed his head to taste her lips, Clarice held him off, but in truth, it was her own nature she struggled to keep at bay. "No . . ."

"Why not?"

"I . . . because I want you too much."

"Good."

He pulled her off balance, so that she had only him to cling to as his mouth came down on hers. Desire came roaring to life as though they'd forged a new existence between them. This was no tentative touch of mouth to mouth nor did it end with a faltering sally of tongues. He seemed intent on conquering all her resistance with a well-planned undermining of her chastity.

With her body in full traitorous revolt and on the point of surrendering to him, Clarice could not retreat and could summon no defense but attack. She slid her hands into the open front of his shirt, surprised by the contrast between his hard-muscled body and the soft prickle of his chest hair teasing her palms. A shudder went through him at this intimate touch, and Clarice felt the tide of battle turning her way.

But then Dominic left her mouth to press his teeth against the side of her neck. She couldn't hold back a gasp of pleasure, though she knew it gave away some of her position. His hands slid down over her full skirt to urge her lower body closer to his.

She hadn't known how much she'd wanted that until it happened. It stole her breath and a good portion of what was left of her reason. She pressed against him shamelessly, and was so lost to propriety as to think his groan the most delightful sound she'd ever heard. She put her chin up in a demand for more kisses, dragging his head down to meet hers, making sounds of her own, eager and wild.

"Clarice . . . ah, you'll kill me."

An admission of surrender? So she thought, until Dominic cupped her breasts in his hands. At some point, he'd slid her gown down, exposing the creamy flesh of her shoulder and the upper slope of her bosom.

She'd been so dazed and drugged with kisses that she'd hardly noticed, even when he'd pressed his lips to the base of her throat before kissing his way out to her shoulder. Then he slipped his hands up her waist and smoothed them over her bodice, lifting her breasts until they all but spilled over the lowered neckline.

"You're so beautiful. I'm hopelessly in love with you," he murmured and lowered his head to steal a taste. The sensation of his mouth on her tightly furled nipple was fugitive, maddeningly elusive, and yet sweetly wicked. She couldn't keep back a cry far louder than those soft moans and sighs which had escaped her vigilance.

It was as if someone had sounded a clarion call of danger in her ear. Her friend and companion, Melissa, raised in an uncaring world, had told Clarice all about the activities of men and women in love when they were but green girls of seventeen. Clarice wondered now how many illegitimate children were brought into the world as a consequence of the hot, urgent feeling of a woman's body when a man touched, held, and worshiped her as Dominic did now.

Taking advantage of his distraction as he touched and

fondled, Clarice propelled herself out of his arms. She retreated a final step, clutching the fallen left side of her bodice with her right hand. He tried to hold on to her, letting his hands slip away at the last instant.

Dominic looked heavy-eyed and slightly dazed as though he'd wakened to a strong light in the middle of the night. She doubted that she appeared any more alert. Even now the heady narcotic of passion was urging her to return to the pleasure of Dominic's touch, hinting that there were many more delights to be found farther along the road they'd begun to travel together.

"I'm sorry," she blurted out as hurt began to replace the desire in Dominic's expression. "We must stop this here and now."

He tried to smile, but perhaps the tide of desire beat too strongly in him still, for his smile died before it was half-realized. "Why must we stop? Didn't you like it?"

"I—never mind. Where . . . how . . . ? Before you did not kiss me. . . ." She found herself having to gulp a few mouthfuls of air before she could finish by saying, "you didn't kiss me before like . . . that."

"There's a saying among the People to the effect that the third time one tries is the mature child of the first two efforts."

"We say, 'third time's the charm.' "

"Much more succinct." His dark eyes were still focused on her with a deeply serious intent. "Besides, I want you more now than I did before. I've tasted how sweet you are and I hunger for more of you, Clarice."

If only he'd smiled when he'd said those things. She could have discounted them as the hyperbole of a man seeking mere physical gratification. But he'd been entirely, dauntingly serious. What answer could be made to such a declaration?

She knew honesty deserved nothing but honesty. "I'm sorry, Dominic. I should have stopped you at my 'no,' rather than continued to make love to you."

"You did say no. *I* should have stopped there. I was wrong."

"So was I. You are, after all, something of a jailer. I always thought those stories of women falling under the spell of such a one were imaginary."

"Your jailer?" He was obviously offended. "Is that what you think of me?"

"I am your hostage, Dominic. There's no sense in wrapping up such an ugly thing in plain linen. If it were not for that, we should never have met."

He said eagerly, "Only say you don't regret it, Clarice."

"No," she said without hesitation. "I do not regret it." She held up her hand when he would have seized her joyfully in his arms. Mindful of what a touch could lead to, Dominic stopped. The desire in his eyes was nearly as arousing as a kiss.

"It's too dangerous," Clarice said. "If Forgall knew. . . ."

"He may know already. You see, I have not even a solitary drop of Fay blood in my veins. I cannot shield my thoughts from the least among them. It has made growing up in Mag Mell something of a challenge as you may imagine."

"Are you afraid of Forgall?"

He did not deny it hotly as a younger man would have done. Dominic deliberated for a moment before saying, "I have never given him cause to be angry with me."

"Until now."

"Until you, Clarice."

In some agitation, she tried to adjust her gown, unable to meet his eyes.

"Let me," he said. With a tender touch that held much of the lover but not uncontrollable desire, he tugged the gown back into its proper position. Then he stood away from her.

"What happens now?" Clarice asked.

He smiled at her so warmly that she lost some of her embarrassment. "I shall help you find Morgain Half-Fay. Then, unless your mother relents, there will be a war."

"Which you and others like you will fight."

"It is what we have been trained for all our lives. You need have no fear for me. In the end, my comrades and I will overcome those who fight on the other side."

"You sound very confident. Is that for my sake? You waste your time." She clutched his hand. "You might be killed."

"No. Even if I am defeated, I will simply return to the time and the place from which I came."

"Yes, Priory St. Windle in 1350!"

"What? How know you that?"

"I read it in a book." She did not mention the circumstances under which she'd found the book. "If you go back there, we will never see each other again."

Dominic covered her hand with his own. "Is it so important to you that we meet again?"

"Yes. No. Stop! I won't be manhandled. . . ."

"Am I being so brutal?" He gathered her close in his arms, pressing her head against his shoulder. His voice was low, thrilling her with its sincerity. "I pledge you, my lady, that I will find you across time, space, and eternity, though the ten thousand devils of hell bar the way."

"A pie-crust promise—easily made and easily broken," Clarice said, her voice obscured by tears that she had no intention of permitting to fall.

He pressed his lips to her temple and released her. "Chadwin has probably already found your nephew for you. I like Morgain, you know."

"He's a scrapegrace."

"Yes, if it weren't for that, he'd be intolerable." He grinned at her and sketched a salute. "I shall go and see."

At the doorway, he paused and glanced back. "I meant it, Clarice. Every word."

A lesser woman would have flung herself into his arms again, giving him, between kisses, a pledge in return. Clarice felt a tremendous impetus to demonstrate how clinging and sweet she could be. She repressed it firmly, letting him go without a word, for if she'd spoken she would have given her heart away.

Too much had proved false of late. Her home was not her home, her trusted servants were strangers, her mother was not lost forever after all. With the foundations of her beliefs shaking, Clarice mistrusted the strength of the refuge Dominic offered. She longed to test it but she dared not try.

The sound of his footsteps had not entirely faded before Morgain appeared in the entrance to the nursery. His finger went to his lips before she had time to more than inhale for her cry of surprise.

"Hist!" he said, his green eyes alight with mischief. He glanced behind him into the hall, then tiptoed in. "I've always wanted to say that."

"Morgain, where have you been?" she whispered.

"I hardly know myself. But I think I can find it again."

"Find what?"

"The forest with the doors. I reached them the first time traveling in my bed. It didn't work this time, but I found another method."

Clarice could no longer think Morgain was out of his head when he talked this way. Ignorance had been more of a comfort than she'd realized. She only asked, "What doors are these?"

"You remember. I sketched them. I—I'm afraid I lied to you about that, Aunt Clarice. I told you I hadn't seen any doors in the trees, that I just wanted to put them there. You see, I had a funny feeling that it wasn't quite the done thing to mention them. Queer, that. But they are quite real and if we can reach them, then we can go home."

"You'll have to explain, Morgain. My head is spinning. How can doors help us leave Mag Mell?"

"I saw Hamdry through the doors. We find them, walk through them, and there we are, safe and sound. Once my father returns, he'll know how to keep us out of their hands a second time."

"You know why we've been placed in this replica?"

"I heard the Fay who are pretending to be Camber and the rest talking."

"That was very careless of them. Didn't they notice you?"

He shook his head with a joking look in his eyes. "Watch what I can do, Aunt."

The hairs on the back of her neck rose like hackles with awestruck disbelief. Morgain had disappeared, gone like a flame when a candle winks out. She looked around the dusty nursery, sure she heard his stifled laughter.

Then slowly, she began to see him. He looked like a drawing of himself in pale pastels, only the figure was not static. It moved with all the boy's awkward grace. He rubbed his nose with the fore-knuckle of his finger and then wiggled all five at her in a funning gesture. The sketchy colors of his clothing began to deepen and Morgain increased in clarity. He passed from a watercolor to an oil in a matter of moments, until he stood before her solid and unchanged.

"How are you doing that?" Clarice demanded.

He shrugged with supple shoulders. "I don't know. I just ask myself to do it, and it's done. Oh, I'm afraid there's a rather big stain on the carpet in my room, Aunt. The manticore I conjured up wasn't entirely house-trained."

Clarice felt glad that Morgain was not slightly older, or he might have conjured up a mermaid or a nymph. "I thought you were trying to control this power."

"I have tried, Aunt, but I'm afraid that . . . I'm afraid. . . ." Suddenly Morgain looked at her with the eyes of a small boy whose longed-for toy broke on Christmas morning. "I haven't been trained for this. I don't really know what I am doing or how to control it. It . . . it frightens me."

Clarice put her arms about him and found him reassuringly solid. "What do you think it means, Morgain?"

"I think I'm becoming one of them, Aunt." He seemed to be looking inward. "I'm losing my human half. I can feel it going even now. The more magic I do, the faster it leaves me."

"Then don't do any more of it, please. Unless . . .
Morgain, do you *want* to change?"

"I thought I might, but I don't. Not really. It sounds
wonderful, but Mother wouldn't like it." He bit his lip,
looking and sounding his age for once. "I wouldn't like
it either. Their hearts are colder than ours, you can tell
by the way they talk. Oh, Aunt Clarice, I so want to go
home."

Clarice cuddled him for a moment, feeling that he
needed her to make a wise, mature decision. Her growing attraction for Dominic belonged to a silly chit fresh
out of the schoolroom, not a woman with responsibilities
and duties. Heartbreak could have nothing to do with
such a woman. "Very well, Morgain. How do we set
about finding these doors?"

"I've made a map. Look." He brought out from his
breast pocket one of his much-folded pieces of paper.
Carrying it over to a sheet-shrouded table, he lay it out
for her inspection. It looked like any of his old maps of
imaginary places but with a difference, for she recognized several names. The great meadow where the
feather-roofed tents stood was in the center with MAG
MELL lettered over the top. A round insignia with a
crown in the center hovered over these words.

Around the map were arrows pointing off to the four
points of the compass. A river here, a shining lake there,
a few mountains rising above the sea, and a distant, jagged peak with the words LA'AL FORTRESS surmounted
by a floating banner empty of all insignia.

"I don't think that this is everything," Morgain said
regretfully. "I had to leave out a lot, but it shows the
main points.

"Did you invent this? How can you know what is
contained in the Living Lands?"

"All those books I've been reading, Aunt Clarice.
There's an awful lot of writers who have either been to
the Deathless Realm or who have written about it.
Maybe it's all make-believe; I don't know."

"That can't be right, Morgain. Why would the Fay

leave those books here for us to find. That doesn't make sense. You don't help an enemy escape."

The boy lowered his voice to a whisper. "I think someone else is helping us."

"I hope you are right. I hope they go on doing it. Come. We'd better dress warmly and I'll try to filch some food from the table at dinner. We'll leave as soon as night falls."

Fourteen

~

They crept out of the house as soon as darkness came. Clarice lead the way at first, for she had been as far as the end of the brick walk. "At least I need not fear the Rider this time," she said softly.

Morgain stole his hand, already cold, into hers. "I thank God Dominic was with you. I should have hated to lose you."

Clarice pressed his fingers. "You will never lose me."

When gravel crunched under their feet, Clarice relinquished the lead. She knew it was the merest folly to trust to a child's imagined map created from a mingling of the wild dreamings of others but it was the only hope she had. She owed it to her sister to return Morgain safe, sound, and as human as he'd been when he'd been given into her care.

"What direction shall we go in?" she asked.

"Wherever the fog is thickest, I assume."

"Ugh. Very well."

Mindful of how cold she'd grown on her previous venture into the fog, Clarice had chosen to wear her riding dress, dragging the trailing skirt around her body and tucking the end into her waistband. The leather breeches she wore beneath her skirt were exposed on the right, a small price to pay for having warm wool co-cooned around her. Beside, it left her stride swinging free.

She left the daring hat with the turned-up brim and feather in her room, choosing instead to wear her shawl again, wrapped and pinned about her head. Her only fear was that these clothes were not what they seemed. Would she arrive at the real Hamdry wearing nothing but cobwebs?

Morgain was snug in his caped coat and best boots, a low, brimmed hat like an officer's forage cap pulled down tightly over his hair. He said, "I believe that there are spells laid on this place to keep us here. If we seek out the most difficult way, then we shall be heading toward whatever they most want us *not* to find."

"We should ignore the warnings, in other words, because the door with the biggest lock contains the greatest treasure?"

"Exactly. For instance, that patch of fog looks much heavier than the rest. I think we should head into it."

Clarice nodded. It was already hard to see her feet. She grasped Morgain's hand firmly, and adjusted her grip on the bandbox she carried in her other hand. It contained four rolls, sliced and stuffed with wild mushrooms, half a dozen small cakes, and three peaches. She'd smuggled them off the table and into the detached pocket she'd held on her lap throughout the meal. The Fay-Camber had noticed nothing, she thought.

Dominic had been harder to fool. He'd sat at the end of the table, smiling at her in such a way that she'd been in one long blush. A man's eyes should not be so intent. Thank heavens Morgain had been at his most distracting. Twice he'd upset his water goblet and once had demonstrated how to skip a new potato across the highly polished table like a stone on a millpond. Clarice had hated to scold him, but thought it would look too suspicious if she did not try to control his antics.

The fog grew thicker with every step they took. Clarice began to feel chilled and, more than that, frightened.

The last time she'd attempted to penetrate the fog, the Rider had nearly carried her off.

"Do you hear anything?" she asked, in Morgain's general direction. He was little more than a shadow.

"There's nothing to hear," he said confidently. "I'd know if there was."

"It doesn't seem to be thinning at all."

"Not yet."

Dominic had said that if the Rider had succeeded, she would have been with her mother by now. The idea had not filled her with delight. Though she knew herself undutiful and unfeeling for admitting it, there was no denying the last ten years without the elder Lady Stavely had been peaceful ones.

When her father had been alive, there'd been a never-ending series of estrangements, shouting, and bitterness. If Clarice dared to speak one word in her father's defense, the same punishments would be laid on her, despite the fact that her mother lavished all the love of which she was capable upon her only child.

Her father had protected her but he had possessed a gift of evading unpleasant scenes by simply not being around when they were occurring. Always, Clarice had been aware that his milder nature would be expected to submit under her mother's implacable will, even on the subjects of education and acquaintance. The merest expression of a counterdesire set Lady Stavely's lips in an unalterable line. Only once had the viscount prevailed over his termagant.

How cold Matilda had been to Felicia, her husband's illegitimate daughter, blaming the child for her own existence. Clarice had loved having an older sister and had taken Felicia to heart from the first day she'd arrived, her common speech and ill-habits not withstanding. Felicia had grown into a delightful, proper lady but Matilda had continued to hate her. Anything that diminished her own child rankled, even though Clarice herself had not felt so reduced.

And there was the dreadful sense that Matilda had

been pleased rather than appalled by the bane laid on
Clarice by Forgall the Fay-King. Had her mother preferred keeping her a child rather than seeing her mature
so that she could at last achieve perfect control over her?
The years between thirteen and sixteen were as blank as
the fog to Clarice yet she felt, somehow, that Matilda
had not been horrified to find her daughter a beautiful,
docile fool.

Clarice couldn't imagine that immortality had cured
her mother of these flaws, any more than it had, apparently, sated her insatiable greed for jewels, gold and
power. She remembered her mother's hands, covered
with rings, so that whenever she grasped her daughter's
hand, it would hurt. They'd sparkled vibrantly, each one
kept scrupulously clean, but Clarice had too often been
scratched by a pronged setting to admire them.

"Morgain, how long do you think we've been walking?" Clarice asked after a long time.

"There's no way to tell. I thought about counting our
paces, figuring half a second per pace, but I lost track
at about a thousand four hundred and seventy-seven. If
only I'd brought my abacus. . . ."

"Don't trouble yourself about it. I'm only wondering
if we're going around it circles, but I suppose there's no
way to tell."

"No. No way at all. Except that we have been walking
on grass for a quite a way. Haven't you noticed?"

"No, I hadn't. What a relief. Are you tired? Shall we
rest a moment?"

"All right. Grass is easier to sit on than gravel and we
might as well rest while we can." They sat down together, knee to knee. "It would be fatal to lose each
other," he said. "I'm glad you're holding my hand,
Aunt."

"I'm glad too, Morgain. It's too lonely without another person. Would you care to eat something?"

"No. But I am thirsty."

"So am I, despite being as wet as a mermaid. We'll
share a peach. The juice will help."

But the string that held the bandbox closed had become involved in a tight knot, aggravated by the fact that the string was also quite wet. She picked at it, breaking a nail. She'd been unable to find her small knife after the struggle with the Rider, so there was nothing to do but to keep trying. It was while she was engaged in this that she first heard the noise.

"What noise?" Morgain asked, looking around.

"Didn't you hear it? A slow scraping sound." She strained her ears. "It's gone now, I think."

"What kind of slow, scraping noise?"

"I don't know." She glanced at her nephew, whose freckles were just visible behind the shifting mists. He wore a most peculiar look, as though he were trying to close his ears to sound without using his hands. "Morgain, what is it?"

"I mustn't think," he said, his voice high with strain. "I mustn't think about what a sound *could* be, Aunt, because I'll make it happen. Oh, why did I have to study mythical monsters! If only I'd studied something safe like . . . like butterflies. The Lepidoptera are so soothing, don't you think?"

The knot slipped free at last. "We shall eat something and then go on," Clarice declared.

But she snatched back her hand just inches away from the lid as it began to rock back and forth. "Morgain . . ." she whispered, drawing his attention to the box. "What is it?"

She clutched him when he would have reached out. "Wait. Don't. Heaven only knows what's in there."

Morgain reached into his coat pocket and brought out the map and a pencil. "I thought I could add interesting topography as we went."

Extending the pencil like a fencer, he deftly flipped off the lid. Instantly, a column of colors arose, in exactly the same size circle as the box. Like a fountain, it shot upward to plume out in a glorious spray. Only this column was made not of water but of brilliant, iridescent insects with wings that flickered and shone even in the dim light of the fog-ridden Wilder World.

Clarice stood, mouth open, looking up, as the fountain ceased. She saw that the breaking spray did not fall at once to earth. Each particular speck floated in the air, higher or lower according to what seemed the merest whim. Then one "speck" drifted near enough for her to see the truth.

"They're butterflies, Morgain! Look."

One had landed on her sleeve, flirting blue and purple wings. He stayed on her sleeve only an instant before flying away, leaving Clarice wondering what he had thought of her.

"Amazing," Morgain said, studying a magnificent orange and black specimen that had landed on his knee. It flew away and he followed its flight with his eyes. "Truly amazing."

"You did say you could conjure things. You must have invoked butterflies just now."

"I did not refer to the butterflies, Aunt. Rather, that."

Looking up, she saw that the fog had lifted as though blown away by the beating of all those tiny wings. They stood in the grass at the edge of a rutted track that lead off into an indistinct distance tinged with blue. Clarice thought she glimpsed snow-covered peaks but it was difficult to make out details at this distance with no clearer light than the moon.

Of one thing alone could she be certain. This was not Devon. Nothing about it looked or felt familiar. The vast rise of the moor did not overshadow this land. Without it to steer by, she felt lost.

"It's a beautiful night all of a sudden," Clarice said warily. The full moon looked like a great water lily in the vast pool of sky. She shamed the stars so that none but the boldest showed themselves.

"I don't trust it," Morgain said glumly. "We can be seen."

"Undoubtedly, but there's nothing we can do about that. Come, Morgain, we'll share this peach. Don't

worry. The butterflies don't seem to have harmed it."
She took the precaution of wiping it off on the satin
reverse of her riding-habit's lapel before biting.

"I don't like peaches," Morgain said. Yet he took a
bite nonetheless. It crunched. The boy's expression
brightened. "I don't mind apples, though."

Clarice brought the fruit close to her eyes to be able
to focus on it properly. She could have made a mistake
in the dining room and taken the wrong fruit, but even
her nose, brushed by fuzz, knew the difference in scent
between apples and peaches. This was, indubitably, a
peach.

Except when Morgain took a bite. Clarice made no
comment. She had a feeling that if she started exclaiming over every peculiar circumstance, her voice would
be down to a mere croak before morning ever dawned.

"Which way now, Morgain?"

He wiped his mouth on his sleeve. "Not the road, I
think. It's too obvious. And we most certainly want to
stay out of those mountains, if you want to avoid your
mother."

"I think that is wise." Clarice closed the bandbox,
wondering what would appear when next she opened it.
There were still butterflies about, though most had gone
off to sup on the flowers in the fields on either side of
the track.

As Clarice and Morgain set off through the field below them, crushing wildflowers underfoot by the scent,
Clarice dared not give her thoughts full rein. Like a
horse galloping back to a familiar stable, they returned
time and again to Dominic. Would he suffer for having
lost her? She naturally discounted his protestations of
undying love. His fancy for her would no doubt soon
burn out, for so violent a flame could not long survive
the loss of its fuel.

Clarice nodded to herself, thinking herself most wise,
though her experience was somewhat lacking. She resolutely ignored the pain in her own heart, attributing it
to the peach. It hadn't been ripe enough, she thought,

though forced to admit that it would be the first fruit of
any kind she'd eaten lately that had proved to be less
than perfection.

No, she was concerned solely with King Forgall's reaction to the loss of his "hostage." She hoped he would
not punish Dominic too severely. She did not pretend to
understand males of any species—except perhaps
horses—but thought that the king and the knight seemed
to have a rapport based on respect. She expected that
Forgall would understand that Dominic could not have
watched her every instant and therefore be lenient. It
would be a great shame if so brave and vigorous a knight
were injured by her escape. Of course, she'd never see
him again. Strange how her eyes could prick with tears
at the thought of never knowing what became of him.

"Watch out," Morgain said, catching her by the elbow.

"What is it?" Clarice asked, coming out of her reverie.

Morgain pointed. The field, smooth and easy to walk
in, came to an abrupt end. A brook, swollen as if with
rain, poured down a narrow defile. Even as Clarice
watched, the water seemed to dig itself a deeper channel.
Mud and stones were falling from the sides of the gully
as more and more water rushed in to augment the brook,
now more of a small river, which in turn created a
deeper and deeper ravine. The water looked black in the
moonlight, save where it boiled white in the presence of
some obstruction.

The two had to jump back as the very bank on which
they stood crumbled into the water. Clarice saw that
across the way, the field continued. The water that
blocked their path was a very new thing. She was willing
to wager that it had not been there five minutes. Surely
otherwise she would have heard the rumble of the rushing water no matter how involved her thoughts.

"As we are judging our route by difficulty, this must
be the right way," Clarice said to Morgain. She had to
raise her voice to be heard.

"There must be a way across. The Fay fight fair."

Clarice saw nothing that could be used to cross. "Go upstream; I'll go down. Look for a fallen tree, some boulders in the water, anything we can use. . . ."

"I can try to conjure a—" he started to say, but Clarice covered his mouth with her fingertips.

"Don't. If every time you 'wish' for something, you lose a little bit of yourself, then don't. We shall manage very well as two mere mortals, never fear."

Morgain nodded and promptly walked away, his eyes turned toward the stream. Clarice followed suit, glad of her boots and glad too that the strange noise she'd heard had been left behind on the road.

She'd not gone far when Morgain came hurrying back, slightly out of breath and with the hem of his coat sopping wet. "What is it?"

"A tree has fallen across the ravine. It's not very big but it held me."

"You've been across already?"

"Yes. How else would I know if it would hold?"

Clarice didn't know whether to shake him or hug him. She did both, briefly. "You foolish child! If you'd fallen in, I never should have known what had happened to you!"

He freed himself, giving an impatient twitch to his coat. "Of course you would have. If you'd gone upstream it would be another pair of shoes, but as you headed *downstream* you would have been unfailingly certain to have seen me float by."

As usual, Morgain left her without a word to say. If she continued to scold him, he'd only think her unreasonable and she could not, for her own sake, agree with him. After a choked moment, she said, "Show me this tree."

He lead her back upstream and pointed with pride to the fallen tree. "That?" she said. "It's not a tree; it's a sapling! You crossed on that?"

"It's easy. I just knelt down and crawled across. There are a lot of branches to hold on to. I'll show you, shall I?"

He scooted across as nimble as a monkey, though the hem of his coat once again fell into the water, now rushing along in a frenzy of white foam only a few inches below the tree. It was not, however, until Clarice herself had ventured out that she realized the water was sweeping through the branches underneath her, making the already-flimsy "bridge" tremble as though afflicted with an earthquake.

She found herself frozen halfway across, clutching to the stem of a branch with tight-clasped fingers. Scolding herself in the harshest of terms did nothing to persuade her hand to loosen. Clarice felt the tree shift beneath her, yet still could not move.

"Aunt! The farther bank is crumbling! Please hurry!"

The sound of Morgain's terror prompted her to move. Very, very slowly, she proceeded. He reached out to help her over the last few feet, but she was so afraid that he would fall in, or that she would *pull* him in when she fell herself, that she ordered him brusquely back.

She crawled onto the solid ground, hampered by her heavy skirt's waterlogged hem. To Morgain's bright suggestion that she should stand up, she gave no reply but the shake of her head. Upon reaching the flowers, she collapsed, facedown. Fortunately, she'd taken the precaution of slinging the hatbox on its ribbon over her shoulder so that it rode on her back.

For a little while, she indulged in a fit of the vapors. At least, she thought that's what this trembling, palpitating, shuddering loss of control was. Even when the Rider had tried to drag her off, she'd not felt so feeble. That had been something to fight; this crossing had only to be accomplished.

She sat up, brushing ineffectually at the stains she'd collected across her bodice and face. Her hand dragged across her cheek with a sticky feeling. She sniffed at her fingers. A scent, sharp, spirited, and clean, caught her notice though she could not place it.

"I expect I am a sight to frighten horses," she said.

"No, except your hair is coming down a trifle," Morgain said, looking her over critically.

She tried to fix it as they continued. "What kind of tree was that?"

"A conifer."

"I beg your pardon?"

"An evergreen. I don't know what kind. Not English, I think. I noticed that the doors stood in a perfect grove of them."

"Then we are coming closer?"

Morgain debated with himself and then, reluctantly, shook his head. "I doubt it. We might be on the way for days."

"I trust not. We haven't that much food."

"Oh, I'm not worried about that. Shall we press onward?"

All Clarice wanted to do was lie on the nice soft ground until her mind stopped replaying those horrid moments above the water. But she considered that she'd shown Morgain enough of a bad example for one march. Assuming a cheerful expression, she sprang up and pronounced herself quite fit.

For a little while, the Wilder World threw no more obstacles in their way. Yet Clarice felt a growing awareness that they were not unwatched. There was nothing to see, and the sounds she'd heard were not repeated, but all the same, she felt *eyes* upon her and had to resist turning about every moment to see who was there. It was an unnerving sensation.

The moon set, freeing the stars from the burden of her light. Clarice felt better too. Perhaps whatever watched them could not see so well without moonlight.

The beauty of the stars was magnificent, yet strange. Here the stars seemed more numerous than at home. She sought in vain for the constellations she knew—the Great Plow, the Crab, and the Virgin. It seemed as though the press created by thousands of other stars had crowded the constellations out of true so that they could no longer be distinguished as themselves.

Clarice saw, out of the corner of her eye, a few shooting stars come flying down. She turned to look with a gasp of pleasure. "Morgain, did you see that?"

"I saw nothing."

"Shooting stars, a whole group of . . . look! More." She raised her hands as though to catch them. "Aren't they beautiful! I've never seen so many fall all at once."

She stopped to stare. Morgain trudged on, never raising his face to the sky. She had almost to trot to catch up. "I always think they should not be silent," she said. "So much strength and beauty . . . I am reminded always of Herr Handel's *Music for the Royal Fireworks*. It would only be right. . . . Look! Even more of them."

These two whizzed round like Roman candles before flying off into the unknown. "Odd," Clarice said, then amended her comment. "Odd for anywhere but here."

"We should go on."

"In a moment," she said absently.

"At least let us reach some cover."

"Cover? It's not going to rain, Morgain."

The star-shower had increased to no less than once a second. Clarice stood with her hands clasped against her heart, a joyful smile on her lips. The light shed by the stars as they zipped past flickered the way a lamp set in a window does when viewed by a rider on a fast horse among trees.

"Let us go on," Morgain said.

Clarice was touched by the nervousness of his tone. "Of course, Morgain," she said, instantly feeling guilty for having wasted even a few moments at a standstill, no matter how awe-inspiring the reason.

No sooner had she taken one step forward than the first fireball zoomed in to land with a stunning crash not a hundred yards away. Clarice staggered backward as a powerful wind kicked up, blowing dirt into her dazzled eyes and roaring in her ringing ears. Flames began to devour the flowers.

"Run!" Clarice shouted.

Fifteen

~

"Hurry, before the flames grow too violent!"

She took the lead, snatching Morgain's hand up in hers and fleeing for all she was worth in the direction of the flames. "You can't mean to go right through," Morgain shouted, suddenly reverting to nine-year-old boy. "We'll be burnt up!"

Another meteor plowed into the earth behind them, setting the land there alight. Clarice caught a glimpse of a glowing red ball, covered over with what looked like burned black lace. "So we will, even if we stay here! Come on!"

Morgain made no more protests. He clung tight to his aunt's hand and ran when she did. He knew how to scramble through a turn too, for one of her lightning changes of direction. The stars were falling thick and fast now. Clarice had little time or taste to admire them. She guessed that they had no natural origin, any more than had the brook. Could the Fay-King manipulate even the heavens?

The fires caused by the fallen stars gave off surprisingly little smoke, yet there was an acrid smell and taste in the air that reminded Clarice of the odor of an oil lamp when the metal grows hot. Ahead of her was an ever-increasing wall of fire that seemed to laugh as it licked out with its many long, red tongues. Clarice looked at it and felt only defiance in her heart. "They couldn't stop me with water; they'll not stop me with fire, though it contain every devil in hell."

She took her nephew's face in her hands. He looked white, his eyes rolling toward the flames like a frightened horse's. She bellowed in a low, intense tone calculated to penetrate the ceaseless roaring of the fire. "It's just another obstacle, Morgain. Don't worry. 'The greatest treasure has the largest lock,' eh?"

His gaze locked onto hers. He seemed to realize that he was giving way to his emotions and tried to pull himself up. His high boy's voice came clearly to her ears. "That theory sounded very comfortable back at the Manor. It brings me no ease now."

"Have you a handkerchief in your pocket, Morgain?"

He groped in them, saying "What have you in mind, Aunt? I don't really want to blow my nose just now." He found a grubby cloth in his coat and handed it to her.

"Not that." She folded the handkerchief into a triangle and tied it around his eyes. "Do you remember two years ago when the Randolphs' stable caught fire?"

"They blindfolded the horses . . . Aunt, I'm not a horse."

Clarice led him by the hand, closer and closer to the wall of fire that raged before them. Though Morgain made no sound, she could tell by the way he dragged on her hand how much he hated this.

When they stood within leaping distance of the fire-curtain before them, Clarice stopped so suddenly that Morgain stepped on her heel. "What a fool I am!" she said in wonder. As though in answer, the noise died.

"What is it, Aunt Clarice?"

"Don't you feel it, Morgain? There's no heat! As near as we are standing, our hair should be catching but there's no heat!"

He yanked the dirty cambric down from his forehead.

Staring with half-closed eyes at the terrifying flames, he held out one thin, wavering hand. The dancing light played over it but it was not only unscorched but not even warmed.

"They don't want us dead," Clarice said. "They only want to slow us down"

"We shan't let them," Morgain said with great determination. "Come along, Aunt."

Despite his grim resolve, he could hardly bring himself to pass through the fire. There was too great a disparity between what his eyes perceived and what his mind told him. His eyes gave him the information that he would surely be turned instantly to ash if he entered the fire, though his mind told him that without heat the fire could not consume him.

"I'll go first," Clarice said.

"No!" He had his arms wrapped tightly about his shoulders as though he were cold.

"Then together?"

"Yes. Together."

Morgain was no lightweight. Naturally stocky, he enjoyed his meals and did not exercise as much as a less-studious boy might have done. Yet with love in her heart to give her strength, Clarice lifted her nephew up, rather awkwardly, his legs dangling, and carried him past. His face was buried against the folds of her shawl so that he did not see the fire swirl about them.

Clarice saw everything as they pressed into the heart of the fire. Red flames were followed by butter yellow, succeeded by a blue like the flash of a diamond, and finally a white so brilliant that it made the hottest summer sun seem dim. All the flames seemed to bow and sway to some internal rhythm of remarkable speed. For an instant, she seemed to be privileged to hear it, taken at a faster tempo than any she'd ever imagined possible, a primitive music of drums and more drums. It would be so easy to fall into step and forget that her goal was to be free.

There seemed to be words in the song, words that

embraced the destructive powers of fire, how even the world's greatest cities were slaves to its powers, both of creation and of destruction. Man cannot build without me, it seemed to say, but what he builds I shall destroy and take pleasure in destruction.

Clarice struggled through, her arms and back aching from carrying Morgain. When she stepped through the last of the fire, she stumbled. Catching herself, she said, "You can get down now."

"I'm sorry," he said bitterly as he stood on his own two feet. He jerked the handkerchief from around his neck and stuffed it into his pocket. "I should be a help to you, not more of a hindrance."

"You are, my love. I never should do these things if not for you. We'd better hurry on."

She realized quickly that, though she could walk, hurrying was not in her power. The muscles of her legs twitched and pulsed every time she tried to go beyond a steady pace. She remembered reading an account of the recent war in France which described how soldiers on the march could lose all sense of feeling in their legs and yet continue on in a kind of trance far beyond what one must suppose they could endure. She did not complain, knowing that her pride would not permit her to plead weakness when her nephew kept on.

After a long time, they reached the shelter of a line of trees. It had been on the horizon for ages, though they never seemed to come any nearer to it. Morgain sank with a sigh onto the mossy ground beneath the first tree. "Thank God," he said. "I've a blister on my heel the size of a shilling!"

"Why didn't you say something?"

"What could you do if I had, Aunt? I'm not going back to that house."

"No, of course not. Are you hungry?"

"Starved. I always wake up hungry in the middle of the night and it must not be far off that now."

Though she approached the now-battered bandbox with trepidation, nothing flew out when she took off the top. She served out the rolls and the cakes. A few leaves swirled down from the tree so she put the lid back on the box.

"It's strange we can't see the fires from here," she said, thoughtfully chewing.

"They've probably gone out. Once the People knew we'd not be stopped by it, they had no further need for it. Naturally, they'd drop it."

Clarice thought again of Dominic. Would the Fay-King decide he had no further use for him? The thought sent a shiver through her. She tugged her shawl more closely about her. "Shall we stay here for what's left of the night?"

"No. I think we should press on."

"You are tired, and so am I."

"If we rest, we'll be caught."

"But we can't go for days without sleep. You rest first and I'll keep watch. Then we'll change. For pity's sake, Morgain," she said in reply to his mute stubbornness, "I'm dropping with exhaustion."

"All right. Pass me a peach, please."

She opened the box and stared in confusion at the contents. Instead of seeing their dwindled supplies, she saw no less than had been there before they'd eaten. Each of them had eaten one roll stuffed with mushrooms. She'd had one cake; Morgain had eaten two. Now everything was in the same quantity as before. Even the first peach they'd eaten had been replaced. In addition, someone had put in a crystal flask stoppered by a cork. The liquid in it sparkled and not just because of the faceting of the crystal. "Somebody is helping us," she said.

"Good," Morgain replied. "I was hungrier than one roll, anyway."

The miracle reoccurred after he'd eaten another. All Clarice had to do was replace the lid of the bandbox. When she removed it, there would be the food replaced. Unfortunately, and she hated to complain, it was always the *same* food. She foresaw a time when they'd be dreadfully fed up with mushroom rolls, pink cakes, and peaches.

Uncorking the bottle, Clarice took a cautious sniff. Something vaguely lemony but with a tingle as of effervescence. Sipping, she smiled. There was no possibility of growing bored with this "lemonade." It danced on her tongue and seemed to put renewed heart into her. Plus, no matter how much she drank, the level in the bottle never grew less.

Morgain drank too, and afterward had an arrested, thoughtful look on his face. After a moment, he started stripping off his shoe and stocking. Clarice didn't even have time to demand of him what he was doing before he'd taken the crystal flask and dribbled some of the drink over the shocking great blister on his heel. No sooner had the liquid touched the skin than it healed, leaving not even a callus behind.

"Who is helping us?"

"I know, I think. But I don't dare say his name. If anyone should be listening, he might be punished."

"Wise." She took another swallow immediately after Morgain finished. "You know, I don't feel tired anymore. Perhaps I was just hungry."

"That must have been it," he said decisively, putting on his footwear. "I'm not tired anymore either and I wouldn't be surprised if we are much closer to the doors than I thought. Don't know why I'm always such a pessimistic ass."

"I don't know why either," Clarice said, and the two of them laughed as though she'd said something anthology-worthy.

She retained just enough sense to realize that their behavior was growing increasingly devil-may-care. She forgot the bandbox when she and Morgain started to press on through the trees and had to hurry back for it. Something moved in the corner of her eyes as she bent down for it, but when she turned her head, nothing was to be seen or heard. "Hello? Hallooo?" she called. "Is anyone there, friend or foe, Fay or mortal?"

No answer came but the rustle of sudden breeze among the treetops. They were very tall, those trees, with feathery leaves that gave the slender trees the appearance of a Directoire female—immensely long, thin bodies with huge bonnets over all. Everything below them was draped in shadows deeper even than the night.

"Oh, well," she said, tripping over tree roots on her way back to Morgain. She couldn't find him which, she dimly felt, should have filled her with terror. Instead, she sang the once-nonsense rhyme of Mag Mell and went wheeling on through the night. The closely interwoven tree branches seemed to open before her, yet when she looked behind they seemed more impenetrable than ever.

Then she came out into the clearing and saw the doors.

They stood alone. No wall touched them, though they were big enough for a cathedral. At least four times the height of a man, they were covered with sinuous vines that crossed and recrossed themselves so often that not even a finger could have traced a single line to its end. When she tried to trace a vine with her eyes, her head spun.

Amidst the vines, she saw small animals and birds, faces mortal and Fay and things that she could not recognize as either animal or sentient but some strange mingling of both. There were flowers among the vines and insects tending the buds. Some flowers looked like the stylized lotus of Egypt while she saw as well the lotus of China. She also saw roses, hibiscus, lilies, and something not unlike the treacherous bellflowers of South America which lure insects to their doom with a combination of sweet sap and irresistible odors.

The doors stood slightly ajar, just as Morgain had drawn them. In the gap, she saw a strip of clear blue sky smiling above a house that she knew as well as she knew her own face. A scent blew through the opening, the concentrated dusty sweetness of the moor in high summer.

Clarice took an involuntary step toward what she was yearning for. But she couldn't leave without Morgain.

"Morgain! I've found them! Come on, Morgain, do!"

"There's no need to shout, my dear."

She knew that smooth, suave voice. Then a dapper creature moved against the background of the dark trees. She could see every detail of his rich costume because he seemed to glow with his own inner light.

"King Morgain?"

"Yes. 'Tis I, myself."

"Where's Morgain Half-Fay?"

"Safe, my dear."

"Has he gone through the doors?"

"Not yet." He came closer. "I see you are admiring our doors. They are magnificent, aren't they? Even older than I myself. Some say they are older than the People, but that's impossible. Boadach saw the first sunrise. He was Eldest and most fit to be King of all our People."

"Are you in league with my mother?" she asked, forgetting to guard her tongue.

"Perish the thought! I owe my allegiance to Forgall; he hath it all. Well, nearly all," he added with a flexible wriggle of his shoulders. "I do save a particle for my family."

"If you know where Morgain is, you must send him through the doors."

"I shall, if it be his desire."

He held out his hand and Morgain appeared just beyond his fingertips. He seemed unharmed, still with a dazzled look in his eyes. Clarice hurried to him and clasped her arms around him. "We mustn't become separated again, dear heart."

"No," he said quite loudly. More softly, almost on the level of thought, he whispered, "Be careful."

Clarice released the boy. "We must thank you, King Morgain, for your assistance tonight."

"I?" he said, with something of a nervous glance at the sky.

"I thought it strange that there should be a convenient

tree fallen across the flood and no heat in the fire? Then there was the food. . . ."

"No one wants you dead, my dear. You have more value living." He smiled at them. "But we were talking about the doors. They are our main portal between the Living Lands and the Realm of Mortality. Some say they should be closed and sealed forever; that this would close all the portals—and we have many and a many throughout your world. But no one has ever succeeded in locking the Great Doors. I, for one, cannot repine, for through the doors I have lost my only son, and found my only grandchild."

He turned to his grandson. "You are the light of my life. I watch you through the Veil between your world and mine. There is so much of me in you. Stay. Let me teach you to control the powers that are your birthright. You may command all material, the birds of the air, the beasts of the field. Stay."

Morgain had been looking fixedly at the opening between the doors until his grandfather had begun to speak to him. "You are kind, Grandsire. But this is not my world and I will not stay in it."

"You don't understand what you are giving up. You can be more than a man."

"But a man is all I wish to become. A man like my father. He made a choice, Grandfather. So must I."

"And I." The lesser king bowed his head. "I have made a bargain with Matilda. The life of my grandson for the return of her daughter."

"What?" Clarice looked up, for suddenly the empty woods were full of soldiers. She caught a glimpse of a banner, pale gray and empty of any device. "Run for the doors, Morgain!"

"Yes, run! Both of you," said a deeper, richer voice. Clarice turned her head, searching for the owner of that voice.

"Dominic?"

As though a black velvet curtain parted, he stepped out of the void. She could see his right leg swinging forward, but the rest of his body was hidden for a moment, until the other half of emerged from nothingness. It was as if he had been born in that moment from the night itself. In his hand, he bore a sword that flickered with the blue flames of the stars.

A hissing arose from the woods. Even King Morgain took a step back.

"Run, Morgain," Dominic growled again. "You, too, Clarice. Run!"

Clarice's nephew was in no doubt as to which Morgain he meant. With a war-whoop he raced across the grass toward the doors. Clarice followed after a stunned moment, snatching her skirt up in her hands.

Contrarily, the opening between the doors looked smaller and smaller as she raced near. Morgain, unhampered by skirts, jumped through the gap first. He disappeared against the blue sky.

Clarice was within a few feet when a whistling sound came through the air. Suddenly, she found herself falling, her feet tangled in some kind of sticky cord. She put out her hands to break her fall and felt a meteor of pain shoot up her arm as she landed hard.

Trying to stand up, she heard Dominic cry out, "Come on, you worthless hounds. See how dies a Son of Men!"

"No!" she gasped. This time, when the whistling came out of the night, the cord wrapped about her upper body. When she fell again, she could not even break her fall with her hands. She struck her head on the edge of a door, and the sounds of battle faded in her ears.

Clarice awoke with a feeling of well-being that had nothing at all to do with how she felt physically. There, she was quite certain that she had a blackened eye at the very least, as well as a tremendous headache. When she moved her right wrist incautiously, it told her in no uncertain terms that it was bruised and swollen. Yet, despite these ills, her heart floated in her breast, light and joyful. Morgain had made his escape.

For the first time, she awoke in a room that was not

even a close copy of her own. She lay in a white-clothed bed big enough for her and all her relations. "Even their horses," she said aloud and smiled. But her happy memory was soon lost as she wondered what had happened to Dominic.

She remembered him standing in the wood, illuminated by the blue fires of the sword he held in his hand. As he raised it above his head, the flames had poured over the blade like oil set alight. He'd proclaimed his willingness to fight and he'd urged her to run through the doors. What had happened to him after?

Clarice fought with her mind. The sense had been knocked out of her, yet images flashed behind her eyes. There must have been moments of waking when she'd looked about her. Now, though, she could make no sense of what she saw. A cold glint as of diamonds, the whisper of a sweeping skirt over a stone floor, a ringing laugh she seemed to know well. . . .

The only thing to do was to go in search of the truth.

Sitting up, she took notice of her surroundings. The big bed was furnished with every luxury, from deep down pillows to silken cream sheets spread over with white cashmere coverlets. The sheer bed curtains were of the finest gauze, scented with honeysuckle, and scattered over with precious gems. The beams of clear sunshine through these were dazzling, something out of a faery tale. As she turned to climb out of bed, the curtains parted as though held back by invisible hands.

Her feet sank into a carpet of silken threads, white, ivory, and silver blended to create a tapestry picture of the goddess Diana and her hounds on a hunt. It was large enough and sublime enough to hang on a king's wall— here it was no more than a bedside rug.

The room was vast and round, with pillars of pale pink marble set in a semicircle around the bed. More gauze curtains hung between them, glittering as they swayed in a draft she could not feel though she wore the lightest of cambric and lace night-attire. As she walked away from the bed, a set of curtains opened magically, to reveal beyond them a fountain playing musically above a pool.

Sticky from her night's battles, Clarice approached with eagerness. The fountain was created entirely of gleaming *blanche-de-chin* porcelain, as white and stainless as a maiden's thought. As she came nearer, the water pouring from the jar held by a statue of a bay-leaved crowned Daphne began to steam lightly. The scent of honeysuckle grew stronger as frothy bubbles appeared in the water.

Clarice had no sooner put her hands up to untie the laces of her pale pink nightgown than they began to untie themselves. It rather tickled. The gown slipped from her shoulders and vanished. Clarice began to feel that she was not alone. She only hoped her invisible servitors were female.

The water was divine. She'd never in her life taken a really hot bath. Water brought up from the kitchen in brass cans was usually no more than warm currents in a by-and-large frigid tub. And this was more water than a hundred servants could have brought in an entire day!

The instant she decided to wash her hair, a crystal flagon of shampoo flew out of nowhere to hover a few inches in front of her. She hesitated, recalling that the last thing she'd taken from a crystal flask had lead to disaster when it made her throw away her common sense.

The flagon just sat there in midair, unwavering, unwearying. She decided that she could take a risk when alone that she could not when someone she cared for was nearby. When she put out her hand, instantly the handle rose, the spout tipped, exactly as though a person held the flagon. A pellucid stream of soap poured into it. When she chose to rinse away the foam, the water from the fountain ceased to cause bubbles and ran clear.

Yet when she arose from the pool, her hair and her body were dry. She felt both clean and refreshed, yet did not require the use of a towel. Putting up a hand, she surmised that her hair had been arranged without her being aware of it in a high knot on the crown of her head, with soft tendrils spiraling down around her face.

"What of clothes?" she asked.

Almost before the words had left her lips, a pair of stockings and a superbly embroidered chemise appeared, closely followed by a huge petticoat-hoop. It was not the same shape as, for instance, English court dress, which demanded a narrow hoop. This was entirely circular and quite stiff.

Clarice thought she'd look a perfect scarecrow in such a strange petticoat, but as there was no one present to argue with, she climbed into the thing. Then came whalebone stays, much more severe than those she usually wore. The invisible hands laced her until she could hardly draw enough breath to say, "Stop!"

Instantly, almost apologetically, the laces were loosened.

Then came the rest—a huge skirt of deep blue satin with a separate bodice to match. The blue was the exact shade of her eyes. It was figured over with diamond-shapes in gold thread. A pearl marked each corner. The sleeves of the bodice were slashed to show puffs of white satin beneath. The top and bottom of each slash bore a square emerald, flashing with a deep blue light, set off with more pearls at each corner.

Clarice had never worn clothes of such richness, or of such exquisite discomfort. The wide hoop about her waist weighed like a hundredweight of stones resting on her hips. Despite these clothes being so very unusual, Clarice felt certain she'd seen them before. Even the shoes that appeared, high-heeled, embroidered, and set with her cipher in pearls on the toes, seemed very familiar.

It was not, however, until the pearl-studded ruff appeared that Clarice understood that she was being dressed in the style of the Elizabethans. She resembled in every detail a full-length portrait of the Honorable Miss Antonia Stavely, whose beauty had won her the enmity of the Virgin Queen. The only difference was that Clarice did not remember Antonia wearing quite so many fabulous jewels.

Diamond and tortoiseshell combs worked their way gently into her hair. A flawless emerald, as big as the palm of her hand, set in rock crystal carved into a dragon's claw, attached itself onto her bodice, linking together the drape of three ropes of pearls, each pearl the size of the end of her little finger. Rings, each formed from a single gem, insinuated themselves onto her fingers. She noticed that there was neither gold nor silver, nor indeed any metals, used in the construction of these marvels.

When yet more jewels appeared, bracelets to peep out from beneath the rich lace cuffs at her wrists, Clarice said, "Enough!"

Rather meekly, a fan and a long pomander showed themselves. She took the fan, for she was hot under all the weight of her dress. The pomander, a beautiful thing of filagreed gold, slunk away. "Now, if you don't mind, I'm hungry."

The "bath" curtains parted and Clarice passed through into the chamber where her bed was. It was difficult to walk until she realized she must take slow and careful steps instead of moving with her usual speedy cadence.

She noted that the bed had been made in her absence. Another pair of curtains parted to show a marble table set with service for one in a room that was draped in pale blue silk, a perfect foil for her gown. A chandelier of exquisite form and style with not only the pendants but also the chains made of crystal hung above the satinwood table.

"What a pity there's no one to admire the picture I make," she said.

The instant she sat down, awkwardly managing her farthingale, harp music began to play. For the first time, Clarice seriously considered whether she were dead. Or perhaps she'd fallen asleep at some amazingly dull London soiree, just as the innocents in their first Season had begun to show off their "accomplishments" for eligible

young men and their mothers. Several of those she'd
known in her own callow days had been prone to inflict
ghastly discords upon her sister schoolroom misses. But
no, that could not be true, since assiduous pinching did
not awaken her.

There was nothing to do but accept what was going
forward and eat something. She did full justice to everything offered, though, mindful of Dominic's warning,
she touched no wine. If the lemony drink of last night
had appeared, she would have smashed the bottle.
Everything tasted so good that it would have tempted a
far less capricious appetite than hers. She would need to
recruit her strength if she was going to search for and
find Dominic.

At the end of her meal, an unnoticed curtain at the
far end of the "dining room" parted, showing a door at
the end. Thus far, no evil had befallen her. She had
bathed, been clothed and fed, in short—all her physical
needs had been met. Some quality in the shampoo or
the water had healed the cut on her head and so soothed
her black eye that she could no longer feel it pull when
she smiled. A long sleep had restored her stamina, of
that she felt certain.

Yet despite being physically improved, the closer she
came to the farthest door, the more nervous she grew.
It was the precise opposite of how she'd felt upon awak-
ening. She would have gladly traded this apprehension
for the stiff wrist and black eye of this morning so long
as they came with morning's optimism.

This door did not open at her approach. Growing fanciful, Clarice thought it looked as though it would like
to, but could not. She raised her hand and rapped on the
door with the largest and least graceful finger-ring. It
made a slight thudding sound, as though someone had
flicked a fingernail against a piece of cracked porcelain.

"Awake at last!" cried the one voice in either world
that she could never forget or mistake for any other.
"Come in, my dearest love, and greet me!"

The door flew open. Greatly hesitating, Clarice

crossed the threshold into a room painted a sweet peach.
Rising from a damask-covered armchair was a little
dark-haired lady, slightly plump, dressed with the awe-
inspiring gorgeousness of Good Queen Bess.

   "Mother?"

Sixteen

～

Matilda Stavely said, "Surely they told you that I am alive?"

"It is still a shock." Clarice came closer, slowly. "I am happy to see you."

"Happy? Yes, but not overjoyed. Not happy as I am happy. Well, I expected that. They have poisoned your mind against me, all of them. It will take time for you to see things as they really are."

Clarice said only, "You look very well, Mother."

"Thank you, my dearest. No. Do not embrace me." Matilda shrank from her daughter's outstretched arms and turned her face away from the kiss Clarice offered. She said, "It is not that I do not wish you to. How I have missed you! But you know, I am one of the People now and you are still a mortal."

"Yes, Mother. I hardly know what I am doing."

"Sit down, Clarice. Here, at my right hand. There is much to discuss."

Another armchair, exactly like the first, slid across the floor. Turning a merry little pirouette on one leg, it stopped next to Matilda. Clarice sat down, looking about her in wonder. Her mother's room was not like the one she'd awakened in, nor was it darkly paneled with rushes on the floor in keeping with their attire. Rather, this was a simple, modern room with every ornament and furnishing the epitome of neatness, propriety, and fashion. It was not a copy of Lady Stavely's own sitting room at the Manor, though it had the same feeling. There were no silver goods or mirrors. Clarice wondered how her mother survived without anything shining in which to observe her reflection.

Matilda turned to her daughter, resting her chin upon two fingers. "I should not have thought it possible that you could grow more lovely than you were at sixteen. Yet I do believe your hair is slightly richer in tone and your figure and complexion are certainly improved."

"I don't eat as many sweets as I did then," Clarice said, wishing she did not feel so defiant. Why was it enough for her mother to say "white" for Clarice to maintain through thick and thin, whether true or false, that "black" was the only choice?

"That's good. You were such a little podge when you were a baby!"

Clarice dredged up a smile. "Mother, what has happened? How did I come here? And where, by the way, *is* here?"

"This is my home and yours too, now. My people brought you here last night. They know how to please me, for they have tasted of my displeasure."

"There was a man there, last night. Dominic Knight. What happened to him?"

Matilda did not seem to hear the question. "We will be together forever now, my love. You have no idea— no one who has not been a mother *could* know—how much I have longed to have you near me again. You are my reason for living," Matilda said, smiling misty-eyed.

"Why, then, did you leave me?"

"Do you blame me for that? What choice had I? My reputation had been blasted, my husband was dead—he who should have protected me!"

Clarice felt she must correct her mother's interpretation of things, no matter what the cost. "Mother, you had taken a lover who robbed you. That was hardly Father's fault!"

"I know who has told you these lies. That slut, Felicia. She's just like her whore of a mother. Has she tried to turn you against me?"

"No, Mother. You forget. I was there when it all came out."

"Ah, but you were a child. You couldn't understand the loneliness of my heart. I will explain it all to you. But not now. Now, let me look at you. My eyes have been hungry for the sight of you. How beautiful you are in that gown! Do you like it? I created it for you myself."

"Yes, Mother. It's beautiful."

"Then you should say 'thank you,' don't you think?"

"Thank you, Mother."

"Charmingly done! I'm so glad you've not forgotten your manners without me there to guide you." She laughed. Clarice could not remember her mother ever laughing before. The most she'd ever done in her mortal life was lift the corners of her thin mouth very slightly and say, "most amusing."

Clarice said, "It's a pity I cannot see myself in it."

"Why can't you?"

"There are no mirrors here."

"No, not as mortals know them. But we can see ourselves easily enough. I will show you later when I give you the other gowns I have for you. That will be a delightful way to pass the time before bed. I have so looked forward to having the dressing of you again. These new fashions—pshaw! No form, no elegance, no art!"

"You keep up with modern taste?"

"Of course. I may be a Fay, but I want to remain à la mode, when I can."

"But these clothes are surely of an earlier time than ours."

"I am not restricted to any one style, my love. Look . . ."

She rose to her feet, her magnificent skirt of pale orange satin rustling. Even the back was embroidered and set with flashing opals. The ruff behind her neat dark head was huge, made of transparent net studded with diamonds. Yet Clarice had hardly noticed her ostentatious display, any more than she would have stopped to admire the beauty of a cobra's rippling scales.

A blink later, her mother wore an Indian sari of the same orange but in silk, shot through with golden threads. A diamond the size of her fist hung about her neck suspended from a graduated rope of other diamonds, while rings not only covered her hennaed hands but also her painted toes.

The next instant, she wore the ruffles and furbelows of a Pompadour, still in orange. Then an Egyptian costume of pleated orange linen, her eyes brightened by blue shadow, the great white and red double crown of the Upper and Lower Kingdoms of her head, sinuous ornaments of gold twisting around her arms and a great collar, intricately laid with bright enamel, about her neck. Even her sandals were of gold.

Returning to the dress of the Elizabethan court, she said, "Anything is possible, my dearest one. I will do anything for you now that we are together once more. Nothing will ever separate us again."

Matilda looked away from her daughter, her eyes growing slightly glazed as she stared at nothing. In a quiet, steady tone, she said, "I'm quite angry with Forgall and his ilk. How dare they keep you from me!"

Clarice could not recall a time when that look, that tone hadn't been a signal that meant "go warily." Not even ten years without her mother had been enough to overcome her instinctive shrinking away as though by meekness she grew less noticeable. But she was not a child now. She need not be cowed by harsh looks or words.

"Mother, where is Dominic Knight?"

"Who? Oh, your guard."

"My friend, Mother."

"He's no friend to you! He was a jailer, mewing you up in a prison for no fault of your own. Oh, Forgall shall pay for his wickedness! Come with me, child. You are free now and you must see what the future holds for you."

She crossed the floor and threw back some heavy damask curtains. A pair of French windows had been concealed behind it. Dazzling sunlight poured into the room as Matilda opened the doors. "Look out here, my dearest. They are waiting to greet you."

"Who are?"

"Look out."

Clarice approached the opening. A semicircular balcony clung to the side of the building. The instant she stepped foot upon it, a great noise of cheering arose. She walked out and grasped the stone railing.

She looked down into a square courtyard full of cheering people. They were a long way down, for her mother's balcony was near the top of the tallest tower. The walls were of gray stone, deeply scored. On the topmost blocks, pennons of silk rippled in a sweet mountain breeze. They bore no heraldic marks.

"Is that your army down there, Mother?"

"Yes, dear. Wave to them. Let them see you."

Clarice acknowledged the cheers of her mother's troops with a sheepish wave. The shout that went up slapped the walls with an echo that seemed to treble the volume. The glass in the French windows rattled.

She looked down, trying to distinguish individuals in the crowd. There must have been several hundred people looking back at her. Glancing at her mother, she said, "You have a great many followers."

"Not so many as Forgall, but enough. Look . . ." One instant, Matilda's be-ringed hand was empty; the next it held a round lens in a carved wooden frame. She handed it to Clarice. The wood felt slick in a very ancient way, as though it had been smoothed by the fingers of many.

Holding it before her eyes, Clarice jumped in surprise when the faces in the crowd became clear. That was astonishing enough but when she looked closely, she saw something else. Where was the astounding beauty of the Fay? She saw pale, pinched faces, dull eyes and hair, and their smiles showed discolored, pointed teeth. Their laughter was full of cruel knives. Some of them were not even Fay but the kind of creatures that filled Morgain's fantastic maps. She saw claws, fur, feathers, beaks, and red eyes, sometimes all on the same being.

"Who are they?" she asked again.

"Fiends, mostly. There are quite a few Fay among them, disenchanted with Forgall's ways. Several of the more powerful Djinn have come to join us, together with their retinues. Wave again, my love. One should never neglect the little attentions that please one's servants."

Clarice concealed her shudder. Her mother's advice had been the same, years ago, when Clarice had first been waited on by Rose. She waved, even more reluctantly than before.

"Later," her mother said, "we shall have a progress through the castle. Many of them have brought gifts for you."

"How kind."

Matilda chuckled. "Don't say that until you have seen the gifts! But don't fret. You needn't keep any of them. Simply show that you are graciously inclined toward them and they will follow you to the seven corners of the Wilder World."

The sun went behind a cloud. Clarice looked up. There were dull, metallic gray clouds sweeping across the sky to the accompaniment of a low, whistling wind. She raised the seeing-lens up and saw with a sick feeling that something horrible was riding in the clouds. They had horses, as bony and desiccated as themselves, and they smiled down on her with bare-toothed approval.

Her mother reached out and slipped the glass from her hand. "Come in now, my love. The night is falling."

Clarice sat quietly while her mother talked about the future. Matilda paced restlessly, her skirt rustling, her hands gliding over each other with tiny *tings* as her rings met. "Everything will be as it was. We shall be together every day. There will be no Felicia to come between us. You will be all mine as you were when you were little. Only better. You can understand me now. You can rule the Living Lands at my side. Everyone will worship you as they once worshiped and adored Boadach's daughter."

"I thought you were intent on bringing Boadach back."

Matilda paused for an instant, as though checked in the mad rush of her thoughts. "I—I have every intention of trying," she said. "I may fail."

Clarice did understand her mother but thought that this was not the moment to say so. "Forgall is afraid you will succeed."

"You spoke with him? What did he tell you?"

"Only that you had barricaded yourself in this fortress and that you were gathering an army to overthrow him."

"So he tried to take you away from me and use you against me. Well, I hope he realizes how futile he has been!"

"Mother . . ." Clarice began, then changed her tone. If Matilda wanted to think of her as the pretty innocent she'd once been, conveniently ignoring the last ten years, perhaps it would be wise to humor her. Her mother's temper had never been even; Clarice doubted whether absolute power had created any softening.

She made her voice high and infantile. "I don't know why you don't like King Forgall. He was ever so nice to you, making you one of his People."

"Yes," Matilda said thoughtfully. "Yes, that was a great kindness. For a time, I was as happy as I had ever been in all my life. To know that no ill can ever touch you, that no harm can ever befall you again is beyond anything any mortal knows."

Matilda's face took on a glow like that Clarice had seen in the eyes of the members of Forgall's court. Her mother looked no more than seventeen, the harsh lines beneath her eyes fading, her chin losing its hard edge, the corners of her lips turning up instead of being grimly tucked back. Even her hair, sternly controlled in a jeweled net, seemed to soften and curl. Clarice saw her mother as she should be, tender, feminine, and attractive. It did not last.

Matilda said, "Yet he refused to grant me the one thing my heart most earnestly desired. There'd already been some talk about his bringing me into the Lands of the Living. I asked him if he were a king or a slave in his own kingdom. He told me that he could not act capriciously more than once every thousand years or so. I knew then that he was a weakling. Boadach would be a finer king than Forgall. Boadach will be grateful to me. He will grant my request."

"What 'request'?"

Matilda studied her daughter for a moment. Clarice found it difficult to keep her wide-eyed expression in place. "Don't trouble yourself over it, Clarice. You have nothing to do here but enjoy yourself. You have only to ask for whatever you want. Be frivolous. Be extravagant. The more you demand of me, the happier I shall be. I could never give you all I wanted before."

"Isn't there going to be a war?" Clarice asked, still artlessly.

"No. Forgall will give way to me now that I have you." Matilda smiled. "Are you happy to be with me again, my dearest?"

"Very happy, Mother. I have missed you." Clarice realized that this was true. With all her faults, Matilda remained her mother. Though she'd been impossible to please in her mortal life—and seemed no easier now— her approval still meant more to Clarice than that of any other person, with one exception.

"You'll never need miss me again. Now come with me. I want to show you those other gowns."

As Matilda had promised, after a time, they left the tower to walk among her people. Instead of descending long flights of stairs, Matilda opened a door and escorted

Clarice through. When she opened it again, they were standing on the hard-packed earth of the courtyard. A wave of sounds and odors struck Clarice with considerable force after knowing little in the past hours but sweet perfume and the tinkling of fountains. She had pleaded exhaustion and the stress of the night before to avoid trying on the roomful of clothes her mother had created for her.

As soon as the door opened, two Fay men stepped forward, bowing low in front of Matilda. They had a cold, dusty look about them. Clarice couldn't tell them apart until the tour was half-over. Then she noticed that Miship always nodded his head when he spoke, while Condigne shook his.

"Everything is proceeding according to plan, my lady," Miship said, nodding emphatically.

"It's a hard, hard task," Condigne added, mournfully shaking his head.

Clarice trailed behind her mother and her two subordinates, despite this tour being nominally for her. She couldn't help knowing that a great many eyes were upon her. Though the people and creatures they passed bowed to Matilda, their eyes followed Clarice. Some were smirking, others stern, some even leered. Those she passed by with a haughty expression, but for the rest she had a half-smile and a nod.

Her mother seemed to be in her element. She knew everyone's name and either knew what position they served in or appeared to know. She entered into everybody's interest, discussing recipes with the cooks or making a suggestion of the best way to resolve a conflict between a centaur and a satyr. After a glance from her dark eyes, the satyr did not look at Clarice a second time.

There were gifts, as Matilda had said. Food and wine for the most part, with a few other things. One footsoldier who came only to her shoulder gave her a cunningly braided thong for her hair while a cook gave her a wooden spoon covered with runes for improved sauces. These she accepted gratefully, while her mother, with surprising tact and gentleness, turned away the more inappropriate offerings.

As they walked down one of a dozen twisting passageways, Matilda said, "Now we come to the guard room. Accept here whatever they offer. They are the backbone of my army; without them, we are all lost." She turned to Miship and Condigne. "Stay without. I shall not be more than a few moments."

"Yes, my lady," Miship said, nodding.

"As you wish, my lady," Condigne said with a sigh and a shake.

Matilda paused before the doorway, breathing heavily. "Mother . . . ?"

"This room is full of iron and steel, Clarice. I bear it because I must yet it is difficult. Follow me."

The guard room was full of human soldiers, all of whom leapt to their feet, chanting some slogan as Matilda entered. She was more than gracious here, taking some extra time to thank them for delivering her daughter to her.

"Some of you have already heard the expressions of my heart. I am sure now that you see her dressed according to her station, you have a greater understanding of my concern."

Their cheers told her that they did. Clarice stood abashed, while Matilda applauded. An officer approached her, a bundle of black cloth in his hands. He bowed. "This belonged to the Rider of Vedresh. We are his heirs and wish it to be yours."

Abashed, Clarice said, "I'm sorry. . . ."

"You have nothing to reproach yourself with," the officer said. He appeared to be about thirty, with a prominent jaw and rather cold light blue eyes. His white-blonde hair was clipped close to his scalp. "The Rider knew the risks."

He shook out the cloak and draped it about her shoulders. Though made of wool, or something similar, it had no weight. The closure was a chain of metal links, each one in a stylized shape like an ear. "It serves to hide whatever sound you make as you pass by your enemies. They can still see you, but not if they do not know you are there."

Matilda said, "How kind! But I hope my daughter has no enemies here."

Clarice tried to thank the officer and men but they started cheering her so that her voice was drowned. Before the cheers died away, Matilda passed on, out of the room. Clarice followed her into a hall but before she could go on she heard a whisper, "Hist, my lady!"

"You want to speak to me?"

By his clothes and broken nose, he was another mortal soldier. He looked past her and listened behind him. "My name is Kevin O'Hannon and I'm as loyal a fellow as you'll find."

"I have no doubt of it," she said, her heart heavy. He looked so ordinary that she could have seen him on any London street corner or danced with him at any Assembly. If only she had . . . "Pardon me, Mr. O'Hannon, but my mother is out of sight and I don't know the fortress well enough. . . ."

"I'm not bargaining for a better position, my lady. It's that I'm a soldier and I have no stomach for torture."

"Torture?"

"Aye. That *werroeur* what came in with you last night. Now it may be that a fine lady like you don't care much what happens to a man once he's outlived his usefulness, but it's the sort of thing as leads to bad feelin' among us who serve. . . ."

"You're mistaken; you are. I do care. Where is he?"

"Held in the dungeon, 'course. No food today, nor water neither and that's the kind of treatment I mean. There's got to be a reasonable adherence to the rules o' combat or what ill befalls one soldier might fall on us all if the position were to be reversed, if you catch my meanin'."

"I do, Mr. O'Hannon."

"Not that I think we'll be undone, no. I'm loyal, I am.

But if Forgall were to get wind of how the boy's been treated, you see . . ."

"Will you show me where he is?"

He deliberated. "It may not be wise, but I will for the sake of your sweet face, my lady. Not just at the moment, though. Your lady mother's a good queen, but I'm not caring to catch the rough side of her tongue. Come back when you hear the doves fly past your window."

"There's no window in my room. . . ."

"Aren't you the silly though! Ask your mother to make you one. She'll do it quick enough to please you."

It was difficult to wait, knowing that Dominic was suffering from hunger and thirst. She'd already noticed, during her tour, that there was a fine grit or dust in the air that dried her mouth almost as soon as she'd stepped outside. She could only imagine that things were worse in a dungeon.

Once again in her chamber, Matilda's eyes lit up when Clarice expressed a wish for a window. She did not even have to state her carefully considered reasons for wanting one. "And a balcony!" Matilda said at once. "One just like mine."

After a brief consultation with herself, Matilda twiddled her fingers in the direction of the outer wall of Clarice's room. Surprised that such magic required neither a spoken spell nor any fierce faces of summoning power, Clarice almost missed the fact that a window had appeared. Triple pointed arches complete with Gothic tracery graced the wall, the center arch larger than the other two and containing the French windows.

"How lovely!" Clarice exclaimed quite naturally.

"Do you really think so? I have improved a great deal since I came to Mag Mell but it takes more practice than I have time for at present."

"You conjure as though you were born here," Clarice said. She could grant her mother that much praise.

She left one panel open so she might hear the whisper of bird wings in the night. Afraid that this would not be enough to awaken her, Clarice decided not to go to sleep that night. If only O'Hannon had been more specific about the time! Clarice didn't know if the "doves" flew at midnight or dawn. She had to be ready, though, the instant they flew past. Fortunately, her mother's method for traveling between her chambers and the ground floor was swift and silent.

Clarice's only worry was that Matilda, deprived of her maternal perquisites for so long, might come into gaze on her sleeping daughter. Naturally, Matilda had not conjured a lock for this bedroom. Passing the time by considering and discarding one excuse for being absent after another made a very poor stimulant. Thinking of Dominic, however, worked quite well.

She would not have thought that he could be defeated, yet if it meant his life had been spared, she could not grieve that he had been captured. She very much doubted that *he'd* see it that way. Smoothing her spotless linen nightgown over her hips, she wondered if she could convince him that life was sweet, then blushed for the wanton implication of her thoughts. She had liked the kiss he'd stolen and wished very much that he'd steal another one tonight. Then she caught sight of the pot of chocolate—kept magically warm—and the biscuits her mother had left in case Clarice grew peckish in the night and she sobered.

"Hunger and thirst," she whispered. "Oh, God, protect him until I can reach him!"

Despite her anxiety and determination, Clarice had fallen fast asleep by the time the doves flew past her window. She was awakened by one that had landed on her new balcony and was tapping its beak insistently against a stained-glass panel. The instant Clarice put her feet on the floor, the bird flew away. Was the expression of hurt disdain on the dove's face just her imagination?

"I'm up . . . I'm up. . . ." she called after the departing dove. It had looked at her the way Pringle did when she lazed the day away in bed under the pretext of a cold in the head.

Among all the apparel her mother had given her, there

had been a quilted overdress and a pair of thick boots. Though the night was not cold, some need inside her demanded warm clothing. The magic hands were quick to guess her needs. A deep reticule served to carry the chocolate and the biscuits. At the last moment, she took the cloak of silence too.

It was only after she reached the courtyard that she realized she had no notion of how to reach the guard room again. There'd been so many twisting corridors, so many flights of steps up and down, that her head had begun to go around long before the end of the tour.

A whisper out of the night roused her from trying to remember. "Is it yourself, then?"

"Mr. O'Hannon?"

A lantern unsheathed itself, showing a thin line of golden light. " 'Tis corporal, if you don't mind, my lady."

"Oh, excuse me, Corporal O'Hannon."

"This way, if you please. Clever of you to bring the Rider's cloak. May prove useful, yet. Mind the cobbles. They're a thought wet after the rain."

"What rain? I didn't notice any."

"You wouldn't a-way up there. But Queen Matilda's quite right to make it rain down here every evening. The filth some of these lads throw down 'ud make a dog sick, so it would. Mind your head here, my dearie . . . pardon me. My lady."

They went down a long flight of stairs, transversed a corridor and then down another flight. Torches hung on the walls, making the air thick with smoke. As they went, Clarice asked, "Is it all right to talk?"

"Oh, aye. But quietly."

"Why do you call my mother 'Queen'?"

"Isn't she one, then?"

"No, I don't think so."

"Ah, me. Well, this is my way of thinkin'. If she's not queen now, my callin' her so is flattery. If she will be queen soon, my callin' her so is but good practice." He chuckled softly. A moment later, he held up his hand to stop her. "Hist, whist! In that dark corner and not a word now!"

She heard the tramping of booted feet a few seconds later. Holding the dark hood of the cloak up to her face so that her pale skin would not be glimpsed, she saw a dozen soldiers tramp by the opening at the end of the corridor. Seeing their faces, she caught her breath.

Underslung jaws with protruding tusks, spiky hair or fur that came halfway down their noses, and short fingers with long, yellow nails was all she had time to glimpse but it was quite enough. A sour smell, like vinegar mixed with spoiled lard, drifted down to her.

Corporal O'Hannon leaned up against the lintel of the arched opening, apparently at ease, cutting his fingernails with a dagger. He raised a casual hand in greeting as the troop marched by. They did not challenge him.

After they'd gone by, he came back to her. "Fiends," he said, and spat. "I hate 'em."

"I can't believe my mother has welcomed such creatures into her army!"

O'Hannon shrugged. "They're good fighters, I don't say they're not. But they've no more sense of honor than does a fighting cock." He went and peered both ways down the corridor. "Come on then," he said.

He led her down a last, shorter flight of steps and then stopped a few stairs from the bottom. "Listen, my lady. There'll be a guard outside. I'll keep him busy. You pull the hood up over your face and creep by quiet as a ghost. When you see your friend, make sure he doesn't speak any louder than need be or his goose is cooked as well as me own."

"Won't the cell be locked?"

"And with what, my lady? Iron bars? Iron locks? You forget where you are."

O'Hannon, it seemed, had brought his own refreshments to the dungeon. As she slipped past the guard, who had his back to her anyway, she saw the Irishman offer the man a drink. The guard seemed only too glad to accept. From the rear he seemed quite human, but his voice sounded subterranean.

Clarice followed O'Hannon's instructions, but neither of them reckoned on the stone hinges of the door. The moment she pulled on the handle, they screeched. The guard started to turn around, saying, "What noise was that?"

Quick as thinking, O'Hannon said, "Sure, I heard it! It came from down the way there." He pointed into an intersecting hall. "An escape, d'you think?"

"I go to see. . . ."

"An' why not? With me here to keep watch over this 'un. I'll be glad to be doin' that for you."

The guard shrugged. "Not my fault if one escapes. This be my post."

"'At's right, my boy. Have another bitty sip now. Good for what ails you."

As the guard raised the flask to his lips, O'Hannon made a fierce face at Clarice. This time before she essayed the door, she sprinkled some of the hot chocolate on the hinges and, to make doubly certain, she held her cloak up before the hinges. She plainly heard a protest from the grinding stone, but the guard heard nothing this time. The cloak had muffled it.

Clarice slipped inside, leaving the door ajar and trusting to O'Hannon to keep the guard's attention. He'd brought her this far despite his proclaimed loyalty to her mother; Clarice did not hope that he'd overlook her smuggling out a prisoner. That would have to wait.

A torch burned with a flickering blue flame on the wall. It hardly deserved the name of light but it was better than nothing. The cell, cold stone on every side, smelled like the inside of a giant's boot. It was silent. Clarice had pictured rats but heard none of their characteristic noises. At least Dominic had been spared that much.

"Dominic?" she called softly, mindful of the guard just outside. "Dominic?"

"Who's there?" His voice was dry and hoarse. Clarice

had not known how worried she'd been until she heard his voice. Tears filled her eyes.

"It's Clarice."

"Clarice? Where?"

"Hush. Here by the door. I can't see you. . . ."

Then he was there before her, the light casting blue shadows onto his face. He looked hollow of cheek and eye, like something dead yet walking. Clarice didn't care. She held out her hands to him and, when he took them, moved close to him.

"I thought you were dead," she said.

"I'm not certain that I am not. Why would your mother keep me alive?"

"Kiss me, and tell me whether you live or not."

Seventeen

~

She couldn't even feel ashamed of her boldness. Not when he pulled her against him with such need, such longing. It was there in his hands, in the unsteady beating of his heart, in the sweet possession of his lips. He pressed his cheek against hers and said, "When I saw you fall, I thought you were dead."

"I thought you'd been killed. Mother wouldn't answer any of my questions."

They kissed again, sweetly, too glad just to be near one another to attempt arousing their passions especially under these circumstance. Her heart too full to speak seriously, Clarice said lightly, "Aren't you starving!"

"In more ways that one, sweetheart." Dominic chuckled. "I don't suppose you brought anything to eat?"

"That's why I came. Just a moment." She carried her bag over to a projection of stone glimpsed in the near-dark. The outside of the chocolate pot was sticky from drips and the sweet biscuits were somewhat crumbled. Dominic stared as though she'd laid out a feast.

He drank from the spout and choked a little. "I thought it was water. . . ."

"No. I didn't think . . . I'm sorry. I should have brought water."

"Never mind. I daresay this will put more heart into me than water or wine. I was told once the warriors of the Incas used to drink it before battle."

He ate nearly every crumb and drained the pot dry. "That's better. Now let's go."

"Go?"

"We'll escape. There's only one guard. . . . How did you get in here anyway?"

She told him about O'Hannon. Dominic sounded puzzled. "Why would he help you come to me?"

"He says he doesn't approve of treating you this way because Forgall might act in kind to his prisoners."

"And you say he's out there now, distracting the guard?"

"That's right." She clutched his arm when he would have gone past her. His muscles bunched beneath her hand as though he'd rip out of her grasp. But he did not. "I don't think he'll help you escape."

"He won't have the chance to deny me."

"Dominic, listen. I can't go now. If you escape, you leave me behind."

"What?"

"I can't go now. There are things I must discover first."

"I know what it is," he said. He took a deep breath. "I can smell strange perfumes on you and . . ." His hands slid over her arms but not in a caress. "New clothes? Are you so enamored of your mother's gifts that you are blind to her real intentions?"

Clarice squelched her hurt. "I hope you know me better than that. Like it or not, for better or for worse, she is my mother. I have to try to understand what she wants."

"Don't you know yet? She wants you. She wants to keep you here forever. That's what this is all about. She asked Forgall to make you a Fay, will you or nil you. He wouldn't do it so she's gone to war to force him."

Though Clarice wanted to tell him he was wrong, everything rose up in her to say that he was right. That was why her mother had been so evasive even while she spoke of their glorious future. What future could there be without her becoming an immortal like Matilda? "How could she have thought Forgall would do it?"

"Forgall was besotted by her from the moment she interrupted their revels. He'd do anything for her, except bring you across against your will."

"I hadn't realized that he felt like that about her."

"He probably doesn't now. Once he'd realized what she was after, it must have killed his affection for her. I don't think she cares for him at all. She only wants you by her side for always. But can you say that she truly loves you?"

"She is my mother."

"But does she love *you*? The woman I love has a soul far more beautiful than her face. Did your mother ever love your indomitable spirit, your sweet heart, your humor? Was she ever eager for you to grow into your strengths? Or did she try always to keep you at her side, dependent and callow?"

Clarice forced out the words, facing the truth. "She loved me best when I was docile. I suppose that is how she wants me to be now. I know it is. I hoped . . . when I heard she wasn't dead, I hoped for something more."

Dominic offered the comfort of his arms. Against her hair, he said, "Perhaps the 'something more' you seek is immortality?"

"Don't be ridiculous. I could never. . . ." But she thought about it, as alluring visions of what she'd seen since entering the Deathless Realm rose up before her.

"It's tempting, isn't it?" he asked, his voice a hard whisper. "You have power over the things of the earth. Whatever you chose to do is effortless. Travel where you will on the breast of the wind, walk on the sea-floor without air, fly to the stars or make them dance to your piping. Your deepest longings fulfilled in the blink of an eye. And you dwell forever in the kind of beauty that mortals only see in dreams. Oh, it's tempting so long as you don't look past the pleasures of it to the pains."

"What pains? What pains could there possibly be?"

"This, for one."

He pushed up her chin and kissed her, driving her passion until she forgot everything except what she found in his arms. His big hands threw back her cloak and he caressed her breasts through the quilted dress. The friction and the pressure heated her blood. It made her restless and eager to have him feel exactly the same frantic yearning that she did.

She slid her hands beneath the tatters of his shirt and ran them over the velvet skin of his flat stomach. He shivered. She smiled against his mouth, taking the thrust of his tongue as a tribute. He tasted of the bitter cream-iness of the chocolate he'd drunk as well as his own unique flavor. Between the two, Clarice felt intoxicated.

Behind them, the guttering torch flared, first greenish, then yellow. Now she could see the color of the beard that she'd felt against her cheeks and chin. His eyes were deep-shadowed yet bright with a hunger that her kisses had only increased. His chest rose and fell with panting breaths.

Clarice shook back her hair. "How was that a 'pain'?" He seemed to have forgotten what he'd set out to prove to her, for he was staring at her without speaking.

He closed his eyes before he answered. "I was told when I was sent out to keep you hostage that the women of your time were meek, modest, and chaste."

"Am I not so?"

He laughed, an all-too happy sound in that dark place. She reached out with shaking hands as she said, "Hush!"

Grinning at her, he said, "Meek? Modest . . . well, perhaps. Chaste? By the Stones, never! Mind you, I'm not ungrateful."

With a proud toss of her head, she proclaimed, "I am a virgin, Dominic."

"I know it," he said deep in his chest as he slipped his hands over her shoulders. "There's never been a chance to set that right. And if you stay here, there never will be."

"What do you mean?"

"The Fay don't make love, Clarice. I've dwelt among them for four hundred years and I'm not sure how they have children. I know it's rare for there to be any children living in the Wilder World at any time. If you stay here, you'll be a virgin forever. You were not made for that kind of life."

"I've done perfectly well as a spinster thus far."

"That's because you never knew *me* before."

She started to laugh at his masculine arrogance but gasped instead as he pulled her against him again. She couldn't even pretend to resist him, not with these moments so fleeting. Pressing her face against his neck, she murmured, "I don't want to be a Fay. I want to be yours."

"Don't tell your mother that. Whatever you do, don't tell her that."

When she left Dominic's cell, Corporal O'Hannon was singing an old Gaelic lullaby to the guard. His eyes when he saw her were expressive. Clarice's heart ached as she slowly closed the cell door. It seemed so final, as though she were bidding Dominic a lasting adieu.

She slipped down the corridor to wait for O'Hannon. He was not long in coming. At first he said nothing, but when they were safely out of earshot of the guard, he exclaimed explosively, "What in the name of the Three took you so long? Did you smuggle him in a five-course meal?"

"I apologize, Corporal. We had much to discuss."

"You must have! And me runnin' out of words which is a thing that don't often happen to one of my ilk, I can tell you."

"I know it must have been a strain on your nerves. I don't know what I would have done without you."

"Ah, now . . ." He ducked his head modestly. "Not that I've any nerves to speak of, mind you! 'Tis only for yourself I was concerned. I daresay you didn't wish to hurry yourself either for the company was pleasant though the room left something to be desired, eh?"

"It is not perhaps the most congenial surroundings."

Clarice tried to memorize the twists and turns of the way back to Dominic. If only she had a piece of paper to mark it down!

O'Hannon broke off in the middle of a complaint about his erstwhile companion to say, "It's no good trying to learn the way, my lady. It changes every time."

"Then how do you know it?"

"Oh, it's just a knack. I ask my heart which way to go and it's never wrong."

"You are *human*, aren't you, O'Hannon?"

"That I am, and proud of it! But any human can do the same with a bit of trainin'."

"Can you teach me?"

"Now why would I be doin' that? You'll never need come down here again in all your long life."

"Does everyone know what my mother has planned for me?"

"Sure, and isn't it known to yourself?"

"No. I had no notion until Dominic told me."

"He's a knowin' one by all I ever heard. I hope it's me as takes him down when the day of battle comes. That'll be a day of glory! There'll be songs sung of the *werreour* around the Great Fire and the name O'Hannon will lead all the rest."

"Will you meet me tomorrow night so I can see him again?"

"No. I don't dare. You've relieved him for tonight and the guard promised he'd give him some food tomorrow. I won't vouch for the quality but I doubt he'll be expecting anything like Mother makes."

"I needn't ask if you'll help me rescue Dominic?"

"Rescue him? He's your enemy now, girl . . . I mean, my lady."

"He'll never be that. I—I love him, you see."

The Irish soldier whistled low in astonishment. "That's bad, that is. If I'd known that, I never would have taken you along to see him. Don't curse me for it after, will you?"

"No, of course not. You've given me a wonderful gift. I thought he was dead."

"But he is. As good as dead, so to speak. Your mother's going to be makin' an example of him. Throw him back to his own time and place, don't you know? I'd rather it was me. I enjoy the Living Lands, but they're not a patch on Dublin."

He stopped, holding up his hand for her to halt as well. Then he walked boldly out into the courtyard. An instant later, after a quick check around, he beckoned to her. "Here's where we part, my dear. When you're happy one day, think of old O'Hannon and bless him, won't you?"

"I will. Thank you."

"Ah, run on now. Use that cloak and go silent."

Clarice was half-afraid she'd find Matilda waiting for her in her room. Knowing that the Fay could render themselves invisible at will, Clarice could not feel herself truly composed until the covers were around her and her head half-buried in the pillow bed. The quiet dark of the night comforted her jangled nerves.

At first, she thought of those stolen moments with Dominic. She hoped O'Hannon would forgive her for being such an unconscionable time but every instant had been too precious to surrender for mere safety's sake.

Thinking of Dominic, of how he'd touched her, she had to clap her hand over her mouth to keep from turning her sighs into moans. This feeling of half-desperation, half-desire was new and thrilling. Had she ever thought herself as cold and uninterested in men? In one way, Dominic was right. She'd never met a man who could rouse her deepest feelings the way he could with one touch.

She'd help him escape but first she had to free him from his cell. Without O'Hannon's help, she'd never be able to distract a guard *and* help Dominic. If only she had the chance again to see him, to plan. A note through the door would be enough to set a time for him to be ready.

The night brought no counsel except for a daring thought that had come upon her while tossing restlessly in her bed. Her mother had promised to do anything she would ask.

"Be extravagant," she had said. *"The more you demand, the happier I shall be."*

Matilda brought her breakfast on a tray with her own hands. "Here you are, my darling! Everything as you like it! Toast with gooseberry jam, tea, and an omelette with asparagus."

"I can't believe you remember that," Clarice said, pleased despite herself.

"I remember everything about you," her mother said, beaming. "How did you sleep?"

Clarice sat up, stretching. Her mother watched her with loving eyes. Then she set the tray on Clarice's lap. "Eat it all up! You need your strength."

"Do I?" As always in the Realm of Eternity, the food was a spiritual experience. "Have you eaten, Mother?"

"Yes, hours ago, sleepyhead. But if I may have a slice of your toast?" She took it between her fingers as she sat down on the edge of the bed. "One of the best things about being Fay is that one can eat and eat without ever gaining an ounce. Why, in ten years, I have not gained a pound! I'm sure if I'd stayed human, I'd be waddling like a plump duck!"

Clarice laughed with her, wishing Matilda could be like this always. "I notice that the Fay eat no meat. Why?"

"Some promise made in the Long Ago Before, when Boadach, Forgall and the harpist Cuar first emerged from nothingness. We take vows very seriously here."

"Dom . . . someone told me that it is possible for a Fay to study human behavior. Did you have to study how to be a Fay?"

Matilda shook her head and looked thoughtful. "That's strange. I never thought of it. When I changed,

Forgall just turned his head and glanced at me and I *knew*. I knew the speech of animals and the words of the wind. I could transform myself, go anywhere, do anything, but no one ever taught me how. I had never known such freedom."

"Freedom?" Clarice echoed. "I always thought that adults did exactly what they pleased at all times. I've since learned differently."

"I'm sorry you had to learn that. I would have given anything to keep you free of the burdens of your position. At least you have had enough sense to steer clear of one snare that awaits women. You didn't marry." Matilda's sharp brown eyes studied her intently.

"I never met someone I could see spending my life with."

"And I was not there to arrange matters. Perhaps that is as well, now."

"I should like to marry one day."

"Don't think of it, my dearest. Take the advice of the one who loves you best. Whether you marry for property or for 'love'—as the modern mind conceives it—the married state leads only to inevitable disillusionment. A man is never what he seems."

Thinking of the several roles Dominic had played since she'd met him, Clarice couldn't conceal her smile. "Sometimes that doesn't matter, surely? If you can see past what he appears to be and find the man inside. . . ."

"What hope can an innocent child like you have of stripping away a man's deceptions? Their lies are like the skin of an onion. Peel one away and there's another beneath it and thus until you find nothing at the heart. Better still to stay free forever. I learned that too late."

"I know that Father loved another, but at one time did he not . . ."

"I was not speaking of your father. I would never be so disrespectful of his memory. But, as you raise the point, your father made every effort to offer me the forms and shows of the marriage tie. For a time, I even hoped . . . but I knew that his heart remained with the woman who'd borne him Felicia. Once she came to live with us, I could no longer carry on the pretense."

Clarice, who remembered how little pretense of affection there'd been between her parents even before Felicia's advent, wondered if her mother was fooling herself or trying to make her marriage sound better than it was for her daughter's sake. "Mother, I loved my father dearly but I knew his faults. I cannot be sorry that you were married to him for where would I be otherwise? Yet I can imagine that he was not easy to live with."

"That was the difficulty. He was too easy. Anyone might impose upon his good nature, even I. When Felicia came . . ."

No one could miss the sharp rancor in her tone whenever Clarice's half sister's name was mentioned. Clarice said, "I must tell you that I have come to rely greatly on Felicia's judgment and that her husband is as dear to me as a brother."

"Oh, yes. Blaic. He threw away a princehood for a girl of no fortune and less name. I met his father, you know. The poor fellow could scarcely raise his head for the shame. How seldom do children repay a loving parent's care." Matilda patted Clarice's knee through the blankets. "I'm sure you would never prove so ungrateful."

"I am very fond of Blaic," Clarice repeated. "He and Felicia are so happy together. They have a son, you know. They named him for his grandfather. He was staying with me when . . . when all this happened."

"My poor darling! Dwindling into a lonely, put-upon maiden aunt with no future but to be used! What a dreadful fate!"

"You make it sound as though I were some penniless dependent, Mother. Besides, Morgain is—"

"Oh, you are a too good to see that you are being imposed upon. They just drop him in your lap whenever they choose, without so much as a by-your-leave I'll be bound!"

"It isn't like that at all. He's my dear nephew. I'm glad to house him whenever his parents wish me to. I could almost wish he were my own. When I do have my own children, I could do far worse than follow Felicia's methods of child-rearing."

"Your own children!" Matilda scoffed. "You're a child yourself! You are too young to even think of such a thing!"

"But I do think of it, Mother." Clarice wondered whether she would have to be less indirect. Though becoming a Fay held temptations, she hoped she was incapable of being seduced by them. She gathered that Dominic had no interest in changing and she would not go where he was unwilling to follow.

"Is there a man?" Matilda asked.

Remembering Dominic's warning, she said, "No. I have never seen anyone to marry. Someday, I hope—"

"You hope! Meanwhile, the years go racing by. Now that I am immortal, I can see what a swift river is human life. You hardly step in the stream before it sweeps you away to your doom. Fifty years are an eyeblink—an eyeblink! Go on as you are, Clarice, and you'll be old and ugly before you know it. The best, sweetest moments of your life will be gone beyond recall and what will you do? Weep? Mourn? Repent? All useless!"

"Mother," Clarice said. "Don't grow so agitated. I am only twenty-seven. . . ."

"Twenty-seven . . ." Matilda gasped, as though her daughter has just announced that she'd been poisoned and didn't expect to see another sunrise. "Twenty-seven . . . As old as that already?"

"I was not quite seventeen when you left. The years do not stop for us all."

Matilda stood up. "I must speak to my generals. Dress yourself in whatever you choose so long as it is splendid. You will show yourself to them in an hour. There is not another moment to lose!"

"Mother, I don't understand."

Matilda glanced at her, with pained eyes. "Twenty-seven! My darling, forgive me. I should have acted sooner."

Distracted, counting what must be done on her fingers, Matilda hurried toward the door. Clarice called after her. "Mother, will you let Dominic Knight out of prison?"

"Yes, dear, whatever you wish. Provisions . . . man and horse . . . a litter for Clarice . . . I shall ride, of course. . . ."

"At once, Mother?"

"Yes, it's done. It's done. Don't bother me now, my love. Just dress and hurry!"

Clarice was happy to obey this behest. The least complex outfit in her wardrobe was a long tunic of red silk with an overblouse, tied at the waist with a wide teal-colored sash. The blouse was gorgeously embroidered in scarlet with dragons and phoenixes juggling real pearls. Matilda had said something about the Imperial dress of China, but Clarice had looked at so many clothes at that point that she'd even given up nodding her approval. She did not accept the triple-level head-dress with the dangling pearl strings, nor did she wear the silken slippers that matched the dress. Rather, she pulled on her own sensible boots with her own hands and traveled down to the courtyard.

Instead of the serenity and silence of last night, the courtyard was overrun by gesticulating, shouting soldiery. It all looked like an ant's nest broken into by an inquisitive child. It was a measure of the soldiers' preoccupation that none of them took notice of Clarice, despite the eye-scorching colors of her dress.

She tried to slip around the edges of the courtyard, scanning the crowd for Dominic. If her mother kept her word, Clarice could not imagine him sitting quietly in his cell until she came to him. He must be looking for her too, or she did not know him.

Then she saw him, standing in a doorway, blinking as though even the dim sunlight that filled the courtyard of the Fortress of La'al hurt his eyes. Clarice hurried toward him, hardly noticing the accidental buffets from hurrying soldiers. "Dominic!"

Her voice did not carry above the echoing noises of wagons rolling, men laughing, or the rest of the sounds that accompany an army preparing to march. Yet his head turned, his eyes found her. He started forward, but where was his free stride, the easy swing of his arms? She hurried to him, taking refuge with him in a corner out of the way of the turmoil.

She saw that shackles bound his hands and feet. They glittered with a strange light, as though they took the meager sunlight and broke it into a thousand colored shards. When he raised his hands, she saw that the manacles were loops of clear crystal, angled and faceted as though they had grown in this form.

She gathered the cold loops in her hands. "I didn't think of this."

"Why should you? A few minutes ago I awoke. The cell door was open, the guard was gone, but these had come in his stead." He raised his hands as one to touch her chin with his fingertips. "Don't cry. At least I am outside in the air—if not perfumed"—he took a deep breath and his eyes watered—"it's better than the air in that dungeon. A thousand years of despair has a definite odor."

"I will ask her to take them off you."

"She won't do it unless I give my parole not to escape."

"Then give it." She leaned closer to speak more softly, though the noise in the courtyard had not abated. If anything it had increased as a barrel-chested, low-centered gnome shouted out orders of march. "We have to escape as soon as we can."

"If I give my parole, then I can't escape. It would be breaking my word."

"The devil fly away with your word," she said, knowing it was futile to argue. Part of the reason she loved him was for his honor; she couldn't ask him to throw it away even to save his life. "O'Hannon told me Mother plans to make an example of you. She'll send you back to your own time in order to persuade Forgall's human soldiers to surrender."

"That won't make them quit. We all know what the penalty is for failing."

"That may be true, but it won't stop her from sending *you* back. And I won't have that happen."

He grinned at her, his devil-may-care smile never more heartrending when it was accompanied by the cold clink of his chains. "You're as autocratic as your mother."

"Yes, I am. You better learn that lesson now, sir!"

"I would kiss you if it weren't for all these . . ." He looked about them and his smile was replaced by a dark frown. "What is happening?"

"I'm afraid this is my fault. Mother and I were talking a little while ago and I mentioned my age. It seemed to throw her into a panic."

"How old are you?"

"Twenty-seven."

"That would explain much."

"As in?"

"Why you are so set in your ways, for one thing." He winked at her. Then he said, "Your mother wants to make you immortal, but she doesn't want you when you are old."

"Twenty-seven is not old!" she said, knowing that she only protested to see him smile again. "It's . . . mature."

"True. In the days of my birth, you could have been a grandmother by now." He looked her up and down. She read desire in his eyes, even now, and wondered what it would be like to give him the children necessary to make future generations. He must have noted her blush, for Dominic missed no detail about her, however small.

But he said only, "Matilda must feel that she has no time left to waste on negotiations. She must march against Forgall now, ready or not, before you age any further."

"Then we must escape, ready or not, and warn For-gall's army."

"You mean *I* must escape."

"No. You and I both. I don't intend to stay here and be forced to make any change so utterly abhorrent to me."

He reached out as though to take her by the shoulders but his manacled hands would not part far enough to permit it. Clarice took his hands in hers. They twisted around and held her hands tightly. "Clarice, it's too dangerous for you to come with me. If I am captured, I may be sent back, or even killed. I don't dare let you take that risk too."

"You'd rather I stayed here to face these risks alone?"

"Here, you have a chance of a future. If Forgall loses, you'll be a Fay and live forever."

"If you die or go beyond my reach, what good is immortality to me? We go together, whether into life or into death. As soon as we break those chains."

"Clarice . . . please." She made sure he saw nothing but the utmost determination in her expression. He sighed and said, "You can't. They're unbreakable."

"Then how far will you get? It may be hundreds of miles to Forgall's army."

"Not so far as that. My own cadre is hidden . . . I won't tell where. But I can reach them." He chuckled low. "I wanted to be in the forefront of the battle. I may well have my chance."

"And you'll leave me here?"

"You'll be safe."

"Oh, yes. There's safety in a broken heart." She left him, pausing to throw him a last look before she traveled to the tower. He bit his lip to keep from calling her back.

Eighteen

They waited through an interminable day. Dominic sat at a refectory table in the nearly empty guard room, eating what Matilda's own *werreour* ate, whenever it was offered to him. Though they looked at him as a curiosity, they gave no sign of hostility. Regardless of personal loyalty, they were all human beings when off-duty.

O'Hannon sat on the table, his feet swinging as he playfully flipped a razor-sharp knife from hand to hand. The man had the reflexes of a juggler and the eyes of a thoughtful killer. As he toyed with his knife, he said, "It's what I don't approve of—I'll not hide my teeth! No gentleman soldier should be subjected to such treatment. Ah, it 'ud make a Turk blush, so indeed."

"You can't blame Queen Matilda for taking no risks. She knows I'm honor-bound to attempt escape."

"Ah, but to put shackles on a man like yer honor! 'Tisn't decent. Nor is it fair to us." He paused for an instant between throws to gesture at those fellow soldiers present but never missed his cue for snatching his knife once more out of the air. A rumble of agreement came from their throats. "Here you sit, yer honor, at your ease, eating well, drinking well, buildin' up the strength of yourself crumb by crumb. Do we begrudge you?"

The others said, "No!" with one voice.

"Do we say 'that man is mine enemy let us use him despitefully'?" Again a "No!" came back in force. "And with all these crafty bastards on watch, what chance have you of escaping us? I'll tell you! None! Absolutely none!"

He slammed his hand down on the tabletop, making all the jugs, bottles, and glasses jump. The others set up a last cheer and then, as a deep-toned bell rang in the corridor, took final swigs and gulps before going off to their duties. O'Hannon kept his perch on the table.

He leaned close to Dominic, his knife stayed in his hand. In a voice that hardly carried, he said, "For all of me, I'd be more'n glad to turn my back and let you escape. I daresay quite a few of the boys feel the same."

"Why?"

"We'd far rather meet you on the field, d'you see? That's what we're waiting for."

Dominic asked, "O'Hannon, have we met before? I have the feeling I know your face."

"We may have done. For a long time I served in His Majesty's Own before I went into the East for a spell. It's no place for a decent man, that. Birds big enough to carry off a horse, an' the cart it's drawin' as well. Sea monsters and girls with six more arms than anybody needs. Them thrice-blasted Djinn everywhere you look. Gets so a man don't dare open a bottle in the hope of finding a bit of cheer in the bottom. That's where I first heard about herself, out there."

"What made you change sides, O'Hannon?"

The slighter man shrugged, as though the answers were too complex to be readily understood. Dominic pressed him. "There must be a reason you abandoned the king's service for Queen Matilda's."

"Every man has his own little reasons. If I had to pick one that we all share though. . . ." His shoulders lifted and fell once more with resignation. "The boys and I all feel that the whole reason for us even being here in the Wilder World is to fight. But who was there to fight?

No one. Everything in the kingdom was peaceable until Matilda. Now there's battle in the offing. I can smell it in the air, the way you can smell the morning coming after sleeping all night in the open. It is as if what we have waited for, trained for, and dreamed of is finally about to dawn. We'd follow worse than Matilda to gain our opportunity at last."

Dominic felt some that drive in his own blood. "To fight at last. To be free . . ."

The Irishman clapped him on the shoulder. "That's the spirit! We've spent years training for this moment, building ourselves and our cadres up with marvelous dedication. And never once have we been used as we should be. Dragons? Bah! Bit of pretend hand-to-hand with the four-armed guards of the king? That was something like, all right, they hate us like fire, but they weren't allowed to defeat *us* and we couldn't kill *them* because of their immortality. So what good was any of it?"

"No good at all."

"Right! We knew there'd never be a good war without the king having some strong enemy to challenge him. When Matilda came along, she saw at once that the only way to challenge Forgall was to build up an army, and an army of mortals at that! We were glad to lend her an ear. Terrible persuasive talker, she is. I'd not be a might surprised to learn her mother came from County Cork. She knows the ones who aren't content before they even know it themselves!"

"But can she rely on you to fight if all you want—"

The words were hardly out of his mouth when O'Hannon slapped the blade of his knife against Dominic's neck. "We'll fight like devils because we're *werreour,* same as yourself! What do we have we to lose? If we are defeated, we go home to our own place and time. Ah, to walk through the streets of Dublin again! To drink the good black beer and taste the rye loaf! There's naught like it here, for all their fancy ways."

Dominic sat with the knife at his throat and breathed shallowly. "And if you win?"

"If we put her on the cedar throne, then she's sworn to send every man-jack of the *werreour* back to whence they came. We can't lose, d'ye see? Either way, we get what we want."

"I was no more than a boy when they took me. My parents died in a plague. There's nothing for me there."

"You break my heart." Coolly, O'Hannon flipped the blade around, releasing Dominic, and began paring his nails. "I was hardly half-grown myself when I was left on the parish. I'm not saying the Fay didn't do me a favor, but I would have been fine on me own. Perhaps if we win, Herself will see her way clear to sending us back to our own times as we are now, full-grown. A fellow who knows how to handle himself in a fight, now, he always has the means to find a full belly. I could just fancy the life of a mercenary soldier, eh? Choose sides and change if the battle don't go to my likin'. Go off to kill for the highest bidder and take the pick of the camp-followers. Ah, that's the life for a boy with a bit of spirit in him!"

"If all you want is to go back, fight me now. *I'll* be sure to give you what you want."

"What? With them chains on? You won't win that way. Otherwise, I'd be more than a little tempted. Ma-tilda might lose the battle and I might survive it. Then I'm right where I am now and I hate it."

"I'll fight you if we can get the chains off. Do you know how to do it?"

O'Hannon's grin was not unsympathetic though its wryness told Dominic the smaller man knew exactly what he was up to. "No, not the slightest. That's magic, that is. I never studied it. Ask Herself, eh? She'll be happy enough to do it, after the battle."

Once again, O'Hannon returned to his game of flip-ping the knife from hand to hand. " 'Tis a pity you won't be fighting. All your trainin' gone to waste."

"Could the king take these pretty bracelets off me?"

"No doubt. But the king is far, far away." He began to whistle "Tom, Tom the Piper's Son" rather shrilly, flipping his knife to the rhythm.

Dominic had sized O'Hannon up from the first as a man who always kept one eye on the main chance. He could not imagine any of his own cadre talking the way the lightning-handed Irishman did. Despite his protestations of loyalty, he guessed that O'Hannon would change sides fast enough if the odds fell toward Forgall. Dominic could think of half a dozen things he could do to change those odds, but they were none of them possible while he stayed shackled in the Fortress of La'al.

"O'Hannon, I have a proposition for you."

"You interest me, Knight. I had a feeling you might. Mind you, I'll not do anything disloyal."

"I'll tell you what I have in mind. You tell me if it's disloyal."

"See me all attention."

Dominic wished that *his* mother had been born in County Cork, for he'd never learned to speak persuasively, except to Clarice. Thinking of her, he found words. "You want to fight me because you think I am the one to send you home."

"I'd want to fight you in any case, me boy. I've heard of you, d'ye see? We've all heard of you and there was not a man-jack among us who didn't want to see if you were as good as they all say."

"I am that good," Dominic said, knowing it was true. Even after a day of starvation and all the bruises he'd taken when fighting at the Doors, he knew he could take O'Hannon and a dozen like him. "You only took me at the Doors because of my . . ."

O'Hannon looked slightly abashed for the first time. " 'Cause of *her*. You don't need to say anything more. I saw her yesterday and did her some little service."

"I know it."

"She's an angel out of heaven. If I weren't such a bad man . . ." He shrugged. "But I am. Not so bad that I can't see how having her taken away by the likes of us wouldn't make a man miss a swing or two. As it is, you sent four of our boys home a mite ahead of schedule. That, plus the Rider."

"So you see, O'Hannon. I am as good as they say. And none of your lot have dispatched me, as I am sitting here now."

"You speak like a Daniel come to judgment, Knight. May I call you Dominic? My name's Jack."

"Listen, Jack. Find a way to get me out of the Fortress. Let me make my way back to Forgall's army. He'll take these 'bracelets' from me and when battle's joined, I'll search you out. You and as many of your cadre as wish to fight me. I'll either send you home, or you'll send me."

"You tempt me mightily, Dominic. Indeed, indeed. But how to do the thing, eh?"

"I must be away before your army marches."

"You'll give the game away to Forgall. We'll have no surprise. Well, there's not much chance he doesn't know we're coming, not while he holds the scrying stones." O'Hannon slid his knife into the decorated scabbard he wore at his waist. He jumped lightly down from the table. "I'll think on it, Dominic, my boy. If it could be done . . ." He chuckled. "Ah, but it'll be a great day come the mornin'! If I had a proper fight to look forward to, I'd sleep like a babe in arms, so I would. I'll think on it."

"Not too long, Jack," Dominic said as the other man's hand went to the door. "If I'm not away before your army moves, they'll recapture me. Then no grand fight."

Dominic could feel the other man's eagerness for the promised "treat." He wished he could feel the same. Before he'd met Clarice, he could imagine that he would have been as eager for combat as any one of Matilda's *werreour*. But with his heart warmed by thoughts of his beloved, he couldn't chill his blood enough to kill. In all probability, if he faced O'Hannon without mastery over those feelings, the Irishman would have no trouble at all dispatching him.

But he was less worried about O'Hannon than he was about Clarice. If he left her with her mother, she would be comfortable and safe, at least until the battle was over. If Forgall won, Dominic did not think the king would hold her responsible in any way for her mother's crimes. He'd just send her back to Hamdry. But if Matilda won, and Clarice were still with her, then she would undoubtedly suffer the change into Fay. Then he would have no choice but to join her for he would not live as a man without her.

Even as he debated with himself, Dominic knew he was wasting his time. There was only one person who would decide whether Clarice undertook the hardship of escape with him, or stayed here. That was Clarice herself. He was very much afraid that he knew what her choice would be. She'd already decided that she owed her mother her presence.

Dominic groaned and raised his hands to rub his face. Every time he moved, the crystal chains gave out musical notes as soulless as the ringing of a water-filled glass. It was a sound he was already heartily sick of. He'd have to muffle it somehow during his escape. It would be simpler with O'Hannon's help, but whether or not he had that, Dominic was determined to escape the fortress before Matilda's army marched away.

Clarice listened, her hands folded demurely in her lap, while her mother and her generals discussed the plans for the approaching battle. Though she didn't understand everything, she was impressed despite herself at her mother's grasp of the essentials of warfare. Where had the daughter of an undistinguished if noble family learned how to conduct a battle? She wondered if Matilda was a reversion to some barbarian princess far back in her pedigree, a Boadicea reborn, who needed only the opportunity to prove what she could accomplish given an army to command.

When the generals, one of whom at least was human-form, finally left, Clarice asked, "Mother, wherever did you learn all that?"

Matilda smiled with some false modesty. "A woman never knows what she is capable of until tried by fate."

"What a pity you could not have gone into the Army in our own time! You would have outshone Marlborough and all the other so-called great military minds."

Matilda seemed to dwell a moment on that pleasant picture, but then sighed. "No, it is not to be thought of. Look what became of Jeanne d'Arc. All because she meddled in affairs better left to men. I do these things because I must for if I do not, who will? But I shouldn't like you or any young woman to be forced to do something so utterly against their natures as join an army. Women should be content with their own sphere."

She had dressed rather simply for the meeting, almost severely, and had left off a good many of her jewels, contenting herself with a string of marrow-fat pearls and her ever-present rings. She raised her hand as though she would pat Clarice's cheek but contented herself by making a gesture of protection and blessing over her head.

"You should rest while you can, my love. Tomorrow we will be on the march at dawn."

"I am to accompany you?"

"Oh, yes. You must be there to cheer on my army and to witness our victory. They are fighting as much for you as for me. Do not forget it."

"I shan't, Mother." She stood up, taller than Matilda. "I wish I could embrace you to wish you good fortune."

"Tomorrow you shall. I will be so delighted to hold my dearest in my arms again."

"I can't help wishing that . . ."

"What? You know I'll grant any of your desires."

"I wish that you might find happiness."

Her mother laughed. "A wasted wish, my dearest! Tomorrow, I achieve it. We will never be parted again."

"No. We will never be parted again, Mother."

Within the hour, Clarice was in the fast-darkening

courtyard again. She wore her riding habit, somehow overlooked in all the hundreds of exotic dresses her mother had conjured up. A heavy shawl of white wool was tied about Clarice's waist, all her luncheon bundled up in it, while the cloak of silence went over all.

Things had changed in the square. Instead of confusion, there was order. Wagons, small and large, covered and open, were lined up neatly, waiting for their beasts of burden. Knots of soldiers stood about under lighted torches, discussing in more or less raucous voices what feats they'd accomplish on the morrow. From time to time, a hustling courier dashed by. Or a preoccupied officer passed, counting wagons or men. No one noticed her, or if they did, no one cried out.

Now to find Dominic. Like it or not, she was going with him. At least in Forgall's camp, if he was killed or sent back she'd know of it immediately. She wasn't about to stand any uncertainty on that point one instant longer than she had too. As soon as the word came, she'd know what to do.

Another officer came by, this one sauntering with deliberate speed. Clarice put back the hood of the cloak. "O'Hannon!"

He whirled, his hand on the dagger's hilt at his hip. When he saw her, his sandy brows twitched together. "Ah, in the name of the Three, what are you doin' here, my lady?"

He glanced around nonchalantly and strolled to her side. "This is no place for you. Not with the dark closing in."

"I must see Dominic Knight again."

"Ah, no. Not again. It's not safe." Then he looked in her eyes. "Curse me for a black-blooded rascal if I ever regretted a good deed more than when I took you to see him the first time!"

"I don't so curse you, Corporal O'Hannon. Do you know where he is?"

"Yes, rot my soul. An' won't he half-bless me when

he sees you. Come on then. And without a sound, else we're all sped."

She raised the hood over her head and followed him. The cloak muffled the sounds she made, but sharpened her own hearing. When O'Hannon held out his hand for her to stop a moment while he went on, she did so, leaning back until her shoulders touched the wall. She heard a strange clicking sound, faint but repeated.

Looking around, she saw next to her on the wall a furry brown spider as big as her hand. She screamed with terror, but no sound emerged from the muffling hood. The spider's eyes leaped out on stalks in surprise. It scuttled away, the tiny pads on its feet clicking away over the stone walls.

Clarice sprang away from the wall, terrified that she'd see the squashed remains of another such creature behind her. But it seemed that this one had traveled alone. Shaken by an uncontrollable revulsion, Clarice tried hard to recoup her poise. As a rule, even the smallest spider terrified her, and she'd never seen one so large that its features were distinguishable before.

She followed O'Hannon again, her confidence wasting away by the moment. She told herself that as soon as she saw Dominic everything would be all right.

"Oh, no!"

The cry was surprised out of Dominic. With no cloak to muffle his voice, Clarice heard the anguish in his tone quite clearly. She heard little else, despite her own cloak. O'Hannon had left her several paces off while he approached Dominic. They communicated with a series of hand-signals so quickly that their fingers seemed to be nothing but blurs. After just a few gestures, Dominic had cried out.

Clarice was not in the mood for further discussion. She walked up to the two men, put back her hood, and said, "I'm coming with you and that's all I have to say. I can go on repeating it for as long as you please but it seems a dreadful waste of time."

"Are you sure it's not yourself that's from Ireland?"

O'Hannon asked. "She makes sense, man. If you're going, you'd best be gone."

"He's still shackled," Clarice protested.

"That's not going to stop Dominic Knight, the grand fellow that he is."

"Dub up, O'Hannon. Clarice, only your mother or my king can get these off me. Do you think your mother would?"

"Not even if I ask her, which I can't. I'm not going back up there again. Can you travel with them on?"

"I can, in a wagon."

"Good. Is there one?"

O'Hannon said, "Just me own. With me lovely mare to pull it along."

"But I thought . . ." Clarice began. Instead, she put her hand on O'Hannon's shoulder and kissed his cheek. The Irishman flushed a painful red.

"You'd best have this as well," he said, reaching for his knife. He dropped it, fumbled it up, and handed it to Dominic. "I'll be gettin' that back," he said gruffly. "With all the rest."

"You have my word on it."

Clarice noticed the guilty glances each man threw her way when they thought she was not looking. She wondered what plot they'd hatched between them, but did not ask. She felt certain that she'd not approve, but at the moment she'd make a deal with the devil himself to get Dominic out of this place. They hung the cloak of silence around his shoulders to muffle the perpetual jangling of his chains. He could only shuffle along, yet managed to keep up with the other two.

They came to the wagon which stood, perhaps by coincidence, in the front rank directly before the gate. Glancing up, Clarice saw guards pacing on the parapet. Their attention, however, seemed directed outward. No one appeared to be watching the wagons.

O'Hannon whispered hoarsely, "Can you be drivin' a horse 'n' cart, my lady?"

"As well as yourself, O'Hannon," she said, trying to

be lighthearted but afraid her chattering teeth gave her away.

O'Hannon's laugh sounded forced as he silenced Dominic's protests. "Sure, you could drive it yourself, man. But with her droppin' in as though by special wish, it's more sensible for her to do it. Or do you want to risk driving right off the mountain with her aboard?"

Dominic growled beneath his breath. Clarice pretended not to know that he wanted to swear and asked him if his bruises were paining him much. "Not as much as my damned pride," he said. "All right, already, O'Hannon. Boost me into the wagon, then go get your bloody horse."

Clarice sat in the hay with him beside her beneath the arched wooden hoops and canvas roof of the wagon. It was small; he had to lie with his knees bent to fit in the bed. The light that came through the loosely tied flaps in the back was dim and flickering. Yet she could see that Dominic wore his fiercest look. She didn't think it was for her; rather, she knew he was trying his best to hide the shame of his limitation.

She said, "I'm sorry to be so adamant about escaping with you. But I cannot stay here any longer."

He reached for her hand, his chains jingling. "I'm sorry too, Clarice. I shouldn't try to make up your mind for you. That's what Matilda is doing."

"At least you both do it from motives of love."

"Don't compare my love to that—"

She pressed her fingers to his lips. "No matter what you think of her, remember she is my mother. I don't approve of what she has done, or her reasons, but she is my mother. I will love her and you both. You'd better accustom yourself to it."

"Even while you try to escape her, you still love her?"

"Once I love, it is for always, Dominic."

"I know it."

She smiled at him. "Put your head down and try to sleep. I don't think you've slept since you were captured."

"I won't until we're free. But I will, with your good leave, close my eyes a few moments." His head fell back and in less time than she would have believed possible, he was asleep. She tugged the cloak of silence up to his mouth, in case he began to snore, and waited for O'Hannon to return with the mare.

Looking at Dominic was a pleasure she'd been too much denied. Watching him sleep, she realized why she'd been so determined to escape La'al with him. It wasn't just for her freedom, or for his. Neither was it because she couldn't bear not knowing what became of him or because she wanted to share his dangers.

He had given her the reason himself, in the dungeon. Her smile widened as she pictured his reaction when she began to seduce him. Then it faded as she realized she had not the faintest idea how to set about it. She straightened as she remembered whose daughter she was. If her mother could learn to maneuver an army, surely she was capable of seducing her own beloved Dominic.

He snapped awake a few moments before O'Hannon brought the horse. There were sounds of others nearby, also backing animals between the shafts of wagons. Peering cautiously out, Clarice saw that not every wagon had a horse. She wondered how she would have managed if O'Hannon had expected her to drive a giant wolf or a *thing* with the hindquarters of a hippopotamus, the head of a crocodile, and the mane and forelegs of a lion. She expressed this in a whisper to Dominic and heard him answer, "Exactly as you will now, probably."

O'Hannon harnessed the horse to the wagon. As though talking to it, he said, "Follow the wagon on your right. When you cross the causeway, you'll see the ones ahead turn left into a field. Don't follow them there. That's where we're massing for the march. Keep going straight until you come to the place where the road splits in three. Take whichever looks most likely to throw them off your track. They'll be after you the minute you fail to turn into the field."

"Thank you, O'Hannon. I hope you won't be punished. . . ."

"No. There's a friend of mine waiting to knock me on the head and drag me into a cupboard where I'll be found in the morning with a blinding headache, no doubt."

"I don't know why you're doing this for us."

"No? You will though soon enough. If we don't meet again, my lady, 'tis been a blessing knowing you." His head turned away. "There's the signal to be ready." More loudly, he said, "Ach, wouldn't you know it, though?"

Someone in the darkness asked him what was wrong.

"The fool I am, I've gone and forgotten me water bottle. Don't start without me, now." He hurried away to the sound of coarse laughter and a few ribald jokes.

"What did he mean 'I'll know soon'?" Clarice asked.

"Never mind now. Be ready."

"Can we trust him?"

"We've no choice."

Clarice half-expected shouts of discovery to attend her slipping onto the driver's perch. She'd left her provisions in the back with Dominic and wore the cloak over her head, more to conceal her hair than for any magical properties. Her hands were shaking. She had to draw several deep breaths before she was calm enough to take the reins. She did not dare let her anxiety be transmitted to the horse or she'd be too difficult to control. She couldn't imagine O'Hannon having any but mettlesome horses.

The groan of the portcullis raising awoke all the hair on the back of her neck. The first of the wagons rolled through the gateway and out onto the narrow causeway. Clarice could feel the sweat gather between her breasts. It trickled down cold as ice water.

Behind her, Dominic whispered, "We're next. Don't hurry it."

"I've been driving to an inch since I was a child," she said proudly, forgetting he could not hear her. She decided her actions would have to speak for her and not just while driving.

Anticipating every instant to hear shouts or shots, she drove steadily and calmly through the gate. The causeway, paved with white stones, stretched out across an abyss so deep that the bottom of it could not be seen from the bridge. It was so narrow that the rims of her wheels on both sides whispered against the stone work of the inch-high curb as she drove over. Any flaw in her control over the horse and they'd go tumbling down to the rocks below.

On the far side it widened out, the road taking a downward dip within a hundred feet of the end of the causeway. The wagon in front of them had already turned off. Now everyone in the fortress would know something was wrong. How soon after that would Matilda realize her daughter had left her?

Clarice stifled a pang for her mother's pain and drove straight on, slapping the reins down on the mare's back. Her hood blew back from her face and she couldn't help laughing at the wind in her hair.

The first shout came from behind them. On instinct, Clarice glanced back. She saw nothing of their pursuers, but Dominic had turned around in the hay so he could peer out between the flaps. "They're not following us," he said, his voice bouncing with his body.

"They're not?"

"No. They've no orders. But the watchmen have seen us and it won't take them long to tell the officer in charge. Then they'll be after us."

The road dropped off even more abruptly after about the first mile. Suddenly, Clarice found herself driving down a twisting mountain road in the dark behind a horse who'd decided that the racing season had begun. She tried to slow her, knowing how dangerous this descent was, but found it hard to convince the horse when every nerve in her body demanded greater and greater speed.

"O'Hannon didn't mention *this*," she called over her

shoulder during a momentary level place. When Dominic didn't answer, she risked a quick glance at him. He sat wedged in the back corner, both hands wrapped around a wooden roof strut. The crystal chains tinkled unceasingly in a way that gave Clarice an instant headache. His neck and teeth were set, throwing his jaw into high relief. She thought of his battered body and tried even harder to slow the horse's pace over this jagged road.

"We're at the fork," she announced anxiously after what seemed eternity. She walked the horse, who had now had the edge taken off her enthusiasm.

"Here already?" He knelt behind her, looking out.

"The horse was in a hurry. Are you all right?"

"Fine. Take the left-hand fork until you come to a large stand of trees. I'll direct you from there."

"Are we going to join Forgall's army?"

"No. They'll be following and I'm not leading them there."

"But I thought—"

"The first thing I'm doing is taking you home. This is no place for you. Don't argue. For once in your life, let someone else take care of you!"

"Everyone is always trying to take care of me, Dominic. You, my mother, even my sister and her husband. Even Morgain tries, when he remembers I'm around. Everyone has done such a wonderful job that I'm tempted to give the profession a try myself. I'll start by taking care of myself and you. We'll go right."

"Clarice . . ."

"Sit back."

She drove in the moonlight until even Dominic, who seemed to have a map of the Living Lands imprinted in his mind, was lost. "If nothing else, you've succeeded in *losing* part of Matilda's army. That's good. Unfortunately, you've lost us as well."

"Then I can stop driving before we find ourselves. There's a stream through those trees. We can water the horse."

She did everything, from unharnessing the mare to rubbing her down with a wisp of hay before hobbling her for the night. She gave her an armload of hay within distance of the small stream and returned to the wagon. Moonlight streamed in the rear, through the tied-back flaps.

"I've always wanted to play 'gypsy,' " she said, settling into the hay. Then a curious look crossed her face. "Ow. What *am* I sitting on?"

She reached behind her and pulled out an opaque amber bottle. Dominic sat up to take it from her hand. "Ten thousand blessings upon the Irish!"

He pulled out the cork with his teeth. With his eyes closed in ecstasy, he waved the bottle beneath his nose. "The one thing even the People cannot surpass."

"What is it?"

"The water of life, my sweet one."

"Oh, good, I'm thirsty." But when she put it to her lips after he drank, she smelled good whisky. She took a healthy gulp and then sputtered, tears coming to her eyes. "That's good," she said, her voice rasping and then she coughed again.

"You've had it before?"

"Once or twice." She suddenly felt a little shy. Would this be a good moment, she wondered, to seduce him? Food first, she decided. "Let's eat. I'm afraid it's not much."

"You are always apologizing for what you feed me. Don't worry so much. I'm a soldier; I can eat anything."

They ate what she'd smuggled away from her uneaten luncheon. She refused to take the lion's share that Dominic insisted on offering. Though she could have gladly eaten three times as much as she did, she made sure there was something left to break their fast on the morrow. Then she left the wagon again to soak a cloth ripped from her petticoat in the stream. She washed her face then brought the dripping rag in for him.

When they were both clean and dry, Clarice suffered another attack of shyness. She had no patience with her-

self! Tomorrow would bring battle—possibly even tonight if her mother's troops found them. Knowing
Dominic as she did, she felt certain he'd find some way
to enter the fray. Tonight—this moment—might be her
only chance to know his love. Dithering wasn't going
to make that happen.

Dominic stretched to the length of his chains, groan-
ing a little. She looked at him tenderly. "I love you,"
she said.

"Clarice . . ." He sat up abruptly, an expression of joyous surprise in his eyes. "I want your love so much. I
was starting to feel like one of 'them' until I met you."

She closed the gap between them, leaning down over
him. "I never want you to feel like that again."

Kissing him, tasting the whisky on his lips, she tried
to show him that she was ready to know everything
about him. Frustratingly, he only brushed her lips. "I
can't even hold you," he said.

"Let me."

She began to unlace the thong at the front of his shirt.
It seemed very natural to press a kiss into the opening.
He groaned again, more sharply than before. She felt his
big body shake in reaction to her boldness. "Clarice . . .
what are you doing?"

"You'll see. I hope."

Nineteen

Several minutes had passed, minutes in which Dominic had not been very cooperative. They had to lie close together, his bound hands between them. She'd put her arms around him and tried to show him with her kisses what she wanted. Though he seemed happy enough to return those kisses, he did not seize her as though he would devour her. Where was the passionate man of their last two encounters, whose desire drove hers?

Frustrated by his question, she sat back on her heels, studying him. He chuckled. "You look like a general planning a strategy of attack."

"I am."

"I don't understand. Won't you explain?"

"Very well." She raised her hands to free her hair, noting how his eyes focused on her uplifted breasts. He was trying not to look, but he couldn't seem to help himself. She took her time searching out the final pin. Then she shook loose the tumbling waves of gold.

His voice was husky and he had to clear his throat halfway through his sentence. "You said you were going to ex—explain."

"Oh, yes. Well, Dominic, the way I see it is this. . . ." She began to open the silver-braid frogs down the front of her riding coat. His gaze followed her fingers. "We have to face facts, unpleasant though they are. We may only have this one night to last us all our lives."

"One night . . ."

"There may not be a tomorrow for us." Taking up her courage, she spread open her coat and peeled it from her shoulders. Shrugging out of it, she dropped it behind her. Now she wore only her thin habit-shirt and the chemise beneath. She felt his eyes there and a tingle began to grow in her breasts. She felt them tighten as they did when she was cold, but she wasn't feeling the slightest bit cold.

"Clarice . . ."

"So I asked myself, what do I want? I know what everyone else wants me to do. Mother wants me to stay with her for always; you want me to go home."

"You'll be safe there."

She smiled at him, tenderly, lovingly, and with just the slightest hint of reproach. "Safety isn't everything, Dominic."

She put her hand to the doubled band of material at her throat, and tugged off the clip that held it together. Breathing a little faster, she untied the knot, and watched his eyes. Not even all her courage would suffice if she saw rejection there.

"Clarice," he said again, "what are you doing?"

Suddenly, there was no more room in her for fear. Undoing each button, she tantalized him with glimpses of soft skin and white linen. She'd been unable to find her own chemise so she'd been forced to take one Matilda had given her. Having made her plan, she chose the prettiest one. It was of linen so fine that it was nearly transparent, lavished with point-lace, much of which was inset over her bosom. Watching the color mount into his face, she wanted to laugh with pure womanly joy but she only smiled.

His voice was very deep now. "Are you trying to kill me?"

"Certainly not."

She leaned forward, returning to kneel over him, starting to kiss him again. Her hair fell down around his face even as the open sides of her shirt fell over his body. Clarice brushed his mouth with her own, recognizing in the way he raised his head as he returned her kiss that he wanted her to linger. But she didn't. She kissed his cheek, his beard rougher than before, his eyelids, his forehead, before returning to his lips.

"I can't even hold you."

"No. And you can't hold me off, either." She couldn't help giggling a little at the look on his face.

"Now you're laughing at me?" The growl in his tone spelled danger but she welcomed that. If she could just push him far enough . . .

He tried scooting back, but she only followed. He raised his bound hands, the crystal links jangling, and said, "Clarice, don't do this."

"Why not?" She sat back on her heels once more, only to remove her shirt. He shut his eyes. "A tactical error," she whispered and ran her fingers over his chest.

He tried to catch her hand with his own. "Clarice, as a man of honor, I cannot allow this to go on."

"Do you remember the first time we kissed? I thought you were such a fatuous person, but I couldn't help wanting you even then. I didn't know what I wanted exactly. I thought a voice outside myself was telling me to kiss you, but I was wrong. It was a voice from inside myself, deep, deep inside. I'd never heard it before. Or perhaps I had but I never listened to it. It told me to take what I wanted. It's speaking to me again right now."

She raised his arms and slipped inside their circle. Reaching up to his face, she gave him the kind of kiss she wanted from him, deep, hard, and completely open. She felt him try to damp out his reaction to her, but he couldn't, not entirely. He was rigid all over with the effort of not responding to the temptation she offered.

Then she broke his defenses. Tears came to her eyes as she said, "Help me, Dominic. I don't want this to end without ever having . . . having known you."

He crossed his arms around her back, looping the chain to keep the cold links off her warm skin. Then he kissed her, so tenderly at first that her tears flowed onto his face. Then some spark flared in the dry tinder of their longing and tenderness fled before a welcome blaze of desire.

The soft slide of her body over his had been driving Dominic slowly out of his mind. Now, even with his hands all but useless behind her, he could show her that madness worked both ways. He knew little of the courtly forms of love but every touch brought its own pleasure. He rolled her over onto her back and for a long time they made no sound but those they drew from one another. Then suddenly she said, "Ouch!"

"What's wrong?"

"This hay is scratching me. Never mind. Kiss me again."

She dragged his head down to hers. He plundered her mouth, she a willing victim. But the glimpse he'd had of the body she pressed so intimately against his had given him an idea.

He pulled her back on top of him. She hung above him, her breasts near to his mouth. He'd kissed her throat already and the smooth rising flesh above her bodice. Now he dragged the fabric down with his teeth. Her breasts were freed, their rose tips tightly furled. Keeping one eye on her face, he took a tip into his mouth and lavished it with his tongue.

Her pink-flushed face was made more beautiful by a combination of surprise and increased pleasure. She propped herself up with her hands on his shoulders and he felt the tiny stings of her nails as she clutched him. "Good?" he asked.

"Oh, Dominic! What . . . what are you doing to me?"

"I don't know," he said, laughing. "But I think I will continue." He did, relishing every panting cry. He was ready for her, and when she rocked her hips over him—

which she could not seem to control—her skirt brushed over his heavy arousal.

Even in the Wilder World, animals still procreated. They did not "make love." Dominic knew that more than any mere completion, he wanted to make love to Clarice. He was still not certain that a gentleman should, but he knew he was going to.

He sought out the buttons riding over her hip, only to find that her fingers were there almost as soon as his own. He reluctantly let her wriggle free of his arms while she slipped off the skirt. She stood up to do it and he could not tear his eyes away from her beauty. Wearing only the provocative shift, she smiled at him, her hair wild in a way he'd never seen before, but nothing about her was more arousing than the gleam in her eyes. That alone would have been enough to make him ardent.

When she slipped the straps from her shoulders, letting the shift slide all the way down, he groaned. The moonlight bleached out her color so that she might have been made of marble. But there was nothing cold about her as she slipped again inside the circle of his arms.

"All my wishes coming true and me with my hands fettered. There is no justice!"

"We're not doing so badly," she said. "Are we?"

"No, love. We're not." He pressed a kiss onto her bare shoulder as he drew his fingertips down the groove of her back. Shivering, she pressed closer against him still. With every breath, he inhaled the spicy fragrance of her aroused body. It was not she alone who shook with need.

"What now?" she asked innocently. "I feel sure there's more to come."

He had to clear his throat. "There is. But we can stop now, if you want to."

"Stop?" She shook her head in wonder. "I feel . . . I feel . . . oh, there aren't any words! I want you to feel the way I do. I want . . ."

Dominic sat up, with Clarice on his lap. He had to bite his cheek to do it without giving in then and there to the urgency that demanded the ultimate expression.

He laid her down on the fallen skirt, hoping the heavy wool would protect her delicate skin from the hay. Then he started to touch her, indulging in his wildest fantasies, while she watched him in wild-eyed wonder. Soon, though, her eyes closed as she writhed beneath his hands.

He couldn't help tasting where he touched. Her reaction startled them both. She seemed to shatter, shaking apart in a way that frightened him a little, but went directly to his heart.

"Are you all right?"

Her eyes slowly opened. She put her hand to her mouth. "Was that me?"

He nodded. "Are you all right?"

Her sigh was a long note of sheer bodily bliss. "What now, my love?"

Somehow they managed together, between giggles and growls, to free him from the confines of his clothes. His shirt hung loose, his breeches were open. Clarice looked down into his lap. Her eyes went wide. "Is that for me?"

"If you want it." She obviously had no notion what her almost-scientific study of his body was doing to him. He dug his fingernails into his palm to keep from seizing her before she was ready. He thought that was the last extremity of torture, until her curiosity drove her to touch.

"Clarice . . ." he ground out. He didn't think he could stand another instant of her gentle exploration. Already his heart felt as though it might pound right out of him.

She lay back, smiling her infinitely feminine smile, waiting for him to take what she offered.

There was a moment's awkwardness as he worked his arms over her head. She did not make it easier by dipping her head quickly to lick the nubbin hidden in his chest hair. Then he had her captured against his pounding heart. She gazed up at him. "Help me, Dominic. I want to please you."

He kissed her until she was gasping, her hands clutching his back helplessly, as her feet ran over his calf muscles. "Your pleasure is all I ask."

Poised at the threshold of her body, he found his way eased by her body's gifts. He wanted to go slowly, give her time to adjust to this strange intrusion, but she moved against him so welcomingly that he knew the image of invasion was only in his mind, never in hers.

He heard her catch her breath as he found the secret impediment within. He stopped, appalled by being the cause of her pain, but again she took them beyond it with her generosity. Embracing him, taking all he had to give and giving so much more back to him, the pain was only momentary, soon forgotten by them both.

Dominic felt chilled and overheated all at once, as he had during a fever long ago. Only the fires she set in his flesh would never go out. As they rocked together, he felt the forces of the universe gathering in his body, as though a great cosmic storm had awakened within him and he and Clarice huddled together at its mercy. They moved together, lost in an all-absorbing rhythm, and Dominic could feel the storm tugging at him, demanding he surrender to it. But he refused to go into the heart of this miracle alone.

He bent his head and took the tight tip of her breast into his mouth. The addition of this pleasure snapped Clarice's eyes open. She clutched at him, moaning his name again and again. He felt the intimate clasp of her body tighten further and together they were caught up in the destruction of time and space.

It was a strangely peaceful aftermath. Realizing that his suddenly boneless body lay too heavily on her fragility, Dominic moved to the side. He felt vaguely surprised that outwardly nothing seemed to have changed. The wagon had not been blown away, nor had the moon exploded into a thousand singing shards. He chuckled deep in his chest as he threw his arms over his head. He'd never felt so well in all his long, long life.

"You sound uncommonly pleased with yourself, Mr.

Knight," Clarice said, propping herself up on her elbow.

"Pleased with you," he answered merrily and then saw that she bore a strange expression. He'd never seen her look frightened before.

"Don't," he said, reaching out for her. "Don't be embarrassed. You were wonderful . . . beyond my dreams."

"Thank you." But the worried lines did not leave her brow. "Dominic, where are your chains?"

He looked at his hands as though he'd suddenly grown a new set. The jangling crystal chains, that had never sounded true, were gone. His feet too were no longer shackled. Unable at first to believe it, Dominic sat up and rummaged through the hay.

"They're not here."

Clarice sat up too, her arms folded around her knees. He couldn't see any of the parts of her that he'd so recently come to adore, but even so he knew she was unclothed and it had an effect on him that was no longer strange. But at the distressed expression of her eyes, he forgot desire in his need to reassure her.

"Dominic, is it true . . . that if the one who worked the spell dies, the spell ends?"

"Your mother isn't dead, Clarice. She's Fay. She does not die."

"Oh, I know but . . . couldn't Forgall kill her?"

"No. He wouldn't even if he could. The only thing he could do is banish her away somewhere. The Desert North, maybe."

Clarice heaved a sigh of relief. "Then what happened to your chains?"

His grin now was tenderly possessive. "At a guess, I would say you happened to them."

"I?"

"Nothing can stand against love, Clarice. You gave me pure, disinterested love, thank you very much, and even magic isn't proof against it."

"But I did want something from you. I wanted to know."

"Did you find out?"

Her cheeks were as delectable a pink as they'd been when he'd claimed her. "Yes. I—I don't know how to thank you."

"There's no 'thanks' between you and me. What we've done was foreordained from the moment Forgall chose me to be your guardian."

"I hope you don't think I should have fallen in love with whomever Forgall sent?"

"No. You were made to be mine, and I have waited four hundred years and more for you."

She smiled at him shyly. "I'm glad you waited for me. If only . . ." He pressed her to finish what she'd meant to say. Dominic felt there should be no "if only" between them. But Clarice only shook her head, her eyes slumberous, and said, after stifling a yawn, "We should probably go to sleep. Won't we have to be on our way very early tomorrow?"

"If we are not captured in the meantime." He lay down on the outspread skirt of her habit. "This isn't very big for two people to lie down on."

"You didn't complain before." She couldn't quite meet his eyes.

"I mean, side by side."

She slept in his arms, his body keeping her warm. For himself, he kept sleep at bay. Though he knew he must do battle tomorrow, these moments were too precious to lose in sleeping. Besides, all he'd ever dreamed of lay sleeping beside him. No other dream, however wonderful, could compare to this living fulfillment. When the pink light of dawn touched her face, he awakened her with a kiss.

"It's morning. We should dress and be on our way."

"Shut your eyes tight and pretend that it is still dark outside." She drew his head down for another kiss, which lasted a long, long time. Almost before he knew he meant to, he was making love with her again.

Dressing, afterward, took longer than it should have done. How could he bear to see Clarice's wonders being hidden one by one without kissing each a fond good-bye? She laughed and tried to keep him from achieving his goals but her efforts were weak on purpose.

He drove the horse this time, Clarice seated beside him, her long hair flying free in the breeze. "Are you taking me home?"

"Yes. Don't worry about me. I can defeat a hundred men so long as I know you are far from danger."

She slipped her hand under the bend of his arm. "I don't want you to think I lack faith in you, but how I wish this battle was unnecessary."

"Most battles are unnecessary but not this one. It's for the very life of the Living Lands."

Her sigh of resignation was not a happy sound. She nodded in reluctant acceptance of what he had said. "Then don't waste time taking me to where I can reach Hamdry. Let us go to your battle. No doubt Forgall can send me back with a snap of his august fingers."

"That is probably true. Very well. We'll go to his camp, but if he cannot or will not, then he will not see me in his army's front rank but standing before the Great Doors, kissing you good-bye."

As the sun mounted in the sky, they turned onto a road that was little more than a rutted track running in the cathedral-like gloom beneath tall trees whose branches touched overhead. Clarice gazed out into the depth of the woods, her attention wandering. The landscape was beautiful but sad, the leaves a palely fluttering silver. She didn't hear so much as a bird singing despite the warmth of the morning. Then a flicker at the corner of her eye made her turn.

She saw nothing then, but a moment later she saw another flicker as though someone or something had suddenly stepped behind a tree out of sight. More attentive, she began to search the woods in earnest. Fortunately, the horse was not going very fast.

"Dominic," she said, "I thought I saw . . ."

An instant later, she saw one plainly. It stood only a few feet off the road and did not seem in a hurry to seek concealment. It seemed almost to smile at her, peering under the bony ridge above its opaque silver eyes.

Clarice reached for the reins and slapped them down hard. Had she been glad the horse didn't want to speed along? Stung by the reminder, it began to hurry.

"What is it?"

"Those things from the sky . . ."

"Things?"

"I saw them flying around the Fortress. They're horrible things, so gaunt you can see through their skin. . . ."

"*Amungasters!* Here? Get up, horse!"

But the mare needed no more encouragement than the thin whinny that sounded from deep in the woods. Clarice, watching, saw white flashing among the trees as a mounted corps of the starveling creatures came riding after them.

She hung on tight as the cart practically flew down the rutted road. Dominic said in a tight voice, "If we overturn, keep running for as long as you can. Better your heart should burst than one of them should catch you."

Clarice's curiosity did not extend to asking why. She'd been frightened enough when she'd seen them at La'al when they'd seemed reasonably well-disposed toward her. Now to be hunted by them—the hollow call of a ghostly horn sighed through the woods, freezing her heart. She looked behind her. The pale shapes seemed to be gaining.

"They're just behind us!"

"Are they?"

"Look, you can see for yourself!"

"No, I can't. Only females can see *amungasters*. They're female themselves, or at least they were once. Get up, horse!"

Faster and faster they went, the cart rocking violently from side to side. Clarice was prey to the horrible idea that the creatures were flinging themselves aboard. Though she looked back every moment without seeing any, she couldn't rid herself of the idea. She realized she was saying Dominic's name over and over under her breath.

"Are they gaining?"

"No. Neither are they falling behind."

"We'll be out of these woods in a minute. The mare is almost done for."

Clarice strained her eyes ahead and let out a scream. "They're ahead of us! Look!"

To her shock and horror, Dominic pulled on the reins. Clarice wanted to plow straight through them, scattering them like ninepins, but Dominic pulled up. Then he leaped down and was greeting the white-robed figures who materialized out of the woods on either side of the road. It was only when they threw back their hoods that Clarice realized that these were mortal men.

She looked behind her. The emaciated figures of the *amungasters* and their bony horses were gone.

Clarice climbed down from the cart, feeling about ten thousand years old, and went to hold the mare by the cheek-strap. She too was quivering in her harness. "There, now," Clarice said, smoothing the sweat-flecked neck. "There, now."

Dominic looked as happy as a boy on the first morning of summer holiday. He talked with great animation to the three men who'd appeared out of the woods, grasping each one by the arm, and clapping them on the shoulders. Then he waved his hand toward Clarice. Each stranger bowed to her with great formality. The tallest of the three pointed up the road in answer to Dominic's eager questions.

He came hurrying back, his stride free as though every step were a reminder than he no longer wore chains. He said, "Back in the cart, my sweet life. Forgall's army isn't half a mile away. By the way, the boys said they're grateful to you for noticing the *amungasters*. They have nothing female with them at the moment and didn't realize the danger."

Clarice dismissed this as an irrelevancy. "We can't go

on yet. The poor mare is exhausted. Have they a horse we can use?"

"This is just a foot patrol, the farthest picket." He ran his gaze over the mare. Her trembling had ceased but she still showed the whites of her eyes. "I can't leave her here; she's O'Hannon's."

"Did you promise to return her?"

He acted as though he hadn't heard. Clarice stepped in front of him, her hands on her hips. "Dominic, what did he mean when he said I would soon know why he helped us?"

When he told her, she stared at him in wordless amazement. He spread his hands apologetically. "It was the only way, Clarice. He never would have helped us escape otherwise."

"You'll not do it!"

"I must. I gave my word."

She would have had better luck trying to destroy the Fortress of La'al by kicking at the ramparts with her bare foot than trying to change Dominic's mind when it came to points of military honor. She walked beside the cart in silence, watching him pull it while the mare followed, tied to the rear.

Forgall's camp was orderly and silent. Silent until the soldiers realized who it was that came into their encampment dragging a cart like a gypsy peddlar. Pandemonium erupted. Suddenly, the shafts were pulled out of his hands, and Dominic and Clarice both were lifted onto willing shoulders and paraded up to the White Pavilion.

It looked exactly the same as it had in the green meadow of Mag Mell. Forgall too looked just as before, except this time he was pleased to see Dominic, dropped down on one knee before him. "I hoped you would come safe home from the Fortress. Glad to see you are none the worse for a little more wear."

He glanced incuriously at Clarice, who suddenly realized her habit was rumpled and soiled, her disordered hair crowned with wisps of hay. As always in the Living

Lands, such things were easily remedied. This time, though, instead of a gown of stainless white, Forgall's fancy had clothed her in scarlet. She wondered with a blush how much he knew of last night.

Dominic asked his king eagerly, "Am I too late?"

"No. Matilda's troops are massing on the other side of Barren Tor."

"Barren Tor?" Clarice asked, astonished. "You're not going to fight in *my* world?"

"Is there such a place in your world? Here it is the site of the last great battle against the Worms, known to you as Dragons. It is a place of ill-omen, for we lost many good knights that day before a lasting peace was won. I can think of many places I'd rather make my final stand."

Dominic said, "My king, I have a boon to ask of you."

"Ask, my son."

"Will you send Clarice of Hamdry back to her own place and time? I wish her to be safe out of the battle-ground when the clash comes."

Forgall looked at her again, his eyes piercing. "Is this what you want?"

Without hesitation, Clarice said, "No." She turned to Dominic, who caught his breath to start an arguement. "No, I will stay until I know what happens to you."

"Very well. You may wait in my Pavilion, my lady. Don't open the silver chest, will you? Powerful magic there." That was the last word Forgall spoke to her, for some of his officers came up then.

Dominic said, "Clarice, are you certain?"

"Yes. Don't lose. Promise me."

"I never lose. Clarice . . . when this is all over, when we're free of the threats that . . . well, will you . . . ?"

Some of his friends came up to them, hardly noticing Clarice except not to step on her. They were boisterous in their welcome and roughly teasing as they talked about the battle to come. Dominic had time only to kiss her hand before he was carried off with them to accoutre himself for combat.

She watched him go, wondering if she'd ever see him again. He loved her with his whole soul, of that she had not the faintest shadow of a doubt, yet he could walk away from her now with hardly a thought for her. The night they'd spent together would be with her for always; was with her now. Her entire conception of the world had undergone a revolution. Now she understood many motivations and drives that had been closed books to her before. From what Dominic had let fall, she knew he'd never made love to anyone before either. Yet he could go back to the world he'd known before, a world of battles, comrades, good against evil, without feeling strange. She did not know if she ever could.

She knew he had no fears. He believed that he could not be defeated. Perhaps he needed that belief in order to face the battle.

Her faith was not so blind. Her fears were all for him. No one here could help her fight them. Could anyone? Clarice knew the answer. Ashamed that she'd never given religion a thought since her troubles had come upon her, she clasped her hands and sent a prayer directly to heaven. She had no doubt that God could hear her in this kingdom of magic as well as He could upon the floor of Westminster Cathedral. "Take care of him!"

Twenty

As if by prior arrangement—which for all Clarice knew it was—the rival armies gathered on Barren Tor as the sun rose to its zenith. Climbing up in the wake of a party of knights, Clarice found it hot, tiring work. Sometimes she used her hands to pull herself up by the long, rank grass that grew on the sides of the hill.

When she reached the top, she found herself standing on ground that looked very much like what would be left if a gigantic knife had sliced off the top of a pointed peak. The sides sloped sharply down toward the lower ground while the top was smooth as shaped clay. No grass or other plants grew there. The earth seemed baked hard, for even the hundreds of soldiers walking over it raised no dust.

In the center, just as on her own Barren Tor, were tumbled black stones, some broken, others leaning at drunken angles. It was the remains of a larger structure than the one she knew, but in its air of desolation it might have been a twin.

Forgall's army ranged on one side of this monument. As the sun shone down upon them, they were brilliant in a dazzling array of clothing, with banners bearing a variety of strange devices fluttered overhead. Laughter and merriment seemed the order of the day. She heard minstrels, saw jugglers, and some of the People, dressed more simply than the others, moved in the crowd offering refreshments. It seemed most disorganized and she saw no somber faces, even among the cadres of humans clustered here and there.

She looked across to where her mother's army had foregathered. A shadow like fog seemed to hang over them. They were standing in serried ranks, weapons at the ready. Teeth were bared but not in smiles. The silence in their ranks was so profound that the flapping of their empty gray banners could be heard clearly.

To her surprise, she saw her mother's short, plump figure step out in front of her army. Entirely unattended, she walked toward the stones. Clarice pressed her palms together tightly, bringing the tips of her forefingers to her lips. She hoped with all her heart that her mother was offering to sue for peace. She started forward, determined to give Matilda whatever support she needed.

Walking behind Forgall's merry troops, Clarice tried to hurry forward, her eyes fixed on her mother. It was only after tripping over the hem of her skirt that she saw the person coming down from Forgall's lines. It was Forgall himself, his russet beard unmistakable even from a distant. Was this a parley?

A voice boomed out, from the sky, or perhaps from under the earth. "Let every voice be silenced!"

Some in Forgall's army apparently believed this did not apply to them. Some Fay ladies laughed at a juggler, while some courtiers lying on silken blankets were singing catches.

"LET EVERY VOICE BE SILENCED!"

Now the only sound on the barren ground came from the pennons of both armies flapping in the breeze. Not even the hawks riding the thermal layers made a cry. Clarice continued to try moving forward through the crowd, determined to reach the stones. No one else seemed to be moving in that direction, though she passed one or two who were hurrying back to some prearranged spot with ribbons or other fairings in their hands.

"Let every eye attend!" the disembodied voice called.
"Let every heart be at ease!"

"Impossible," Clarice muttered.

"LET EVERY VOICE BE SILENT!" the voice ad-
monished, apparently for her alone. Some of the ladies
who had been laughing earlier gave her a haughty look.

"Sorry."

"Attend well the word of Forgall!"

She hurried on and came to stand opposite the fort.
There was a greater press of people there, eager for a
quality view. Clarice wondered how she'd ever get
through to see. Then the Fay directly in front of her
glanced back and saw her. He paled and stepped aside,
tapping the one before him on the shoulder. Everyone
between Clarice and the front rank moved out of her
way, some bowing, others sneering. They left her a
wide-enough aisle to drive a horse and cart through for
fear of her touch.

Forgall had just seated himself, gathering his heavy
golden cloak about him. Clarice hadn't heard a word
he'd said, though several Fay standing around had given
each other nods of approval. She didn't dare risk the
displeasure of the voice again by asking what had been
said.

The voice seemed louder now but also deeper and
colder. Was it coming from the stones themselves?
"Heed the word of Matilda!"

Her mother stood up. Her voice carried. "I accept Forgall's suggestion with this condition. If there is no decision after the fifth effort, the battle becomes general."

Forgall nodded. "As my champion, I name Dominic
Knight!"

At that announcement, a deafening cheer rose from
Forgall's ranks. It was like a thunderclap, yet was not
quite loud enough to drown out the voice. "The King's
Champion! Dominic Knight, come forward."

Clarice searched the crowd desperately. At first, she
couldn't see him anywhere. Had he decided not to fight?

She didn't want him to fight and yet . . . She couldn't
have borne it if he was ever reduced in his own eyes.

Then he came forward from less than ten yards away.
He wore no armor, beyond a vambrace on his left fore-
arm. He wore no shirt or breastplate, nothing to turn a
weapon but his naked flesh. In his right hand, he bore a
scabbardless sword. It did not burn with blue flame as
had the one he wielded at the Doors. This sword was
unadorned by magic or gems. Clarice saw that the blade
was battered and not terribly straight. Was he mad to
contemplate battle attired like this?

In front of the two rival powers, Dominic bowed low.
Forgall and Matilda in their turn bowed to him. Perhaps,
she thought in wild relief, this is all ceremonial. No real
fighting will take place. That's why they all wear such
a holiday air and why he isn't wearing armor. No one
will really die or be "sent back."

Matilda stood to announce her champion. Before the
words approached her lips, there arose a commotion in
her army. Everyone pointed, though no one whispered,
at this break with discipline in the stone-faced army.

A man came running out of the ranks, but there
seemed to be something wrong with his feet. He fell,
rolling over and over across the very slight downward
slope to the stones. He raised himself up, his hands
clasped in front of him. She saw with horror that he wore
the crystal chains. Though his face was bruised and
dirty, Clarice recognized O'Hannon.

"My queen, I ask the privilege of combat with this
man. Let it prove my guilt or innocence of the suspicions
you bear toward me."

Matilda was seen to consult with Forgall for a few
minutes that seemed no less interminable to Clarice than
it must have seemed to O'Hannon. Dominic stood facing
the king, his sword's point on the ground, his position
easy. He gave no sign of having noticed O'Hannon,
though the Irishman was kneeling within six feet of him.

"I accept!" Matilda said.

On the empty ground between the two armies, a huge

circle appeared with a small group of stones in the center. Clarice had not noticed them before. They seemed
to have risen up from the earth in the last moment. Two
of these stones were upright, square and true, looking as
though they'd been set into place only yesterday. The
third was laid over the tops of the other two. There
seemed to be deeply incised markings on the capstone,
but Clarice couldn't see them very well. Perhaps it was
just the strong sunshine, but the pictures on the stone
never seemed to stay the same from one moment to the
next.

The two men stepped over the line and stood before
the stones. O'Hannon's chains had disappeared the moment Matilda had accepted him as her defender. Someone brought him a sword and a vambrace to encase his
arm.

There was no signal given to start. The two men
crouched low to keep from exposing any vulnerable
flesh. They began to circle about each other with a kind
of deadly patience.

"I wish I knew the rules," Clarice sighed in the voice
with which one speaks to one's own soul.

"There's only one rule."

Clarice couldn't bear to take her eyes off Dominic,
now leaping back as O'Hannon tried a slash across the
belly. She couldn't look around for the kindly person
who tried to alleviate both her anxiety and her ignorance.

"What is this rule?"

"Win." Silence for a few long moments before the
clash of steel on steel broke it. As the two men returned
to circling each other, the voice spoke again. "There's
one more. Don't fall through the portal. You return to
where you came from and dreadfully savage it must be."

At the same moment, Clarice realized that the "person" explaining all this was the voice she'd heard making the announcements. But this time it was only in *her*
head.

On the field, Dominic and O'Hannon were circling
each other. The slightest opening or negligence of atten-

tion brought a slashing swipe from the other. The sound
of the two blades colliding in parry after parry carried
over both armies. Clarice saw several Fay looking ill,
but she hardly glanced at them as they sank down in
faints. They were only a nuisance, getting in the way of
her line of sight.

One nearly fell right on top of her. Only the quick
action of one of the fainting one's friends prevented a
collision of skin between Clarice and the Fay. Another
one pointed to a clear spot farther away from any possibility of her enthralling one of the Fay to do her bidding. She moved reluctantly but found she had a much
better view near the main group of stones than in the
crowd. She could even hear her mother's whispers of
"Good show!" and "Nearly had him!" Forgall was silent.

Clarice didn't care what her mother was saying, but
she could see Dominic's lips moving. She wished she
had her cloak of silence to enhance her hearing. Why
didn't O'Hannon take a jump through the portal of his
own accord, since he wanted to go back so badly? Then
she recalled that Dominic had said O'Hannon wanted to
go back as he was now, fully grown and ready to do
battle for whatever lord would fill his purse.

Dominic was stronger, with a better reach, and, to her
partially tutored eye, seemed to have a greater knowledge of sword-play. All this was countered by the
smaller man's incredible speed. Time and again, it
would look as though Dominic had him at his mercy,
only to find the Irishman was not where he'd been the
instant before.

Clarice found herself bobbing and weaving with every
move Dominic made. She echoed in miniature his
sword-play and arm work, felt the sweat forming in
beads on her forehead, felt her heart pounding as though
it were she in the ring. She knew she watched a fight
between two unsurpassable masters of the art. Her father
would have enjoyed it, but she could not admire the finer
points when at every instant she expected to see her
lover go beyond her reach forever.

From Forgall's ranks, someone cried out, "They're too evenly matched!"

Clarice heard her mother and Forgall conferring. She wondered at him speaking so warmly and even with a mild teasing note to a woman who was doing her very best to unseat him. Matilda wanted a fresh challenger, while Forgall was determined to retain the same champion. Clarice couldn't allow Dominic to face a different opposer, one who'd been resting all this while. Besides, it might be a troll or a fiend. All was fair in love and war.

With that thought came the answer. It had been born of several things, but the final spark had been the look of fear on the faces of the Fay when it seemed she might touch them. These supposedly all-powerful creatures were afraid of the lightest press of her fingertip on their bare skin. In a way, she was more powerful than any of them.

Very deliberately, Clarice circled around the stones, coming up on her mother's right. Down the arena, Dominic fought for his life against a desperate opponent. All her hopes were pinned on the outcome, but she no longer watched. If she could stop it herself, stop it now . . . !

Matilda's attention was fixed on the circle. Her lips were loose, her eyes brilliant. She looked no more than a girl, caught up in excitement. Her fist was clenched, lightly pounding the stone beside her. "Come on," she said softly but urgently under the breath. "Come . . . oh, my. Close with him, come on."

Clarice stood just slightly behind her, hoping that she did not reach the edge of Matilda's peripheral vision. Matilda's hand went flat on the stone as something exciting went forward in the circle. Fighting against her own need to discover if Dominic were hurt, Clarice sprang forward, covering her mother's hand with her own.

"Clarice?"

She felt the shudder that passed through Matilda's body and wanted to cry for having betrayed her. But then her mother's hand twisted under her own and held on tightly. Clarice looked down into Matilda's eyes and saw great happiness shining there.

"Oh, my sweet love," Matilda said, as she stood up and reached out to embrace her daughter with her free arm. Though she'd outstripped her in inches while still young, Clarice felt like a small child again as she rocked in the arms of the one, for all her faults, who had always loved in her a way no other person could. To hold her again seemed to wipe away all the pain and trouble between them. She felt her heart slip the bonds of bitterness that she herself had hardly known for what they were. She forgave Matilda in that instant for everything, even for abandoning her in exchange for immortality.

Thus far, the only one who'd seen what had happened was Forgall. He smiled indulgently at mother and daughter, then rose to his feet. Throwing out his arms, he shouted, "Halt!"

In the circle, dripping with sweat, Dominic and O'Hannon paused, still eyeing one another and not relinquishing their warlike crouches for an instant. Forgall pointed two fingers at them. Clarice, held out at arm's length by her beaming mother, saw two figures come out of the crowd.

They were taller than the rest of the Fay and bore bows and staves in their hands with a quiver of arrows on their backs. In their second set of hands, they carried . . . Clarice looked again, staring. These must be the four-armed guardians of the king's person. They moved with stately grandeur through the crowd and ranged themselves between the combatants.

Only then could Dominic look up and try to find Clarice. She could have laughed with joy when she saw his jaw fall as he found her. Releasing her mother's hands, she waved to him. He dropped his sword and started up the hill.

Then Matilda said, in an odd, muffled tone, "Command me."

"I beg your pardon?"

Forgall said, "By our Ancient Law, when a mortal touches a Fay, the Fay must perform a task for the mortal. Throughout our history, there are many tales of foolish mortals throwing away their wish on some useless or ill-considered frivolity. Be thou cautious, my lady."

Dominic had reached her side. She saw that at some point he'd been injured. A cut over his ribs bled sluggishly. "Are you badly hurt?"

"No. O'Hannon's just faster than I expected. What have you decided to wish for, Clarice?"

She searched his face. "What would you wish for?"

"I have no desires left, but one. To be with you." His eyes told her that he also wished to repeat the affections of the night before.

It was with heightened color that she turned to Forgall. "And you?"

"I? I have nothing in the two worlds to wish for. I am King of the Living Lands, Wielder of the Right, Keeper of the Immortal Wonders. There is nothing I want that I cannot have without a moment's difficulty."

Clarice glanced at her mother, then back at the king. "Nothing?"

Forgall frowned in his beard. "Some things are only valuable if they come of their own free will."

"True," Clarice said. "I thought, you know, that I would wish for my mother's happiness, but now I think that is not something that can be created through any wish of mine. What she believes she needs to make her happy would only make me miserable for I cannot stay here. I believe that one can find happiness with another person, but only if the happiness is in you to start with. I love Dominic and if we were not to be together, I should never love any other man who would come into my life. I would certainly never marry. But I could be happy with my family, my friends, and my existence."

She smiled at him, hoping she hadn't hurt him. "You'll be happier yet with me," he promised.

"As for you, sire, I cannot wish for her to love you. That is something you have to create between you. All

I can do is make it possible for you to try."

Clarice looked deep into her mother's eyes. "Mother, I wish for a lasting peace in the Living Lands."

Matilda bowed her head. "So shall it be."

A wailing scream arose from the nonhuman and the non-Fay troops mustered behind Matilda's generals. The fog bank that had seemed to hover above them began to whirl and spin, creating a great funnel in the sky. Clarice saw Djinn, fat, fabulously jeweled and turbanned, rising into the sky, followed by all their retinues, some still carrying baskets of fruit or leading cheetahs on silken ribbons. Giants, trolls, and fiends were sucked up, bellowing, while strange monsters from fables tried to outrun or outfly the funnel, only to be scooped in with the rest.

Even the *amungasters,* as Clarice was relieved to see, did not escape, despite being so gaunt that they blew this way and that before being drawn up. Clarice wondered what these creatures had done to be turned into something so horrible but decided she was better off not knowing.

When all the creatures had been collected, the vast cloud collapsed in on itself until it was a puffy disk. Like a gyroscope, it began to rotate on a fine-drawn axis, faster and faster, compacting itself more and more until finally it winked out. "Are they all dead?" Clarice asked.

"Certainly not," her mother replied. "They've been returned home. Whether it's a cave in the Augean mountains or a palace on the moon, they are all home now. I feel . . . I feel surprisingly good about that." Matilda turned to Forgall. "What about you? Or shall the goodwill be all on my side?"

The Fay-King crossed his arms. "What do you suggest, Matilda?"

"Whatever Clarice thinks is best. This is her wish, after all. Besides, she has always been more than a pretty face. She has a good heart and a very level head."

Clarice honestly thought she would have fallen down

in a dead faint if Dominic had not been there to take her arm. "What should Forgall do, Clarice?"

She said, after taking a deep breath, "I think you should have no more *werroeur* in the Living Lands. You will just have to manage without a standing army."

Forgall stroked his beard. "I don't know that we can do without them entirely—there will be disgruntled goblins and such after today—but perhaps a greatly reduced force?"

"Only if they are free to go if they wish it. No one should be kept against their will to fight another's battles."

"Is that what I've done?" He looked at Dominic, who nodded with great reluctance.

"I am grateful to the Fay for saving my life and for prolonging it until I could meet Clarice. But I long for the life of an ordinary man."

Clarice laughed. "You'll never have that! You'd have to *be* an ordinary man."

Forgall laughed. "I have done you a favor, my son. Very well. Let Matilda and me discuss terms, and then we shall see."

Several hours later, while the Fay armies feasted and toasted one another on the new-christened field of Clarity Tor, Forgall and Matilda were still arguing the terms of her surrender. Though perhaps she had not entirely accepted the fact that Clarice did not want to be immortal, she was willing to waive that demand. Without it, her reason for fighting Forgall ended.

Clarice and Dominic strolled arm in arm through the torch-lit encampment. The night was scented with the thousands of flowers that had sprung up on the barren ground the moment Matilda's surrender had been formally announced. The two sides had rushed together in what had looked like a violent battle-charge but had turned into a splendid party. Even the sourest of Matilda's supporters seemed to be having a wonderful time.

They passed Condigne and Miship arguing about the quality of the beer. "It's not what it was ten thousand years ago," Condigne said, sighing as he shook his head.

"No, that's true. But there's so much more of it," Miship said, nodding to the *Wyrcan* maid who was pouring out refills.

They both bowed to Clarice when they saw her. Everyone did, from either side. Some of that, she thought, might have to do with Dominic striding along beside her. He had put on clean clothes such as he'd worn when they'd first met and she thought him by far the best-looking man there. "I wonder how many of them are really pleased the war is over."

"Most of them. Even if the cause is just, war is a dreadful thing to inflict on a peaceful land. I hope there'll never be another, either here or in our own place."

"If only it were so easy among mortals."

They turned around for they were being called. O'Hannon, clean, neat, but with miserable eyes, came up to them. He left waiting for him a group of soldiers. They wore a variety of bits and pieces of uniforms, from Russian white with braid on the sleeves to the buckskin and blue of the American experiment. "What is happening? Have 'they' up there said anything about us?"

"Not yet, Corporal O'Hannon," Clarice said. "It won't be too much longer, I'm sure. Would you like me to go find out?"

"That's right; they'd tell you. Speaking for the fellows, we'd be forever in your debt, my lady." He spoke more softly. "It's been terrible difficult keepin' their spirits alive. Some of the wilder ones want to go down to the circle and toss over the guardians that are waitin' for orders, then step through the portal on their own. I'd let 'em try it, too, were it not for the fact they'd be slaughtered like flies. *Nobody* dares to quarrel with a guardian."

One of the four-armed ones was waiting outside the White Pavilion. Clarice felt strangely shy about approaching him, for she'd never come close to anything like him before. She didn't know how to act without being accidentally insulting.

As it turned out, she did not need to embarrass herself. When she approached, the guardian bowed low. He used one hand to sweep open the front flap of the tent, another one made a graceful gesture of welcome, and the third and fourth kept the ever-present bow and stone-tipped arrow at the ready. Dominic too was permitted to enter. But the curtain fell and all four of the arms assumed a defensive position when O'Hannon and his friends tried to enter. Clarice could hear him at intervals trying to bully, bribe, and beg his way in.

The moment Matilda saw her, she came toward her, smiling softly. "My dearest . . ."

"Mother," Clarice said, rather shocked, "were you sitting on his knee?"

Matilda's cheeks were suffused with rose. "Well . . . and why not?"

"It's something of a sudden change, is it not?"

"I'll tell you." She glanced over her shoulder at Forgall, who pretended not to be listening. "It was never the king himself I had any objection to. From the moment I first saw him, I thought . . ." Matilda looked prim. "Well, it's not really very unusual. Rather banal and vulgar. Persons of our order do not believe in such a thing as love at first sight."

"Why not?" Clarice asked. "It's magic, isn't it? You must believe in that."

Matilda smiled again, revealing a hitherto undiscovered dimple. "Perhaps I do, even that kind of magic. After all, creating a diamond out of nothing is really much easier than falling in love."

"What will happen?"

"I can't say. We've been discussing that."

"I thought you were talking about creating peace."

"Oh, that we did in the first ten minutes." Matilda's blush deepened. "Since then, we have been . . . talking about other things."

"You'll marry him?"

"I shall certainly give it some thought. A hundred years or so," she said roguishly, tossing a teasing glance at Forgall. But when she looked at Clarice, sorrow filled her eyes. "A hundred years . . . you'll be . . . you'll be . . ."

"I'll be where I belong, Mother. With my ancestors in Hamdry churchyard, letting the grass grow green. I hope to delay that day as long as I can—I have much living that I want to do. But I'm not afraid of it. It's *right* for me, as this is right for you. Don't cry. You can come to see me sometimes, can't you?"

Matilda could only nod, as she dabbed her eyes with the silken handkerchief that appeared between her fingers. "And I shall give you a trousseau such has never been seen in the history of mankind!"

Clarice said, "He hasn't proposed yet, Mother."

"What!" Her eyes dried as if by magic. "I shall have Forgall speak to him at once! The gall of the . . ."

"No, Mother."

"But you have no one to protect you, no one to look out for your interests. He may be trifling with you!"

Clarice caught Dominic's eyes across the richly carpeted Pavilion. He was discussing the matter of the other *werroeur* with Forgall, but still had an instant to flash her a loving smile. "He's serious. As serious as I myself. But there are other things that must come first. He will not abandon his cadre, nor even O'Hannon, until they all have what they want."

"Men! Though I live ten million years, I will never understand them!"

"Think how I feel."

When Forgall, Matilda, and Dominic went out to talk to the soldiers, they found that every one of them had a slightly different idea about what should be done and they were not backward in expressing their feelings. Dominic took Clarice aside after a while and said, "This will take forever!"

"What's amiss?"

"Some want to return to their homes just before they

were orphaned to warn their parents. Others want to go back as grown men, like O'Hannon, with money in their purse and a sword in hand. Others want to pursue dreams of wealth, or knowledge, and at least a few want women. Every one of them will have to be sounded separately, dealt with individually, and then some kind of plan developed for each man. And this group isn't an eighth of all the *werroeur*. Some will have to be recalled from every corner of the Living Lands."

"Dominic," Clarice said, gazing down at the circle, "I want to go home."

"I know it. I will try to hurry matters along as quickly as I can but it's not easy hurrying immortals. But I can't just walk away. . . ."

She put her arms around his waist and stepped close, putting her head on his shoulder. "I know it. I don't want you to. But I want to go home. There's so much to be done, so many explanations I'll have to make. I'll go now; you follow me when you are free."

"No. I don't want you going back alone."

"There's nothing *there* you need to protect me from. I shall be waiting."

Thinking of that parting, Clarice walked on the snow-covered grass of the moor. The first snowfall of winter had come late, dusting all Hamdry with white. Down at the Manor, Christmas preparations were going forward, with much singing and merriment. The orphans had come from Tallyford and had promptly set the rafters ringing with their escapades, while Camber, Rose, and Cook tried to keep up with their demands for refreshments. Blaic and Felicia were there, still marveling over how much Morgain had grown in just the few months since they'd seen him off to school. Doctor Danby, scowling with vibrating eyebrows, argued philosophy with Mr. Hales and Mr. Henry while Mrs. Danby quizzed Melissa about every detail of her pregnancy.

Clarice had borne it all as long as she could, smiling until her cheeks ached. Then she'd bundled on her coat,

swirling a shawl over her head, and gone out through
the garden to the hills.

Six months had passed since she'd bid Dominic a
tender farewell in the morning after the peace celebration. He'd held her hard against his heart, whispering
promises in her hair. His tears had mingled with hers as
they kissed farewell again and again. They had made
love again in the night, strong and sweet. Leaving him,
even for the little time they'd promised, had been like
tearing herself in two. Even leaving Matilda, though
hard, had not been so painful. But the urge to go home
beat insistently in her blood as though she were being
summoned and could not resist.

She found herself lying on Barren Tor with a five-
mile walk ahead of her, wearing a scarlet dress and slippers on what surely must have been the hottest day of
high summer. When she reached a road at last, the slippers were slung around her neck by their strings and the
dress was dusty and torn. She didn't blame the first several wagons that passed for not stopping for such a disreputable female. But then a shiny black gig did, with a
slewing, sliding stop. Mr. and Mrs. Yeo sat on the seat,
staring at her.

"How are you?" she cried cheerfully, limping up.

"You'm not a ghost then?" Yeo asked.

"I don't think so."

"Nay," Mrs. Yeo said, bumping her spouse's ribs with
her elbow. "It's her laidyship raight enow. Get down and
help her in. We be on our way to the trial this very
minute."

"Bah. T'ain't nothing in this world but one of these
inquests."

"What inquest?"

That was when she heard that Camber had been taken
up for murdering her and burying her body so cunningly
that no one had been able to find it. "Searched myself,
I did. All 'long the moor. Big job that."

"Iss, fai!" his wife said. "Comin' home covered in
muck, two days out of three."

"I can't believe they'd think *Camber* murdered me. Surely someone has spoken up for him."

"Oh, iss. T'other zervants been loyal to him. Then they was clapped up too. Don't worry. Your zister routed 'em out. That man of hers is in a fair way when he's riled. Thought the constable'll drop down dead after he come to visit."

"Thank God Felicia and Blaic have kept their heads."

If she'd been fond of creating a sensation, she would have gotten all she wished when she walked into the common room of the Ram's Head tavern. Doctor Danby was the coroner and was handing the constable his head. "I put it to you that in the course of your blundering investigation you have discovered no evidence whatsoever that Lady Stavely has been done away with! Not a drop of blood, not a scrap of torn clothing, not a hair from her head!"

Constable Wroxhall was fighting back, his broad face red, drops trickling down over his plump cheeks. "Him and that Knight feller did away with her ladyship, then Camber killed his accomplice. He's mortal clever is Camber. But he can't answer me one question. Where's Lady Stavely? If she be not dead, then where is she?"

"I'm here!"

Blaic said, that in terms of sheer pandemonium, the French Revolution played second fiddle to the riot at the Ram's Head. She had not realized how much she was loved by her tenants and the townspeople until she came back from the dead. As for her servants, Camber could only put his head down on the table and weep while Rose and Cook threw their aprons over their heads and couldn't speak for fifteen minutes by the clock.

Though she'd tried to think, in Yeo's cart, of a tale to tell to explain her absence, she couldn't come up with anything that wouldn't leave her open to the worst kind of suspicions. So she told the truth. "I went walking on the moor and was taken by the pixies."

In the heart of even the most cynical, the most sophisticated of those who dwell near the vast emptiness of the moor there lurks a belief in the power of the "good folk." Some may have had their doubts, especially after some months passed, but no one dared call her a liar, for what would happen if the tale she told were true?

Clarice too had her doubts. Sometimes she thought it all a strange dream. Perhaps during those six days that she was missing, she'd struck her head and fallen into a dream.

As she walked in the snow on the edge of the moor, she put her hand on her gently rounded figure. In response, she felt an upward kick, faint as yet but growing stronger day by day. It had been no dream.

There'd been no way to tell Dominic she was pregnant. She'd seen no trace of any Fay since she'd returned. Morgain had not seen his grandfather, nor had Matilda come to visit her. Blaic could no longer pass through the secret ways that riddled the mortal world. So Clarice waited for Dominic with nothing to support her except faith and her sister.

"Time is different there. What seemed like weeks to you was only days here."

"So months to me is—what? Years in Mag Mell? He cannot have forgotten me so utterly."

Felicia sighed sadly. "I'm trying to help and all I do is make it worse. I don't think there's any formula for it. Time speeds up and slows down there so strangely. It may have been six months for you but only three days to him. There's no way to tell."

"Forgall could tell him. My mother could tell him. Why haven't they?"

For this, there was no answer. Felicia did her best to keep her sister's spirits high, but Mrs. Gardner could not be there always. The nights were the worst. Clarice would lie awake, longing for Dominic. She remembered how proudly she'd said that she didn't need him for her happiness. If that were true, why wasn't she happy now?

Overhead, the sky looked low and gray. Knowing full well how dangerous it was to be out on the moor when the weather turned, Clarice thought about returning to the house. But she simply couldn't face that much merriment. She walked along, her eyes on the ground, remembering the night of Melissa's wedding, how she'd found herself on Barren Tor with a man on horseback leaping over the stones. She wondered, and supposed she always would, if that had been Dominic or the Rider.

But that had been nighttime and now it was broad daylight. As the first fat white flake melted on her nose, she looked up and realized she had no idea where she was. This wasn't Barren Tor, or any hill she'd ever seen in all her years of wandering on the moor.

The top was rounded and so deep in snow that her feet were quite buried. Towering before her, unsupported by any wall or lintel, were a pair of doors. The black stone of which they were carved had a glossy shine, unmarked by any rune or carving. They were closed, but she could see a line running between them and, faintly, a keyhole showing as a dull speck against the black stone. The keyhole was just big enough for her fingertip.

Clarice inserted her finger, wondering if she'd ever get it back. A chime, incongruently soft to come from such hard things, sounded in the curlingly crisp air. Clarice tugged her finger out and jumped back clumsily as the doors began to open. They swept aside the snow, piling it up before them.

Inside, there was darkness. Standing there, Clarice called, "Hello?"

Her voice echoed back hollowly.

Was something trying to tell her that the Living Lands were gone? Had all that wonder and beauty been lost somehow, in some terrible cataclysm? She did not want to walk into that echoing emptiness.

Then she heard the clatter of hooves—not racing frantically to escape, but coming along at a considerate pace. A rider appeared, sitting tall in the saddle, a bag or two slung on behind him. He wore a black cloak, the hood fallen back to reveal his dark hair and the intent look that squared his jaw and deepened his eyes.

The dark horse came all the way through the doorway, and the doors closed with a click. Clarice was looking only at Dominic and didn't even notice when the doors sank silently into the ground. She waited for her beloved to come to her. As yet, he hadn't even seemed to see her.

"Dominic!"

She saw surprise strike him. "Clarice!" He swung down effortlessly. "What are you doing here?"

Laughing, she said, "Waiting for you."

She was in his arms at last, having the breath kissed out of her, while all her doubts and fears were washed away on a tidal wave of joy. As when they had parted, their tears mingled but this time so did their laughter.

She laid her head on his shoulder and said, "I was wrong. Being with you is my only happiness."

But he wasn't listening. His hands were on her hips as he tried to see down between them. "Clarice, is that . . . ? Are you . . . ?"

"Yes and yes."

"I'm just sorry I'm so late."

"I was meaning to ask you about that, but later. Right now, all of a sudden, I seem to feel the cold."

"Oh, stones! Yes. Come on. You can ride the horse. I thought I'd have to travel for miles because even Forgall didn't know where these doors would put me, whether in your garden or in the Forbidden City half way around the world. They're new."

"New?"

"Specially created just for me. The method had been all but lost. Took some time to find the right kind of stone too. But let's get you out of this snow first. What are you doing, tramping around in this with nothing on but a shawl?"

"I was lonely so I went looking for you. I've been doing that quite a bit."

"I am sorry, Clarice. You see, I couldn't come here at first. Every time I went through the portal, I wound up at Priory St. Windle in my own time. The first several times I was six years old again. I wouldn't wish it on my worst enemy. Then when I was sent through as I am, I still found myself standing in back of my house at Priory St. Windle. Apparently, a *werroeur* can only go back to his or her own time, not another. It's some kind of safety control."

"Did O'Hannon go back all right?"

"He *danced* through the portal, leading that mare. I promised I would look him up in an encyclopedia when I came home, to see if he made a noise in the world."

"And now you are home."

"Now I'm home." He gave her that grin that never failed to make her heart turn over. Gazing at him, thinking that there was no magic that could create such a feeling, she again missed the moment when she went from a place she did not know to the place she did. Moreover, the gravel they walked on was her own drive.

Just as before, Drake and his sons came up to take the horse to the stables. When Dominic handed the head groom the reins, Drake couldn't speak. Dominic lifted Clarice down. She paused an instant to put her hand on the groom's sleeve. "It will be all right, Mr. Drake. Don't worry."

The groom was not the only one left speechless by Dominic's reappearance. But the crowning moment for Clarice was when she introduced him to Felicia and Blaic. The two men from another realm shook hands, sizing each other up. Dominic said, "I hope you can show me how to adapt myself to life in this century."

"If you'll marry my sister, it will be a pleasure. If not, I'll take pleasure in our next meeting, but you won't."

"Blaic!" Clarice and Felicia both exclaimed. But Dominic only said, "We won't need to fight each other— at least, not for that reason."

This did not bode well for their future meeting, but when Mr. Hales read the marriage ceremony over them a week later, Blaic stood up with Dominic. The banns had been waived, due to the condition of the bride, but for all that, it was an exuberant wedding. Clarice wore one of the gowns that had "mysteriously" appeared in her wardrobe shortly after Dominic's arrival. It had even been cut to fit a pregnant figure. With it, she wore Forgall's wedding present, a rope of pearls that a queen would sell her teeth for. Clarice thought that her mother must have told the king what to send.

In addition, she wore a chaplet of spring flowers that looked as though they'd been picked that morning, despite the extra three inches of snow that had fallen in the night. They were a gift from Morgain and his grandfather who had, at last, paid a visit.

After a party that rivaled the best the Fay could show, the bride and groom were at last alone.

"They meant well," Clarice said as he carried her over the threshold of her bedroom. "There's been so much talk already; they didn't want any more."

"I don't blame them. But it has been impossibly difficult to see you alone."

Dominic pulled her onto his lap and started kissing her. Clarice gave herself up to the delightful sensations he aroused. Though it had been so long, the feelings had merely been lying dormant until he came back to reawaken them. As he kissed and nibbled on her throat, she said, "Dominic, you're not jealous of Blaic anymore, are you?"

He stopped and stared up at her. "You knew?"

"I guessed. You were always so sharp when you spoke his name."

"I'd been told you were in love with him."

"Those Fay! I do love him, as my dear brother. That's all."

"Now that I know Felicia I can see that he never would have been in love with you."

She raised her hand, feigning a slap. "Thank you so very much, Mr. Knight!"

He caught her hand and began kissing the fingers. "You were waiting for me," he said.

"Yes. I would have waited forever, but I was starting to get a little impatient."

"*You* were impatient. The *Wyrcan* who made the doors would hide whenever they heard me coming. But they didn't have the incentive that I had." His hands were roaming over her body, noticing the changes. "I'm in awe, Clarice. What an amazing creature you are. I'll never think anything a Fay did is miraculous again after the miracle of you and our baby."

As Clarice lay down against the pillows she seemed to have a vision of the future. There would be long, wonderful years of life with the man of her dreams and his children. They would live together in this house of Hamdry, which had seen so many strange things. The moor would shelter them forever, yet give them those mysteries that added so much interest to life.

Dominic asked, "What are you thinking of? You have the strangest smile. . . ."

"I'm thinking of the future."

"To the future," he said, kissing her.

The future, she thought, her lips being otherwise employed.